Love WILL FIND *You*

William McNulty

ISBN 979-8-88616-155-7 (paperback)
ISBN 979-8-88616-319-3 (hardcover)
ISBN 979-8-88616-156-4 (digital)

Christian Faith Publishing
832 Park Avenue
Meadville, PA 16335
www.christianfaithpublishing.com

Printed in the United States of America

CONTENTS

ACKNOWLEDGMENTS

Mary Dick, my sister, and to my late brother-in-law, Paul Dick (1933–2022), who had always been more like a brother to me. Your combined incredible encouragement, love, and support made it possible for me to write the books God allows me to write.

To my living children, Laura Billue and Cynthia Leigh Powell, and the loving memory of my son, William Martin McNulty Jr. (1975–2008).

To my grandchildren Alex McNulty, Ryan MacGloan, Jake Coughlin, and Nick Coughlin.

Samantha Mitchell for reading the manuscript of my first book and suggesting I use Christian Faith Publishing Company to launch my writing career, and for being a very special Christian friend.

Shalanda Gilliland, President, Allie Lasher, Vice President of Operations, Christian Faith Publishing Company, for their beautiful cover designs, their amazing editors, and their labor of love.

My heart is full of love for each of you.

CHAPTER 1

Rachel Rice

Rachel Rice is a beautiful twenty-two-year-old levelheaded woman, who stands 5'4" tall, weighs 121 pounds, has shoulder-length blond-color hair, blue friendly eyes, pretty teeth, and outgoing personality. She learned from her dad how to be a goal-oriented person who sets goals and works hard to achieve them. She is known as an achiever.

Henry Rice is a board-certified orthopedic surgeon, forty-seven years of age, who stands six feet in height, weighs 180 pounds, with brown-color hair, brown-color eyes, and the father of his only child, Rachel.

Dr. Rice is methodic in both his personal and professional life. His daily schedule is always penciled in on his office and home calendars for Rachel and the people he employs to follow.

Friday afternoons are always reserved for him to spend time with Rachel. She enjoys riding with him to his office every Friday to sit in his waiting room to speak with his patients and read magazines. One Friday, when she was fourteen years of age, she picked up a magazine to read about a prestigious college by the name of MIT, Massachusetts Institute of Technology, located at 77 Massachusetts Avenue in Cambridge, Massachusetts, just outside Boston. Something clicked inside her mind and heart that told her she would one day graduate from MIT.

MIT was founded as a private research university in the year 1861, to specialize in laboratory instructions in applied science and engineering. Each undergraduate class normally had about 4,500 students.

In 1976, MIT became a *grant college*, reaching out to students looking for an education in math, oceanography, and marine science. To be considered for MIT enrollment, you must have a GPA of 4.16. MIT requires each applicant to be at the top of his class and to compete with other students who are also A students. She read where the annual cost to enroll now into MIT was $51,832, with only seven students out of one hundred who applied being accepted.

Rachel requested brochures from the eight Ivy League colleges of Brown, Columbia, Cornell, Dartmouth, Harvard, The University of Pennsylvania, Princeton, and Yale. Harvard piqued her interest but not quite enough to dissuade her from her initial decision to apply and graduate from MIT. People perk up when anyone mentioned the name MIT, which has a reputation for not only being difficult to gain admission into but equally difficult to maintain acceptable grades to graduate and earn an MIT degree. Once she allowed her mind to visualize achieving one of her goals, it was embedded firmly into her heart and mind.

Since she was fourteen years of age, she told everyone, "I will apply and graduate from MIT." And she did!

Being a graduate from MIT University instilled a lot of pride within her and gave her added confidence to consider applying for a vacant position as math coordinator of a large local high school located near her home. The ink on her degree from MIT barely had a chance to dry when she read about the math coordinator position and the seventeen applicants from local and nearby states who had already applied for the position. She held the newspaper article in her hand when she walked into a local coffee shop-deli to eat breakfast, drink a cup of coffee, and consider her chance of success to be hired ahead of seventeen other qualified applicants.

Her mind was focused on an empty booth only a couple of steps away from her when she reached out her hand, holding the newspaper article to lay it on the table, when she collided with a young man approaching the same booth from the opposite direction with the same intention. The newspaper article and her notebook fell to the coffee shop floor. The young man wrapped his arm around her to prevent her from falling onto the floor as he apologized profusely. They both stooped down to pick up the newspaper and her notebook. Slowly they rose to their feet, giving each other the once-over with their eyes. She knew from the look in his eyes that he approved of her. She would later learn that when their eyes met, his heart leapt in his chest. Admittedly he had a very handsome face, and she approved of him and the words he chose to use for his apology.

"I have to admit to you that this is my first experience of meeting anyone this way. It is one way to obtain your name and phone number." He looked at her and smiled, showing her his beautiful white teeth.

"It hasn't worked yet," she said, smiling back at him.

"Spoke too soon, eh?"

"Maybe?"

"Thank you."

"For what?"

"For giving me hope that I have not ruined the slimmest of chances to obtain your name and possibly your phone number. May I please have your name and, hopefully, your phone number?"

"I know nothing about you to release my phone number to you. Sorry."

"Excuse me, do you mind if we take this empty booth to eat today? We are in a hurry."

Rachel looked at the two people looking for a booth in a very crowded coffee shop and said, "We just got here and were about to sit down." Rachel sat down on one side of the booth and motioned for the young man to sit on the other side. "Sorry." She looked apologetically at the two people looking for a place to sit down to eat.

"I did not pay them to come along when they did, but now I feel blessed." He laughed out loud.

"Why do you feel blessed?"

"Why?" He watched her shake her head up and down. "You are a stunningly beautiful woman."

She could not resist bursting into laughter. "You are something else. Probably a real ladies' man with all the perfect cute things to say. Right?"

His laughter stopped, and his face turned serious as he spoke honestly, "No. You honestly make me a more confident person. For the first time in my life, I feel there is nothing I cannot do with you near me. The person who coined the phrase 'behind every good man is a great woman' must have had you in mind when this was inked for history. I bet you do not know and do not believe you are beautiful, do you?"

"No."

"My mother always said, 'If a woman doesn't know how beautiful she is on the outside, she is twice as beautiful on the inside.'"

"Your mother sounds like a very sweet person. I would love to meet her. She has done a great job raising you." Rachel blushed.

"You are the most beautiful woman I have ever met. And even more beautiful when you blush." He smiled and looked lovingly into her beautiful blue eyes. "Please tell me your name."

"My name is Rachel Rice."

"May I ask what position you hold in life today?"

"Interesting way to phrase your question. Why today?"

"People change vocations to better themselves, so what you may do today may not be what you will be doing a month from now. I say this because of the newspaper you held in your hands when we met."

"Clever. You must be a detective?"

"No. Today I am a pharmaceutical representative with higher aspirations. What business do you bless daily where you work?"

"I recently graduated from MIT. I found an article in this newspaper advertising for a math coordinator position for Lincoln High School. I wonder—"

"Sorry to cut you off. Go for it. I would hire you on the spot even without a résumé. You have a gift that needs to be shared. You will be an inspiration to every person who crosses your path."

"Looks only get you so far."

"Not just looks with you, Rachel. You are deep. Do you know what I mean by deep?" he asked excitedly.

"No. I am just Rachel."

"Please do not say that in the future when you describe yourself. You are not *just anything*."

"You do not know me." She stopped talking and stared into his beautiful hazel eyes. Before she relaxed her guard too far with him, she had to find a way to be sure he was for real and not just a guy wanting a one-night stand or using his charm to relax her into a quick sexual fling that she would never do with any man. A slow courtship, engagement, and marriage would take place before she slept with any man for the first time. She knew nothing about him and didn't want to rush into a relationship. Too many of her friends have done it, and now they are nursing broken hearts while the men in their lives notched their belts and departed for parts unknown. She waited patiently for him to speak.

"Go ahead. Ask me anything. I will never tell you a lie."

"Oh. That's right. Silly me. Men do not tell lies, do they? May I have your name?"

"Robert Wilson. Thank you for asking. I was afraid you were going to let me walk out of here and not ask for my name. That would bother me all the way home."

"I am cautiously optimistic about you, Robert Wilson. You seem too smooth and quick for me to handle."

"Remember you said this to me. Okay?"

"Why?"

"Because after you get to know me and meet my family and friends, you will swear they are telling you things about a totally different man. They will describe a man who is kind of laid back and incapable of saying the things I am saying to you."

"How do you explain this sudden change in your demeanor to say these things to me?"

"My heart."

"Your heart?"

"Yes. I have never felt this way before. My heart reacted to you the minute my eyes fixated on your beautiful face and heard you speak from *your heart*. My confidence level around you is off the charts. I love how I feel around you. I have this feeling that I need to speak up if I want a chance to experience any part of my life with you in it. I cannot believe I am saying this to you. But the only other alternative is to say nothing and let you walk out of my life. I know if I did this, my heart would prove to me it was right, and we both would be the loser. Take a chance on me."

"How?"

"Trust me with your phone number and suggested times for me to call so we can talk, or at least set up a future meeting for a cup of coffee, lunch, or dinner. I want to give you my work and home numbers for you to call me 24-7. I would love to hear from you any time of day or night."

"I won't give you my phone number, Robert. I cannot take that chance without knowing you better. I will agree to a future meeting for lunch since I see from this meeting, I can trust you with a longer meeting than a cup of coffee. I have a lot on my plate right now and do not have room for a relationship. Please try extra hard not to make me sorry for squeezing you into any part of my life."

"You are going to squeeze me into your life? Those words just made my heart do exciting flips."

"Lunch. Not into my life. You know—"

"Sorry to cut you off again. I am truly sorry. I know exactly what you meant and nothing more, Rachel. You will never have anything to worry about with me today or ever. I will always be a perfect gentleman and try my best to never make you feel uncomfortable around me. I will treasure every minute I get to spend with you. Will you do me one big favor?"

"That depends on what it is. What is your big favor?"

"Go for the interview. They will hire you over others because of your MIT degree. I have a very strong feeling about this, Rachel. You must apply so you never look back and wonder what if. Okay? Apply. You got this, hands down. Please tell me you will at least apply. You have nothing to lose by applying. When they see your beautiful face and sit and speak with you for a minute, the job is yours."

"You sound like my father. Thank you for saying these nice things about me, Robert."

"You are welcome. I meant every word, and I will always have your back."

"Always?"

"Yes."

Rachel looked into his eyes for the longest ten seconds of his life. She didn't know why she suddenly wondered if he would be there for her if she had a major medical emergency. A life-threatening emergency that would consume most of his available free time for months or even years.

He seemed to read her mind when he spoke before she continued speaking. "Yes, Rachel. Even then, I will always have your back."

"You have no idea what I was thinking, so how could you—"

"Sorry, cutting you off seems to be a habit. I do not know what you were thinking specifically, but I believe your vision into the hypothetical future was serious enough to make you wonder if I would still be there for you. My answer is unequivocally yes. Unless I do something to chase you away from me, which I will not do. If you decide to leave me once we become an item, I am going with you."

Rachel had some coffee in her mouth when he spoke these words to her, and she spontaneously spit some across the table as she burst into laughter. Sheepishly she looked around the restaurant to see how many people she disturbed with her outburst. He was surprised and shocked to see Rachel's reaction to his comment. He burst into laughter of his own. He could not take his eyes off her beautiful face. When they stopped laughing and just looked at each other, it sparked more laughter. He loved everything he just learned about Rachel, and now he also loved this fun side of her too. They both sat on their sides of the booth enjoying this unique spontaneous fun time together. She never felt so relaxed with a man before.

Unintentionally, and simultaneously, they each put one hand in the center of the table at the same time. Rachel's hand landed on top of his. "Oh, sorry."

"Please do not move your hand from mine, Rachel." His words froze her hand in place.

"May I say something without upsetting you in any way?" Rachel asked.

"Only if I may go first. It is important for me to tell you something that you need to hear from me."

"How bad is this going to hurt my feelings?" Rachel asked.

"I hope it will not. I do not want what I have to say to ever become an issue between us."

"You are scaring me. I need to go. Keep whatever you were going to say to yourself. Okay."

"Rachel."

"No. I need to go. I do not need to hear anything upsetting in my life now or ever." Rachel started to slide out of the booth when he came over to her side of the booth and slid in next to her.

"Please trust me this one time so you will learn to possibly trust me in the future when I ask you to."

"Please let me out of this booth."

"I am not gay. I want to tell you that I believe in marriage before making love with the woman of my dreams. I will never put my hands in forbidden places, so you can relax and be yourself around me. If we progress to the point of marriage, I want our wedding night to be beautiful, special, and romantic and not just another day. I want to take you all over the world to wonderful places to eat, shop, play, and have fun. I want to experience the world with you. I am sorry if the way I feel about this issue is not the way you feel."

Rachel felt her female emotions reacting to every word spoken by him. She was attracted to him at first sight, and now hearing him tell her how he will always respect her and treat her like a lady until the day they marry made her feelings for him escalate. She did not want to be groped or spend any evening fighting any man off her. She looked into his eyes and saw the respect he spoke about. She looked down at his lips and surprised herself when she leaned closer to him and kissed him passionately on his lips.

Rachel was levelheaded and a grounded young woman who knew what she wanted in life. Today her heart told her it wanted him in her future life.

He had never been kissed like this in his life. Every male passion within him was suddenly alert and begging for more. He could get used to this euphoric feeling every minute of every day. The second their lips separated from each other, he leaned back toward her for another kiss. She put both of her hands on the sides of his face to ensure that this second kiss was closer to a peck than their memorable passionate first kiss. They both felt the passion of their first kiss, and it would forever stay on both of their minds the remaining days of their lives. This gave them both something to look forward to on their wedding night. Robert Wilson knew he would one day marry Rachel.

"I came in here to eat something without any thought of meeting a man. God brings all things and people together for a divine purpose. I hope our meeting is for something good that will last our lifetime and not bring either of us sadness or pain. I want you to remember the things you just told me every day. One slip up will forever destroy your credibility with me. No forgiveness on this issue. Do you agree?"

"I agree, Rachel. I will never do anything to lose your love."

"I will take you at your word until you break your word to me. Do you want to meet me for lunch or for dinner?"

"Any time, any day, any place. My heart is racing in my chest at the mere mention of spending time with you. Please tell me where and when."

"Cheddar's Restaurant, this coming Friday at noontime or evening. You choose the time. Please do not break my heart."

"Your future days and my future days are uncertain for a variety of reasons, so choose evening for us to handle daytime unexpected interruptions. May I pick you up, or do you want to drive your car and meet at Cheddar's?"

"Do you mind if I drive and meet you at Cheddar's?" she asked.

"No. Always follow your heart and your instincts."

"I love the words you chose to use for your advice to me."

"Take a minute to consider your day and the traffic to Cheddar's and choose 5:00 p.m. or 6:00 p.m. or 7:00 p.m. to meet me."

"Can you break away to get ahead of the traffic on your end to meet me at 5:00 p.m.?"

"Yes. May I ask you to clarify something? Our meeting and parting ground rules for us to live by?"

"Okay." She gave him a questioning look with a half-smile. "Please ask me your question."

"I have no experience in this area. You are my first love. Do you prefer just a hug when we meet and when we part? Is it okay for me to give you a small kiss when we meet, and perhaps both a hug and a

9

small kiss when we part? I would never embarrass you with a public passionate kiss. I would like the last thing we remember about each other to be a kiss in the event God places His loving hand on one of our shoulders and whispers, 'Come home,' before we have the chance to meet again on earth, if you do?"

"Wow! May I give some thought to this and tell you when we meet on Friday?"

"Yes. I agree in advance to whatever decision you make for us."

"Okay. Thank you. Before we slide out of this booth to leave each other today, may I have one of the greeting and parting kisses you have in mind for us?" She didn't wait for his reply before she leaned closer to him to allow his lips to press softly against her lips for two seconds. "That is a perfect kiss. I agree to these kisses when we meet and part. Okay."

"Do you want the keys to my car? I won't need them anymore. I will float on the cloud you just created for me. You are beautiful and truly amazing. You started to say something to me, before I went first and interrupted you. Please tell me what you were going to say?"

"Trust me, after you told me everything you had to say followed by everything that transpired, I forgot what I was going to say."

"Okay. If you think about it, write it down and tell me Friday."

"Okay. If I remember, I will write it down and tell you when we meet on Friday."

Robert slid out of the booth and helped Rachel to her feet. They looked at each other for a few seconds with mutual respect and love in their eyes. "It really was a pleasure meeting you and having something to eat with you. I do look forward to seeing you this coming Friday."

"Thank you for agreeing to meet with me again, Rachel."

"I am counting on you to never break my heart." She gave him a serious look, then smiled, turned, and walked away.

He watched her walk through the door and disappear as he put his hand over his heart, thinking he now felt two hearts beating inside his chest. His heart had never felt so full of love.

CHAPTER 2

Robert Wilson

Robert Wilson is a handsome young man, twenty-four years of age, who stands six feet in height and weighs 185 pounds, with sandy brown-color hair, hazel-color eyes that have a soft and friendly look.

Robert mastered the art of speaking from his heart with a perfect volume and tone that made people pay attention to him when he spoke. He was gifted with a brilliant mind that enabled him to skip a grade in high school and graduate at the age of only sixteen.

He never considered the impact of his request when he asked God to take the reins of his life to guide his choices of enrollment into the best college and best medical school available to him. God did guide his college and medical school decisions. He graduated from the number 1 medical school in the USA.

"Thank you, God," he whispered out loud with his medical school diploma in his hand.

He decided to sit down with a cup of coffee to reflect upon the challenging events he hurdled to achieve his successes that now has put him in a position to really enjoy his life. His journey started with a dream of becoming a medical doctor. He loved acting like a doctor when he bandaged up his friends and put their arms in slings to treat their imaginary injuries. When he was fifteen years of age, he focused all his available time on reading books written about the medical profession. Because he was not from a wealthy family, he would have to work to pay his way through college and medical school, and those costs would be unmanageable unless he found employment with flexible hours and a paycheck way beyond what he could imagine earning without a skill. He was a positive guy, who always saw the glass half full and never half empty. He first researched the total cost of his education before he looked for high-paying outside sales jobs that gave him options for more study time to cram for major exams.

Upon graduation from high school, he immediately sent an application, with a copy of his high school transcript, to Duke University in Durham, North Carolina, and asked if they would consider offering him a full scholarship to include tuition, boarding, books, and any miscellaneous expenses associated with these requested items.

Ten days later, he received a letter from Duke University offering him a full scholarship, paying everything he had requested. He immediately accepted their offer, packed his bags, and enrolled.

Four years later, he was a proud Duke University graduate with honors at the age of twenty. Duke University was God's gift to him, and he will always be eternally grateful.

God then led him to answer an ad for a pharmaceutical representative that offered a salary with a generous commission that would easily pay his way through medical school. This job required a lot of short-distance traveling, with flexible hours that would be ideal for him, so he applied for the position and was immediately hired. Being a pharmaceutical representative proved to be everything he had hoped for. The monthly salary plus commissions exceeded his wildest expectations. The flexibility in his hours, along with the money he made, would allow him to attend the best medical school located along the East Coast of the USA.

He began researching medical schools located along the eastern parts of the United States, hoping to find the perfect medical school for him to attend. If he wanted to be one of the best doctors in the USA, he knew he had to graduate from one of the best medical schools in the USA.

He made a list of the ten best medical schools located reasonably close to his home and sent each one a letter requesting their brochure. Some of the top 10 medical schools were located too far out West for him to attend. So his plan was to only visit the top 10 medical schools located near his home. He never dreamed he would find the number 1 and number 2 medical schools located so close to his home.

All top 10 medical schools responded to his letter by sending him a brochure, so he visited (1) Johns Hopkins University School of Medicine, located in Baltimore, Maryland; (2) Harvard Medical School, located in Boston, Massachusetts; (4) University of Pennsylvania Medical School, located in Philadelphia, Pennsylvania; (5) Duke University School of Medicine, located in Durham, North Carolina; (7) Columbia University, located in Upper Manhattan, New York City, New York; (8) Washington University, located in St. Louis, Missouri; (9) Yale University, located in New Haven, Connecticut; (11) University of Michigan, located in Ann Arbor, Michigan; (12) Mayo Medical School, located in Rochester, Minnesota; (14) University of Chicago, located in Chicago, Illinois.

Robert was torn between Johns Hopkins University School of Medicine and Harvard Medical School. He chose number 1, Johns Hopkins University School of Medicine. He enrolled at the age of twenty.

Johns Hopkins required a fee of $100 just to apply. The annual tuition cost is $69,863 for all students regardless of residence location. The breakdown is $52,700 for tuition, $15,410 for room and board, and $1,230 for books and supplies. No other fees.

Applicants must submit a four-year college diploma from a credible college with excellent undergraduate grades, achieve exceptional scores on the medical school entrance exams (MCAT), and submit impressive personal and academic references to gain admission into Johns Hopkins medical school.

Robert was returning from one of his short pharmaceutical trips when he decided to stop to get a cup of coffee. He was on his second sip of coffee when he finally relaxed to blow out a long breath of air and impulsively whispered out loud, "Lord, looking back at my life now, I do not think I could ever do all this over again."

He then glanced around him to be sure no one was within earshot of him when he felt this unexplained emotional rush that hit him so unexpectedly to cause such an unusual verbal outburst. He was so triumphantly relieved that the hard part of his quest to be a medical doctor was now over, happy tears filled his eyes. He did not feel embarrassed over what just happened, impromptu. Conversely he felt blessed when he quickly took a few seconds to think about his career choice and what God has allowed him to achieve. Simultaneously more tears slid down his face when he thought about Rachel. It was then that he really felt like standing up and screaming, "We did it, Lord. We did it. Thank you for the life I will live as a medical doctor with Rachel. But why me?"

The kind of emotion he was now feeling was uncharacteristic and foreign to him. It was the kind of emotional feeling one gets when they sit down to reflect long after they scored the winning touchdown or hit a home run to win an important game for their team. The strong similarity is in the fact that he has now successfully accomplished everything asked of him. God put him into a position to take his medical boards to officially become a licensed physician to make his childhood and early adult dreams come true. Euphoric, exhilarated, jubilant, triumphant, or just giddy is how he feels right now. "Yep, this would be a hollow victory if I did not have Rachel to share this and my life with. Thank you, God."

His mind drifted to his medical board exam and dinner with Rachel. The exam is scheduled for a few days after his dinner with Rachel. He decided not to tell her about graduating from medical school or his medical board exam until he passed it. He did not want to jinx the exam.

Before he left the coffee shop, he wanted to spend a few minutes thinking about his future as a doctor after he passed his boards. New doctors are required to work under supervised medical training for one year before choosing a field of medicine. Most new doctors at this point will choose to specialize in one area of medicine, such as family practice, pediatrics, general surgery, or training in emergency room medical care. To obtain additional follow-up training in any of these areas of medicine, a *three-to-seven-year residency* program is strongly suggested, especially if you wanted to be later assigned to a hospital or major clinic.

After the residency program, doctors who want to become more specialized in a field of medicine will eagerly accept a post-residency program called a *fellowship*. These programs offer specialized training in oncology (cancer treatments), cardiology (heart and blood vessels), or gastroenterology (digestive system) which can take one to four years to complete after your residency.

Establishing your own medical practice where you are wearing your own stethoscope in your own medical practice could take from eight years upward to sixteen years.

Robert was now feeling overly anxious to see Rachel on Friday.

Rip Van Winkle went to sleep for twenty years. I would give almost anything for me to sleep for two days to make Friday come quicker. Holding Rachel in my arms and looking into her beautiful blue eyes as I kiss her lips will consume every conscious thought in my mind until I see her.

I am anxious to learn if she submitted her application to be the next math coordinator at Lincoln High School and if she missed me half as much as I missed her?

CHAPTER 3

Rachel's Job Interview

Rachel Rice was nervous but feeling hopeful when she drove her vehicle into the Lincoln High School faculty parking lot, per the instructions she was given, and parked her car. Before she alighted from her vehicle, she closed her eyes and said a prayer, "Lord, please let me feel your presence when I meet with the people of Lincoln High School. Please continue to be the center of my life and guide what I say to be truthful and pleasing to you. I want them to like me, and I want to be everything they are looking for in a math coordinator. Please let me be relaxed to be myself. I ask this in, Jesus's holy name."

She hoped her excellent college credentials from MIT University would be enough for her to be hired on the spot to fill this position offered by Lincoln High School. She took a big breath of air and slowly blew it out as she walked inside the front door of Lincoln High School. She swallowed hard and took another big breath of air before she opened the door of the principal's office. After she announced her arrival, she went into the waiting area and sat down to wait for further instructions.

"Ms. Rice." Rachel looked up at a young woman who was looking at her with a big smile on her face, holding a clipboard. "You may go in now." Rachel raised her eyebrows, and with a slight smile on her apprehensive face, she slowly blew out a short breath of air. "Relax, you got this," the woman told her.

Rachel was stunned to hear these words. She stopped walking and looked back at this young woman and said, "From your lips to God's ears." Both ladies burst out laughing at this comment. "Thank you. I really needed to hear what you said to me. And I needed to laugh to relax me. May I have your name?"

"Yes. My name is Joy Winter. Welcome to Lincoln High School. I look forward to working with you and getting to know you. Please contact me for anything you need after you get settled in here at Lincoln."

Rachel started to speak when Joy raised her right hand toward her mouth, joined her index finger with her thumb, and slid these two fingers horizontally across her lips. "Our secret."

Rachel stepped closer to Joy and gave her a big hug. "I won't ever forget you." Joy nodded her head and smiled before she turned away from Rachel to open the door to the principal's office for Rachel to walk through to begin her interview.

"Good morning, Rachel Rice. My name is Ben Howard. For the last twenty years, I have been the principal of this high school. Let me take a few minutes to review your résumé and information received from your high school and MIT."

Rachel nodded her head. She guessed him to be about fifty years of age, six feet in height, and probably 180 pounds. He appeared to be in great physical shape with a slim athletic body, black hair, blue eyes, and white teeth, without cigarette or coffee stains. She quickly formed the impression that he was a confident man, probably honest, and a man she could trust. She liked him instantly and that was so unlike her.

Mr. Howard cleared his throat. "I am looking for the best qualified people to teach at our school. And since we are looking for a math coordinator, the best qualified math applicant will fill this position. Does this make sense to you, Ms. Rice?"

"Yes, Mr. Howard. It makes perfectly good sense to me. I hope to be the person to fill the position."

"MIT graduates are hard to top. The best of the best. Congratulations on your choice of schools."

"My primary reason for choosing MIT was their math program. I love math."

"Lincoln High School loves people who love math." Mr. Howard smiled at Rachel. "Many qualified applicants applied for this position. My job is to pick the best applicant and not play favorites. I am sure you agree with my task. Right, Ms. Rice?"

"Yes. I do understand this Mr. Howard." Rachel got a bad feeling in the pit of her stomach. She feared the next words to come out of his mouth would not be the words she wanted to hear. She closed her eyes for only a second as she mentally got in touch with the Holy Spirit that she knew resided within her, and silently prayed, *Lord, please let him select me to be the next math coordinator of Lincoln High School. I ask this in, Jesus's name.* She opened her eyes and looked at Mr. Howard for only a brief second as he opened his mouth to speak. She held her breath.

"Welcome to Lincoln High School, Rachel Rice. You are the most qualified and the woman we want to head up our math coordinator position at Lincoln High School. Do you want to work with us?"

Rachel jumped to her feet to grab the extended hand of Mr. Howard, who had walked halfway around his desk to congratulate her. "Yes! I do! Thank you very much. You won't be sorry for hiring me."

"I do not have a doubt in my mind that you will make us proud, Rachel. May I call you, Rachel?"

"Yes. Please call me Rachel."

She could not remember a time in her life when she experienced a similar adrenalin rush that felt this good to her. Hiding or controlling the happy tears filling her eyes never crossed her mind. She believed moments like these were meant to be enjoyed and relived later as treasured flashback memories, and she wanted to savor every minute of this euphoric feeling that was now filling her heart.

Robert Wilson's bold prediction came true, just as he said it would, and she could not wait to tell him about her good news. She was bursting at the seams and felt like screaming with joy. She visualized Robert's handsome face breaking into a big smile when she told him about her good news.

The door to the principal's office opened with Joy Winter peeking into the office with a big grin across her face. She tilted her head slightly and raised her eyebrows in a questioning gesture, looking from the face of Rachel to the face of Mr. Howard to confirm Rachel's tears were happy tears.

Rachel did not hesitate to turn and walk toward Joy with her arms open to receive a hug.

Mr. Howard said, "Do I detect a little conspiracy between you two? Did a cat get out of the bag?"

Rachel and Joy simultaneously joined their index finger with their thumb and slid these two fingers horizontally across their lips and, in unison, said, "Our secret." They both burst into laughter and hugged each other like two happy sisters.

"Just what I thought. I better keep a close eye on you two." When he smiled, they all laughed. "Rachel Rice has accepted our offer to become the math coordinator of Lincoln High School. Please welcome her and show her everything you had to learn when you came here to Lincoln High School. Please help her choose a private parking space for her vehicle, help her select a locker in the teacher's faculty lounge, give her a credit card to pay for her free lunches, and give her anything else I have failed to mention. Okay?"

"Yes, sir. It will be my pleasure." Joy turned toward Rachel, who had been standing next to her and said, "Mr. Howard just confirmed that we officially have hired you as our new math coordinator of Lincoln High School. Welcome to our team, Rachel. I hope you will be always happy with us here at Lincoln High School. Are you ready to walk with me to pick out your parking space, select your locker in the teacher's lounge, and meet the cashier in the cafeteria, where we will eat our daily lunches?"

"Yes," Rachel answered excitedly.

Rachel and Joy had smiles on their faces as they turned to walk out of the principal's office, and as they disappeared, they closed the door to the principal's office behind them.

Joy handed Rachel a tissue. Rachel dabbed the tissue against her eyes to dry her happy tears as she looked through her tear-filled eyes at Joy, who is thirty years of age, 5'4" in height, about 120 pounds, with blond-color hair, green eyes, and beautiful skin.

"Mr. Howard might be right to call us Bobbsey Twins. We definitely could pass as sisters," Rachel said with a giggle.

Joy opened her arms to welcome a hug from Rachel as they did a happy dance in each other's arms to symbolize their close instant friendship of sisterhood created as an answer to prayer.

CHAPTER 4
Rachel Takes a Chance

Rachel Rice was awakened by the sound of her alarm clock ringing from her bedside table. She instinctively reached over and shut it off as a smile spread across her beautiful face, thinking about the new love of her life, Robert Wilson. She laid back on her pillow for a few more minutes before she rose to her feet. She even laughed out loud at feeling kind of giddy with butterflies in her stomach.

Am I in love? Is this what it feels like to be in love? Robert is the first man I have ever felt like kissing, and I did spontaneously kiss him passionately. I still cannot believe that I was the instigator of the kiss, she thought embarrassingly to herself. *Will he think less of me for being so forward? How could he ever believe I have never done such a thing before? I must talk to him tonight about that kiss to make him understand it was impromptu and so unlike me.*

Rachel wondered about a possible future life with Robert. *I know nothing about Robert Wilson. The only thing I know about Robert is that he works as a pharmaceutical representative. How often would he be traveling on the road and not be home with me? Before I get too head over heels with him, I need to find out his future plans. Will he always be a traveling pharmaceutical representative?* She remembered his comment to her about his having higher aspirations and now wished she had followed up and asked him a few more questions about his aspirations. This was one of her shortcomings, where she missed too many opportunities to satisfy her curiosity when people made comments she should ask questions about. Now she did not know how to address or approach the subject with Robert without his thinking she was not happy with him being a traveling pharmaceutical representative.

She closed her eyes and whispered, "Lord, please encourage Robert to talk to me about his future occupational aspirations when we meet today, without me having to bring up the subject. I do not want to make him feel uncomfortable or make him start to question any ulterior motives that I do not have. Please guide everything I say or do with Robert tonight. I ask this in Jesus's name."

*****

Robert tossed and turned all night long. He could not sleep a wink during the night thinking about the love of his life that he was meeting tonight. He finally realized that looking at the alarm clock every few minutes was not a way to get it to speed up, so at 5:00 a.m., he decided to surrender any hopes he had of sleep. His thoughts shifted to Rachel as he got up and walked into the shower. He knew in his heart she would be a blessing to everyone at Lincoln High School if she submitted her application to become the next math coordinator. The most important thing to him was her happiness. He planned to allow her to speak first about her life and plans before he told her about his now being a medical doctor.

They both stayed busy during the day and lost track of the racing hands on the wall clocks that were mounted in rooms where they worked. They walked quickly to their respective vehicles and hurried to be on time for their first dinner date.

Robert arrived first and parked his automobile near the front door of Cheddar's Restaurant. He went inside the restaurant and reserved a booth in a corner so he and Rachel could talk more privately, and waited just inside the front door for her to arrive. Not knowing the color or make of her car, he watched each vehicle park and anxiously watched to see the first glimpse of her beautiful face, when she slid out of her vehicle and started walking toward the front door of Cheddar's Restaurant.

Rachel pulled into a parking space near the front entrance and checked her hair and lipstick in the rearview mirror before she opened her car door. She rubbed her hand over her stomach to see if she could feel the wings of the butterflies flying excitedly in every direction. She giggled out loud at the thought of her being in love, before she opened the door and stepped out.

Robert stepped outside the front door and waited for her to walk into his arms. He put his hand over his heart to see if he could feel the love he felt for her. He loved this feeling of being deeply in love for the first time in his life.

Rachel remembered his pledge to always be a gentleman, which allowed her to dismiss any concerns about restricting their kiss to two seconds. As his arms wrapped around her, she wished they would stay around her forever. She gave no thought to a two-second kiss when their lips met. Feelings she had about kissing a man were immediately surrendered along with any pretense of being reserved or discreet. She was in love. Her heart and her kiss were telling him, *I am yours for as long as you want me.*

Robert was in uncharted waters, with this being the first love of his life. He waited all his life for a woman like Rachel. The minute their lips met, he pulled her closer to him and released every emotional passionate feeling he was feeling for her. He did not hold anything back. The more he gave to her, the more she responded in kind. She never tried to hold anything back.

They were now both in uncharted territory and too inexperienced to know how to harness the emotions they were feeling for each other. It did not take long for him to start experiencing almost animalistic emotions that seemed to scream with excitement. He wanted all of her, now.

Rachel's knees buckled for the first time in her life. She felt faint and a little frightened knowing she was close to that emotional state where it would be difficult for most women to say no to the desires of men. A flashback of an earlier conversation with her dad telling her it was up to a man to try, and a woman to put him in his place gave her the strength to focus on the Holy Spirit that she knew lived inside each of us. She found the needed strength to focus on the guidance of the Holy Spirit telling her to place her fingers between her lips and his

She whispered, "Stop, Bobby. Save the rest for our wedding night. Okay?" She focused on God and whispered, "Thank you, Lord."

Robert was a true gentleman when he allowed her soft hands to separate their lips. This is the kiss he will remember the rest of his life. He now knew how a woman's passionate kiss could take control of a man's mind.

Rachel kept her fingers on Robert's lips and continued to look up into his eyes. Her face was flushed, and her heart was racing like she had just run a marathon race. Seeing the look in Robert's eyes was something she hoped to see on their wedding night but never before that sacred night.

Robert started to speak when Rachel put one finger from each of her hands over his lips. "Please allow me to speak first, Bobby." He looked disappointed, thinking he was in trouble with her. "You are not in trouble with me, Bobby." His disappointing look changed to an inquisitive look, with her fingers still over his lips preventing him from speaking. "You are a man. My dad tells me it is up to a man to try, and it is up to a woman to put him in his place. You were not trying anything with me. We love each other. We love kissing each other. I believe we always will. I started the kissing between us when I gave you a passionate impromptu kiss the first day we met. I had never done anything like that before and feared you might think less of me for doing it. You implemented the two-second kiss rule that I approved when we met, but I was so happy to see you today, I threw caution to the wind and surrendered my heart and my kiss to you, just like you did to me. We both learned it only takes one minute or two at the most to ruin good intentions wanting to wait for a wedding night. I never felt my knees buckle from a kiss before today. I was emotionally in trouble trying to resist what your kisses do to me. I love you."

"Thank you for stopping me when you did. I was caught up in the emotions of that kiss. I wanted all of you, and I have never experienced those feelings with any woman. I only want that feeling with you, so I need to follow the two-second kiss rule. I want to save everything else for our wedding night. God gave each of us a special love when He crossed our paths together. I will try to live each day showing you how much you mean to me and how much I love you."

"Give me one of our agreed-upon two-second kisses before we go eat. Okay?"

Rachel already had her lips against his before he started talking, causing her to laugh as they kissed.

"I will take your kisses any way you give them to me." Robert laughed before they both turned to walk inside the restaurant to eat.

They followed the hostess to their booth. Rachel sat down and slid into the booth on one side of the table. Robert was not sure if he should sit alongside of her where he wanted to sit or if he should sit across from her. The waitress had placed his menu on the opposite side of the table from Rachel, who was now looking at the menu and not paying any attention to Robert or his seating dilemma. She looked up from her menu and looked at Robert, saying, "I prefer you sit next to me, if I get a vote on where you sit?"

"Thank you. I will follow your suggestion." Robert smiled at her.

"How do I make this one of my rules to go along with your two-second-kiss rule?" Rachel smiled.

"You are in luck."

"I am in luck? How am I in luck, Mr. Wilson?"

"I have a house rule."

"Am I going to like your house rule?"

"Yes. I believe you will, my dear."

"It is starting to sound good if I am your dear." She chuckled out loud.

"If somebody asks me who is the boss of our home, I will tell them I am. I do everything she says." Rachel was not expecting that answer and was very glad she did not have any coffee in her mouth this time. She and Robert gently slapped their hands together to complete a happy high five as they laughed out loud.

"Thank you for being in my life, Bobby. You are good for me. I know we will be good together."

"And what do I owe this bit of gratitude to?"

"The faith you have in me. You strongly recommended that I send in my application to be the next math coordinator of Lincoln

High School, and I did. They hired me on the spot. So thank you, sir."

Robert turned toward her and pulled her into his arms. "Congratulations. I am so happy for you, Rachel. You will be the voice of reason and the leadership Lincoln High School has been looking for."

"Why do you think they are looking for a voice of reason or leadership?"

"Because you were not there. You complete what the school needs."

"You have me on such a high pedestal, Robert. I fear and dread the day I fall off."

"I will catch you."

"You already caught me. I am yours for as long as you want me, which is both an exciting and a scary position to occupy. I never want to disappoint you in any way. I ask myself if I will measure up as our lives unfold."

"You bring up a good point. Try to remember we are both young, which means we have the chance to slowly build a great life, feeling our way together through experiences, problems, and whatever life throws at us. We do not have all the answers, so we should not have any high expectations of each other. I will always look upon you as my wife, who can never do any wrong in my eyes. You can never slip or fall off any pedestal. You deservedly occupy the pedestal you are on in my heart, mind, and soul."

"When you get mad at me for something, will you still feel this way about me?"

"Always. Do you have anything else you want to tell me about you?"

"No. Why?"

"Because I need to tell you something about me that I failed to say when we first met."

"If this is going to hurt me, please do not tell me. Please do not tell me anything negative. Okay?"

"Okay." Robert chuckled out loud, looking at her. "This is not negative."

"Okay. I am trusting you, Bobby. Please do not break my heart."

"Where did you develop this fear you have about me breaking your heart? Please tell me honestly?"

"I am just afraid to lose the feeling I have in my heart and stomach when we are together. I have never been in love before, and I want to always stay in love with you. And you in love with me."

"Every morning when I wake up, and every night before I go to sleep, I think about you. You are also in my thoughts a lot in between my morning and night. I love dreaming about you. Please remember, I am aware of your biggest fear. I will never consciously do anything to lose your love or your faith in me."

"I will look into the mirror every day when I wake up, and every night before I go to sleep, to tell the girl in the mirror, 'Bobby loves you with every emotion within him, and he will never break your heart.'"

"Perfect. And please say this to yourself several times each day until your heart believes it."

"Okay. Thank you for putting my fears to rest and for talking to me about this, Bobby."

"Thank you for letting me know how strong this fear is within you. I never want you to worry about anything. Promise me, if something ever bothers you, no matter how slight, you will talk to me about it before it grows unnecessarily into a wall between us. Okay."

"Okay. I promise. And now that you have removed my fears, please tell me what you did not tell me the day we met?"

"I am a Johns Hopkins medical school graduate. I will soon pass the medical boards to obtain a license to be a medical doctor." He stopped talking and watched her eyes dilate before she screamed.

"What! Why didn't you tell me about this when we first met, Bobby?" she excitedly blurted this out before she covered her mouth and looked around the restaurant to see who she disturbed.

"I love it when you call me Bobby. Only my mother called me Bobby."

"You are dancing around my question? Fess up. Tell me why you held this fantastic news from me."

"I would love to dance with you. I—"

"Bobby."

"Okay. Sorry. I wanted to tell you about my professional plans when we first met, but I didn't want to take away from any part of the conversation we were having about your life. Your future and your plans are much more important to me than anything going on in my life."

"How in the world can you put my life ahead of your plans to be a medical doctor? How?"

"To remove you from my life would also remove my motivation and my aspiration to do what I do."

Rachel felt her eyes filling with happy tears as she leaned her head against his left shoulder, with a tissue dabbing at her eyes. "Nobody has ever loved me like you do, Bobby. Nobody. I don't understand it. I will just accept it until I catch you telling me a lie. Please don't ever break my heart, Bobby." She looked sheepishly at him and tightened her face playfully like she was about to get hit. "I know, hand me a mirror," she said with a giggle. "It will take practice but worth saying every day and every night."

"In addition to that suggestion, if I ever say or do anything—and I do mean anything—that rubs you the wrong way or hurts your feelings, tell me immediately to avoid any walls being built between us."

"Okay. I hope my question was not too curt. I would never want to hurt your feelings. I should have asked you about your future aspirations when we first met. You did mention how a person may be working in one field today but not necessarily working in that same field a month from today. I take full blame. It is my fault."

"In your defense, it is not your fault or my fault. If we had more time when we met, you would have asked me all the questions on your mind. I had not taken my medical boards when we met, so that conversation would have been premature anyway. I am not a person to boast or brag, but I never would have kept this from you. God is allowing me to be a medical doctor to protect, care, support, and love you the rest of your life, if you will have me?"

"You already know the answer to that question." She looked up into his eyes and watched him lean down to give her a two-second kiss that they both enjoyed. Their eyes smiled at each other as they finished their dinner over light conversation.

"Please turn on your phone and let me have it for a couple of minutes."

Robert reached into his sports jacket to retrieve his cell phone and handed it to her, saying, "I have no secrets from you. My life is an open book. My phone is your phone to use any time of day or night without asking. If you see it and need to use it or inspect it, you don't have to clear it with me. I want you to get very comfortable reaching into my pocket to take a credit card, money, my cell phone, or keys to my car and use them for whatever reason you have at the time. What you have is yours and what I have is yours. Does this tell you how much I want you to be in my life and not just a part of it?"

Rachel's mouth fell open as she stared at him with love in her eyes. "You just want to see me cry."

Robert laughed. "Only if your tears are happy tears. I never want you to be sad or want for anything."

"Do you think we will ever be able to live a life where we will never want for anything?"

"Yes. I know we will be able to live life that way."

"May I ask how you know this to be true?"

"I have to work for one year under a licensed physician, earning around $70,000 annually, before I am eligible to be assigned to a clinic or a hospital, earning a starting pay of $187,200 annually."

"Wow! Bobby, that is a lot of money to make in one year. You will no doubt earn every penny you are paid. I am so proud of you."

"After I work from three to seven years in a fellowship program, I can choose a specialty where the annual salary is mind-boggling even to me. Money will never be an issue with us."

"My dad made good money and made sure we had everything we needed to live within our means. He often said, 'It is wise to live a balanced life with money in safe places for a rainy day. Never try to live beyond your means or up to the standards of your neighbor, who might be borrowing his way into debt.'"

"Your dad is a smart man. You have a level head, Rachel. We will buy a nice home, raise good kids, have date night one night weekly to keep our love alive, join a good church, and retire old together."

"God blessed me beyond my wildest dreams when He led me into the coffee shop to meet you."

"Women like you are rare and not easy to find. I didn't meet anyone like you in four years of college or four years of medical school. I knew instantly when I looked into your eyes and heard you speak when we met that God was blessing me with you, and I will never do anything to lose your love."

"You're exceedingly kind to say these things about me, Bobby. I can truthfully say the same things about you. Can we agree to say that we were both blessed when we met, since it is a truthful statement in my heart?"

"Okay. But I will always add that I was blessed more than you," he added with laughter.

"You are a mess, Dr. Wilson," Rachel said with a smile.

"Thank you, Rachel. You are the first person to address me as Doctor."

"Besides deserving, how did it feel after eight years of schooling?"

"It felt good. Thank you. And I will always remember you being the first person to address me as doctor. That memory will always be special to me. I love you, Rachel."

"I love you, Bobby." Rachel looked into his eyes and saw that familiar look she saw outside when they met earlier today. She put her hand gently over his lips. "Bobby. Please look into my eyes." He did as she requested and felt the need to blink his eyes several times to focus. "Two-second-kiss rule, Bobby. I love you with all my heart. But one two-second kiss, and then we need to go. Okay?"

"Okay." He leaned down and gave her a two-second kiss. "I cannot get enough of you. I could kiss you all day and all night. Just the thought of kissing you makes me want all of you. Thank you for keeping me emotionally under control. I love you."

He slid out of the booth and held out his hand to help her. She wrapped her arm around his arm as they walked to her car and stopped to face each other. She stepped into his arms and squeezed him tightly, with the left side of her face lying flat against his chest. "I could get used to this and having you around me all day and night. Thank you for a wonderful night, Bobby. Thank you for talking to me the way you do and for treating me like I matter to you. It means more to me than you will ever know. My heart is full for the first time in my life because of you and your love for me. Thank you."

"I will sleep deep and good tonight after spending this time with you." He blew out a big breath of air and looked down at her. "How do I function during my days and nights without you in them?"

"Hold on to that thought and cherish it every day. I share this same feeling, Bobby. Thank you for telling me what your heart feels. I do not think most men can share what their heart feels with a woman."

"You have my heart and my love." Robert reached out and pulled her close to him and, while hugging her tightly, said, "I feel like we just crossed a big gap, and you filled it with trust and your love. Thank you for trusting and loving me, Rachel."

"I trust you with my love, my heart, and my life." She looked up at him as his lips found hers, and a rewarding kiss was allowed, longer than their two-second-kiss rule. He opened her car door and helped her inside. She started the engine of her car and rolled down her car window, smiled, and said, "Bye, Bobby."

"Bye, Rachel."

CHAPTER 5

Dr. Mary Dee Sharp

Rachel Rice stopped to put the strap attached to her purse over her left shoulder and adjust the two packages in her arms before she continued walking toward the fast-moving revolving exit door that led to her car and the outside sidewalk. She was apprehensive about her ability to successfully exit out of the fast-moving revolving door with two awkward packages in her arms. She had a genuine fear of stepping out of the revolving exit door onto the concrete sidewalk, dropping her two packages, and falling face-first on the concrete sidewalk.

With the packages in her arms and nothing for her to hold onto, she quickly discovered the pace was too fast for her to control the packages and her balance when she stepped out of the revolving door onto the outside sidewalk. The minute her foot touched the outside sidewalk, she lost her grip on the packages and fell onto her hands and knees. The momentum from the pace of the exit door, that seemed to push her forward out onto the concrete sidewalk, caused her to begin sliding forward, ripping away skin from her hands and her knees. She was almost in a prone position, with her hands stretched so far out in front of her, when her face and elbows dropped down to collide with the concrete sidewalk. When she saw a drop of blood on the sidewalk, she yelled out, "No! Please, Lord, not my teeth." She was still on her hands and knees when she ran her tongue over her front teeth to confirm her biggest fear. She had just broken off a portion of her front tooth.

Her immediate thought was about her students at Lincoln High School and about Bobby, the new love of her life. She never wanted them to see her this way. And these thoughts made her begin to cry and become very emotional and distraught.

She looked up when she heard a female voice speak to her. The woman had kind green-color eyes, shoulder-length blond hair, and an exceptionally beautiful smile.

"May I help you to your feet?" the unidentified woman asked.

"Yes. Thank you so much for taking your time to help a total stranger. I am so clumsy. Please help me," Rachel answered as she was being gingerly helped to her feet.

"You would do it for me," the kind stranger said with a smile.

"Yes. *I* would, but why do *you* say this about me?"

"The friendly Christian look in your eyes."

"Christian look. Thank you for that nice compliment. May I ask your name?" Rachel asked.

"My name is Mary Dee Sharp. My friends call me Dee."

"Dee? I love it," Rachel answered with a smile.

"Thank you, Rachel."

"You are welcome."

"My dad was going to name me Charm. He felt I would be a good luck charm to every person God blessed to be a part of my life. My mother told me he laughed out loud when he thought about making Charm a part of my official name. He loved to joke with people and be the life of the party." Dee giggled.

"The name would have been a conversation starter for sure," Rachel said while laughing.

"Yes, but not as big of a challenge to a boy named Sue." Dee laughed out loud and rolled her eyes.

In spite of her injuries and her broken front tooth, Rachel burst out laughing. She loved listening to Dee's comments and loved hearing her cute laugh. "You have a very contagious cute laugh. I would consider it an honor if you would permit me to be one of your friends. May I call you Dee?"

"Yes. Please call me Dee."

"Thank you, friend."

"You are welcome. My car is parked against the curb, only twenty yards from us. Do you feel you are able to walk over to my car for me to put something on these injuries?"

"Yes. That would be exceedingly kind of you to help me."

"May I ask your name?"

"Yes. My name is Rachel Rice."

Dee took out her automatic car door opener from her purse and aimed it at her vehicle and pressed the button to release the locks on the doors. She wrapped her left arm around the back of Rachel and gently used her right hand to hold an area above the elbow abrasions on Rachel's right arm to help her walk. An unidentified woman picked up the two packages from the sidewalk and opened the passenger door of Dee's vehicle for Rachel to sit on the front passenger seat. Dee took the two packages from the Good Samaritan and thanked her for her help. "I have an emergency kit in the trunk of my car. Let me get it. I will be right back."

"I do not want to hold you up from doing anything more important, Dee. I can drive home and tend to my wounds."

"Nonsense. Like we discussed before, you would do this for me or anyone else in need. This time, it is my turn to be your Good Samaritan." Dee smiled at Rachel.

"How can you say this about me so assuredly, Dee?"

"The kindness in your eyes gives you away, Rachel." Dee and Rachel looked at each other for several seconds, forming a special bond between them, before they smiled and nodded affirmatively.

"Thank you, Dee."

"You are welcome. You know, you also have a beautiful smile, Rachel."

Rachel took out her mirror to see how badly her lip was cut and started to cry when she saw how badly her front tooth was chipped. "Oh, no! Wow. I have really done it this time. I just started a new job as a teacher and also just met the love of my life, and look at me. How do I find a good dentist who will see me on short notice?"

"God has a vision way beyond our understanding, Rachel. He will guide you to the right dentist."

"I wish you were a dentist, Dee." Rachel glanced up toward heaven.

"God is prompting me to reveal to you that I am a dentist." Dee looked at her without expression.

"I wish that were true." Rachel shook her head slowly, wondering what to do next when she caught a peculiar look in Dee's eyes, like she was trying to tell her something. Rachel quickly looked back at Dee and laughed out loud when she saw Dee's eyebrows lift with a big smile on her face. "Are you serious? *You are a dentist?*"

"Busted and guilty."

Rachel ignored her pain and spontaneously reached out her arms to wrap them around Dee. "I have great insurance. Please tell me you can fix my tooth?"

"I can fix your tooth and make it look like nothing happened to it."

"When? Please tell me you can do it soon. Please?"

"Is tomorrow soon enough?"

"Oh, yes! Oh, bless you, Dee. May I still call you Dee?"

"Yes. All my friends and my patients call me Dee. Please call me Dee.

"Thank you," Rachel answered while slowly shaking her head from side to side. I would love to see God's day planner."

"Me too." Dee laughed.

"There are about 7.9 billion people in the world. How does God do it? How does God arrange for you to be here to help me before I need you?"

"We serve an amazing God who is all-knowing," Dee answered with total conviction in her voice.

"I agree." Rachel noticed that Dee had applied triple antibiotic ointment and bandages to her knees and both elbows. "I wish you could add this to your invoice tomorrow. Thank you, Dee."

"You are very welcome. This is one of those things we keep paying forward to someone in need. It always comes back to us. It is impossible to outgive God."

"I agree with that statement. May I have one of your business cards?"

"Yes." Dee took out a business card and handed it to Rachel.

"Thank you very much. Do you work alone in your practice?"

"I am the only dentist in my office. I do have a staff, consisting of dental hygienist, dental assistant to me, and a great receptionist. Do you have far to walk to your car? May I drive you?" Dee asked.

Rachel used the index finger of her left hand to point to the car parked directly in front of her. "That is my car. I did not realize it when I first sat down here in your car. I can stumble and fall that far."

"No. You already tried that one." Rachel and Dee laughed out loud. "I can meet you an hour before my first patient is scheduled to show up in the morning, if this works for you?"

"Yes, ma'am. That will help me in so many ways. I will find a way to properly thank you."

"Bring your insurance card or insurance information with you in the morning. If for any reason, you cannot make the appointment, please call me before I leave my home to come in early to meet you. Okay?"

Rachel smiled, showing Dee her broken tooth. "You have no fear of me not showing up. None."

"In the morning, please tell me about your new job and the new love of your life."

"Okay. He is a new medical doctor who graduated from Johns Hopkins School of Medicine."

"I cannot wait to hear more, and I look forward to meeting him."

"I am confident you will like him when you meet him. I will see you in the morning. Good night."

"Good night, Rachel. Drive carefully"

Rachel thought about Dee during her drive home. The Holy Spirit just told her Dee was going to make her broken tooth look like new in the morning, which prompted her to reach down to touch her bandages and think about Dee, as a happy tear dropped from her eye, and a smile spread across her face. Because Rachel was now feeling overwhelmingly grateful, she whispered, "Thank you, Jesus."

She climbed into bed to lie back on her pillow and mentally paint a picture of Dee to be about 5'2" in height, about 110 pounds, pretty soft-green eyes, shoulder-length blond-color hair, a contagious laugh, and a cute smile as her eyes slowly closed for her to fall asleep.

CHAPTER 6

Dr. Robert Wilson

Robert Wilson was now ready to begin living his life as a medical doctor. He received a letter from Northside Medical Complex letting him know he will be working out of this complex starting tomorrow under a licensed physician, who will supervise every medical decision and every medical procedure he makes for the next year.

Pinch me to make this feel real, he thought to himself as he glanced into his bathroom mirror. He decided to visit the complex a day early to learn how to navigate the complex and learn his way around.

The first year of a doctor's life flies by almost too quickly before it is time to choose their medical specialty in family practice, pediatrics, general surgery, or emergency room medicine where they will be trained, on the job, in a *three-to-seven-year residency* program working from a hospital or major clinic.

After one year of training, new doctors must choose to be trained in a residency program from three to seven years in family practice, pediatrics, emergency room, or general surgery.

Following the completion of the three-to-seven-year residency program, doctors have an option to accept a fellowship for more elite specialized training in oncology (cancer treatments), cardiology (heart and blood vessels), or gastroenterology (digestive system), which normally takes an additional one to four years of additional medical training to complete.

It takes from eight years to sixteen years of medical training before a new doctor can hang his own stethoscope around his neck working in his own medical practice.

Robert drove to the Northside Medical Complex to look at the building directory to see if it provided a clue where he should report tomorrow. His heart fluttered just for a brief second when he spotted a familiar name on the directory—Dr. Robert Wilson, MD. Every emotion raced to unfamiliar levels. He was so overwhelmed he couldn't take his eyes off seeing his own name listed as a medical doctor on a directory outside this huge medical complex.

Seeing his name with the initials MD following it added credibility to his lifetime dream of being a medical doctor. He remembered the feeling he experienced when he passed the medical boards to be a medical doctor. That feeling put him temporarily into a state of euphoria. God and the Holy Spirit within him guided him to graduate from the finest medical school in the country, Johns Hopkins School of Medicine, and guided him to meet the love of his life, Rachel Rice.

Rachel suddenly popped into his mind. He had a strong desire to give her a call and tell her about his good news. He reached his hand into his jacket pocket and pulled out his cell phone, searched his contacts, and saw her name and phone number that she previously typed into his phone the last time they were together. He touched the red button to call her.

After the second ring, she answered excitedly, "Hi, Bobby. I was hoping you would call me since I do not have your phone number."

"Let me give it to you now. Punch it into your phone so you will always have it to call me 24-7. No time is too early or too late for you to call me. Okay?"

"What did I ever do to deserve you, Bobby?"

"Not fair stealing my line, Rachel. It is me who does not deserve you."

"If we both feel this way about each other most days of our lives, we will live a happy blessed life. You never need a reason to call me, but I am curious if there is a specific reason for your call before I tell you my news."

"I am standing outside of a medical building where I am to start working under a medical doctor, to start my one-year training program. I am looking at the names of doctors and different specialties when I saw a name that temporarily made my heart skip a beat, like it does when I look at you."

"Oh, you are so kind. Okay, I give up. What was the name that had such an effect upon you?"

"Dr. Robert Wilson, MD."

"On the medical board outside the office building for everyone to see?" she asked excitedly.

"Yes. It choked me up, Rachel."

"You just choked me up, Bobby." Rachel giggled into the phone.

"Look who is being kind now. I love you so much, I had to share this moment with you."

"I am so glad you did. Thank you for not only thinking about me but calling me, Bobby."

"I always think about you, Rachel. Did you say you have news to share with me?"

"Yes. I am okay, so do not get concerned or alarmed when I tell you my news. Okay?"

"I cannot promise that in advance until you tell me what you want to share with me."

"I fell today and skinned up my hands, knees, and my elbows on a concrete sidewalk. I also—"

"How bad are those injuries? Now I know why I had a strong premonition to call you just now."

"Please have more premonitions to call me. Abrasions and torn skin in the areas I mentioned."

"Triple antibiotic ointment is good for those types of injuries. I should have been there to possibly protect you from falling. I would—"

"I have not finished telling you the worst part."

"There is a worst part?

"Yes. I also cut my lip and broke off a part of my front tooth."

"Oh, Rachel. I am so sorry. I know you do not want your students at Lincoln High School to see you all banged up. We need to get you to a dentist. I can check—"

"God has it all under control, Bobby."

"I know God has everything under control, Rachel. But we need to get your front tooth fixed immediately. I can make some calls and find you a great dentist who will see you this week. Okay?"

"A woman helped me up from the sidewalk and walked me over to sit on the passenger seat of her automobile while she doctored up the abrasions to my hands, elbows, and knees. She told me what to do for my swollen lip when I got home. She happened to be a—"

"I am glad this woman was there, and I am grateful for her helping you the way that she did. There are a lot of good people in this world. What are you going to do about your front tooth?"

"That is the best part of my story, if there can be a best part. The woman who helped me is a dentist."

"For real?"

"Yes. How does God move us around to be in a place to help people like He does, Bobby? How?"

"God is all-knowing and never makes mistakes. God knows what you are going to ask Him before you ask. One of the most amazing things to me about God is the way He forgives and forgets our sins. I forgive people, but I never forget what they did to me. How does He forgive and forget? Talk about sending a dentist to you before you even break your front tooth. Awesome story, Rachel. Can she fix your front tooth to where it is not noticeable?"

"Yes. She told me I would never be able to tell where my tooth had broken."

"Tell me about her."

"Do you have time? Do you have to go inside the building you are standing outside of to work?"

"My first day is tomorrow. I came here today to scope it out. I am sitting on a bench, so I am okay."

"Okay. Her name is Dr. Mary Dee Sharp."

"Do you like her? Do you trust her? How does she—"

"I am not sizing her up to marry her." Rachel laughed into the phone. "Trust my instincts, Bobby. I feel really good about her, and if you looked into her eyes and talked to her, you would too."

"Okay. You are right. I need to rely upon you to handle everything God puts in your path to handle when I am not with you. I do trust your judgment. After all, you did choose me."

"Boy, what does that say about the errors in my judgment?" Rachel said, laughing out loud.

"Good one, Rachel. I like the humorous side of you. I want to see and hear more of it."

"You have been too busy kissing me to hear the humorous side of me," Rachel said jokingly. "And I am not complaining."

"Tell me your plans for tonight?"

"Now that you made my day complete by calling me, I am going to take a bubble bath, read a little bit, and get a good night sleep for my dental appointment in the morning."

"Have you notified your school principal that you might run a little late in the morning?"

"I may not have to. The dentist is meeting me an hour before she normally sees her first morning patient. I will be fine. But thank you for that concern for me."

"You're welcome."

"What are your plans for tonight and tomorrow?" Rachel asked.

"I am going to walk inside to meet the people I will be working with tomorrow and then go home. I will cook something for me to eat and get a good night sleep."

"Text me the name of the building where you will be working when you get a chance. Okay?"

"Okay."

"Remember the permanent marching orders I gave you from my heart to your heart."

"I know your orders, Rachel. Do not break your heart."

"You learned the second part of your orders. The first part of your marching orders were to never allow a cute nurse or pretty doctor to steal your heart away from me to break my heart."

"How can they steal what I do not have? You have my heart, and you always will, Rachel."

"I will hold you to that, Bobby. I love you, Bobby. Good night."

"Just as long as you hold me, Rachel. I love you too. Good night."

CHAPTER 7

Robert Meets Allison Hope

Robert finished his conversation with Rachel and walked into the Northside Medical Complex to learn which doctor he would be working under during his one year of supervised medical training, which is required before he is eligible to enter a follow-up three-to-seven-year residency training program.

Once he opened the outside door to the Northside Medical Complex and stepped into the lobby, he immediately spotted a young woman sitting behind a desk underneath an information sign hung above her head. She appeared to be about twenty-three years of age and probably 110 pounds, distributed perfectly for any man to be proud to have her in his life. She had black-color hair that was styled nicely away from her face down to the top of her shoulders. She had dazzling blue-color eyes that shined brightly. She smiled and waited for him to speak as he approached her desk. Her smile seemed natural and effortless as she revealed her bright white teeth.

She watched him giving her the once-over with his eyes before she said, "Do you have me all sized up?"

Robert burst into laughter, which made her laugh too. "Busted. Not on the job five minutes, and I am already busted." He was still shaking his head sideways and smiling at her when he managed to say, "Hi."

"How may I help you, sir?"

"I am not sure why I came in here?" Robert laughed. "You have disarmed me with your question?"

41

"You were so obvious. I could not resist teasing you. I always wanted to say that to a man. You guys all give us the once-over. I know. It is a man thing." She giggled. "Your friendly face made me reminisce back to my college days with some of my friends who looked like you." She giggled. "I will now put my serous face on. How may I help you?" She stopped smiling and looked at him with her serious face.

"My name is Robert Wilson. I am new to the medical profession and assigned to work in this building for the next year under a licensed physician, but not sure which one. Can you help me?"

"Nope. I quit before you have me fired." She got up with her purse and started walking for the front door.

"Stop. You are safe."

She stopped, turned around to face him, and eyed him cautiously without speaking. She raised her eyebrows and pressed her lips together and looked at him as she slowly blew out a long breath of air.

"This is our secret. Your face and smile belong back here." Robert pointed to her desk chair.

"You swear on whatever is sacred to you?"

"I swear on whatever is sacred to me. I am your friend today and always. You quickly sized me up and felt comfortable and safe enough to tease me. Thank you. I will always remember this and laugh about it."

"Okay." On her way back to her desk, she paused long enough to do a high five with Robert and sat back down behind her desk. Looking up at him, she smiled and said, "Yes. I can help you, Dr. Wilson."

"Thank you, ma'am."

"Dr. Joe Drake employs everyone who works in this complex. You will be working under him. To find his office, you need to walk down the hallway behind me to suite number 33."

"Thank you very much. May I ask your name?"

"Uh-oh. Here it comes. Need a name to turn me in." She giggled out loud.

"You belong on a stage with your comedy act. You are good. I want a front-row seat at your shows."

"See what things you make me do?" she teased him again, and he loved it. "My name is Allison Hope."

"I bet that is the one of the best things you give to all your friends."

Allison gave him a confused look. "Teasing?"

Robert smiled at her. "Hope. You have the ability to inspire people and give them hope."

The look in her eyes really said it all, but she could not resist saying, "That is one of the nicest things anyone has ever said to me. Thank you, Dr. Wilson."

"I always speak the truth. God will bless you abundantly, Allison Hope."

"From your lips to God's ears. I will always remember your words and pray to be an inspired ray of hope for everyone to see. Thank you for saying this to me. It means more to me than you will ever know."

"I had a strong feeling that God wanted you to hear those words from me. I trust you are a believer?"

"Yes. I believe in Jesus. I pray and walk with him daily. Do you?"

"Yes. I do. Thank you for asking me that question."

"You are very welcome. Please let me know if I can ever help you after today."

Robert's eyes seemed to smile while looking into her eyes. Allison Hope was now convinced she made a new friend. The loving look she had in her eyes would be the look Robert would always fondly remember.

"Stay safe, inspiring, and happy, Allison Hope. Bye."

"Bye, Dr. Wilson. I look forward to seeing a lot more of you."

"That future pleasure will be mine." Robert smiled as he turned and walked away.

CHAPTER 8

Robert Meets Tiffany Dawn

Robert opened the door to suite number 33 and stepped inside the lobby to observe a woman standing inside the receptionist window, speaking on the office telephone. He sized her up to be about 5'2" in height, 120 pounds, probably in her early twenties, blond-color hair, green eyes, pretty teeth, and contagious friendly smile as he walked closer to the receptionist window and waited for her to finish her call. She hung up the telephone before she looked up at him with her contagious friendly smile and asked," How may I help you, sir?"

"My name is Robert Wilson. I was told to be here tomorrow to begin a one-year supervised medical training program under Dr. Joe Drake. I came a day early to learn my way around the complex and to find this office. I hope that is okay?"

"I am impressed with the way you introduced yourself without telling me you are a doctor. That is the first thing I hear from most new doctors." She reached out her hand toward him and said, "My name is Tiffany Dawn."

She reminded him of one of his former attractive female classmates. He and his close buddies liked hanging around her, and they would undoubtedly love Tiffany.

"Welcome to our staff, Dr. Wilson. I look forward to working with you. If you need anything, please let me know. I serve as your receptionist, your concierge, your reservationist, and your friend. Okay?"

"You are the epitome of indispensable, Tiffany."

"I do not think I would go that far, but thank you, Dr. Wilson." Tiffany laughed out loud.

"I bet the things you do every day encompass most of the twelve steps to be indispensable."

"Now you have me curious to learn these twelve steps."

"Sometime when you have time, I will tell them to you."

"I have time right now, if you do? I am the only one here. Everyone has gone home for the day."

"I am sorry to pop in so late in the day. I do not want to hold you up."

"How long would it take to tell me the twelve steps?"

"Good point. Not long. Okay. I have a copy of them in my briefcase. May I read them to you?"

"Absolutely. I would love to hear them to see how I measure up."

Robert took out a tablet from his briefcase. "These are the twelve steps to be known as indispensable."

1. Help others without expecting anything in return. Take pleasure in watching others succeed.
2. Dedicate yourself to always live by a higher standard. Do your best at everything you try to do. Constantly strive to keep raising the bar for yourself.
3. Do what you tell others you will do and try to do more. Do not make commitments you cannot keep.
4. Be of value to others. Be the one people reach out to. Be the one from whom people seek mentorship, coaching, information, and solutions.
5. Be open and adaptable. Learn to embrace change and help others see the benefits of change.
6. Be honest. Admit a mistake, a missed deadline, or a bad judgment call. Communicate openly and work hard to find solutions to any problems you may have caused. Never engage in blame-placing.
7. People who are indispensable usually expand their role by going the extra mile. Whatever your job requires of you, make it a point to always do your job well and be available to help others.

8. Learn more by being more. Do everything you can to make more of yourself. Volunteer for tasks outside your usual role; be eager to step up and take on more than your share. Do it with openness and effectiveness and a willing heart and mind. This will make you invaluable and indispensable.

9. Learn from every failure and every mistake. Regardless of how bad the experience might be, learn to look at it and learn how to grow from it.

10. Focus on inclusion and collaboration. Learn to become the person who thrives on working with others.

11. Acknowledge and appreciate those around you. There's no surer way to gain respect than to acknowledge and appreciate others around you.

12. Stay positive. It's easy to become so focused on the finish line that you fail to enjoy the journey. Be positive and a joy to be around as you're building your success. Being indispensable does not come from having an ego but from what others think of you as you help them succeed.

"Would you like to make a copy of this that you can critique and condense?"

"Yes. I would love to make a copy. Thank you." Robert handed the printed list to her. "Thank you, Dr. Wilson." She handed the original list back to him. "It was my pleasure to meet you. I look forward to seeing you in the morning and introducing you to Dr. Drake and our staff."

"Thank you for spending part of your after-hours time talking with me. It was a pleasure to meet you. I look forward to working with you. Good night."

"Good night, Dr. Wilson."

Robert nodded and smiled at her before he opened the office door and disappeared.

Robert drove back to his hotel, ordered something to eat, read a few pages from a magazine, and climbed into bed to fall asleep.

CHAPTER 9

Dr. Robert Wilson Injured

The sun rose slowly over the horizon, casting a ray of light above and around Robert's bedroom curtains to light up his room. The bedside radio clicked on to the sound of music at precisely 6:00 a.m. Robert rolled out of bed and started walking toward the bathroom to take his morning shower when he abruptly stopped to listen to one of his favorite songs being sung by Kris Kristofferson, titled "Why Me Lord." This song was special to him because he often wondered to himself, *Why me, Lord?*

He stepped into the shower and allowed the hot water to roll off his head and down his back for a few minutes, before he joined his soap bar with his washcloth to finish a very relaxing shower to begin his day. He was almost finished dressing when he thought about Rachel. "Lord, let Rachel be relaxed and love all the people she will meet in Dr. Mary Dee Sharp's office today. Please bless the hands of Dr. Sharp and guide her professionally to restore Rachel's broken front tooth to make it look so new even Rachel will not be able to tell which front tooth was the broken one. In Jesus's name, I pray. Amen."

Robert entered the office of Dr. Joe Drake and was greeted warmly by Tiffany Dawn. "Good morning, Dr. Wilson. May I get you a cup of coffee?"

"Yes, please. You are exceedingly kind."

"I do try."

"Try? You should teach the class."

"Oh. Look who is being kind now." She laughed out loud, making Robert laugh.

"After you have had a chance to drink your coffee, I will introduce you to our staff. Deal?"

"Deal. Are you always so chipper early in the morning?" He leaned his elbows on the reception window ledge and looked up at her.

"I am trying to show you that I can be indispensable." Tiffany laughed and promptly raised her left hand to lightly slap his open left hand to complete a joyful high five with him.

"Trust me, Tiffany. You are the epitome of the word *indispensable*. I am betting you are the glue that holds this clinic together."

"You are exceedingly kind, Dr. Wilson. Thank you for your vote of confidence."

"Earned vote of confidence." He continued to look at her, smiling. "Okay, that first cup of coffee hit the spot. Please lead me to whomever you want me to meet."

"Okay." She took his empty cup from him, scribbled out a short note, and set the cup and her note on her desk before she looked back up at him. "Please follow me."

Tiffany introduced him to every member of the nursing staff before she turned to him, asking, "Are you ready to see your office?"

"I get an office?"

"I am not sure you will be able to enjoy it very much during business hours, but you will have plenty of time to enjoy it in the evenings."

"A little?" Robert held up his index finger and his thumb, showing a little space between these two fingers. "This little?"

"You get the idea." They both laughed.

"I love hearing your contagious laugh. I hope to hear a lot more of your laughter."

"I love to laugh, Dr. Wilson, especially when I have reasons to laugh." Suddenly her mind took a mental trip back through her past, trying to remember the happiest times in her life.

"Wow. I bet that mental trip you just took has a lot of interesting stored memories."

"Stored and locked in my secret mental vault that is marked 'Private, no public access.'" She did not laugh.

Robert continued to watch her facial expressions, trying to figure out if those memories were happy or sad ones, but could not tell. He noticed that she seemed to be also studying his expressions, which promptly made him say, "Which one of us is going to blink first?" He smiled at her.

Nodding her head in agreement, she smiled back at him, saying, "It does not happen often with me. Occasionally someone will say something, like you just did, that will make me think about a past happy experience. I love wonderful memories. Nobody sets out to make sad ones, but sadly they do happen."

"I love how you speak from your heart, Tiffany."

"I believe you will fit into our small office group nicely, Dr. Wilson." She waited for his response.

"I felt it last night when we met. You have a beautiful face and lovely smile. People are comfortable when they are around you. I am comfortable being around you."

"What a nice thing to say. Thank you very much. Please follow me to your new office." Tiffany walked down two long hallways and took right turns at the end of each before she stopped at his office. Robert was impressed when he saw the name "Dr. Robert Wilson" on the outside of the door that she opened wide. She stepped aside to allow him to be the first between them to walk into his new office.

He took one step into his new office and immediately stopped to look at the most gorgeous wooden desk he had ever seen in his life. Seeing his name centered on it made him do a double take. There is something to be said about seeing your own name on the outside of an office building, on the outside of an office door, or on a twelve-inch beautiful brown wooden plaque with your name inscribed in gold, centered on your desk. *Mesmerizing* is one key word that could be used to describe what Robert was feeling at this very moment. Seeing his name in all these places served to confirm to him that he really is a board-certified medical doctor. To someone else, this might not seem like a big deal, but to him it is. Directly in front of his new desk were two beautiful high-backed green-and-brown upholstered cushioned chairs that flanked an expensive-looking brown table with its flat surface about three feet above the ground, measuring about twenty-four inches wide and thirty inches deep. This is a perfect height for a guest who is sitting in one of the flanking chairs to set a beverage on. The brown table accentuated and brought out the brown colors in the green and brown chairs. "Nice touch."

"Yes. I thought so too," she confessed while looking at him and nodding her head in agreement.

"Tiffany would never miss such a thing. Right?" he teased.

Shaking her head sideways with a big smile, she said, "No woman would miss those sorts of things."

"Of course not. What was I thinking?"

"You were thinking like a man. But you are forgiven." Laughter quickly erupted between them.

"Ah, I love this gorgeous plush green couch and the way you positioned it perfectly against the wall on the left side of the room as a person enters the office. The color of it helps beautify this entire office."

"Yes. And I love how everything matches the carpet. The clinic did not spare any expense when it came to purchasing your office furniture or the carpet. The goal was to make your office beautiful. Do you like what you see?" Tiffany asked.

"Yes, ma'am. I do love everything. You did a great job."

"Thank you, Dr. Wilson. I am glad you approve. I am especially impressed with these accessory items."

"I was just about to mention the accessory items—"

"You were not." Tiffany burst into laughter, seeing Robert's stunned reaction to her teasing him.

"I was too," he adamantly replied, then burst into laughter. "You and I are going to be good friends."

"I believe so." She smiled, shaking her head, marveling over how God brought her such a special friend.

"You remind me of my sister, the way we teased each other with did too, did not. I needed that laugh. Thank you, Tiffany."

"You're welcome. I figured you to be a kidder like me." They did a high five and smiled.

"Back to the accessories, hmm." He looked at her and smiled before he continued speaking.

"Go ahead. I will not comment or interrupt you much." She could not help laughing.

"Hmm." After clearing his throat, he continued, "I love how these pictures seem so real to life to me. I love the colors chosen for the horses, dogs, and the riders on horseback depicted in these pictures. Observers who are trained or even untrained would definitely think these pictures are awfully expensive."

"Sounds like you are speaking with experience." She looked at him while tilting her head slightly.

"No, ma'am. Before you even ask, while I do love beautiful pictures, I am an untrained person who does not have an eye to spot a gem from a beginning artist. These are great finds."

"We aim to please."

"Mission accomplished. I am very satisfied. Thank you very much."

"Would you like some time to yourself right now?"

"No. Not really. I look forward to interacting with patients and giving them my diagnosis and prognosis. If I am not rushing things a bit?"

"No, not at all. Dr. Drake assigned his best nurse to stay by your side. She will introduce you to each patient and be at your beck and call to assist you. Let me hand you this clipboard that contains the names of each patient you will see on this floor. Please note that this chart does list the patient's name, diagnosis, and treatment plan. Eventually you will enter your own prognosis for each patient."

"Everything sounds great to me. Thank you for being so thorough and for making me feel so welcome, Tiffany."

"Meeting you has been an extreme pleasure. Welcome aboard, Dr. Wilson." She reached out her hand.

Robert accepted her hand into his and gave it a firm handshake with a smile.

"Follow me to meet Nurse Kim Holly."

Robert nodded. "Please lead the way."

He followed her down the length of the hallway, where they made another right turn and stopped at the nurses' station. "Hello, Kim Holly, guess who I would love for you to meet and work with today?" Tiffany smiled and turned slightly to her left to look at Dr. Wilson.

Nurse Holly looked up at Dr. Wilson, nodded with a smile, and said, "It is my pleasure to meet you, Dr. Wilson. You are already quite a legend around here." She reached out and shook his hand.

"Legend? I am afraid you have me mixed up with someone else. I graduated from medical school and just passed my medical boards to qualify being here today. A legend? Not me."

"He does not have a clue." Tiffany volunteered as she looked from Kim to Dr. Wilson."

He wrinkled his forehead and looked from Kim to Tiffany with a confused look on his face. "Please help me out here, Tiffany."

Tiffany looked at Kim. "Shall I explain, or would you like to?"

"Rank has no privilege on this issue with me. You met him before I had that honor, and I like how you are building a friendship with Dr. Wilson. The floor belongs to you."

"Why would I expect anything less from you, Kim?"

"I do not want to steal your thunder. Tell us about our newest team member," Kim said with a smile.

"Dr. Wilson graduated high school at the age of sixteen, and college at the age of twenty. He started a demanding job as a traveling pharmaceutical representative to earn enough money to pay his own way through medical school. Nothing came easy for him, and he would have it no other way, which is why he enrolled into the number 1 medical school in the United States of America. He subsequently graduated with top honors from Johns Hopkins School of Medicine, which we all call Johns Hopkins medical school. He took and passed his medical boards on his first try to obtain a license to be a medical doctor. Please welcome, Dr. Robert Wilson." Tiffany smiled and started to clap out of respect for his achievements. Kim also chimed in by clapping, smiling, and welcoming Robert to their team.

"Your kindness is a bit overwhelming to me. I was not ready for this kind of warm welcome. But thank you for making me feel so special and welcome. I will do my best to be the doctor and friend you hope I will be. It might be a challenge to balance and navigate from this high pedestal you have mysteriously put me up on. If I let any of you down in any way, please let me know immediately. Deal?"

"Deal," they both responded at the same time.

Tiffany cleared her throat and prepared to speak, "Do you have any questions?"

"No. You have covered everything thoroughly. Thank you, again, very much."

"You are welcome. I will be at my desk. Remember, I am always within earshot of you. Bye."

"Bye."

"Ready?" "Kim looked over his shoulder to review the names on the clipboard he held in his hand.

"Yes, I am ready. Please lead the way."

Robert was surprised at how comfortable he felt going from room to room with Nurse Holly closely by his side. She watched and listened to him ask each patient pertinent questions about their injuries that brought them to see Dr. Drake. He made sure each patient was comfortable with him before he examined them to form his diagnosis. From out of his peripheral vision, he became increasingly encouraged to see his nurse nodding her head in agreement to each diagnosis and treatment plan he discussed with each patient he examined.

Robert could not wait to tell Rachel about his first day working as a medical doctor. Three hours had passed quickly before he stepped out of one treatment room into the hallway on his way to another treatment room when he heard a loud noise that sounded like a skirmish in one of the adjacent patient rooms. He heard an angry male voice, followed by a female voice, yelling, "Help."

A nurse suddenly appeared in the doorway of the adjacent treatment room. She looked at Robert and screamed, "Help me." Just as she tried to step out of the treatment room to run toward him, a handle of a wooden cane wrapped around the front of her throat from behind her and pulled her forcibly back into the room.

Robert ran to the doorway of the treatment room and saw an overly obese white male, about 6'7" tall, and weighing well over three hundred pounds, holding the nurse down on the bed with his left hand and holding a thick wooden cane in his right hand raised high into the air, about to be used to hit her with it, when Robert yelled, "Leave her alone."

The big guy grabbed the nurse by her neck and yanked her off the bed and shoved her into the path of Robert. Robert instinctively used both of his hands to grab and protect her from falling to the treatment room floor, which forced him to turn his back to this patient, who never hesitated to use the thick wooden handle cane to forcibly strike the back of his head. The protected nurse Robert had just saved from being hit by this same cane turned her head in time to see Robert's knees buckle, and his eyes roll back into his head as he collapsed face-first onto the treatment room floor. Simultaneously he was struck forcibly a second time along the left side of his head, causing blood to spurt from both of his head injuries.

Nurse Kim Holly dropped down onto her knees and fell on top of Robert to use her body as a shield and simultaneously screamed, "No! Leave him alone." Impulsively she covered the rear of her head with both of her hands, thinking she was about to be next to be hit with the thick wooden cane.

The huge angry patient stepped closer to Robert with a death grip on his thick wooden cane, and while looking down at Robert and Kim, he raised his cane into the air to inflict more pain when Tiffany Dawn charged into the room, running at full speed like she was a professional football player, to tackle the huge angry man. The big guy fell onto the treatment room floor with Tiffany Dawn on top of him.

Two police officers rushed into the room just as the big guy rolled Tiffany off his body and stood up. He glared at the two officers, contemplating his next move while clinging tightly to the thick heavy wooden cane in his right hand. He was a mountain of a man who looked like a beast towering over the two officers.

One of the officers pulled his pistol from its holster and pointed it at him, saying, "Listen to me very carefully big guy. You have not killed anyone here today. Do not make your temporary problem a permanent problem. I will shoot you. Drop it, now. This bullet will travel a lot faster to you than your cane can come to me. Last warning. Drop it. Now!"

The thick wooden cane made a loud noise when it landed on the floor. The police officer kicked the cane under the bed and put handcuffs on the big guy before assisting him into a chair. He used his radio to call the local police precinct to send a police van to take this big guy to jail.

Nurse Holly used her call button to summon an orderly to come assist her with Robert. Then she used her nursing skills to stop blood from spurting from Robert's multiple head wounds before she rolled him over to take his blood pressure and pulse. The available room space quickly filled up with nurses and the requested orderly.

Dr. Joe Drake rushed into the room and ordered police officers to remove the big guy sitting on a chair with his hands cuffed behind his back. Dr. Drake then asked the male orderly to carefully help lift Dr. Wilson onto the bed.

Dr. Drake looked at Nurse Holly. "What are his vital signs?"

She pressed her lips tightly together as she showed him her written nurses notes showing his vital signs, revealing him to be in a coma and his prognosis listed as guarded and extremely critical. She leaned closer to him and whispered, "I took these vital signs twice. He needs a neurosurgeon, EEG, and a miracle." She watched Dr. Drake read her notes and nod his head in agreement.

"He lost a lot of blood. His vital signs do not look good." Dr. Drake blew out a long breath of air as his eyes became misty, thinking about this being Dr. Robert Wilson's first day as a medical doctor. "Do you know why this big guy with the wooden cane went so crazy?"

"Yes, sir. He is addicted to heroin and demanded a prescription from me. He demanded an immediate hit or fix. I had to be honest with him. I told him no. He went ballistic. He shoved me down onto the bed and was choking me. I rolled off to one side and ran. I got to the doorway and made eye contact with Dr. Wilson and yelled for him to help me. This patient reached out that big thick wooden cane and wrapped the handle around my neck and yanked me back into the room."

"Dr. Wilson rushed into the room to help you. Right?"

"Yes, sir."

"I am so sorry you had this experience. Thank you so much for protecting Dr. Wilson by using your body as a human shield. You might have saved his life by risking yours. I hope I get the chance to let him know his rescue of you was a two-way street. You saved his life too."

"Not quite accurate. I only shielded his body from being hit again. Tiffany Dawn saved both of us."

"Tiffany Dawn?"

"Yes. Tiffany Dawn saved his life by rushing into the room and tackling him before he had a chance to hit Dr. Wilson one more time, or me with that thick heavy wooden cane."

Dr. Drake turned to face Tiffany. "We are all in your debt, Tiffany. Thank you very much."

"I never met anyone quite like him. He would do it for me. I know he would."

"Did you know him before he came to our clinic to work?"

"She and Dr. Wilson talked a long time last night when he came by to check out where he would be working today. Today they just picked up where they left off last night. They have a unique chemistry and a good friendship. They kid each other like they have known each other for years," Kim responded for her.

"I can understand it. You are friendly and easy to talk to. An asset to our clinic. Thank you for being so kind to our newest member and for your help today. Please pray for him to recover and come back to us."

"You are very welcome. Thank you. I will pray for him, Dr. Drake."

"Thank you, Tiffany."

"You're welcome. It is scary how fast our lives can change. Isn't it, Dr. Drake?"

"Yes, it is very scary, Tiffany. Nurse Holly, do you have time to do a couple of favors for me?"

"Yes. What do you need for me to do?"

"First, please start Dr. Wilson on IVs and put him on oxygen."

"Okay." Nurse Holly looked over at Nurse Pat Johnson and nodded her head.

Nurse Johnson hooked up an IV and put Dr. Wilson on oxygen. She turned back to Nurse Holly and nodded her head, confirming her instructions have been completed.

"IV and oxygen have been started on Dr. Wilson. What else can we do?"

"Have a member of your team check Dr. Wilson's employment records and give me the contact information for his next of kin. I need to let them know his condition and where we will likely send him."

"Okay. I will get that handled immediately." Kim looked at Tiffany, who nodded her head and left the room to follow those instructions.

"The Mayo Clinic and Johns Hopkins Hospital employ the best neurosurgeons in the country. Call their neurosurgery department and let them know his medical condition and obtain their availability to admit and treat Dr. Robert Wilson today."

"Okay. I will be right back with answers and a choice for you to make an intelligent decision."

"Thank you, Kim."

"You're welcome, Dr. Drake." Two physician assistants asked Nurse Holly to explain an EEG brain test.

"EEG exam is electroencephalogram test to read the electric activity of Robert Wilson's brain. No oxygen for more than six minutes means Robert could be irreversibly brain dead. The human brain regulates breathing, eye movements, blood pressure, heartbeat, and swallowing. It is sometimes referred to as a muscle of thinking since the brain tells your muscles what to do. The brain controls all things in the body that make us human. Therefore, it is arguably the most important organ in the human body. The brain stem oversees all the functions your body needs to stay alive, like breathing air, digesting food, and circulating blood. Some of the structures of the brain could be working, such as the brain stem, but when not all the brain is working, this could cause a person to slip into a coma. And knowing Dr. Robert Wilson is in a coma gives us cause to have a major medical concern. The EEG brain test will tell the neurosurgeon why."

Nurse Holly walked back into the room holding a sheet of paper with answers to the questions Dr. Drake had asked, and waited until she had his undivided attention before she spoke.

Dr. Drake looked at Kim while adjusting Dr. Wilson's IV tube. "What did you find out?"

"Dr. Wilson never filled out his contact information on his employment records. Lamar Benson said he allowed him to skip that part if he agreed to do it later. He was eager to start examining patients on his first day working as a licensed physician. He told Mr. Benson he would do it today on his lunch hour, but as fate would have it, this happened to him before he took a lunch hour."

"That is not good. Lamar must not allow this to ever happen again, especially not to a new employee."

"Okay. I will let him know and follow up to ensure that all new employees complete this form."

"Thank you, Kim. Dr. Wilson's next of kin, or friends who know him, will not know anything about these injuries or how to begin finding him." Dr. Drake disgustingly shook his head, looking sadly down at Robert.

"Do you have anything else you would like for me to do?" Kim asked.

"Yes, I do. Refresh my memory by telling me the name of the medial school he graduated from?"

"Johns Hopkins School of Medicine, with honors. They have nothing listed for his next of kin. He paid his own way through medical school. The Johns Hopkins Hospital always rolls out the red carpet to treat one their own graduate doctors who needs medical attention. Their neurology department is ranked number 2 in the country. Mayo Clinic is number 1."

"That is very interesting."

"Which part?"

"The Johns Hopkins University School of Medicine is ranked number 1 in the country, while their hospital neurosurgery department is ranked number 2, behind the Mayo Clinic. Do you happen to know the ranking numbers for these two hospitals?"

"Yes. I made a note of it." Kim looked down at her notes. "Mayo Clinic in Rochester, Minnesota, is ranked number 1 in neurosurgery with a neurology and neurosurgery score of 100/100."

"Impressive. Can't get any better than one hundred."

"Johns Hopkins Hospital is ranked number 2 in neurosurgery with a neurology and neurosurgery score of 95.7/100."

"Very impressive and very thorough research, Kim."

"Thank you, Dr. Drake."

"You are very welcome. If I decide to send Dr. Wilson to Johns Hopkins Hospital, do you have the contact information for me to make the referral?"

"Yes, sir. Everything you will need is on this one sheet of paper. May I put this on your desk?"

"Yes, but first, please call Johns Hopkins Hospital and apprise them of his condition and let them know I have decided to transfer him immediately to their hospital for medical care. Obtain the name of the person who will receive him and possibly the name of the neurosurgeon I will be communicating with."

"Okay. I will meet you in your office with the answers to these questions for you to dictate the letter."

Dr. Drake walked into his office and blew out a short breath of air as he looked at Kim. Kim said, "These are the answers to your questions about Johns Hopkins Hospital. They did ask me to call them with his estimated airport arrival time. Their medical team will meet him at the airport to fly him by helicopter into their hospital. Their best neurosurgeon, Dr. Metzger, is on standby, waiting for him to arrive."

"Everything that could be done medically will have been done by the time Dr. Wilson gets checked into Johns Hopkins Hospital. I like how this is coming together. Please ride with him in our helicopter to the airport and stay with him until he is accepted as a passenger on their helicopter. Our helicopter pilot will then fly you and the orderlies back here. Any questions?"

"No. I am ready to go when you say the word."

"Thank you for everything you do for me and this medical complex, Kim."

"Thank you for the trust you have in me to do the things I am permitted to do, Dr. Drake."

"You have earned that trust, Kim. How many orderlies are you taking with you?"

"I have two orderlies on standby to fly with me to help me with Dr. Wilson."

"Great. Here is the letter you will need for the helicopter pilot who just radioed me that he was on the landing pad upstairs, waiting for you and Dr. Wilson. Have a safe flight. See you when you return with the orderlies. Thank you again for everything you have done and for what you are about to do."

Kim nodded her head, turned, and waved to the orderlies standing in the doorway. They waved back and pointed toward the upstairs landing pad, reminding her the helicopter was waiting for Dr. Wilson.

Kim helped them to get Dr. Wilson onto a gurney for the orderlies to push it up to the waiting helicopter.

Kim handed the pilot Dr. Drake's letter of authorization and walked around the helicopter to take her seat on the front passenger seat next to the pilot. The two orderlies jumped into the back seat and buckled up.

Upon approaching the airport, the pilot tapped her leg with his finger and pointed to the waiting helicopter from Johns Hopkins Hospital. He set the helicopter down, close to the Johns Hopkins Hospital helicopter, and waited for the two orderlies to successfully complete the transfer of Dr. Robert Wilson.

Kim Holly signed the transfer documents before she and the orderlies flew back to Dr. Drake.

CHAPTER 10

Rachel Rice and Dr. Mary Dee Sharp

Rachel slept peaceably and woke up without the help of an alarm clock. She felt refreshed and ready to start her day that began with a dental appointment to repair her front tooth and ended with meeting Robert for dinner.

For the first time in her life, she now knew how it felt to have unmistakable feelings of love in her heart. These kinds of feelings were foreign to her before today. She knew, without a doubt, that she loved Robert Wilson and knew he loved her for the woman she had become. She would never trade this feeling of love for any amount of money. She was deliriously happy.

I need to keep pinching myself to make sure I am not dreaming, she thought to herself. She closed her eyes and whispered, "How could I ever make myself believe I am worthy of this blessing, Lord?"

She opened her eyes, shook her head, and got inside her automobile to drive to her dental appointment.

Rachel was suddenly apprehensive and extremely nervous about her dental appointment. Before she could think another negative thought, she turned her car into the dental parking lot and drove right up to the front door of Dr. Mary Dee Sharp. She opened their front door and stepped inside the lobby to see Dee standing behind the receptionist desk. She gave Rachel a friendly smile that immediately seemed to calm most of the fears in her mind.

"Good morning, Rachel. I can set my clock by you. Thank you for being punctual."

"Hi, Dee. You are welcome. And it is indeed a good morning now that I am standing here, looking at you and knowing what you are about to do for me. Thank you for meeting me so early this morning. I will find a way to repay your kindness by sending a bunch of my friends to you."

"I do accept new patients." Dee laughed. "Thank you for that thought, Rachel. You are exceedingly kind." Dee cleared her throat and reached for a clipboard on the receptionist window and turned to face Rachel. "Please do me a favor by filling out this short patient information form so I can create a file on you. Okay?"

"Okay. I did bring my insurance card. I also brought my personal and business addresses and phone numbers for you. I made copies, so you can have those documents."

"I wish all our patients were so thorough. Thank you very much."

"You are welcome," Rachel replied.

"Set the clipboard on the reception window when you are finished so I know when to come get you to begin fixing your front tooth. I bet you are ready to get it fixed. Right?" Dee asked.

"Right. I am ready. And thank you again for meeting me so early."

"You are very welcome. No problem. And thank you for being on time and not throwing off my entire day by being late."

"Now that would have been very ungrateful on my part. I am so appreciative of you and your time."

"See, I was right about you. Okay, now please give me a few minutes to get myself ready to begin working on your front tooth. I will be right back. Okay?"

"Okay. I will fill out this form and be ready."

Dee saw the clipboard on the ledge of the receptionist window before she walked into the patient waiting area to get Rachel. "Please come back into the first room on the left so we can get a closer look at your front tooth and make it look new."

"I feel like a kid at Christmas. The famous song 'All I Want for Christmas Is My Two Front Teeth' has played repeatedly in my mind all night and during my drive here this morning. That is the gift I want for Christmas. I am overwhelmed with joy and incredibly grateful for the gift you are about to give to me. I cannot wait to show Bobby my new front tooth tonight. He is cautiously optimistic about what my smile will look like after my tooth is repaired."

"Please call me and let me know if he gives me an A+." Dee laughed, looking at Rachel.

"I will call you and pass along his approving comments, along with your suggested A+ grade."

"Have you known Bobby long, Rachel?"

"I feel like we have known each other all our lives, but no. I recently met him. My heart is convinced he is the love of my life and the man I will one day marry and happily have his children."

"I am happy for you, Rachel. What does he do for a living?"

"He just passed his medical boards and is now a medical doctor. He graduated with honors from Johns Hopkins School of Medicine, which is rated number 1 in the USA. Today he begins working from a medical complex to begin his one year of supervised medical training."

"Do you know the name of this medical complex?"

"No. He was supposed to text the name of the complex to me last night and forgot to send it to me. I have no idea where he is working. He called me to let me know he was excited to see a familiar name on the outside directory of this medical complex, Dr. Robert Wilson, MD. He was acting just like a happy kid would act at Christmastime. I will ask him the building name tonight when he meets me for dinner."

The injections given to Rachel to deaden the area around her front tooth were now ready for the dental work to begin. Rachel dug her fingernails into her folded hands, bracing for pain that never came.

"That's it? You are done? Wow. I do not know how much pain I expected from my front tooth, but I never expected zero. I am afraid to look into a mirror. What if I have been expecting too much, and

I am disappointed. The last thing I want to do is hurt your feelings if I do not show the excitement you may be expecting me to show. Maybe I should look at my tooth when I get home."

"Thank you for thinking about my feelings, Rachel. That shows me the compassion in your heart."

Rachel reached up to take the mirror being handed to her. She closed her eyes and seemed to be saying a prayer to herself before she opened her eyes to look into the mirror, at her front tooth. If you did not know any better by the sound of her outburst, you would have concluded she was at a ball game watching her favorite player score the winning run.

Dee was a bit overwhelmed by Rachel. Dee smiled and said, "I take that to mean I get an A+?"

"Yes!" Rachel could not stop staring into the handheld mirror. Oh, yes. A thousand times yes. Merry Christmas and happy birthday to me. Thank you so much."

Rachel got home and immediately went to her bathroom mirror to see a miracle smiling back at her.

"Oh, God, thank you so much for bringing Dee into my life. I could not be happier. Please let this happiness continue."

She walked into Joe's Crab House and asked for a booth that faced the front door. The booth selected for her was perfect. She sat down on one side of the booth shaped like a half-moon and slid around to sit in the center so she could spot Robert the second he walked through the front door. She was anxious to see his face light up when he noticed her beautiful face and new front tooth smiling back at him.

Dee not only restored her broken front tooth but made it blend so nicely with her other teeth, it is impossible to tell which tooth had been broken. No matter how close someone got to her front tooth, nobody could tell it had ever been broken. Dee had kept her promise to make her tooth look like new. She would not hesitate to refer all her friends to Dee.

The waitress came to the table holding two menus and two place settings. "May I set the table for you?"

"Yes, please. I am waiting for the love of my life to join me. Please set his place next to me. I do not want him to sit across the table from me. Okay?" Rachel requested.

"Okay. Isn't love wonderful when you find the right one? Love is supposed to bring us happiness."

"Yes, ma'am. I hope you have a good man in your life, and he brings you happiness?"

"Hearing you tell me to set his dinner place next to you and seeing the glow in your eyes gives me hope and a little faith that one day it will happen for me too. May I take a drink order?"

"May I have a glass of water? I will order our food and drinks when he arrives. Is that okay?"

"Yes, ma'am. I will bring you a glass of water and check back periodically."

"May I ask your name?"

"Mary Shipley." Mary stood about 5'6" tall and appeared to weigh about 150 pounds. She had black hair, hazel eyes, and a cute face. She appeared to be self-conscious about her chipped and stained front tooth the way she either turns away when she smiles or uses her hand to block her tooth. Rachel wanted to refer her to Dee but did not know how to get into that conversation without hurting her feelings.

"Thank you very much, Mary Shipley. If you are a praying person, keep praying. God will send you the right man."

"I pray every day. I do believe in prayers. One day." Mary stopped talking and rolled her eyes.

"May I ask you to read a Bible verse, Mark 11 verse 24, when you get time to read it?"

"Could you tell me briefly what it says? I do not want to be in suspense all day until I get home?"

"Yes. Mark 11 verse 24 basically says, 'Whatever you ask for in prayer, believe in your heart that you have received it and it will be yours.' See it. Feel it. Believe it. Okay?"

"Did you do this to find the man of your dreams?"

"Yes. I did pray to meet someone who I could trust and who would love me unconditionally. One day I literally bumped into him inside a coffee shop. I was not expecting to meet anyone that day."

"Honestly. This is how you met him?"

"Yes. We were both trying to reserve the same booth, and we never saw each other before we ran into each other. We ended up sitting there in that booth together, talking and eating. He asked me out, and I took a chance and met him, one on one, for dinner to see how the two of us would interact, and that skeptical decision was the best decision of my life."

"Wow. You should sell that story to a magazine. Do you have any other words of wisdom for me?"

"One caveat. If you hurt someone's feelings, tell them you are sorry. If you are holding a grudge against someone, let them know you forgive them so God can forgive you of your sins and grant your future prayer request."

"I am so glad we met. I cannot wait to meet the love of your life and serve you both tonight."

"Speaking about the love of my life, where is he?" Rachel looked at her wristwatch and took out her cell phone to give him a quick call. Robert's phone rang several times before the call went to voice mail.

"Bobby, this is the love of your life looking for the love of my life." Rachel giggled into the phone. "Did you remember we switched our dinner plans to Joe's Crab House? Please call me when you get this message. I love you. Bye."

Rachel waited thirty minutes before she again picked up her cell phone to give Robert another phone call. She listened to it ring several times before it went into voice mail. Rachel also sent him a text message and waited for his response.

She was getting worried when her next call also went straight to voice mail. "Bobby, I never passed mind reading school, so please call me. I am getting more than a little concerned about you. Could you at least text me if you cannot call me?"

The waitress came by the table once again and asked Rachel, "Do you want to order dinner, a drink, or perhaps dinner to go?"

"No. Thank you. I will wait another thirty minutes. If he does not show by then, I will order my dinner and eat slowly to give him ample time to make his appearance and calm my anxieties."

"Okay, I will check back."

"I am sorry about occupying your table all night. I promise to leave you a generous tip to cover this table for the time I am here tonight."

"Oh, that is so sweet of you. Please don't worry about my tips for the night. My concern is for the love of your life. I will say a prayer for God to protect and shield him against anything bad. I will keep an eye on your table. Flag me when you are ready to place a dinner order. Okay?"

"Tonight I desperately needed an angel like you. Thank you for being so understanding and kind."

"May I ask you a personal question?"

"Yes. Ask me anything."

"You have beautiful teeth. How do you keep them looking so beautiful?"

"If you saw me this morning, you would have seen a broken front tooth."

"Seriously? I chipped the corner of my front tooth. A small stain is now in that spot."

"Let me give you the telephone number for my dentist. She is a miracle worker." Rachel wrote down the information for Dee on a small notepad she kept in her purse, and tore out the sheet and handed it to her. "Do you have dental insurance?"

"Yes, and I prefer women doctors. I need to do something with this front tooth. I keep putting it off. Meeting you and discussing my front tooth is a sign that it is time for me to get it fixed. Thank you."

Rachel decided to err on the side of action rather than more patience when she lifted her cell phone to her ear and placed another call to Robert. His phone went straight to voice mail. She sent him a text begging for his immediate reply.

Two hours had now passed without a return call or text message from Robert, so she raised her hand for her waitress to come to her table to take her dinner order. She ordered crab cakes, with two side items and decaffeinated coffee. She fought off a negative thought from Satan's demons as she ate slowly.

Rachel's mind was racing with negative thoughts and possibilities that kept Robert from calling her, texting her, or meeting her for dinner. Suddenly she had an idea that was worth exploring to help find Robert. She looked in her purse and pulled out a lined tablet and a pen to use when she called for the name and phone number of all hospitals and twenty-four-hour emergency clinics within a fifty-mile radius. She called each one and asked if they treated Robert Wilson in their emergency room or if they admitted him as a patient in their hospital. The phone calls proved to be a bittersweet pill to swallow. Robert Wilson was not treated or confined to any hospital within a fifty-mile radius.

Rachel picked up her dinner check for $7.99 and then reached into her purse to pull out a $20 just as the waitress approached her table. "Any luck finding your man?"

"No. I checked every hospital and clinic without success."

"That could be good news. One positive way to look at this is to believe, like you do, that he would rather be with you than any other place on this planet. So if he is not here, something justifiable and explainable occurred to keep him temporarily away from you. The love you have in your eyes and your heart for him, I know, tells me if he could, he would be here with you."

"If I knew you had this calming, reasoning power inside you, you would have been sitting across from me sharing the evening with me, instead of watching me make frantic phone calls to hospitals."

"I learned from you. Mark 11 verse 24 is great wisdom. Thank you. The love in your eyes when you speak about meeting the love of your life is something I have never experienced, but I want to. The faith and conviction you have in your heart, knowing a man you recently met was going to walk through the front door of our restaurant, any minute, to meet you struck a chord with me. I want to find that kind of love and faith. I want to find that kind of man you found. After meeting you, I now know he does exist. I have renewed reason to pray and hope God will also send that kind of special man to me. I will now be a different person because I met you."

Rachel slid out of the booth and handed the waitress the bill for her meal and $20.00. "I occupied your booth a long time. Please keep the change."

"This is way too much. Let me give you some change."

"Nonsense. I wish it were $100. Maybe one day, I will return and be able to leave you a larger tip. Please tell me your phone number so I can stay in touch with you."

"May I hold your phone for a minute to type my number into your phone?"

"Yes." Rachel watched as Mary typed her number into her phone.

Mary finished and handed the phone back to Rachel and asked, "May I have your name?"

"Rachel Rice. My boyfriend's name is Dr. Robert Wilson. I am the math coordinator at the Lincoln High School." Rachel took Mary's phone and typed her phone number into it and handed the phone back to Mary. "Please stay in touch with me." Rachel looked at her and smiled.

"Okay. Come see me if you get hungry. Call me anytime. Could I impose upon you to let me know when you contact Robert Wilson? I will pray and worry about him every day until I know he is okay."

"You are very sweet. Yes. I promise to let you know. Good night, Mary."

"Good night, Rachel."

CHAPTER 11

Rachel's Long Miserable Nights

Every evening for the last ninety days, Rachel cried and beat her pillow with her fist, screaming things even she did not understand. Every morning, she routinely cried in the shower for the water to hide her tears. She demanded to know from God what she did to deserve this cruel treatment by any man, much less by the man she thought was the love of her life sent to her by God. Every evening, she begged and pleaded with God to let her die or let her know why Robert left her without telling her what she did wrong. She even resorted to talking to her mirror by asking, "Why? What sin did I commit, God? Please tell me."

Rachel merely existed from one day to the next. She dreaded being alive the day her biggest fears would be confirmed that Robert was alive and enjoying his life as a medical doctor with a new love in his life and married or about to be happily married.

She had gone from being the happiest woman in the world to a woman feeling so low, she felt like she needed a stepladder to see over the grass. Losing a perfect love like Robert made life too unbearable to even think about another romantic relationship with anyone. She prayed every night for God to show His mercy by letting her die in her sleep.

Robert was making her bitter and resentful for refusing to accept her phone calls or return any of her phone text messages over the last few months. *How do I get him out of my daily thoughts?* she wondered to herself. She used to love math and working with math students. She often reminisced about her future with Robert and her students, but her life has changed drastically overnight, leaving her without any vision for today, tomorrow, or her future. Her tormented mind is simply a blank screen.

Her family and friends knew her to be a happy person who never seemed to cry, but her red and puffy eyes today told a different story. Because she never liked to see anyone sad, especially herself, she often asked Robert to never break her heart. Because he did, she looked forward to slapping his face and giving him a piece of her mind before she walked out of his life to see how he liked it.

The school faculty, her students, and the school principal were running out of things to say or do to help her return to the happy person they knew her to be. The entire student body believed that Robert dumped her for a new love in his life, leaving her to mend a broken heart.

The school board was keeping an eye on Rachel through the school principal. They had real concerns about her ability to keep her personal life private and her ability to focus solely on teaching her students. The school board finally did send Rachel a letter sympathizing with her loss and gave her thirty days to start giving her classroom students her full undivided daily attention or resign.

She dressed for work and went into the kitchen to pour herself a cup of coffee, thinking about the letter she received from the school board. She thought maybe she should resign and stay at home with her dad until something positive happened in her life. This thought made sense, so she decided to submit her resignation just as her cell phone, lying on the kitchen counter, rang.

She picked up the telephone and said, "Hello."

"Rachel?"

"Yes."

"Hi. This is Mary Shipley."

"Hi, Mary. How are you?"

"Good. It has been three months since we met. I am finally ready to visit the dentist you referred me to, Dr. Mary Dee Sharp, and I was wondering if there was anything you wanted me to tell her for you?"

"No. Perhaps you can tell her I said hello. I am sure she will do a great job on your tooth. Please let me know how pleased you are with her."

"I will call you and let you know. May I ask about Robert?"

"I have not heard from him."

"Seriously? Nothing?"

"Nothing. Not a peep. Thank you for the call. I need to get to work."

"How many days do you work each week, Rachel?"

"Five."

"Monday through Friday. Right?"

"Yes."

"Do you know that today is Saturday?"

"No. I lost track of the days. Glad you called to let me know. I would have looked foolish."

"Do you want to meet me for a cup of coffee since you are already dressed?"

"Another time. Okay? I am lousy company these days."

"I am dead tired after working a double shift, but something in my mind will not let me lie down until I called you. I am glad I did, but I do not know what to say or do to make you feel better. Will you meet me?"

"Another day, please, Mary."

"I will pray for you, Rachel."

"Good luck with that one. I have lost favor with God. I still believe in Him. And I love Him with all my broken heart, but right now, He is busy with other people. Tell Dr. Mary Dee Sharp I said hello."

"Okay. You told me the name of the school where you work, but the name slips my mind. Do you mind telling me the name again?"

"Lincoln High School."

"Yes. That is the name. Thank you, Rachel. I will call you after my dental visit. Bye."

"Bye, Mary."

CHAPTER 12

Rachel Resigns

Rachel cried until she fell asleep, as she had done for the last three months, still not hearing one word from Robert. One hour later, when her eyes opened, she lacked the ambition to get out of bed, so she continued to lie there, staring at the ceiling, wondering what she should do to get Robert out of her mind and out of her life. "God, will I ever find happiness the rest of my life?" she whispered.

She knew it was time for her to come to grips with reality—Robert had left her for another woman. He was a big important doctor now, and she was just a teacher, below the level of achievement expected for a man of his status. Thinking these thoughts, which she believed to be truthful thoughts, ripped her heart from top to bottom and from side to side, just like Zorro had sliced it open with his sword.

Suddenly she thought about Humpty-Dumpty, which prompted her to spontaneously whisper, "Yep, I agree. It is my whole body and not just my heart that is beyond repair. I now have reason to question, for the first time in my life, if I can be fixed?" She turned over and buried her face into her pillow. If she were a betting woman, she would have taken bets that she no longer had the ability to cry these tears she was crying. She was so angry at Robert over the way he discarded her like a bag of trash, she could not resist punching her pillow with both hands before she buried her face deeper into it to muffle the sound of her childlike sobs and the angry words she screamed, "You win this first round, Robert. I only asked you for one thing. Remember? Do you remember?" She screamed louder, "I only asked you for one thing. Do not break my heart. Why did you break my heart? Be man enough to at least tell me why. Tell me!" She screamed into her pillow and punched it nonstop with both hands for a full minute, like she was a professional prizefighter punching her opponent pinned into one of the four corners of a boxing ring. "Darn you, Robert. I wish I could see you one more time to slap your lying face and have the satisfaction of being the one to turn and walk out of your life to see how you like it."

She sat up in her bed, fluffed and straightened out her pillow, and blew out a breath of air, feeling like she had just fought a ten-round fistfight with Robert, and lost. She felt exhausted but surprisingly better after releasing some of her pent-up tension. The inner voice within her head was silent. She was on her own without a script or game plan to guide or dissuade her actions. She sat on the edge of her bed for about five minutes before she shook her head in agreement to the thoughts she was thinking in her head as she whispered low, "Three months is enough, Bobby. Goodbye."

She pulled her pink towel angrily off the bathroom wall hook when she stepped out of the shower at 4:00 a.m. to dry herself. After putting on a robe and slipping into her comfortable plush shower shoes, she walked into the kitchen to pour herself a cup of coffee and began writing her letter of resignation with bittersweet feelings.

"My dream job and the love of my life both ends today. Jesus, if I did not honestly love you and know for a fact that you are my Lord and Savior, I would question if you were supposed to be a part of this farewell, the way my life is falling apart. But I am not that stupid, I will always love and need you, Lord," she admitted this verbally to herself out loud as she took another sip of her hot coffee.

*****

"Good morning, Rachel. You were up very early this morning. A special occasion I should know about?"

"Good morning, Dad. I hope I did not wake you?"

"I could not help hearing some angry comments coming from your room. Anything we need to talk about? You are my only daugh-

74

ter and the only love that is in my life now that your mother is no longer with us. I know you miss her like I do. How can I help you?"

"I am thinking about resigning from my job. Would it be okay with you if I stayed here with you until I find a reason to get up each day, to put one foot in front of the other, to live some semblance of a life?

"This is your home, Rachel. I want you to live here the rest of your life. Your room will always be your room, even after God calls me home."

"Thank you, Dad," Rachel answered without looking at him.

"I remember when you were just a teenager telling me you wanted to attend MIT University. This was a dream of yours, to graduate from such an upscale prestigious school, and you did it. You graduated with honors. Lincoln High School, which is another upscale prestigious school, advertised in our local newspaper that they were looking for a math coordinator. Math is your forte and your best subject. Notwithstanding all the applicants who already submitted their résumé for this one position, you applied and got hired. I know you are not a person who chases a dream, achieves it, and then walks away from it. So talk to me, Rachel. Tell me what is going on inside that pretty level head of yours."

"Not so levelheaded right now, Dad." Tears welled up in her eyes.

Henry Rice is a board-certified orthopedic surgeon, not a psychologist. He slowly let out a long breath of air, searching for the right words to say. "Please start somewhere to make me understand why you are so upset. Right now, my world stops until I know what is going on in your life for those tears to be in your eyes with such a beautiful day outside. Talk to me, Rachel."

"Robert Wilson, the young man I met when he was a pharmaceutical salesman, disclosed to me that he was a recent graduate of Johns Hopkins University School of Medicine, and he passed his medical boards to become a new medical doctor."

"That is great news, Rachel. Why are you so upset about him disclosing this to you?"

"He was really excited one night when he called me, standing in front of a medical plaza building directory that displayed the name

Dr. Robert Wilson, MD. He wanted to meet me for dinner the next night to tell me about his first full day as a medical doctor. I chose a booth in front of the door so I could watch each person who came in the door. I left him a voice message on his cell phone every thirty minutes with no callback. I waited to order my dinner for two hours. He never called or showed up."

"Did he have a good explanation when you got a chance to speak with him?"

"That is my problem. We—"

"I don't understand. If he—"

"Please let me finish, Dad. You are interrupting me."

"I am sorry. Please finish."

"I haven't spoken to him. It has now been three long months, going on four months. He obviously met a good-looking nurse, and this is his way of throwing me away like yesterday's newspaper and dumping me. I have never been dumped by any man before. It is cruel and devastating to be dumped this way. I cannot function. I cannot get excited about my job. I just want to slap his lying face and be the one to walk out of his life to show him how it feels." Tears were now flowing freely down her face and dropping onto her bathrobe.

"This does not add up, Rachel. There must be something else."

"Men." Rachel stood up. "Forget it, Dad. I am going to get dressed and go to work."

"Rachel. I was just trying to say—"

"I know, Dad. Maybe we can talk later." Rachel turned and walked angrily out of the kitchen.

"Talk with me tonight. Okay?" Rachel shook her head in agreement and kept walking.

None of the clothes in her closet appealed to her. What does it matter? *Put on anything*, she thought to herself. She chose a beautiful red top and a gray skirt that looked great together. With her purse and resignation letter in her hand, she walked out the front door of her home and got into her automobile and started driving toward Lincoln High School.

Ben Howard has been the school principal at Lincoln High School for the last twenty years. Mr. Howard is fifty years of age and very athletic at six feet tall and 180 pounds, with black hair, blue eyes, and perfectly shaped and aligned white teeth that shows every time he smiles or opens his mouth to speak. This morning, he sat in his office thinking about the school board's ultimatum given to Rachel Rice. This posed quite a dilemma to him. He has two daughters of his own, and while he has not known Rachel very long, he treated her like a daughter. He valued his ability to correctly judge character, and he knew Rachel to be of good character. She had class and was born to stand out and not just fit in. He was a religious man and prayed every day Rachel would snap out of moods of depression over being dumped by a man.

Every time he prayed about her being dumped by the love of her life, it never felt right, which made him wonder if she really was dumped. How could any man dump a woman like Rachel? She is not your typical run-of-the-mill woman. And Rachel and her boyfriend were not teenagers. He is a new doctor, and she is an MIT graduate. Two levelheaded educated people who met and spoke to each other long enough to fall deeply in love. *If I loved someone as deeply as she believes he loves her, what would keep me from meeting her for dinner or at least calling her over the last several months? Bingo! Yes! No other answers are even possible. He was tragically killed without newspaper coverage, or he was seriously injured,* he thought to himself. *I need to check this out without telling her. Where would I start my search to find him? I need to get his name from Rachel, but how?* he wondered.

Rachel opened the front door to Lincoln High School and walked down the hallway that led her to Principal Ben Howard's office. At 7:00 a.m., she took a deep breath before she opened the door to his office and walked inside to tender her thirty-day notice of resignation.

Mr. Howard looked up with surprise when his office door opened and saw Rachel walking through the doorway when he was just sitting there, thinking about her.

"Good morning, Rachel." He stood out of respect for a woman, like men are supposed to do.

"Good morning, Mr. Howard. May I talk with you a couple of minutes?"

"Yes. What can I do for you?"

"I want to tender my resignation to you this morning, effective thirty days from today." She reached out her hand toward him, holding the envelope containing her resignation.

Mr. Howard reached out his hand and accepted her letter of resignation. "Please give me a couple of minutes to read this."

"Okay."

The one-page letter did not take long for him to read, but he kept his eyes on her letter, hoping time would give him a chance to think of something to say to make her change her mind. His mind was a blank screen void of ideas. The words needed for him to make her see the importance of her teaching career and her students over being dumped by the love of her life were lost in the sea of jumbled thoughts within his mind.

He looked up from the letter he held in his hands and looked into her eyes to see her deep sadness. "You dedicated many years of your life to earn the position you now hold as math coordinator of Lincoln High School. I want you to pray hard about this decision over the next thirty days before I turn your resignation letter into the school board for them to accept and act upon it. I will be praying for you blindly because I am not privy to the details of what has really caused your stress, pain, and sorrow to change your life so quickly and drastically. It is almost inconceivable for me to believe how you could be so happy four short months ago and now see you standing here, a mere shell of yourself, resigning your dream job. Please tell me how I can help you, Rachel?"

"You helped me when you hired me. I thank you for hiring me." Rachel turned to leave his office.

"Rachel, in the educational field, you are a rare gem. MIT University is crème de la crème to me. Personally you are the complete package and the real deal. May I offer one suggestion for you to ponder over the next thirty days?"

"Yes."

"I heard you sat in a restaurant for two hours waiting for a young man you recently met to meet you, and for some unknown reason, he failed to show up. Is this story true?"

"Yes."

"You were convinced he would show up and having this feeling made you call several hospitals and clinics looking for him. If this is true, it tells me you not only had a lot of faith and confidence in a man you just met, it tells me two hearts made a serious love connection. Do you agree with my assessment so far?"

"Yes," she blushed and answered weakly. She transferred her weight from one foot to the other foot, feeling embarrassed. She was trying to resist a rush of tears that would soon turn into a monsoon if she did not quickly get out of his office. She could not get her feet to respond to her mental message ordering them to move. Her mind was glued to the things he was saying about Robert.

"You are a unique beautiful woman. Everyone here at Lincoln High School has grown to know and love you. I believe the man in your life saw a deep love in your heart for him, and no man in his right mind could willingly resist that kind of love, unless an injury or something drastic kept him from meeting you."

Rachel wondered where in the world the tears she was holding back behind her eyelids was flowing from, as she pressed her lips tighter together and closed her eyes.

Mr. Howard realized the kind of deep heartfelt emotions she was fighting back as he held up his left hand toward her, signaling her not to speak and just listen to him as he opened his mouth to speak, "If woman better than you do exist, they must be next to impossible to meet quickly and randomly, so my gut tells me he did not suddenly fall in love with another woman, and your man did not just drop off the face of the earth. He had a good reason for not meeting you, and I am betting it was not another woman."

Rachel looked at Mr. Howard trough tear-filled eyes. She opened and quickly closed her mouth and pressed her quivering lips tightly together. Her body shook slightly as she looked down at her feet, trying to think of something to say. "I am sorry..." The tears flowed down her face.

Mr. Howard walked around his desk and wrapped his arms around her to console her. "I will support you as your principal and your friend. I will always be here for you to speak to in confidence. You have nothing to be embarrassed or sorry about, Rachel."

"Do you believe the things you just said to me?"

"Every word."

"Where could he be?" She looked at him with pleading eyes, expecting an answer.

"May I ask his name?"

"Dr. Robert Wilson."

"I believe you mentioned to one of our staff members that he is a new doctor."

"Yes. He called me the night before from outside a medical building where he was to start his first day. He was excited about seeing his name on the outside building directory. He was going to tell me all about his first day when he met me for dinner, but he never showed up."

"That is a great place to start. Do you remember the name of the medical building?"

"I asked him to call me later that night to tell me the name of the medical building, but I guess he forgot."

"This is going to be like looking for a needle in a haystack."

"I should have asked him more questions."

"I did not know how God would lead me into this conversation with you. I want so much to be able to help you find Dr. Robert Wilson. Thank you for speaking with me, Rachel."

Rachel allowed her eyes to meet his. She nodded her head, turned, and walked toward the door with her head down, and disappeared into the hallway.

CHAPTER 13

EEG Test

Dr. Robert Wilson was a graduate of Johns Hopkins University School of Medicine, so it was only natural for him to be airlifted to The Johns Hopkins Hospital, which is also located in Baltimore, Maryland, to be carefully examined from head to toe and admitted into their intensive care unit.

Considering the popularity of Robert Wilson when he was a student walking the halls of the medical school, it was not that shocking to learn how fast the news of his brain injury and comatose condition circulated throughout both Johns Hopkins University School of Medicine and Johns Hopkins Hospital. There was an immediate round-the-clock outpouring of affection, with vigils and prayers for his recovery.

Updated reports circulated each campus to let people know that his condition was still listed as comatose and critical. Sadly he was entering his 124th day or four months of round-the-clock treatment without so much as a twitch or a blink of an eye. Doctors, nurses, and several members of the hospital staff frequently used the time allotted for their breaks or part of their lunch hour to visit his room to encourage him to fight hard and tell him how much he is loved. His body mass was shrinking and will continue to shrink daily, until he regains the use of his arms and legs. His extended inactivity will make it necessary for him to again learn the many things he did unconsciously, such as walk, talk, and feed himself before his injury. *Use it or lose it* is a medical term used often to explain why patients lose their ability to ambulate, feed themselves, or even speak following catastrophic injuries that temporarily cut off the communication between their brain and affected parts of the body.

Johns Hopkins School of Medicine and Johns Hopkins Hospital classmates loved Robert Wilson enough that they did not care who saw tears flowing down their faces when they stepped out of his room, into the hallway, after their visits with him. They knew he loved life and lived it as a humble and kind person who inspired others with his positive attitude and his gift to lift your spirits with appropriate truthful complimentary words. Classmates were having a hard time watching him now lie motionless like a mannequin.

Daily prayer vigils with lit candles continued over the last four months. His unchanged condition was advertised in newspapers and on social media, hoping a relative of Robert Wilson or close friend would call the phone numbers listed on the television screen, but no one called. It is now understandable why the enthusiasm is waning after 124 days without any improvement from him or a single phone call from a relative or a close friend. His prognosis continues to be guarded and extremely critical.

Lisa Phillips is a licensed registered nurse who stands 5'7" tall with a beautiful face, brown hair, green eyes, 123-pound athletic conditioned body and a caretaker's heart filled with compassion for both animals and people. Her first career choice was to be a veterinarian, so it is not a huge surprise to find her working as a trained licensed registered nurse in the intensive care unit of a major hospital. She was in the process of taking Robert's temperature, pulse, and his blood pressure when a young man visiting a patient in a nearby room walked into Robert's room.

"May I ask you a question about him?" He pointed to Dr. Robert Wilson, then focused his attention back on Lisa.

"Yes, but first, I need to ask for your name and your relationship to this patient? Okay?"

"Yes, ma'am. My name is Billy Owens. I do not know him. I am visiting a patient next door and heard about this patient, and I have questions I do not know the answers to. Will you help me?"

"I will try. Please ask me your questions," Lisa asked.

"I heard he was in a coma. Do you know how long he will be in a coma?" Billy asked.

Lisa heard a noise and glanced toward the doorway to observe Sadie Sand walking into the room. "I am saved by the one person more qualified than me to answer your question."

"I plead guilty. What did I do?" Sadie laughed out loud as she looked from Lisa to Billy.

Lisa and Billy both laughed at her comment. When she was about three feet from them, Lisa said, "I was about to explain Dr. Wilson's condition to Billy Owens."

"Please proceed while I take notes," Sadie said while still smiling and looking at Lisa, then to Billy.

"Oh. I see. Okay, go ahead and throw me under the bus?" Lisa's face displayed a sad pitiful expression before she peeked with one eye up at Sadie before glancing at Billy Owens, saying, "I thought she and I were friends?"

Sadie stepped closer to Lisa. "Not only are we friends, but you are also one of my best friends. I love you like a sister, and I also love teasing you. Give me one of those memorable hugs of yours." Sadie and Lisa hugged each other and rocked back and forth like they were Bobbsey Twins.

Lisa stepped back, looked at Billy, and said, "Let me tell you something about Sadie Sand. She literally learned everything required of her to know about EEG machines that made her in demand as an assistant to a neurosurgeon. EEG machines are in a very specialized field all their own. These machines reveal to a neurosurgeon what is going on inside the head of a patient. Sadie literally learned this field of study from the ground floor up without her having a premed background."

"For real. Is this really true?" Billy asked.

"Yes. She reminds me of a beginning swimmer who dove into the deep end of a swimming pool, so to speak, and learned how to swim with the sharks. She was that determined to learn and be one of the best in this prestigious field of medicine, and she did it."

"Wow. Hearing this story has literally choked me up," he said as he blinked his eyes several times. "I am sorry. I was not prepared for that story. And to know it is true gives me hope for *my* future. Thank you for sharing this with me." Billy looked from Lisa to Sadie. "It is my pleasure to meet you, Sadie Sand. You have an inspiring story to tell the world."

"Thank you, Billy. Thank you very much for your kind comments. May I call you Billy?"

"Yes. Please call me Billy. How do you wish for me to address you?"

"Sadie. And thank you for asking." Sadie glanced at Lisa. She said, "I am impressed. A young man with manners. Your mother did a fine job raising you, Billy."

"Thank you, Sadie. You are exceedingly kind." Billy quickly sized up Sadie Sand to be about 5'1" tall, with hazel-color eyes, and her weight to be about 120 pounds. Her gorgeous smile revealed white perfectly shaped teeth that told him she must have worn braces at some point in her life. She had brown-color hair worn at shoulder-length, and he loved how she styled it in such a way not to hide any part of her beautiful face. The friendly soft look in her eyes immediately put him at ease. Billy liked Sadie Sand.

"Please ask me any medical questions on your mind, Billy."

"I heard this patient is in a coma and has been in it for a long time. When will he wake up?"

"Normally a comatose patient comes out of a coma in a few days or a few weeks. On occasion, however, a person stays in a coma for a much longer time. Most coma patients can breathe on their own.

"The ones who cannot need to be on a ventilator. On occasion, some people come out of a coma and return back to the lives they lived before they got hurt. Does this answer some of your questions?"

"Yes. Thank you for telling me these things that I did not know before. Is he sleeping?"

"A good question. A coma has nothing to do with sleep. You cannot shake and wake up someone who is in a coma like you can someone who has just fallen asleep. Someone who is in a coma is unconscious and normally not responsive to voices, sounds, or activity around them. The brain of a person in a coma is functioning at its lowest stage of alertness. Do you understand what I just told you?"

"Yes, ma'am. Thank you very much."

"You are very welcome."

"I often hear about the medical term *EEG test*. Do you mind explaining to me what EEG means and what this test does? I am more than a little curious. I am interested in medicine."

"Good for you, Billy Owens. I would love to explain this term to you and answer all your questions about it while I work on this patient. Is that okay?" Billy nodded his head in agreement.

"The EEG test is referred to as electroencephalography. EEG helps us record the activity of cells in the brain called neurons. We can measure the electrical activity of brain cells by placing electrodes inside a cap placed on a person's head. Visualize a swimmer's cap with a lot of holes in it. Electrodes are inserted into these holes to touch the patient's scalp, causing them to react each time the patient hears something. The neurons in the brain are what is reacting or firing at each noise it hears. And each time a patient reacts to a sound, the electrodes in the cap measure it on the EEG machine. It is much easier to administer the EEG test at the patient's bedside where he is comfortable. The brain of a coma patient is capable of processing sounds and capable of telling the general area around them where the sound is coming from but unable to identify the person speaking to them. By studying brain responses to sounds, medical doctors can evaluate whether a patient is likely to soon awake from their coma. On occasion, the doctor can determine what the patient's neurological condition will be after they wake up. Neat, huh?"

"Oh, yes. What an interesting way to study the brain activity and help someone when they are not able to speak to the doctor. This is fascinating to me. Thank you very much, Sadie Sand."

"You are very welcome. Any more questions while we still have time?"

"I am full of questions." Billy laughed. "Do all patients in a coma look like this man?"

"No. Some comatose patients look like they are getting ready for a rocket ride to the moon when we hook them up to a ventilator, because they cannot breathe on their own—"

"You mentioned this before, and I should have asked you then. What is a ventilator?"

"A machine that pumps air into a patient's lungs through a tube placed in a patient's windpipe."

"Cool. Sort of like an oxygen mask. Right?

"Yes. If the patient dislodges or removes the ventilator, the nurses' station is automatically alerted for them to check on the patient and put the ventilator back in place and back on his face."

"How does he eat or get nutrients while in a coma?"

"That is a great question, Billy. That is a job for Nurse Lisa Phillips and Lauren Jaco, to give coma patients their nutrients and other medicine through a tiny plastic tube inserted into a patient's vein. This tube allows these nutrients to flow directly into their stomach. Cool, huh."

"Yes. Awesome. What else do you do for a comatose patient?"

"My job and my expertise begins and ends with the EEG test."

"I understand. That is your chosen field of expertise."

"Nurses Lisa Phillips and Lauren Jaco have a more encompassing job taking care of patients like this one. The longer this patient lies in one place without moving, he is likely to get bedsores on the areas of his body that lies on top of a mattress all day. These nurses are well trained to also treat bedsores."

"What is the best thing a family member can do for a friend or relative in a coma?"

"Talk to your loved one about fun things he or she did with you. Paint a picture with your words to make their mind visualize trees, blue sky, a dog, their children, a time they hugged you, or the time he or she made you laugh. If you are a female visitor, discuss the circumstances of your first kiss and how you both felt about it. Paint a picture clearly enough with specifics only the two of you know about. Tell the patient to wake up if he wants another kiss. The voice of a loved one is priceless and does makes a huge difference in the patient's recovery. Eventually he will react favorably to the sound of that voice."

"All the suggestions you just mentioned are priceless to me. I have a good friend in another state who has a brother in a coma from a diving accident. May I share the things you just told me with her?"

"Yes. By all means, use my words and improvise on them cre-atively to help your friend."

"Thank you very much for taking this much time to speak with me."

"You are welcome. Keep your conversations around a patient positive. And thank you so much for speaking with me and for ask-ing several interesting questions, Billy."

"You are welcome, Sadie."

"Several ideas to help your friend's brother come out of his coma would be to get a CD of his favorite songs that could encourage him to move his hand or foot to the music. Put a television in his room turned on to his favorite station and keep it playing 24-7. We never know what that one thing will be to help someone who is in a coma come back to us."

"May I ask you one more question?"

"Sure. You are on a roll. Do not stop now." Sadie and Lisa laughed, making Billy laugh too.

"Is there something special a family member can do for a loved one when they come out of a coma?"

"You just asked one of the most important questions a friend or family member could ever ask.

"Wow, you know how to make a guy feel good. Thank you! I love praise."

"*That* question deserves my praise. In the movies and on tele-vision, a person wakes up from a coma, looks around the room, and bingo, they can think and talk normally. But in real life, this rarely happens. Coming out of a coma, your loved one will probably be confused and slowly respond to his surroundings. It will take time for a coma patient to react to life and start feeling better. Sometimes people who come out of comas are lucky to be able to remember what happened to them before they went into a coma and lucky to bounce right back to do everything they used to do."

"May I ask about the other people?" Billy asked hesitantly.

"Yes. Other people may need therapy to relearn basic things like tying their shoes, eating with a fork or spoon, or learning to walk all over again. They may also have problems with speaking or remembering things. Over time and with the help of therapists, most comatose patients will bounce back to enjoy a good life. They may not be exactly like they were before the coma but close enough to enjoy life.

"I am betting you will touch other people's lives and make a positive difference, Billy. I am glad we met. Good luck to you. Always strive to be everything God created you to be."

"I will try my best. Goodbye, Sadie Sand. Goodbye, Nurse Phillips."

"Goodbye, Billy Owens." They both smiled, waved, and watched him disappear out the door.

"I enjoyed meeting Billy Owens. I feel good about our next generation if he is an example of it. Give me a call next week so we can catch up and talk over lunch. Okay?" Sadie asked.

"Okay, Sadie. Friday of the next week for sure. Thank you for helping me with Billy."

"My pleasure. Good to see you. I look forward to seeing you again next Friday. Bye, Lisa."

"Bye, Sadie." Sadie smiled, waved, and walked out the door.

CHAPTER 14

Mary Meets Dr. Mary Dee Sharp

Mary Shipley had worked up enough courage to make the dreaded call to Dr. Mary Dee Sharp to schedule a long-overdue dental appointment to get her front tooth fixed.

Dr. Sharp's phone was answered on the second ring. "Good morning, Dr. Sharp's office, Janice Buchanan speaking, how may I help you?"

"Hello. I was referred to you by a patient of yours by the name Rachel Rice. May I make an appointment with Dr. Sharp to have her repair my broken front tooth?"

"Yes. Please give me a minute to check our appointment calendar. I have an appointment available two days from now, unless you are experiencing pain and need the doctor to work you in to see her today. Are you experiencing any kind of pain?"

"No. I broke my front tooth a long time ago and lived with it broken until I saw Rachel smile without trying to hide her front tooth when she smiles, like I do. I knew then it was time for me to deal with my dental fears and get my front tooth fixed. I want to smile without feeling so embarrassed about people seeing my broken stained front tooth. I had forgotten how it felt to smile without worrying about the things I worry about. I am finally tired of seeing the embarrassing reactions I see in the eyes of people who see my front tooth when I smile. Plus the stain on my front tooth gives people the impression that I do not regularly brush my teeth. It gets old using my hand to shield my tooth during conversations. And it gets old having to turn my head when I smile. This behavior has changed my bubbly outgoing personality, and I want my outgoing personality back. Do you understand?"

"Yes. You have come to the right place to restore your self-confidence and recapture your beautiful smile. Thank you for sharing those embarrassing moments with me, Mary. We will see you in two days to make your broken and stained front tooth look brand-new. Bye, Mary."

"Thank you very much for talking with me. Bye, Janice."

The real dreaded part now is getting through the next two nights before I have to face my fear of needles and dental drills. Thinking her face might be swollen with unbearable pain following her dental procedure, Mary decided to take an extra day off work.

The night before her dental appointment, she tossed and turned all night without getting one hour of sleep, until she finally stopped trying to sleep, got out of bed, and took a shower.

Driving to her scheduled dental appointment, she realized that today is going to be the day she will man up and face her fears of dental needles and drills that have frightened her since she was a child. Her past negative experiences of wishing for things that never came true for her were common thoughts. For these and other reasons, she knew she could never be as fortunate as Rachel Rice to have a beautiful front tooth that looked like hers. *Fairy tale*, she thought to herself. *My face will look like a balloon tonight, and I will be as high as a kite, with my level of pain through the roof. I should have taken more time off work instead of only one extra day. Dumb, Mary. Dumb*, she thought to herself.

A comforting thought suddenly came to her. *I can use my fingernails to dig into my legs as the initial needle shots are given to deaden the area around my front tooth, and the dentist will never see what I am doing to mask the pain. I will also tightly squeeze the armrest of the chair to tolerate the pain during the procedure. Oh, why did I ever agree to do this. Just because Rachel had such a beautiful result does not mean I will. What a dummy. I would rather take a beating, not quite like Jesus did prior to His crucifixion, but just a couple of light licks to avoid this whole dental visit and dental procedures.*

"Darn, there is the office building. Too late now. Oh, yes, indeed. Naturally a vacant parking spot right at the front door just for me," she whispered to herself out loud. She shook her head sideways a couple of times, parked her car, and just sat there breathing big breaths of air in and blowing them out slowly to calm her nerves. "Darn, it isn't working. Nobody from her office has seen me yet, so why not back out and go home. Why did you do this, Mary? You are talking to yourself again, stupid. Either go inside or back out and go home, now. Okay, okay, I am going inside." She opened the front door of the dental office and stepped inside and walked to her left toward the receptionist, and because of her previous conversation with Janice Buchanan two days ago, she did not feel like a *total* stranger.

In fact, she enjoyed her phone conversation with Janice. *She even commented on my last name of Shipley because she loved beautiful boats and ships. People love to look at beautiful boats.* The name Shipley has always been a conversation starter. Kind of an icebreaker.

The receptionist looked up and smiled at her and said, "Welcome. How can I help you this morning?" The receptionist had a very friendly look in her eyes and a big smile on her face that calmed every fear within Mary.

"You must be Janice?"

"And you must be Mary Shipley. Right?"

"Yes." They took to each other like a fish takes to water, as they instinctively completed a high five with smiles on their faces.

"Would you do me a big favor by filling out this short patient information form so we know how to get in touch with you?" Janice handed her a clipboard with the form and a pen.

"Yes. I would be glad to."

Mary turned and sat down on an amazingly comfortable high-backed cushioned chair and filled out the form. Minutes later, she stood and walked a couple of steps back up to the receptionist window and set the clipboard on the ledge and returned to her chair to wait her turn to be seen. It had been years since she had been to a dentist, and her anxieties were fever pitch with fear, not excitement. She only had to wait two minutes with her anxieties running wild before she heard her name called.

"Mary Shipley."

"Yes." Mary stood up and looked into the friendly eyes of a young woman holding the same form she had previously filled out. "I am Mary Shipley."

Janice stood at the reception window with her arms fully extended toward Mary. Her hands were open with her palms facing up. "Please put your fears and anxieties in my hands. You got this."

"From your lips to God's ears." Mary laughed out loud as she put both of her closed fist into the open hands of Janice before she opened them. Janice withdrew her arms, intending to take her fears away.

"Genius plan. Who thought this one up?"

Janice touched her index finger to her temple and smiled. "I have your back. I will hold both your anxieties and your fears. Now go get your new tooth."

"Wish me luck. Thank you, Janice."

"Hi. My name is Millie. I am the dental assistant to Dr. Sharp. Are you ready to come back so we can make your front tooth like new? You can even take it home with you today?"

"Now that would be a dream come true if you do that for me. It is nice to meet you, Millie." Mary followed Millie into Dr. Sharp's dental office and stopped when she saw the dental equipment. She felt some of her childhood fears starting to stir. Fears she had tried extremely hard to forget.

"Hi. Come on in and have a seat. My name is Mary Sharp. Thank you for coming in and allowing us to remove all your dental concerns. May I look at your front tooth?" Dr. Sharp lifted Mary's front lip slightly with one hand and gently brushed her gums with a Q-tip before she lowered her lip and stood back to talk with her for a few minutes.

"I was referred to you by Rachel Rice."

Dr. Sharp seemed surprised as she raised her eyebrows. "Yes, Rachel. How is she doing? I have often wondered about her. She came in to see me. We gave her a brand-new front tooth, and then she just fell off the face of the earth. How is she doing? How is the new love of her life?"

"I am a waitress, and I waited on her the same day you gave her a brand-new gorgeous front tooth. She could not wait to show her new tooth to her fiancé that night. I was so happy for her and envious at the same time. I wish I could find the man of my dreams like she did."

"What did her fiancé say when he saw her tooth?"

"He never showed up."

"What? You are kidding me. Right?"

"Nope. She waited for him for two hours. His cell phone went straight to voice mail. But she was still in good spirits when she left me to go home. I told her to call me when she contacted him, but when I never heard a word from her, I called her this past Saturday. She still has not heard a peep from him."

"Let me check your upper lip for a minute before you talk again, okay?"

Dr. Sharp inspected the area around Mary's front tooth and confirmed it was ready for her to proceed to inject this area so she could begin to work on her tooth.

"How long did you wait to call her after you first met her at your restaurant?"

"Almost four months. She does not sound anything like the woman I met. She told me she was dressed to go into work the day I called her. She had to check her calendar to confirm the day was Saturday and not Friday. She seemed sad or depressed. She refused to meet me for a cup of coffee."

"That is very concerning. I need to give her a call."

"I am sorry. I am running my mouth preventing you from injecting the area around my front tooth. I will hold onto the armrest while you do it. I hate pain."

"I already injected the area."

"You did?"

"Yes. I am ready to work on your tooth."

Mary closed her right hand, and when she raised it into the air, she quickly opened her fist and said the word *poof* to allow imaginary air to escape. "There goes part of my fears. I never felt anything. And here I am sitting here, scared to death, waiting to feel pain that is not coming."

"Sorry to disappoint you."

Mary laughed out loud along with Dr. Sharp. "Trust me. You did not disappoint me. I was sitting here worrying about nothing."

"Millie will hold this small tube in the corner of your mouth to ensure that everything runs very smoothly. Are you ready?"

"Yes, ma'am. I am ready."

It did not take long for Dr. Sharp to make Mary's dreams come true. Mary was now the owner of a brand-new front tooth that looked just like Rachel's front tooth.

Mary did not have the identical reaction Rachel did when she looked at her tooth in a handheld mirror, but her excitement level and appreciative comments sounded remarkably similar.

"I take it you approve?" Millie asked, giggling.

"Oh, yes. My customers are going to think I am nuts, the way I am going to be smiling and laughing like a hyena. No more having to do half smiles or using my hand to hide my front tooth when I talk or smile. Thank you so much. I will tell everyone what you have done for me and give them your name and number. Hard for me to believe I never felt any pain. I worried all that time for nothing."

"I am glad you are pleased, Mary."

"I am Dr. Sharp. Thank you very much. You just improved the quality of my life immeasurably."

"If I can be of service to you in the future, you know where I am. Please call or come see me."

"Do you have time to speak with me for about fifteen minutes?
"Now?"

"Yes. If you have time."

"May I ask the subject matter?"

"Rachel Rice."

"I will make time right now. Come with me back to my office."

"Okay. Thank you very much." Mary followed to her office and sat on one of the office chairs in front of the desk. Mary was surprised and glad Dr. Sharp chose to sit on the other chair alongside of her, instead of sitting on the chair behind her desk.

"Okay. Tell me about Rachel. Do you mind telling me what she did to make such a big impression upon you?" Dr. Sharp asked.

"No, I do not mind telling you. It was the way she spoke about her love for him and the way she watched the front door of the restaurant, so confident he was going to be the next person to walk through that door every time it opened, for two hours. The love in her eyes when she spoke about him was something for everyone wanting to be in love to see. I want to feel that kind of love in my heart, like she felt and feels in her heart. She confirmed to me that men like Robert Wilson are out there in the world hopefully looking for me."

"Wow. You just described a one-in-a-million kind of love. I am intrigued and interested in helping you any way I can. What exactly do you expect or hope I can do to help you?"

"I need ideas because I do not have a clue where to start looking for Robert Wilson. My heart and my gut instincts tell me something catastrophic happened to keep him away from the kind of love Rachel had waiting for him. I am convinced of it but do not know where to search. Please help me?"

"Let me recap what you have already told me so I can get my brain to focus on new ideas. Okay?"

"Okay. That makes sense to me. Thank you."

"You mentioned that Rachel had called every clinic and hospital within fifty miles of here and was told that they had not treated a Robert Wilson, and he was not confined within their facility. Right?"

"Yes. That is correct. Robert Wilson was not one of their patients."

"And they had not treated a Robert Wilson?" Dr. Sharp asked.

"That is correct. He was not an inpatient on their premises, and they had not treated him as a patient before or up to the time of Rachel's call."

"Okay. That eliminates local hospitals and clinics," Dr. Sharp said.

"That is correct," Mary confirmed.

"If he is in a hospital further away, how did he get there?" Dr. Sharp asked rhetorically.

"Good question," Mary said as she looked up at the ceiling, thinking. "Rachel did say Robert had started a new job as a medical doctor in an unknown clinic. He was supposed to text her the name of the clinic but must have forgotten."

"Forgot or was not able to send her the name of his new clinic before he got hurt?" Dr. Sharp raised one eyebrow as she turned her head to think, as she stared out the window.

"Now that makes sense to me. These two were and are deeply in love with each other. Something along the lines of what you are thinking must have happened, or he would have been with her the night he was supposed to be with her." Mary was getting excited just thinking about the possibilities of finding Robert. "I really like your train of thought so much, I would bet the farm you are 100 percent correct, if I had a farm to bet."

"What do you know about Robert Wilson?" Dr. Sharp watched the facial reactions on Mary's face as she thought about her question. Mary's face lit up, which hopefully meant she could answer the question.

"He is a new doctor," Mary answered with a big smile. "He graduated medical school from Johns Hopkins School of Medicine."

"Great. You can start right there to find him." Dr. Sharp nodded her head as she smiled at Mary.

"I would speak with the dean of the school and ask him to help you find Robert Wilson."

"That makes sense to me," Mary said as she shook her head in agreement." This is a great idea."

"I just thought about something that might be very important, and it could save you a step in the process of locating Robert Wilson."

"I would love to hear it."

"I am familiar with that area around the school, and I remember they also have a hospital."

"They have a hospital in the same area?" Mary asked excitedly.

"Yes. A hospital by the name of Johns Hopkins Hospital. They are either the largest or one of the largest hospitals in the world, primarily because of the number of people they employ as a training hospital. My gut tells me you might want to make your first call to the hospital to see if they treated him recently or possibly have him listed as one of their patients."

"Stroke of genius. Thank you. Everything inside me says we will find him listed as a patient in their hospital. Thank you so much for this suggestion. Do you want to be on the phone with me when I tell Rachel if he is in their hospital?"

"This is your miracle to deliver to her. Out of caution, if you do find Robert Wilson in their hospital, please tell Rachel in person and not on the telephone. Sit close to her in case she faints when you tell her the news that the love of her life had a medical reason for not showing up to meet her."

"Thank you for that advice. I would hate to hear her fall and rebreak her front tooth."

"We definitely do not want that to happen." They both laughed out loud.

"And if I do find him, I will let you know. I will tell her I found him using your suggestion. I will hopefully call you soon with the good news."

"I will pray for your success and look for your call."

Mary stood and looked at Dr. Sharp with a hopeful look on her face. "Thank you, Dr. Sharp."

"You are welcome. Good luck, Mary."

"Thank you for my beautiful front tooth that will make me not only want to smile more often but have my self-confidence and self-esteem restored to make me the social person I want to be."

"I am glad everything turned out the way you envisioned it before you came in today."

"Me too. Thank you for taking so much of your time to speak with me about ideas to find Robert."

"You are welcome. Bye, Mary."

Mary stopped at the door to the dental office where she had the work done on her front tooth and peeked in at Millie. "Thank you, Millie. Pleasure to meet you. Have a great day."

"You are welcome. It was my pleasure to meet you. I hope you also have a great day."

"I will now." Mary giggled and smiled big to show off her new front tooth. "Bye, Millie."

Millie laughed out loud. "Bye, Mary."

Mary stopped at the reception window. "See my new front tooth. Thank you for everything. Your plan worked so well. You can keep my discarded anxieties. May I get a goodbye hug?"

"No. But I will give you a see-you-later hug." Janice walked into the outstretched arms of Mary. "It sure was good to meet you. I look forward to seeing you again. Take good care of yourself, Mary.

"You will definitely see me again. See you later, Janice. Bye."

"Bye, Mary."

CHAPTER 15

Mary Shipley Finds Robert Wilson

Mary Shipley was not feeling confident making a call to Johns Hopkins Hospital, searching for a man she never met nor was she related to him. Notwithstanding her reservations, she picked up her home phone and dialed the phone number for Johns Hopkins Hospital, and while listening to it ring in her ear, negative thoughts encouraged her to hang up. Just as she was about to obey these negative thoughts to hang up, she heard a voice say, "Good morning, Johns Hopkins Hospital, how may I direct your call?"

I am trying to locate a friend who might be a patient in your hospital, by the name of Robert Wilson. Will you help me, please?

"Yes, ma'am. Let me check for you. We have two patients by the last name of Wilson. We have an R. Wilson, who is a woman. The other patient was airlifted into the hospital about four months ago and admitted into our intensive care unit under the name of Dr. Robert Wilson."

"Dr. Robert Wilson is the man I am looking for. Is he still a patient at your hospital?"

"Yes, ma'am. He is still a patient in our intensive care unit."

"Can you tell me anything about his condition?"

"No, ma'am. May I transfer your call to Nurse Lisa Phillips in our intensive care unit?"

"Yes. Please transfer my call to her. Thank you very much."

"You're welcome. Please hold while I transfer your call to Lisa Phillips in our intensive care unit."

"Intensive care, Lisa Phillips speaking. How may I help you?"

"Hi. My name is Mary Shipley. I am a friend of Rachel Rice, the fiancé of Dr. Robert Wilson who is a patient—"

"Yes. Thank you for calling. I am sorry to cut you off. We have been looking for a relative or a close friend of Dr. Wilson for four months. We advertised on social media and in all the local networks asking for a close relative or loved one to call immediately. *Why has she not called us?*"

"She lives near Nashville, Tennessee."

"Nashville, Tennessee?"

"Yes, she met Dr. Robert Wilson inside a restaurant in Gallatin, Tennessee. He asked her to meet him at their favorite restaurant after he finished working his first day as a medical doctor. She sat in a booth for two long hours, without placing her food or drink order, watching every face that walked into the restaurant, expecting to see his handsome face. I was her waitress. She just knew he was going to be the next person to walk in. She called and left a voice message on his cell phone at thirty-minute intervals for two hours without one return call or text message back to her. She concluded, after two hours, that he was not coming to meet her before she finally ordered and ate a shrimp dinner and went home."

"She sounds like a woman who was deeply in love with this man."

"She is *still* sadly and deeply in love with him. His unexplained departure from her life has changed her drastically from a bubbly, charming, outgoing personality to a woman without a smile or reason to crawl out of bed to begin each day. She is a shell of herself. She only does what she is required to do to get through each day before she withdraws from people to live like a recluse. Without a call or any word from Robert Wilson over the last four months, she believes the negative message her broken heart keeps telling her—that Robert found another woman and dumped her. According to her, he is a big medical doctor, and she is just a dime a dozen run-of-the-mill teacher from a local high school."

"None of that matters to most women. We love men who are kind, honest, and trustworthy."

"Please tell me what you can about Robert and what you would like for me to do next, Nurse Phillips."

"Your call will make hundreds of students, nurses, and doctors up here extremely happy. This man is one of their own, and they love him dearly. Thank you for calling the hospital and making our day."

"I almost hung up when the phone was ringing because I am not related to him, and I never met him. I was only the waitress who served Rachel when she waited for Robert for two hours. I would have met him that night if he showed up. When you meet her, you will see how kind and sweet she is."

"Your job is to get her up here. I have experience with patients in a coma."

"Robert is in a coma?"

"Yes. He was in a coma when he came into the hospital. Since you are not family, it is best for me to only discuss his diagnosis and prognosis with family members or his fiancé. I hope you understand."

"I do. Can you at least tell me what caused him to go into a coma so I can tell Rachel?"

"Yes. The assault is a matter of public record that has been aired on all the local television stations and in all the local newspapers, so I can brief you on their reporting. Okay?"

"Okay."

"Robert spent three hours seeing patients in one of the wings of a medical building. He stepped out into the hallway to walk to the next room to treat another patient when a nurse appeared in one of the adjacent doorways screaming for him to help her. An angry 6'7" three-hundred-pound male, who was a walk-in patient, hooked the handle of his thick wooden cane around the front of the nurse's throat from behind and pulled her back into the room. This patient was high on drugs, demanding a heroin fix and a heroin prescription. Robert ran into the room he had seen this big guy jerk the nurse back into, and witnessed the nurse lying facedown on the bed, about to be hit in the back of her head with the same wooden cane. He saved her life. While Robert was making sure she was out of danger, he was forcibly struck in the back of his head, and a second time along the left side of his head, causing serious multiple head injuries. Robert fell face-first, unconscious, onto the floor and in a nonresponsive coma."

"Wow. Thank you for talking with me. I will talk with Rachel and get her up there to see Robert. She will see you soon. Thank you so much for talking with me. Okay?"

"Okay. Tell her everything we discussed to prepare her before she sees Robert lying there, motionless, in a nonresponsive coma. Family always want the people they love to say something to them. And as the days click off, they get depressed and start losing hope and stop visualizing that magical day when their loved one might come back to them after possibly hearing their words of encouragement."

"I will talk with Rachel and give her your phone number. Thank you, Nurse Phillips."

"You're welcome."

Mary dreaded the next call she had to make. *Now what? I work in a restaurant as a waitress. A female paying customer, who is a math coordinator of a prestigious high school and dating a medical doctor, came into my section to eat. They are both way above my pay grade. I am not his or her social buddy. While she waited for her fiancé to show up for two hours, we got to know a little about each other. That qualifies her and me as casual friends, not hangout buddies. The information I need to discuss with her is life changing, and this is the kind of information normally discussed between two social or business personality types that hang out together. I had no business getting involved in her personal life. Now what do I do? This might be a very short conversation when she tells me where I can go and how to get there. Here goes nothing.*

She picked up her five-hundred-pound receiver and dialed the number for Rachel Rice and listened to it ring.

"Hello."

"Hi. Is this Rachel Rice?"

"May I ask who wants to know?"

"Mary Shipley."

"How can I help you, Mary Shipley? This is Rachel speaking."

"I am a waitress at the Joe's Crab House restaurant where you came in to eat one night. You gave me the name and phone number for your dentist while you waited for two hours for your fiancé to meet you. Do you remember me?"

"Yes. I remember you and our previous conversation about Robert. How are you, Mary?"

"I am fine. Thank you for asking. I need to talk with you. Please tell me when you can meet me?"

"Can't you tell me over the phone?"

"No. It must be in person. Please meet with me."

"I lose track of the days. I am dressed for work, and I do not work on Saturdays.

"You got dressed for work the last time I called you on a Saturday."

"I did?"

"Yes. But today, divine intervention got you dressed."

"I am not so sure divine intervention knows where I am these days."

"Trust me. It knows exactly where you are, Rachel."

"Not to be mean, but I do not trust anyone these days. Not even you."

"I aim to change your mind on both fronts."

"What both fronts?"

"Divine intervention and trusting me."

"Good luck with that. What time do you want to meet and where?"

"How about now at the Donut Hole while my courage is up."

"Not sure why you need courage, but okay, I will meet you in thirty minutes."

"Thank you, Rachel."

"This better be good," Rachel said, sounding exasperated.

"God tells me it is a partial answer to your prayers."

"You do not know what I pray for, Mary."

"Roger that! I did say partial answer to whatever you do pray for."

"Okay. I now pray that your partial answer to my prayers is worth leaving my house and driving to meet you."

"I do have confidence in delivering to you a good partial answer to your prayers."

Rachel blew out a long breath of air into the phone. "See you in thirty minutes. Bye."

"Bye."

Rachel walked into the Donut Hole and waved at Mary. She walked over to her booth and slid into the opposite side and looked at Mary without any expression of joy; she only had sadness in her eyes.

"I am not trying to be mean, but I don't think it is fair of you to lure me here by telling me this meeting would be a partial answer to my prayers when you should know I only have one prayer, and that is to find Robert so I can walk up to him and give him a piece of my mind, slap his lying face, and be the one to walk out of his life to show him how it feels to be dumped."

"I do not think you will do any of those things to Robert."

"You wait and see. The minute I see him with another woman, trying to replace me, he will witness a scene like he has never seen before in his life. I was so taken in by him. I was so—"

"Stop! Rachel, please stop and listen to me."

"You cannot defend what he did to me. I will not let him—" Rachel stopped talking when Mary held up both of her hands, with her palms facing her as a signal for her to stop talking.

"Robert would never hurt you if he had a choice, and I know you believe this to be true. You are justifiably angry and lost without the man of your dreams, and that is understandable, but—"

"I am out of here. I did not come here for a pep talk from you, Mary. I know you mean well, but this meeting and subject matter falls into the category of being none of your business." Rachel grabbed her purse and started to slide out of the booth when Mary quickly moved around the table and slid into the booth next to her to block her from leaving.

"Before I met you, it was not my business. After meeting you, however, it became my business in more ways than one. Look at your watch and give me five minutes. If you have no interest in what I am saying after five minutes, I will let you walk out of here, and you will never see or hear from me again. Okay? I need five minutes to tell you everything I need to tell you. Five minutes. Do we have a deal?"

Rachel glanced at her wristwatch. "Five minutes. I will only listen for five minutes."

"I was touched by the love you felt in your heart for Robert Wilson and equally touched by the way you expressed this love, which saddened me when I did not hear from you after you promised me you would call me when you contacted him. You seemed too kind and sweet to break your promise to me, so I figured something had happened to Robert, and I knew if that were the case, you would be too devastated to call me. I did go see Dr. Mary Sharp to have her fix my front tooth and make it new, like your tooth. See."

"Did you bring me here to show me your front tooth?"

"That is one reason. Did she do an excellent job on my front tooth or what?"

"Move out of my way, Mary. I am glad you went to see Dr. Sharp, and I am happy she did such an excellent job on your tooth. I do not have time right now for this. It is good seeing you again. Now, please get out of my way or I will cause a scene you do not want to witness."

"Time-out! We have a deal. You promised not to interrupt me for five minutes."

Rachel folded her arms in front of her and put them onto the tabletop in front of her before lowering her forehead onto her forearms, shaking her head from side to side. "Please finish, Mary."

"I spoke to Dr. Mary Sharp about Robert Wilson."

"My doctor? You spoke to my doctor about Robert? You have a lot of nerve, lady."

"Yes. But please remember, your doctor is now also my doctor."

"I do not like anything you have said to me thus far. Nothing. You have wasted my time."

"Trust me, you will."

"No. With all due respect, I do not trust anyone. And I will definitely never trust you again." She glared at her for a long second before she disgustingly lowered her forehead back onto her folded forearms on the table. "*Finish*," she said as she lowered her forehead back down onto her folded forearms and slowly blew out a long breath of exasperated air.

"Do you want to order a cup of coffee and have something to eat with me?"

"No. I will not be here that long. Besides, your five minutes is almost up."

"Well, let me see if I can change your mind about trusting me and about eating."

"Never happen."

"Oh, Rachel, you are justifiably bitter but admittedly even more than I envisioned you to be."

"Mary, darn it, get to the point, *now!*"

"Okay. I did not sleep very well the night before I was to visit Dr. Sharp. I went to bed thinking about the day you and I met. I sat straight up in my bed about 3:00 a.m. thinking about the calls you had made to all the hospitals and emergency clinics within a fifty-mile radius. I began to wonder why I was thinking about this at 3:00 a.m. I did not have a clue, but I was being led by a little voice inside my head telling me to speak with Dr. Sharp about Robert when she finished working on my front tooth.

"She finished working on my front tooth, did not hesitate to invite me back to her office to discuss you and Robert Wilson. She jumped right in, asking me all the right questions. I was able to form a clear image or picture inside her mind to enable her to depict the one-in-a-million love you and Robert found in each other. She visually soaked up the information that I told her about you to conclude that men like Robert Wilson would never stand up a woman like you, Rachel. Dr. Sharp was convinced that something serious must have happened to Robert Wilson to keep him from meeting you. She used the lack of a single phone call in four months to confirm her suspicions of a serious injury to Robert. She gave me a great suggestion where to look for him."

Rachel slowly raised her head off her arms and sat up in the booth and turned to look at Mary. And for the first time in four months, Rachel had a hopeful look in her beautiful blue eyes that locked onto every word Mary was now saying to her.

"Dr. Sharp told me to check with the dean of the medical school Robert Wilson graduated from before she remembered seeing a Johns Hopkins Hospital in Baltimore, Maryland. It is a teaching hospital, with around thirty thousand people on staff, which makes them the largest hospital in the world. I would start making your inquiries at this hospital."

"I said, 'Wow. They are huge and probably perfect to treat an alumnus with serious injuries.'

"'Yep. I would start right there in your search to find, Robert. Good luck and keep me posted.'"

Rachel grabbed Mary's right arm with both of her hands, anxiously waiting to hear the next words to come out of her mouth as her mouth started to quiver and hopeful tears started forming in her eyes.

"I went home and made the call to the hospital. I asked for a patient by the name of Robert Wilson. The woman told me they had two patients by the last name of Wilson. They have an R. Wilson, which is a woman. The other patient was airlifted into the hospital about four months ago and admitted into their intensive care under the name of Dr. Robert Wilson."

Rachel collapsed into Mary's arms. Mary held her close and used the menu to fan her face. After several minutes, Rachel's eyes slowly opened. She looked up at Mary. "Did I dream about you telling me you found my Robert?"

"No. I found him."

"Why did you not tell me over the phone instead of bringing me here?"

"I was following orders."

"Who gave that order?"

"Dr. Mary Sharp. She told me not to tell you over the phone. And if I met with you, make sure I was sitting close to you in case you fainted like you just did. If I were not sitting next to you, Dr. Sharp would be fixing all your front teeth. That table would not have been too forgiving."

"My emotions are all over the board with a thousand questions," Rachel said excitedly.

"I know. And now we both know he never dumped you."

"Please tell me everything you know about Robert."

"Okay. I talked to Lisa Phillips, who is the head nurse of the intensive care unit and asked her why he was admitted to the hospital so far away from his home?"

"She told me about Robert starting his first day working as a medical doctor in a medical complex."

"That is the same building he was standing outside the night he called me, so excited about seeing his name Dr. Robert Wilson, MD, on the outside of the building directory. I'm sorry. Please continue."

"Robert spent three hours seeing patients in one of the wings of a medical building. He stepped out into the hall to walk to the next room to treat another patient, when a nurse appeared in one of the adjacent doorways and screamed for him to help her. An angry 6'7" three-hundred-pound male, who was a walk-in patient, hooked the handle of his thick wooden cane around the front of the nurse's throat from behind and pulled her back into the room. This patient was high on drugs, demanding a heroin fix and a heroin prescription. Robert ran into the room he had seen this big guy jerk the nurse back into, and witnessed the nurse lying facedown on the bed, about to be hit in the back of her head with the same wooden cane, and Robert saved her life. While Robert was making sure she was out of danger, he was forcibly struck in the back of his head, and a second time along the left side of his head, causing serious multiple head injuries. Robert fell face-first, unconscious, onto the floor and stayed in a nonresponsive coma."

"Wow. He could not call me, and I am giving him the dickens under my breath every day. Shame on me. Is there more to the story?"

"Yes. Nurse Phillips told me Robert does not have a next of kin or someone to notify if he is sick or injured in his employee file. He worked to pay his own way through medical school. He has had a parade of alumni visitors from his medical school, and most of the medical personnel from the hospital take turns visiting him on their breaks or part of their lunch hour. He is well-liked by everyone."

"Thank God."

"Yes. But the nurse told me he desperately needs someone he really cares about to start whispering sweet nothings into his ear to hopefully bring him back out of his coma."

"Will he remember me?"

"Nurse Lisa Phillips hopes you can come up to see him. The love he felt for you is still in his heart. Hearing your voice and all the private things you have said to each other will work miracles to bring him back to you."

"I am so sorry for the way I talked to you, Mary."

"I will make a list of ways for you to make amends to me." They both burst into laughter. "It sure is good to see you smile and laugh again. Watch out, world, Rachel is back." They comforted each other and shared perhaps some of the most endearing hugs ever shared between two friends.

"How do I contact the nurse at the hospital? She can give me their address and also suggest the best place for me to stay for a couple of months."

"Everything you need is inside this tablet. You are all set. Your man awaits hearing your voice. Go whisper into his ear the things he needs to hear from you to bring him back to you. I will walk you out to your car and give you a good-luck hug."

"How in the world will I ever repay you, Mary?"

"Well, I will make a list and ask Dr. Mary Dee Sharp to also make you a long list. Okay?"

Rachel smiled, shook her head, blew out a long breath, and smiled once again at Mary. "God will hear from me tonight. I will be on my knees thanking Him for the two of you."

"I only have one request," Mary said.

"Granted. Anything. Ask me."

"Please keep me informed. Please?"

"You bet. Give me a hug. Bye."

"Bye."

CHAPTER 16

Rachel Cautiously Optimistic

Rachel reached over and silenced her bedside alarm clock at 5:00 a.m. She continued to lie on her bed a few more minutes, staring up at the ceiling, thinking about Mary Shipley. She had her head on her pillow, with her arms crossed behind her head and her fingers intertwined. *Was it a chance meeting that brought our paths unexpectedly together, Lord? What are the chances of my meeting someone with a broken and stained front tooth on the very day my front tooth was restored to look like new? One other thing that has been bothering me is the restaurant where I met Mary. I was about to leave Lincoln High School to meet Robert at Cheddar's Restaurant, which is the only restaurant he and I ate at together, and it is the restaurant I told him the night before on the telephone that I would meet him at, when a coworker suggested I try eating at Joe's Crab House. Why did I even consider following the suggestion of a coworker one hour before I left to meet Robert and switch the restaurant from Cheddar's to Joe's Crab House? My coworker did not twist my arm or give me a command to obey, so why did I do it?*

Rachel suddenly sat up on the side of her bed. "It was you, wasn't it, Lord? You told my coworker to tell me to eat at Joe's Crab House, because you knew Bobby was already airlifted to a hospital and not able to meet me. The Holy Spirit within my head told me to make the switch to Joe's Crab House for me to meet Mary. Right? It was always you, right, Lord? How do you keep track of each of us? How do you select which person to use at a specific time and day so far in advance? I know you do not cause injuries or illness to any of us, but you sure are right there by our side to comfort us and walk or

110

carry us through difficult times, aren't you? Boy, I sure would love to see your day planner."

Before meeting with Mary Shipley yesterday, the vision I had of my future contained a lot of gloom and doom. Gone were the days I expected to be happy. Not remotely possible with my pessimistic attitude and severe depression. During the last four long months, depression robbed me of the life I was accustomed to living, where I smiled and frequently had a kind word for my friends and even strangers. I had given up all hope of ever having that kind of happy life again, before I met with Mary Shipley.

Rachel felt her heart suddenly fill up with feelings of love that she used to feel daily before the disappearance of Robert. Simultaneously with these thoughts, her room suddenly glowed so brightly she expected to see angels everywhere. Now she was convinced that God had heard her daily cries and heard her tearful prayers over the last four long months. She was also convinced that her coworker, Dr. Sharp, and Mary Shipley were chosen by God to lead her to Robert.

Because she did not remember getting up from her bed or walking into her shower, she laughed out loud and whispered, "Angels must have carried me in here and turned on the water, or I floated on my own special love cloud. Right, Lord?" She giggled out loud. "Please do not take these happy moments away from me again, Lord. Please say the word and bring Bobby out of his coma and let him remember me when you wake him up. In Jesus's name I pray."

Rachel grabbed her pink towel off the hook outside of her shower door, dried her body, and wrapped the towel around her head to allow her hair to dry before she walked back into her bedroom to get dressed. When she passed by the full-length mirror in the corner of her bedroom, she stopped and backed up for a second look at her body.

She disappointedly shook her head, blew out a breath of air, and whispered, "Look on the bright side, Rachel. It is a lot easier to gain weight than it is to lose it."

She smiled as she got dressed and thought about going into the kitchen to enjoy her first cup of coffee of the day. The last time she walked into her kitchen for a cup of coffee, she sat down and wrote out her letter of resignation for Lincoln High School. She allowed herself to mentally drift temporarily into deep thought, thinking about that day and how curt she was with her dad. *I will do my best to never allow depression to make me mean to my dad or anyone I care about. I never want to become that person again.*

This morning, she walked into her kitchen humming one of her favorite songs. Just as she started pouring herself a cup of coffee, her dad walked into the kitchen.

"Good morning, Rachel. Do I detect happiness in my little girl once again?"

"Yes, Daddy. Your little happy girl is back." Rachel walked over and gave him a big hug.

"May I ask what brought happiness back into your life without assuming anything on my part?"

"I found Robert."

"Thank, God. When are you going to bring this lucky man home for me to meet him? Perhaps I need to wait for my turn to be told all the details?"

"Your turn will always be first in my life. Were you always so considerate of others, Dad?"

"You know what they say, Rachel. You get more with honey than you do with vinegar." Rachel nodded and smiled.

"I do not know all the details, but I will tell you what I do know today."

"Okay."

"On the same day Robert was to meet me for dinner, he was working his first day as a doctor in a medical complex that had a lot of patient rooms flanking a long hallway. A nurse appeared in one of the doorways and yelled to him for help. She was being attacked by a large angry man holding a thick-handled wooden cane, and demanding she give him heroin. Robert ran into the room and saved her from being hit by that thick-handled wooden, cane but in the process, he was forcibly hit in the back of his head, and again along the left side of his head, by this wooden cane. He fell face-first onto the floor, into a nonresponsive coma. He was airlifted to Johns Hopkins Hospital in Maryland and admitted into their intensive care unit. He is still there today and still in a coma."

"I will pray he is one of the lucky ones to wake up to remember you and able to resume his life."

"Can you tell me the best and worst-case scenarios?"

"I just gave you the best scenario. The worst is he wakes up not remembering you and unable to remember his medical training that qualifies him to be a doctor. There is so much doctors do not know about the brain. Pray hard every day, Rachel."

"Hearing what you just told me, I will put his name on several prayer lists and pray for him every day. Thanks, Dad."

"You are very welcome. Keep me posted. Okay?"

"Okay. May I cook breakfast for you this morning?"

"No, but thank you, sweetie. I have a business breakfast meeting this morning. How about a rain check for another day?"

"You have an open invitation." Rachel smiled and giggled as she stepped closer to her dad and gave him a big hug.

Rachel picked up her cell phone and dialed the phone number for Dr. Sharp to thank her for talking with Mary Shipley and giving her the suggestion and the inspiration to call Johns Hopkins Hospital to find Robert.

"Dr. Sharp's office. This is Janice Buchanan. How may I help you?"

"Hi. My name is Rachel Rice."

"Yes, hello, Rachel. I did not get a chance to meet you when you came in to have Dr. Sharp make your front tooth look like a new tooth. Your praise made her day. And you were an early bird that day."

"Yes. I jumped at the chance when I learned that the kind lady who helped me up and put ointment and bandages on my abrasions was a dentist. I was mentally blown away when she offered to meet me the very next morning, one hour earlier than her established office hours, to work on my tooth. I sure dreaded the next day having to teach a classroom full of students with my broken front tooth. I never dreamed it was possible to see a dentist only hours after I broke my front tooth."

"I heard you were very pleased with the work she did on your front tooth."

"Oh, yes. I reacted both gleefully and embarrassingly." Rachel laughed into the telephone. "I looked into the handheld mirror Millie handed to me and yelled like I was cheering at a football game."

"You did not? Did you, for real?"

"Yes. Embarrassing so." They both laughed. "But I have more reason than my front tooth to be thankful for today. I met and referred Mary Shipley to Dr. Sharp to repair Mary's front tooth."

"Yes. I remember Mary Shipley. I made a comment to her about her last name since I love beautiful boats and ships. I still have her worries in a jar if she ever wants them back?"

"She told me about your clever idea that she said actually worked. What a hoot."

"A spur-of-a-moment idea that worked. I am happy she loves her new front tooth. Did you also mention that you were thankful for something else?"

"Oh, yes. Thank you for steering me back to my train of thought. Mary talked with Dr. Sharp about the missing man of my life."

"Yes. I heard about him not showing up to meet you for dinner at a restaurant and subsequently dropping out of sight a few months ago. Any word?"

"You haven't heard?"

"No. Good news, I hope?"

"I thought Mary might have called and told everyone."

"No. We have not heard from Mary since her last visit."

"I was calling to thank Dr. Sharp for spending so much time with Mary Shipley to discuss Robert."

"Robert is the name of the love of your life who went missing?"

"Yes. Sorry."

"Oh. That is okay. Do you mind telling me the news?"

"No, I don't mind telling you. His name is Dr. Robert Wilson."

"A doctor?"

"Yes. A brand-new doctor who passed his medical boards a few days after we met."

"Neat. You will be by his side from the first days of his becoming a medical doctor to build a great life together. Please tell me I am not jumping the gun on the news you have yet to tell me?"

"I hope your words were inspired by our Creator and turn out to be a future prediction."

"We will both hold that thought. But is there any question about this in your mind?" Janice asked.

"Let me answer you by revealing my news. Okay?"

"Okay?"

"The night Robert did not show up to meet me, I called all the hospitals and clinics within a fifty-mile radius and did not find him. Mary took it upon herself to ask Dr. Sharp for suggestions on where to start looking for someone who might be seriously injured. Dr. Sharp stopped whatever she was doing and took Mary back to her office to listen and help. Hearing the love story between me and Robert, she concluded only a serious injury would keep Robert from meeting me for dinner. It literally took her five minutes to do what I could not do in four months. Mary told her Robert graduated from Johns Hopkins University School of Medicine, located in Baltimore, Maryland. This triggered a memory with Dr. Sharp, who was aware of a Johns Hopkins Hospital being, perhaps, a training hospital and the largest hospital in the world, located in the same area. Dr. Sharp strongly suggested she start her search there, and she found him."

"Wow. Now that is a story for the tabloids. Hopefully you two have reconnected, and all is well."

"Not exactly. There was a good reason why he never showed up to meet me for dinner. On his first day at work, a nurse was being assaulted by an angry patient wielding a heavy wooden cane, demanding heroin from her. She yelled for Robert to save her from being attacked and he did, but in the process, he got hit in the back of his head, and again alongside of his head, with this heavy wooden cane. He collapsed face-first onto the floor in a nonresponsive coma. Instead of meeting me, he was being airlifted to Johns Hopkins Hospital and immediately admitted into their intensive care unit and still there today in a coma."

"I am so sorry. I will put him and you in my daily prayers."

"Thank you. You are kind. I will drive up tomorrow to speak with the doctors and nurses to assess his medical condition for myself and spend quality time with him. Hopefully my voice will make a difference and wake him up."

"I hope so. Thank you for talking with me, Rachel. If you do not mind holding for a couple of minutes, I will tell Dr. Sharp you are on the telephone and get her to speak with you. Okay?"

"Okay. Good talking with you."

"You too. Bye."

"Bye."

"Hello, Rachel. This is Dr. Mary Sharp."

"Hi, Dr. Sharp. I just called to thank you for speaking with Mary Shipley about Robert and guiding her to Johns Hopkins Hospital to find him."

"You found him? Oh, praise the Lord. That is great news. How are things between the two of you?"

"The night he did not meet me, he was being airlifted to Johns Hopkins Hospital in a nonresponsive coma. I do not have all the details, but from what I do know, a nurse yelled out for him to help her from being attacked by an angry patient wanting her to give him heroin. Robert ran into the patient's room and saved her from being hit by a heavy wooden cane, but while he was saving her, he was forcibly struck in the back of his head, and again along the left side of his head, with this thick heavy wooden cane. He collapsed facedown on the floor in a coma. They airlifted him to Johns Hopkins Hospital in Maryland the same afternoon he was to meet me for dinner."

"Four months ago?"

"Yes. No wonder he did not show up."

"How is he now?"

"He is still in a nonresponsive coma."

"Do you have new information on his prognosis?

"No. I am going to drive up in the morning and talk with his doctors and nurses to assess his medical condition for myself and then spend quality time kissing him awake."

"Your voice is what he needs. And the love in his heart for you will wake him up. You are the best medicine for him right now, Rachel. Let me know if I can help you in any way. Okay?"

'Okay. Thank you, Dr. Sharp. My heart is full of gratitude."

"You are welcome. Please bring him with you to see us. That will make me very happy. Okay?"

"Okay."

"Thank you for calling me, Rachel."

"You are very welcome. Thank you for speaking with me. Bye."

"Bye, Rachel."

Rachel started to pack for her trip when she remembered waking up this morning thinking about Mary Shipley, and now her thoughts are back to thinking about her again. She always heard that nothing is a coincidence, and she also heard that no one is sent to anyone by accident.

The Holy Spirit lives inside each of us. Divine intervention is another name often associated with the Holy Spirit. It often tries to mentally guide or influence our decisions when we are about to do something harmful or beneficial to us, especially if we are a Christian. Why am I thinking about Mary Shipley? The voice inside my head seems to be wanting me to ask Mary to ride with me when I visit Bobby. I can feel it. She would be great company for me. But I am betting there is more to your plan, God.

CHAPTER 17

Mary Remembers Her Parents

Mary Shipley was now home and thinking about her meeting with Rachel earlier today, wondering how Rachel will react after four long months seeing Robert lying in a comatose state. The little voice inside her head was telling her that Rachel will soon become her close trusted friend. And that would almost certainly lead to her having to reveal her hidden past life, which is drastically different than the life she lives today as a waitress in a restaurant. It has been a year since she allowed herself to think about her past, but now, she decided to take a few minutes to reflect over the year of life-changing events.

She grew up in an upper middle-class home with professional parents. Her mother was a professor at Harvard University. Mary was gifted with a photographic memory and had the grade point average to be accepted as a student at Harvard University. Harvard students never stopped to connect her last name with her mother, Professor Shipley. Mary's dad was a very successful engineer for a Fortune 500 company. They were a close-knit family who enjoyed laughing, joking, and sharing stories about things of interest, as they traveled together as a family. When people asked about their relationship, they referred to themselves as the Three Musketeers.

Mary graduated from Harvard University with their highest honors or summa cum laude. She immediately enrolled into Harvard Law School and fell in love with many different subjects of the law, which explains why she graduated from Harvard Law School with high honors. Career decisions were something she took very seriously. She was unable to decide if she wanted to work for a law firm as an associate or open her own law firm, so she placed this part of her life on hold, until her heart, her subconscious mind, and her conscious mind united to make that decision for her. If she was ever uncertain about what to do, she did nothing until she was certain.

Late one night, over a year ago, tragedy struck her life and threw her into a temporary state of depression when a police officer phoned her with the news that both of her parents were instantly killed when their vehicle was struck head-on by a driver who fell asleep and crossed over the dividing center line of a very busy four-lane highway in Atlanta, Georgia. It took several months for her to continue with any semblance of her life after adjusting to the sudden death of both parents.

She was thankful that the legal details about the deaths of her parents had been handled quickly and confidentially, away from the public eye. Only a handful of people knew about the $2 million wrongful death settlement she received from the death of her parents.

She sat on her recliner and reflected on the day she met the woman charged with killing her parents. On that day, the woman who caused their deaths was scheduled to be sentenced to twenty years in prison for two counts of vehicular homicide. She never dreamed she would ever do what she did that day.

Amy Evans is a single twenty-one-year-old Yale college graduate. She was excited about being accepted into Yale Law School the night she decided to go out with a few of her friends to celebrate. She was a walking zombie and exhausted from burning the midnight candle at both ends, cramming to pass her final exams to graduate from Yale. Unfortunately she ignored all the warning signs from her body, drank her first drink of alcohol, and tried to drive her car home. She fell asleep behind the wheel of her car and crossed over the dividing center line to hit an oncoming vehicle head-on. She woke up unable to breathe, with her body pressed tightly against the steering wheel and unable to open the driver's door. Smoke was coming from underneath her vehicle and forming a cloud over the area.

Bystanders were able to use crowbars to get her car door open, shut off her engine, and help her out of her vehicle. She walked on wobbly legs over to the vehicle she hit and immediately fell onto her knees and screamed, "No! Please do not let them be dead, God. This is all my fault for drinking and driving. I am so sorry. Help me, Lord." She laid facedown on the grass, crying, until the police put handcuffs on her wrist. She stood motionless with a blank look on her face, like she had just seen an alien from outer space. This glass look she had in her eyes remained frozen without expression as she continued to cry and shake her head from side to side while she walked along the side of a police officer and followed his orders to lower her head to sit down on the back seat of a police car that took her to jail. She was not physically injured but mentally felt like she was living in hell.

Police officers from the jail told the judge she ate like a bird over the last year while she sat in a jail cell, waiting for this hearing and showed no desire to defend herself of the crimes she is charged with. Her court-appointed attorney informed her that he had worked out a plea deal to send her to prison for the next twenty years of her life.

The next words she heard had to be frightening for any defendant sitting in a courtroom.

"ALL RISE. The Superior Court of Fulton County is now in session, Judge Faith Cross presiding."

Judge Cross is forty-six years of age, 5'5" tall, 123 pounds, with brown sandy color hair, and blue eyes. She is a mother of four children with a reputation of being fair, compassionate, but a no-nonsense judge.

She took her seat on the bench and looked out at her court prosecutor, who is David Powers—6'2", 220-pound athletic-built man, age forty-five, with black hair, blue eyes—and asked, "Is the state ready to proceed, Mr. Powers?"

"Yes, Your Honor. The state is ready to proceed in the matter of Amy Evans."

"Is the defense ready to proceed?"

"Defense is ready to proceed, Your Honor."

"Any matters to be addressed before we begin, Mr. Powers?"

"No, Your Honor."

"Is there a family member of the deceased in court today? If so, are they aware of the plea deal reached in this case between the state and the defense counsel for Ms. Evans?"

"Mary Shipley is the only surviving relative of her parents, Mr. and Mrs. Shipley, and we have just been informed she is now in the hallway waiting to be asked to join this proceeding, Your Honor."

"Please bring her into the courtroom."

Mary walked into the courtroom and shook hands with the prosecutor and nodded to the judge.

"Are you Mary Shipley?"

"Yes, Your Honor. I am Mary Shipley."

"Are you the only living relative of Mr. and Mrs. Shipley, who are the deceased listed in the matter pending before the court this morning?"

"Yes, your honor."

"Have you been informed that Amy Evans, who is seated at the defense table, has been charged with two counts of vehicular homicide?"

"Yes."

"Are you aware of a plea deal Amy Evans has accepted in this case?"

"No. May I ask the terms of the plea?"

"A ten-year prison sentence for each death, for a total of twenty consecutive years in prison. Do you agree with the terms of the plea?"

Mary remembered looking over at the defense table and making eye contact with Amy Evans for only a brief couple of seconds when she immediately lowered her face and looked down at the table in front of her. "May I have a couple of minutes to speak with her, Your Honor?"

"Yes. Take all the time you need."

"Thank you, Your Honor."

She walked over to the defense table and stood next to her. She continued to look down at the defense table. Finally she looked up at me with a very frightened look in her eyes that immediately started to fill with tears. "I am so sorry. I will go to prison for the rest of my life to pay for what I have done to end the life of your parents and ruin your life. I know you will never forgive me in this lifetime, but maybe in the next one, will you?" Tears flowed down her face like water running down a waterfall. A voice inside my head whispered to me, Hug her. *She held out her open arms to encourage Amy to get up and give her a hug. Amy blinked back tears.*

"I don't understand what you want. Do you want to hug me or hit me?"

"A power much higher than either of us wants me to hug you. Will you stand for me to do this?"

"How could you possibly hug me after I murdered your parents?"

"If you used a gun, then I would agree with you that you murdered them. I know God is telling me I should hug you. Will you allow me to hug you?"

Amy Evans stood and looked at Mary Shipley through tear-filled eyes and a skeptical look on her face. The very second they hugged, a voice within the head of Mary Shipley said, Do not send her to prison. Check her blood-alcohol content. Ask the court for first offender status. *And upon hearing these words, she impulsively blurted out,* "Oh yeah, right. We are going to go from a twenty-year agreed-upon plea deal to the first offender program."

"We are? What does that mean?" Amy asked her question excitedly into Mary's ear.

"No." Mary answered Amy. She was about to dismiss the idea as being ludicrous when the voice within her head seemed to yell, Do it. It was an accident. Do not send her to prison.

"What is going on?" Amy whispered to Mary.

"What was your blood-alcohol content? Do you remember?"

"Yes, it was 4.5 percent. Why?"

"Because you weren't legally drunk. It takes blood-alcohol consumption of 8.0 percent to be DUI or impaired. It is a long shot, but do you trust me enough to see if I can help you?"

"Why?"

"God wants me to. Please don't ask me about this now. Just trust me. Okay?"

"Okay. But I thought He was mad at me."

"Do you read the Bible?"

"Yes. Sometimes. Why?"

"Lamentations 3:22–23 says, 'God's loving-kindness never ceases. And His compassion never fails but is new every morning. God loves all of us, all the time and not just sometimes."

"Ms. Shipley, are you ready for the court to proceed?"

Mary turned to look at Amy Evans. "Do you trust me?"

"Yes."

Mary turned her attention to Judge Cross. "Yes, I am ready, Your Honor."

"Are you ready to proceed with the plea reached between the state and the court-appointed attorney for Amy Evans?"

"Not with the plea you have before you, Your Honor. May I address the court?"

"Yes. What would you like to say?"

"Amy Evans didn't use a gun to cause the death of my parents. She made a mistake any of us could have made. I am aware of the 'implied intent' if a driver knowingly operates a motor vehicle after he voluntarily consumes enough alcohol to impair his ability to drive a motor vehicle. I would like for the court to consider and re-evaluate an important aspect in this case."

"And what aspect would that be? Are you not wanting the state to punish Amy Evans for the wrongful death of your parents? Don't you wish to see the state give her the maximum criminal penalty allowed by law for her choice to drink alcohol and then drive a motor vehicle to kill your parents?"

"I would like for the state to consider the alcohol content in Amy Evans's blood system when this accident occurred, which I believe was 4.5 percent. She would need an alcohol level of 8.0 percent to be considered legally drunk. Remove the alcohol aspect in this case, and we are left with a degree of negligence. And while she did not have a conscious intent to commit this crime, she is still guilty of vehicular homicide. Facts of this case would prove that she was exhausted cramming for final exams, chose to drive a motor vehicle home, and fell asleep, causing this accident. So—"

"Are you an attorney, Ms. Shipley?"

"Yes, Your Honor. I am a Harvard Law School graduate. I also passed the bar and was about to open my own office to begin my practice when my parents were accidentally killed. I know in a case this serious, it is a stretch to ask for the first-offender treatment, but since I am the daughter and the only living relative of my parents, I am asking the court to give Amy Evans this stretch of a chance to learn from this tragedy by helping her begin a life instead of permanently destroying it with a prison sentence that will preclude her from ever practicing law or having any

semblance of a decent life. She will always have a job with me when she passes the bar exam to practice law."

"You will hire her to be an attorney in your office after what she did to cause the death of your parents?"

"Yes, Your Honor. Amy Evans will have a job working with me during any breaks she gets from her law school and when she becomes a licensed attorney. God forgives our sins, and He also miraculously forgets them. I can never forget the wonderful memories of my parents nor will I forget how Amy Evans accidentally caused their death. But I forgive her. I am not without sin."

"I do not think any of us are. You are the only one who has been damaged in this tragedy. Amy Evans has served one year in jail waiting for her trial or this hearing. She has certainly shown a lot of remorse for causing the death of your parents. Let me hear from the prosecutor in this case."

"Your Honor, the court has the authority to reduce or modify any of the sentence guidelines."

"Is the state of Georgia in agreement with me giving Amy Evans first offender status in this case?"

"Based on the argument presented by Mary Shipley this morning, yes, Your Honor."

"You are the only injured party in the death of your parents. Do you need time to consider what you are asking this court to do, Mary Shipley?"

"No. I am sure of my decision and just as sure of my request that I ask this court to grant."

Judge Cross shook her head and raised her eyebrows as she studied the expression on Mary's face before she said, "Okay. You are the sole heir of your parents. I will never understand your reason, but the court is going to grant your motion of first offender status for Amy Evans."

"Thank you, Your Honor."

"Do you have anything you want to say, Amy Evans?"

"Could you explain the first offender status to me?"

"Yes. The First Offender Program can prove to be a dangerous program, or it can be a blessing, if you stay out of trouble for three consecutive years. If you do, your record will be wiped clean, like nothing hap-

pened. If you get into any trouble over the next three years, however, your probation status under the First Offender Treatment Program will be revoked, and you will be sent back to this court for me to sentence you for both of these vehicular homicide crimes you are charged with today, plus I will sentence you for the length of time called for in your new crime. Do you now fully understand the First Offender Treatment Program?"

"Yes, Your Honor. I do understand it."

"Do you want this court to sentence you as a first offender?"

"Yes. I am asking the court to sentence me as a first offender."

"This court sentences Amy Evans as a first offender for the crimes of vehicular homicide."

"Thank you, Your Honor."

"You're welcome. You would be starting a twenty-year prison sentence today if Mary Shipley did not show up to convince the court to reconsider the agreed-upon plea deal. You should thank Mary Shipley."

"Yes, ma'am. I am still in shock at her kindness and mercy to not only forgive me but to help me begin a new life with this second chance."

"I think we saved a good one today, Your Honor," Mary said as she stretched out her left arm across Amy's back to gently grab her left shoulder and pull her closer to her. "God and I both believe you are worth saving, Amy. Please do not prove us wrong." Mary looked at her and waited for her reply.

"I will not. I promise you. I will not prove you wrong. I will work hard for you. I will find a way to repay your kindness and belief in me. I still cannot believe this is real."

"One small correction. You will work with me, not for me. We will become a successful team. I will walk you out." Mary looked up at the judge. "Are we dismissed, Your Honor?"

"Yes. I look forward to seeing a lot more of you, Mary Shipley."

"I look forward to that, too, Your Honor."

"I am deeply sorry for the loss of your parents, Mary."

"Thank you, ma'am. I honestly believe it was their day and time to see the face of God."

"Now that is an interesting and beautiful way to look at the death of a loved one."

"Amy Evans was the vehicle, or the person, chosen by God to send them home. I honestly believe God is pleased with our combined efforts to change what would have been a terrible ending for Amy."

"Do you want to walk your client down to the probation department for the release papers to be signed?"

"Yes. Thank you very much. Does the prosecutor want to go with us?"

"Mr. Powers. Do you want to accompany the defendant and her new lawyer down to probation?"

"No, Your Honor. But I would like to ask Ms. Shipley one question, if I may?"

"The court has no objection, if Ms. Shipley does not."

"No. I have no objection. I will answer the question, if I know the answer."

"Why didn't you tell me, when you first came into the courtroom this morning, you were going to ask the court to consider giving Ms. Evans first offender status?"

"I did not know it myself."

"When did you know it?"

"The thought was not even in my mind until I hugged her. We hugged and a voice within my head said, 'Do not send her to prison, ask for first offender status.' My first reaction to this thought in my mind was, 'Oh yeah, right. We are going to go from a twenty-year agreed-upon plea deal to the First Offender Program. Just as I considered rejecting the voice in my head, the same voice screamed, 'DO IT!' The rest of the story you know. I cannot explain the inner voice other than to say I believe in my heart it was the Holy Spirit guiding me to ask the court to help Amy Evans."

"May I borrow this voice when you are not using it?" Mr. Powers laughed out loud.

"It lives in your head now. God will turn it on for you, if you ask Him." She didn't laugh.

"You are serious?"

"Serious as a heart attack."

"This has been a very interesting and amazing day," he said, looking up at the judge.

"Once the probation papers are signed, you are free to go. Good luck to you, Amy Evans."

"Thank you very much, Your Honor." Judge Cross nodded her head and smiled at Mary Shipley.

"Court is now adjourned." Judge Cross turned and disappeared through the door behind her bench.

Mary looked at Amy and asked, "Are you ready to go with me?"

"Yes. Anywhere you want to take me." Amy smiled for the first time in one year before she looked down at her skinny arms and body. "I need to start eating again to regain the twenty-five pounds I lost."

"I know where you can find the twenty-five pounds you lost," Mary said, looking down at her own body. "I need an exercise program, pronto." They both laughed out loud as they walked out of the courtroom.

CHAPTER 18

Amy Evans Gets a Second Chance

Happy tears ran down the face of Amy Evans the minute she stepped outside the courthouse a free woman. Not one friend or relative wanted to witness her being sentenced to twenty years in prison, so no one knew she was a free woman, allowed to mingle back into society. She was borderline in shock with happy feelings to sort through. She wanted to always remember this day, so she made no attempt to wipe away or stop the flow of her happy tears. She looked up. "Thank you! You did hear me, didn't you? You heard me at the accident scene when I cried out, 'Help me, Lord.'"

Mary remained quiet when she quickly realized this was a special moment between Amy and God. She also seemed to understand the polarized emotions running through Amy's mind, so she stood silent, allowing Amy to process the extreme emotional contrasting feelings of one minute realizing she was going to spend the next twenty years in prison, beginning today, to hearing the judge tell her she was a free woman. And it must have been overwhelming to hear the judge tell her once she signs probation papers and stays out of trouble for three years, her criminal record would be wiped clean, as though she never committed a single crime.

Mary knew it would take many months or perhaps years for Amy Evans to comprehend how the Holy Spirit was able to miraculously and instantaneously touch Mary's heart to not only forgive the accidental deaths of her parents but simultaneously convince the judge, who was about to put her in prison today for twenty years, to give her probation.

"May I hug you one more time? I was scared thinking about prison life and what those ladies and guards were going to do to me." Amy blew out a long shaky breath of air, watching Mary step closer so she could give her a thank you and goodbye hug. Amy did not have a clue where she would spend the night or how to get her life on track to live the rest of her life but knew she could not ask anything more of Mary Shipley.

They both smiled as they stood a couple of steps away from each other. Mary asked, "Anything else we need to discuss, Amy?"

"I will call you with my cell phone number, and I will mail you the address for the law school so we can stay in touch with each other. I have your address and your cell phone number if I need you. Thank you so much. I do not know how, but I will spend the rest of my life trying to repay you."

"Call me 24-7 if you need anything. How are you fixed for spending money?"

"I will make do and get by."

"Please tell me honestly how you will make do? This is not the time to be modest. If you need my financial help, I can help you. Consider it a long-term loan to be repaid monthly from the salary you will earn working with me. Okay?"

"Are you serious about hiring me?"

"Yes."

"Why? You can hire a better student who is fresh out of law school or hire a seasoned lawyer. You have done way too much for me already. We both know you don't need me."

"I have done my homework on you, Amy Evans. You need my connections at Yale Law School."

"Why? And why?"

"I follow the suggestions given to me by the little voice inside my head who told me to check you out. I did not know why I was doing it then, but I do know now. God knows. God knows everything we do, now and everything we will do in the future, before we do it. He is the most important person in your life. Pray to Him every day, and thank Him every day for the life He allows you to live."

"How did you get so religious?"

"Prayer."

"I will pray to Him every day."

Mary studied Amy's facial expression for a few seconds before she said, "I believe you will."

"I promise."

"We learn from our mistakes, or we should. Eleanor Roosevelt once said, 'A woman is like a tea bag. She never knows how strong she is until she is in hot water.' Show the world how strong you are, Amy."

"God has people all over the whole world asking Him for help. I wonder what I did to get God's attention to send me a person like you to rescue me."

"I can answer that one easily."

"I would love to hear the answer to my question. Please tell me what I did?"

"You said, 'Lord, help me,' while you were on your knees at the accident scene. Right?"

"Right."

"God hears all prayers. *And He answered that prayer that you spoke from your heart.*"

"It truly was spoken from my heart."

"He sees what is in your heart, and He knows what you will ask Him before you say a word."

"Thank you for all the nice things you say to me and about me."

"Do you have a fully paid scholarship to law school?" Mary asked her.

"Yes. I graduated from Yale University, so it only seemed right to apply to Yale Law School which is rated number 1 in the country by a company called BEST who rates all law schools. Yale has 621 full-time student enrollments at an annual tuition cost of $64,267. Harvard was a close second with 1,737 full-time student enrollments at an annual cost of $64,978. I sure was lucky to receive my scholarship."

"Does your scholarship pay for your living quarters, books, and food?"

"No. My scholarship pays for my books and all of my tuition."

"How will you pay for your housing and food? How much do you have saved up?"

"I have $500 in savings. And I have a credit card with a limit of $1,000. I plan on getting a job."

"Yale will only allow their students to work twenty hours weekly. You cannot earn much in twenty hours. Do you have a place to stay after being in jail for a year?"

"No. Not off the top of my head, but I will find a place to stay."

"Do you have clothes, toothbrush, and other things in storage?"

"I defaulted on my lease, and they took all of my personal property in lieu of the back rent I owed."

"Your car? What happened to your car?"

"It was an old car with no collision coverage. The salvage yard scrapped it. No money to me."

"Please bury your pride, Amy. I cannot help you without knowing your whole financial picture."

"You have done so much for me, Mary. I cannot allow myself to impose on you financially."

"The big point you're missing is you will pay me back for every penny you spend for the food you eat, the clothes on your back, cosmetics, your housing over three years, gasoline for your car, and your spending money. All these expenses will be kept on a ledger in your file to be repaid to me over a ten-year period. Spreading the total over 120 months will be like paying pennies from your salary, plus your commissions you will earn working with me. These payments to me will not affect your lifestyle or put a dent in your ability to live a very good life. I am not offering you charity. You are not a charity case to me. You will pay your way through law school on a deferred payment plan through me. I need good people to work with me in my new law firm. Please stop thinking of this offer as charity. Do these business terms appeal to you, and do they meet with your approval?"

"Yes, ma'am. I am a tad overwhelmed. Please be patient with me."

"Okay. I understand this is a sudden reversal from the pits of hell you envisioned for yourself only an hour ago to become a possible dream come true. Remember, God does not make mistakes. We do not know His

plan for you or me. We both need to block out our negativity and put our trust in Him. Okay?"

"I feel so guilty every time I look at you."

"You need to pray and ask God to show you how to forgive yourself."

"I need Him to tell me how to do that."

"He will tell you how. He knows you have serious work ahead of you, Amy. Your mind must be clear to pass law school and the bar exam. How badly do you want to be a lawyer?"

"I have wanted to be a lawyer for as long as I can remember. I will rise to the task and apply myself 24-7. I will pray daily, asking God to show me how to forgive myself and guide my life."

"That is all you need to do. Focus on God and your future. Pray every day and more when you feel your mind drifting to think about something negative about your past. Think of this as a baseball game, with you standing on first base. Can you run to second base with your foot still standing on first base?"

"No."

"Every time you think about something negative from your past, try to remember the baseball story about first base."

"Okay. It will take time for me to block out all the negative thoughts about my past. I especially want to block out thoughts about prison gates closing behind me, knowing they would not open again to let me out for twenty years." Her eyes teared up as she glanced over at Mary and quickly looked away.

"I understand. This just happened to you, and understandably it will never fade away completely, but it will be manageable if you keep praying and leaning on me and God."

"Thank you for understanding and for being patient with me. I will be okay, knowing I have you, who I do not deserve, and God to guide me and lean on. I have more than just a chance to get it all together."

"I have total confidence in you, Amy. You have always been an A college student."

"Yes. I was blessed with a great mind and memory. Thank you for your confidence in me."

"Please remember that we are forming a business relationship where you agree to work with me for an agreed-upon annual salary, plus commission. *I will give my accounting firm the total amount of money I advanced to you over your three years in law school and ask them to spread the total amount you owe me over ten years, or 120 months, excluding the automobile, which will be my law school graduation gift to you. The total expenditures over three years will not be as astronomical as one might expect, once the automobile payments are removed from your list of things to pay. You will not feel a financial pinch from the payroll checks you will receive."*

"Okay. I accept your offer of employment. I also accept your generous repayment terms over ten years that allow me to pay you back with money I earn working with you. Thank you so much for structuring my repayment over ten years."

"You are welcome. Do you still have your scholarship?"

"Yes. I kept in touch with Yale Law School. Even after I told them everything that happened, they held my scholarship for me. I just need to enroll and choose my Yale Law School housing plan."

"God is the one who had them hold your scholarship for you. And since you do not have any personal belongings to worry about here in Atlanta, will you let me drive you up to New Haven, Connecticut, now to get you checked in for the next semester?"

"I am in a partial state of shock believing people like you exist. Compound that thought with my thinking you are really going to walk out on a limb and do all this for me. You are, aren't you?"

"Yes. If you will let me? If I do not do it, who do you have to help you?"

"Nobody. I have nobody to help me. I worked my own way through college. I cannot explain the feelings I have inside me telling me to trust you. I know everything will be okay for me if I not only trust you but do right by you in everything I am asked to do. Does this make sense to you?"

"Yes, it does. I will tell you about a voice inside my head that talks to me. *I know this voice is from one third of the Trinity of God. The voice is* the Holy Spirit, *who told me to help you."*

"So you were speaking honestly when you said God told you to help me?"

"Yes. God has His eyes on you and will always be with you, if you allow Him to be with you?"

Tears filled her eyes just thinking about God wanting to always be with her, as she looked at Mary. She could not speak. She nodded her head in agreement and looked down at the pavement.

"My car is right here." Mary pointed to her car parked along the curb. "Since we have a lot to talk about, is it okay if we get into my car and talk on the way up to Connecticut?" Mary did not wait for her reply when she retrieved her car keys and automatic door opener from her purse to unlock her vehicle. She pulled open the driver's door and stood waiting for Amy to ease into the passenger seat before she slid behind the steering wheel and started the car engine.

Amy looked over at Mary with gratitude in her eyes. She was filled with too much emotion to speak. Sitting in the passenger seat of Mary's car, knowing she was about to travel to Yale Law School to begin an incredible dream she thought she had hopelessly lost less than one hour ago, was an overwhelming happy feeling she never envisioned ever feeling again in her lifetime. To keep from crying out loud and bawling like a baby, she pressed her lips tightly together and just stared at Mary, who was studying her expression with a curious but understanding look in her eyes. She was determined not to speak until Amy found a handle on her emotions. Amy slowly blew out a long breath of air, refusing to look away from Mary until she whispered the words, "Thank you." She finally looked away toward the car floorboard.

"Before I put the car in gear to start our new journey together, why don't we both take a minute and give thanks to God for allowing everything to turn out so favorably for you in court today, and ask God to guide and bless everything we do together to make everything work for both of us. Okay?"

"Will you say the prayer for us?" Amy asked Mary.

"Yes. I would be happy to say a prayer for our future together. Our Father in heaven, I want to thank you for speaking to me through the Holy Spirit today in the courtroom of Judge Cross. You gave me the ideas and the words needed to save Amy Evans from a twenty-year prison sentence to enable us to work together to make a difference in your kingdom. Please put your shield of protection and guidance around Amy Evans during her next three years at Yale Law School. Be with her and guide

her to pass the bar exam and to build a successful law career with me in my new law firm. I ask this in Jesus's name, amen."

"Wow. The words you just said echoed every thought in my heart. Thank you, Mary."

"You're welcome. Now let us get on the road to make all of this happen for both of us. Okay?"

"Okay." They smiled at each other and held each other's hand for a few seconds before Mary put the car into drive to begin their road trip to Connecticut.

"After we get you enrolled, we will decide on a house for you in a good neighborhood."

"Do you know anything about their housing?"

"Yes. Matter of fact, I do. My father attended Yale and lived in their housing. They have housing all around the school. You can choose East Rock, Wooster Square, or other areas closer to the school."

"Do you remember very much about the areas?"

"Yes. East Rock is considered their suburban area with a lot of cafés, bodegas, and a deli on every block. Students with families will choose to live in this area. Great place to live if you have a car to drive. The negative is the twenty-minute walk to law school without a car or bike. A great option for students to ride are the shuttles, which are plentiful and reliable. Without a car, it gets mighty cold standing outside in the snow waiting for a shuttle ride."

"East Rock sounds like a neat area for me to live. Should I even consider other options?"

"Wooster Square, which is further out than East Rock, is another option for you to consider. It has a lot more for you to choose from. They have plenty of houses in this area close to pizzerias, bakeries, and a farmer's market that is only open part of the year. With your personality and what I detect of your heart, you will love it there in the spring, where you will enjoy seeing the pink and white cherry blossoms bloom and cover the neighborhood to make this a very beautiful place to live during your three years there."

"That sounds like the best area yet for me, unless you have more choices for me to consider?"

"Anywhere else that you choose will be between a five-minute to a fifteen-minute walk from the law school. All the areas to choose from will be close to a grocery store, restaurants, and bars."

"I never want to walk inside a bar the rest of my life. If I meet a guy who drinks alcohol, he will never get to first base with me. I will never break this rule when it comes to men who drink alcohol."

"I understand, Amy."

"Is that my options for my condo or house choices?"

"Yes. You have the option to choose a house, condo, or school dorm."

"Please guide me to make the right decision."

"Okay. I would suggest you call Elm Campus Partners and let them guide you to a temporary home to get you off the street tonight. Tell them you want to immediately upgrade to your own private home to live in the best available area over the next three years. Tell them the daughter of Professor Shipley referred you to them."

"Did your mother or father know these people?"

"Yes. My dad attended Yale University and used them to find his living quarters. I used to come here with them when Dad wanted to visit his Yale buddies. I love this area of the country."

"I am sorry to dredge up painful memories."

"Nonsense, Amy. Learning that you were a Yale graduate immediately put a soft spot in my heart for you. This place brings back wonderful memories being here with my parents. I feel them with me. This trip and the follow-up trips here to see you will bring back more wonderful memories of my parents. I will relive a different fun time with my parents each time I come here to see you. I am so excited about doing this with you."

"I will always feel sad about what I did to cut your time short with your parents."

"Thank you for saying that to me. My next words to you are gospel true. My parents were going to die at the same hour of the same day by something you or another person did, so you did not cut their life short. Forget about that part of your guilt. You were the one chosen by God to send them home."

"You were being honest when you said this to the trial judge?"

"Yes."

"Thank you for telling me. I need to let that sink into my brain. Wow."

"This is a good time for you to use my cell phone lying on the console to make your living arrangements for tonight while I am here to confirm financial responsibility. Try for a two-bedroom home so I have a room to sleep in when I come to visit you. Tonight I will sleep on the couch"

"I will sleep on the couch. You get the bedroom, if they only have a one-bedroom."

"We will do it the American way and flip for it." They both did a high five and laughed out loud.

"I sure hope to see a lot more laughter coming out of you." They both smiled at each other and nodded.

"Do you have the time to spend up here helping me?"

"I will take the time. This is important to both of us. Tomorrow will be a busy day. You need to choose an automobile you want to drive and own three years from now. I will cosign for any automobile you choose up to 45K. The automobile insurance on the vehicle will list you as the principal driver. We will then open a bank account for you. I will make a deposit into it for you to buy your own clothes, your own food, and hygiene products. I will keep everything in a file for you. Every month, I will send you an accounting for your records. Paying me back over the first ten years you work with me will not create any financial hardship for you. In the end, you will have paid your own way. Do you have any questions about anything?"

"How much interest on your money will I pay you?"

"I will not charge you one penny interest. Working with me over ten years is repayment enough."

"I am speechless by your kindness and hearing how you always refer to me working with you and never for you. I cannot stop thinking about the way the prison guards talked so hatefully to me only a few hours ago, and now I am on my way to accept a Yale Law School scholarship that I thought I had lost this morning. Unbelievable. And this dream keeps getting bigger and bigger. I lost my only car, and here I am, on my way to pick out a new car that I will own in three short years. And the biggest thing is I get to choose a place to live all by myself instead of sharing a prison cell. To make this incredible dream even more incredible, I will have my own checking account with money in it to buy my own clothes, hygiene items, and food to regain the weight and strength that I lost over

the last year. If you lay around without exercise over a period of a year, you lose a lot of elasticity in your body. Only exercise and continued use will wake up these sleeping areas of your body for you to ever use them again. The area of the knees on any long pants that I buy will be worn thin from the amount of time I will spend on my knees thanking God for His mercy and you. Okay. I will shut up now."

"I love to hear you talk about things on your mind or in your heart. Everything you just said will happen for you if we stay closely connected over the next three years. If you do the normal things expected of you, the automobile you select for me to cosign, for you to drive, will belong to you. If you do not do the things expected of you, or if you get into any trouble over the next three years, you will lose your car, my financial support, and me."

"I will gladly slice my own throat in death before I ever cross or disappoint you."

"God sees something special in you, Amy. I do not think you will let either of us down."

"I will die, if I do."

"God does not make mistakes. I only wish it were possible to reverse time for me to have been there to remind you of the consequences of driving an automobile after you took your first drink of alcohol, when you were so exhausted from burning the midnight oil studying to pass college exams."

"This is a big ask from me when I ask you to believe that I will never drink another drop of alcohol as long as God allows me to live nor will I drive an automobile when I am physically exhausted.

"I believe you. Wow, we made great time. Let us go inside and get you checked into school."

"You do know your way around Yale. And without GPS. I am impressed." Amy giggled.

"I spent a lot of time up here with my parents. I know the area like the back of my hand."

"Before we go inside, let me say thank you, one more time, for everything you have done and will do for me. You have my promise and my word that I will never let you down."

LOVE WILL FIND YOU

"I trust you. God loves you. Once we get you checked in, we will drive over to see the people at Elm Campus Partners to find out what section they selected for you to live temporarily, or possibly permanently, over the next three years."

"I hope I do not wake up tomorrow inside of a prison cell to realize all of this has been one big dream?"

"Do you want me to pinch you?" They laughed out loud, followed by a quick hug and laughed some more as they got out of the car to check Amy into Yale Law School.

"A dream has just come true," Amy said out loud as she walked outside the law school exit door.

She turned to face Mary. "Thank you so much, Mary."

"You are very welcome. I am happy for you. And I am happy God selected me to help you."

*****

Elm Campus Partners' front door was wide open when they parked in one of their reserved parking spaces for visitors out front of their office building. They walked into their office and stood at the counter, waiting for a woman to end her phone call to help them.

"Hello. How can I help you today?"

"My name is Mary Shipley, and this is Amy Evans, we—"

"Yes. Hello. I remember your dad and you as a much younger little girl who was frequently with him. My name is Eleanor Whitley." Ms. Whitley appeared to be about sixty years of age, who stood 5'6" tall, about 130 pounds, with blue eyes, silver hair, and sparkling white teeth that were almost mesmerizing. Her eyes sparkled and had a wonderful glow, almost angelic, as they made you feel welcome and comfortable speaking with her. She was truly a people person How is your dad?"

"Both of my parents were killed in a car accident over a year ago. Dad loved this school and this area. He raved about how kind you were to him and told everyone about the ideal home you selected for him that made his stay here so memorable. Thank you for everything you did for my dad."

139

"You just made my day saying the kind things you just told me. Thank you for that."

"You are very welcome. It is your professionalism and your kindness that brings me here. I am sure many other people who have experienced the wonderful things you do refer their friends to you too."

"Like you. Not only do you refer people to me, you are bringing Amy Evans. Right?"

"Right."

"Hi, Amy. May I call you Amy?"

"Yes. Please."

"I have arranged for you to live in the same housing section not too far from the same house Professor Shipley lived in when he stayed with us."

Mary said, "Thank you very much, Ms. Whitley. I love that area. How many bedrooms does it have?"

"Two."

"Perfect. And is it possibly available now?"

"Yes. It has already been cleaned and ready for occupancy. How would you like for me to handle the billing?"

Mary opened her purse and pulled out her wallet to hand her a credit card. "Could I get you to debit this card monthly or quarterly? And may I ask for you to send me an invoice with each debit at your convenience?"

"No problem. This will work for me. May I be nosy and ask if there is a special relationship between you and Amy?"

"You will not be nosy. Yes. There is a special relationship between us." Amy lowered her face to look at the floor and braced for the embarrassing comments she knew were about to come out of Mary's mouth. "I am an attorney now. Amy will work for me when she finishes law school and passes the Bar."

"Oh. That is wonderful news. Congratulations, Amy."

Amy looked up at Ms. Whitley with the look on her face one gets when they just walked into a surprise birthday party thrown for them. Choked up would be a very mild explanation for her expression as she glanced at Mary with too much gratitude to speak. She kept looking at

Mary as she pressed her lips tightly together and blinked her eyes rapidly, fighting back a tsunami.

"Amy is now a little overwhelmed by my recruiting her ahead of the other law firms that will be after her services. Snooze you lose, and I am not snoozing." Ms. Whitley and Mary burst into laughter. "Well, we better get going. Thank you so much for taking care of Amy, which also takes care of me."

Ms. Whitley handed Mary a set of keys and a map of the area. "These will get you into the home, and the map will guide you around the area. She stuck out her hand and shook hands with Mary before she glanced at Amy. "Do not be a stranger, Amy. I am here for you 24-7 if there is anything you need. Please remember, you will never be imposing on me. Okay?" She stuck her hand out toward Amy.

"Thank you very much. I will call you before I come by if I need anything. Knowing you are here for me means a lot to me. Thank you very much for finding a nice place for me to stay," Amy said as she accepted Ms. Whitley's hand into her hand and noticed the friendly look in her eyes.

Amy and Mary walked out of the office, and when they sat on the front seat of Mary's car, Mary looked at Amy and said, "That went very well. Wow! She even gave you a home close to the home my dad lived in during his three years living up here. How do you feel?"

"Not speaking about the time, you have already taken to get me registered into law school and being here with me to arrange for my housing over the next three years, you are the most courteous, thoughtful, amazing human being I have ever met."

"Whoa! What did I do to rate this compliment?"

"You gave me dignity I did not deserve. Since Ms. Whitley knew your dad, you had every right to tell her I was responsible for ending his life and the life of your mother. I braced myself for you to tell her, and I could not believe how you kept that information between us. She deserved to know."

"No, Amy. She did not deserve to know. Please do not ever tell her or anyone else what will always stay between us. Okay? What I told her was true. I did not tell her a lie."

"That one protective moment did more for me than I could ever explain to you. Thank you."

"You are welcome. We must put this behind us, and we will over time. I learned many things going through my depression for many months, and one thing I learned is everyone comes into the world to pass. Nobody comes into the world to stay. It was in my depression stage that I researched my feelings about death, and somewhere I read where God entered the day and hour of our death in our book of life. We all have a time and date certain to exit this world. And since God has given each of us free will, we were each given the choice to commit suicide and take our own life. But my question about these people who do commit suicide is, did they choose a permanent solution to their temporary problem? And more importantly, did they also end any hope they might have had to live the promised life of eternity with God and their loved ones by prematurely ending their life before God wanted their life on earth to end?"

"So again, you were being truthful with the judge. If it was not me, somebody else would have been chosen by God to do something negligent that day and hour to send your parents home to heaven."

"Yes, Amy. That is correct. They were both going home to heaven that day and at that precise hour."

"What a revelation this is to me," Amy admitted to Mary.

"Okay. Let's walk inside your home and see what it looks like." Amy exited the car and, for the first time in over a year, joyfully walked up to the front door of her next temporary home for the next three years, grinning from ear to ear while looking at Mary.

"Ah. Somebody is happy. That is a good look on your pretty face. Keep smiling, Amy."

"Awe. What a sweet thing to say. Thank you, Mary. I cannot remember anyone telling me I had a pretty face."

"You will hear it a lot from the guys in your classes," Mary said assuredly.

"My heart will not be open for a relationship with any man until I pass the bar exam and start working with you. I cannot let that happen. Men want women to get behind them and support their career. I cannot afford to let my emotional guard down when it comes to men and a romantic relationship."

They took one step into the foyer of the home and noticed a coatrack to their right next to a hall closet door. To their left was a spacious room stylishly furnished with a couch, two chairs, magazine rack, an oval-shaped coffee table and a television set. To their right was a dining room with a large oval table surrounded by six chairs. To the left of the dining room was a kitchen they chose to ignore for now to see the rest of the home. They walked further down the hallway and saw a hall bathroom for guests and, only a few steps further, they found the two bedrooms that flanked the hallway.

Mary said, "The master bedroom is huge, and I am glad this room is all yours. This second bedroom is not that much smaller, and it sure beats a couch." Mary and Amy laughed out loud. They turned and walked into the kitchen. Mary said, "Impressive. I love a spacious kitchen with a lot of kitchen cabinets, and your kitchen sure has everything I love, including this five-foot countertop with four stools in front for people to sit and talk while you prepare something to eat." Mary looked to her right to view the adjoining small kitchenette table with four chairs. And further to her right was a dining room with the beautiful hardwood flooring. "That dining room is a nice touch, as well as the screened in front porch that you will enjoy. Birdfeeders would also be nice touch for you to install. You will enjoy the different birds who come to your home to eat the bird feed you put out for them, and as a reward to you, they will lay eggs in your birdhouses to make your home their home."

Amy shivered. "You just gave me goose bumps picturing me having birds come to my home to eat bird feed that I will have money to buy for them. Visualizing the rest of your graphic story where birds will come to lay eggs in birdhouses that I will install for them, so they can make my home their home, just touches my heart and flirts with my tsunami switch. I love birds. This is way more than I deserve."

"I am very happy for you on one hand and envious of you on the other."

"You can always enroll again and enjoy this with me." Amy chuckled, looking at Mary.

"Do not tempt me. I would not be the first person to graduate from two major law schools."

"I would sure welcome having you doing this with me."

"Do not temp me." Mary giggled. "It is your turn. I will live this through you, so take pictures and send them to me."

"Okay. Thank you for making my new life possible."

"I do not know about you, but I am tired and need a few hours' sleep. Are you ready to turn in?"

"Absolutely. I am naturally wired with excitement, but sleep does sound good."

"I know of a great pancake restaurant close by for us to eat a big breakfast in the morning. Are you game for an egg pancake breakfast before we open your checking account and buy your automobile?"

"Yes, ma'am."

"Good night, Amy."

"Good night, Mary."

*****

The sun peeked around the closed window blinds hung on the windows in both bedrooms to usher in a new day. Amy slipped off the edge of her bed and immediately dropped down onto her knees to say a few prayers and to give thanks to God. She walked into the kitchen area and looked into Mary's smiling eyes. "Early bird gets the worm is the only cute saying I know to say in the early morning hours."

"I like that saying. Good morning. How did you sleep?" Mary asked.

"Like a newborn baby. I could not believe it, as keyed up as I was, I slept deep and restful. How about you? Did you sleep good?" Amy asked.

"Yes. I did. Thank you for asking. Are you ready to eat a big breakfast, open a checking account, and pick out your new car?"

"I am, Mrs. Claus." Amy giggled and smiled at Mary.

"I am about as excited as you. We are about to add onto our history together."

"To protect your investment in me, may I ask you to consider getting a life insurance policy on me."

"God was not wrong about you, Amy. What a brilliant idea. Where is my business brain? I am going to enjoy working with you. That is one coverage I never want to collect on, but it is prudent to get you covered in case. Thank you very much, Amy."

"You are very welcome.

The breakfast was scrumptiously delicious. They ate until they could not swallow another bite. "I can tell we are getting used to each other to be able to eat and not feel like we had to fill the quiet moments with nervous conversation. I like you, Amy."

"You seem to have that special way about you. I am now more comfortable around you."

"I am glad. That is how I want you to be. Ready?" Mary asked.

"Yes."

They drove only three blocks from the restaurant and pulled into the parking lot of a local bank. One of the bank officers, sitting at a desk off to their left, nodded and smiled at them as she rose from her chair to come greet them. "Hello. My name is Rosemary Cash. How can I help you?"

Rosemary Cash had a cute face with beautiful skin, who appeared to be about thirty years of age, about 5'3" tall, and probably 140 pounds, with a bubbly personality to go with her contagious smile that shown a perfect set of white teeth and friendly hazel-colored eyes. She is a people person.

"Hi, Ms. Cash. My name is Mary Shipley, and this is your new neighbor, Amy Evans." Mary shook hands with Ms. Cash and stepped slightly to one side for Amy to also shake her hand. We would like to open a checking account. Could you assist us?"

"Absolutely. Is this a joint account or an account for my new neighbor?"

"A checking account for your new neighbor."

"Okay. Please walk with me to my desk. Let me give you this form to complete for me, Amy. May I call you Amy?"

"Yes. Please call me Amy."

"Please call me Rose. A nickname that stuck. I am now used to it, and like it."

"Okay, Rose. I like the name Rose."

"How do we want to handle a small deposit to open the account?" Rose asked.

"May I give you a debit card to draw the funds needed for the account?" Mary asked.

"Certainly. Please list the amount you want me to debit on this sheet of paper so we have a paper trail of the amount you are requesting

me to debit to make sure I don't misunderstand and draw the wrong amount from your debit card. Does this work for you?"

"Yes." Mary took the form and entered the amount of $7,500 and handed the form back to Rose.

Rose got to her feet. "Amy, may I have the front sheet you have completed that shows your name and address so I can open your checking account?"

"Yes. I have finished with it." Amy handed the first page to Rose.

"Please excuse me for a few minutes to get this account opened." Rose walked by Amy and Mary to walk behind the bank tellers so she could use the bank phone to debit the card Mary gave to her to open the account for Amy.

"I got your account set up and ready for use. I am going to give you these temporary checks to use until you get your printed checks in the mail. Also here is a debit card that you can use for purchases that the merchant will automatically debit what you spend out of your checking account. Welcome to our area and bank. Let me know if I can ever do anything for you." Rose stood and stuck out her hand to Amy.

Amy stood to accept the hand Rose extended to her and said, "This was quick and painless. Thank you very much, Rose. I will look forward to seeing you again," Amy replied.

"The pleasure will be mine, Amy." Rose glanced toward Mary. "It was a pleasure to meet you, too, Mary."

"Thank you, Rose. You are a people person and an asset to any business. Bye."

"What a nice thing to say to me. You made my day. Bye."

"This is your deposit slip," Mary said as she handed it to Amy.

Amy took the deposit slip and, while looking at it, said, "This is way too much money, Mary."

"The money is for you to purchase clothes, personal essentials, and food for to live comfortably for a few months. You do not have to spend it all today. Besides, I do not want you worrying about money. I need for you to concentrate on your exams. You will be living on your own up here, Amy. Okay?"

"Okay. I will show you I am a good budgeter of money," Amy vowed.

"I will notice when your account is running low on funds and make another deposit for you. You mentioned wanting a GM car to own. There is a Chevrolet dealership about a mile down the road. We will browse their lot to see if you happen to see a vehicle you might want to own. Okay?"

"I am not picky, Mary."

"I want you to be. You will be stuck with this car for a few years. You do not want to own a vehicle that you are not excited to own or feel comfortable for you to ride in. Take your time and choose wisely."

"Okay. I see a car right there on their lot that looks good to me. Can we test drive it?"

"Sure. There are two salespeople milling around the lot. One is a man, and the other is a woman. Do you want to ask one of them to help you?"

"Can you guess which one I will choose?" Amy giggled and raised her eyebrows, looking at Mary.

"Cute. Go get her, tiger."

Amy opened her car door and walked up to the woman salesperson and asked to test drive the new Chevrolet SUV with the sales price listed on the windshield for $29,900. She drove it and immediately loved it. This is the automobile I want to own in three years. Amy got out of the vehicle and found Mary.

Amy walked up to Mary and said, "Mrs. Claus. I found the vehicle of my dreams. What I need to purchase this vehicle is beyond my abilities. May I pass the purchase baton to you, ma'am?"

"Remember how this feeling feels in the future. Be frugal with money that you earn with me. Never allow yourself to be in a position where you have to depend upon anyone to buy you things you want to own. Let's go talk to the salesperson so I can get this purchase done for you."

"Thank you, Mary."

"You are welcome."

Amy drove her new car out of the dealership and followed Mary back to her new home. Amy kept saying, "Thank you, God," repeatedly until she arrived back inside the home that she will live in over the next three years.

Amy and Mary sat on the barstools in front of her kitchen counter.

Mary said, "I am going to give you a gasoline card for you to use any time you need gasoline or oil for your car. Anything else, take it to the dealership. Call me if you experience any problems you cannot handle. It is now time for me to leave and resume my life. Please walk me out to my car so I can give you a see-you-soon hug."

"I will pray daily asking God to guide my study habits to teach me how to be the best lawyer I can be. I am admittedly apprehensive."

"If you were not, there would be something wrong with you, Amy. I am a phone call away, and I can be here quickly if needed. Pray every day and talk daily to Jesus. He is the one who saved you. You two have a lot to discuss. He showed you He loves you. Show Him you love Him by putting Him first in your life. God will be with you when you walk into your first classroom, when you take your first and last exams, and when you walk across the stage to accept your Yale Law School diploma."

"God will also be with me every time I drive my new car," Amy said excitedly.

"The reason God will be with you wherever you drive and wherever you go inside Yale Law School is because God, in the form of the Holy Spirit, lives in your heart and in your mind. Talk to Him. Okay?"

"Okay. Thank you, Mary."

"You are welcome. You cannot fail with God guiding you. I am also available 24-7. Concentrate on your grades and your future as an attorney with me. You will be fine. Okay?"

"Okay. Thank you for my car, my place to live, my checking account with money, and my new life."

"Call me immediately if you need anything. You have my permission to call me 24-7. Your job is to pass your exams and earn your law degree. Give me a see-you-soon hug. Okay."

"Okay." Tears trickled down Amy's face as she watched Mary drive away from the Wooster Square two-bedroom house that was located only a stone's throw from a pizzeria and a bakery where Mary's father used to live when he went to Yale. Amy did not have to wait for a home upgrade. She was living in permanent housing now for the next three years, thanks to Mary and Mary's dad.

Mary was pleased that they had set up a schedule to talk by phone every week just to say hello and stay in touch with each other. Mary believed Amy would be a trusted close friend and a welcomed addition to her life and her new law firm. She felt Amy was now starting to believe this very same thing.

Amy sat down on a chair at her kitchen counter, trying to wrap her mind around why she had been given this enormous gift. She closed her eyes and began talking out loud, "God, it is me again. How do I begin to thank you for saving me from a brutal life inside a prison? How?" Tears were now flowing down her face. "I know you never make a mistake. I accept all of this as a blessing for me that is not deserved. Please help me to stay focused on you. Thank you for giving me this unbelievable second chance."

CHAPTER 19

Rachel and Mary Visit Robert

Mary woke up from her two-hour catnap feeling hungry. She walked into her kitchen to decide what she wanted to eat for dinner when her cell phone rang. Her caller ID listed the caller as Rachel Rice.

"Hello, Rachel."

"Well, aren't you the smart one with caller ID? You do have a smartphone. Right?"

"Technology is my game. Ask me again, and I will tell you the same." Mary giggled into the phone.

"Cute. What have you done with Mary? May I speak to her, please?" Rachel asked.

"Oh, I am sorry. That requires a special high-security clearance. Do you have one?"

"Oh, yes. She and I are Bobbsey Twins, and nobody alive has a clearance higher than the two of us."

"In that case, let me put her on the phone for you. Hello. Is this Crabby?"

Rachel was taken aback but quickly played along by saying, "Joe's Crab House, Crabby speaking."

"There you are and not too crabby. Did someone do something to make you nice? Eh?"

"Okay. I will admit it. You managed to turn my dark world bright. You are the best!"

"What? I have a bad connection. Could you repeat what you just said?" Mary teased Rachel.

"Cute, again. I treated you horribly, and instead of resenting me for it and doing nothing to help me, you devoted a lot of your personal time to interview Dr. Mary Sharp and used her suggestions to find Robert. You even went the extra step to confirm it was my Bobby, and he was alive by speaking with Nurse Phillips before you called me. No matter what happens up there, you have initially given me hope that I have not had in four months. You temporarily changed my life, and hopefully this will turn out to be a permanent change. I will always remember what you have done for me, and I will be in your debt."

"You would have done it for me. This is what friends do, right?" Mary asked.

"I am nervous about traveling to Maryland and seeing Bobby. Do you want to go with me, since you are the one who found him? Plus, you are the one who spoke to Lisa Phillips. What do you say? Do you want to go with me?"

"Okay."

"What! That is it? No begging, pleading, or conditions?"

"That part comes later, or do you want to hear them now?"

"No. I will quit while I am way ahead."

"Who was the lame brain who said all blondes are dumb?" Mary laughed into the phone.

"Oh, I can tell you loved that one." Rachel also laughed into her phone.

"Okay. I admit it. I did so I will score one for the brunettes—me." Mary laughed.

"Brunettes score 1, blondie score 0. Temporarily but I will get even," Rachel teased with a giggle.

"Do you have travel details that you want to share with me, blondie?" The phone was silent on both ends for quite a few seconds. "Hello. Was that too much for you to handle so quickly?" Mary teased.

"Sorry. I had to get the phone away from my mouth while I regained my composure. You are a riot."

"I do not have too many of those, so you are safe. That one I could not resist. Okay, give me your travel itinerary please, ma'am."

"We can drive up together and get a couple of hotel rooms or share one if you are limited on funds."

"I will help you with the gasoline expenses and pay for my own room from my penny jar."

"I do not need help with gasoline expenses, but since I am asking you to come with me, I wanted to offer to pay for your room, or we can share a room."

"No on both counts. I want to snore in private. Have you selected the hotel?"

Rachel burst into laughter. "Funny. You really are a riot. Snore in private. Cute. I wanted to wait to call the hotel until I confirmed you would go with me and then select how many rooms I would need."

"Why don't we do a three-way call. We can ask for connecting and adjoining rooms or rooms close to each other."

"Great. That sounds like a good plan. When can you be ready to travel?" Rachel asked.

"I need to pack a few things. I can be ready to come meet you in about an hour. Sound good?"

"Perfect. I never dreamed you could be ready that fast. Bless you."

"Thank you, Rachel. I need all the blessings I can get. If it were the man of my dreams, which I do not have, I would want to be there yesterday to kiss him out of his coma."

"I am glad we met."

"Me too."

"Do you ever think about it?"

"About?"

"The way we met?" Rachel asked.

"Probably not as deeply as you, but I do think about our chance meeting."

"It was not a chance meeting, Mary."

"What are you saying?"

"Remove all distractions for five minutes and listen to the following sequence of events. Okay?"

"Okay. You have my curiosity piqued. Please explain," Mary requested.

"Before I met you, the only place I had dinner with Robert was at Cheddar's Restaurant. The night Robert and I talked, before he disappeared, he told me to meet him the next night at Cheddar's. A friend of mine at school told me about Joe's Crab House only one hour before I was ready to walk out the door to meet Robert. But after that conversation with her, I changed from Cheddar's to Joe's Crab House. Why would I do such a thing?"

"Because you are a blonde?"

"No. Well, yes. I am blonde and keeping score to get even. Listen, follow this next part very closely, and if the hair on your neck does not stand up, you are not listening closely enough to me."

"Okay. I am tuned into you. Please continue."

"Okay. Knowing what we both know now about Robert, my coworker must have gotten a message from a spiritual voice inside her head for her to even mention Joe's Crab House to me, especially one hour before I was ready to leave to meet Robert, who had his mind set on meeting me at Cheddar's. I did a blonde thing when I impulsively changed the restaurant from Cheddar's to Joe's Crab House."

"I cannot wait to hear your reasoning behind this one."

"You do not get it? Really? Wow, which one of us is really blond?" Rachel sighs into the phone.

"Watch it, blondie. Brunettes, on occasion, are a *little* justifiably and *unexpectedly slow.* Blondes on the other hand? Well, you know." Mary laughed hard into the phone.

"You also loved that one. Okay, just for you slow ones. God knew Robert was already airlifted to Johns Hopkins Hospital, and for me to possibly find him, I had to meet you at Joe's Crab House. If I did not meet you—"

"Bingo! I got it! Wow! This is huge. Oh, yes, I see it all clearly. God knew Robert was not going to show up at Cheddar's Restaurant. The only possible way for you to find Robert was for you to eat at Joe's Crab House to meet me to see my cracked and stained front tooth for you to refer me to Dr. Mary Sharp, who would refer me to Johns Hopkins Hospital to find Robert. It really was a short putt from there to find Robert. Do you like how I used the word *putt* instead of a long shot or leap?"

"Oh, yes. You are so brilliant, OB 1." They both laughed hard for a couple of minutes.

"Scary and downright frightening to think about the *what ifs*. If anything were removed from this chain that led us to Dr. Mary Sharp, we definitely would have a different ending that did not include us being the people to find Robert."

"You are right. The most amazing part to me is how God used so many necessary people to lead us to find Robert. Unbelievable. I came so close to run out the front door of my school without listening to my coworker about Joe's Crab House."

"God is awesome and amazing. I need to sit down a minute," Mary said out loud. "I have goose bumps covering my arms and my neck. Neither of us—"

"Me too. Sorry to interrupt you," Rachel admitted.

"I cannot get over how God moves people around like chess pieces. He had multiple people lined up to help me find Robert. Unbelievable! My goose bumps have goose bumps. I am serious. You should see my arms and my neck," Mary admitted.

"We will have fun discussing this on our drive up to Maryland. Do you need to get a pen to write down the directions to my home?"

"I keep a pad and a pen next to all of my phones. I am ready to write when you are ready to talk."

"I am always ready to talk," Rachel answered with a giggle into the phone.

"I am not touching that one. This is your only reprieve," Mary teased.

"You are so good to me. Okay. Let me give you the directions to my home."

"Okay, Rachel. I wrote down the directions to your home. And I do not have any questions."

"I have one. Why would a waitress keep a pad and pen next to every phone in her home?"

"I could be a lot more than just a waitress. You do not know about my secret life."

"Do you have a secret life?"

"Doesn't everyone?"

"Not me. You are the only one in this crowd. You can leave your car here unless you prefer for us to drive up in your car. I am so glad you are coming with me. Thank you, Mary."

"You are most welcome. And one day, we will discuss my secret life. And responding to your earlier comment, we can decide about which car to take once I get to your home."

"Okay. Pack some clothes to stay for a few days and call me with any questions?"

"I will not have any questions."

"Great. See you in about an hour. Bye."

"Bye."

CHAPTER 20

Robert Opens His Eyes

Dr. Robert Wilson was a graduate of the Johns Hopkins University School of Medicine, so it was only natural for him to be airlifted to the Johns Hopkins Hospital to be examined and immediately sent to their intensive care unit to be treated for a nonresponsive coma, because it could take weeks, months, or years for him to wake up.

Robert Wilson has now been in a coma for four months without showing any progress.

Lauren Jaco is thirty-one years of age with an attractive face, 5'2" tall, 115 pounds, with light-brown-color hair, and hazel eyes. She is half of a nurse team assigned to handle the intensive care unit with Nurse Lisa Phillips.

Both nurses hold the highest ratings given to any nurse within the medical industry. The hospital considers both nurses to be crème de la crème skilled nurses trained to handle all medical and trauma situation. Every hospital in the country would immediately hire one or both nurses on the spot.

Rachel Rice and Mary Shipley stepped out of the elevator on the intensive care floor and stopped at the nurses' station to announce their arrival and request permission to see Dr. Robert Wilson.

"Hi. How may I help you, ladies?" Lauren Jaco asked.

"Hi. My name is Rachel Rice, and this is Mary Shipley. We would like to see one of your patients by the name of Dr. Robert Wilson. Could you direct us to him, please?" Rachel asked.

"May I ask your relationship to him?" Lauren asked.

"I spoke with a nurse by the name of Lisa Phillips. She told me—" Mary stopped talking abruptly.

"Yes. Sorry to interrupt you, Ms. Shipley. Lisa did tell me. I am sorry. Dr. Wilson gets so many visitors from the college and medical school, it is hard to keep track, but we try. You are a very good friend of Rachel Rice, who is Dr. Wilson's fiancée." Lauren looked at Rachel. "Right?" Lauren asked.

"Yes," Rachel and Mary both answered.

Lauren turned her full attention to Rachel. "It is my pleasure to meet you, Ms. Rice."

"Please call me Rachel."

"And please call me Mary."

"Only if you both call me Lauren. Deal?"

"Deal," Mary and Rachel both answered at the same time, making the three of them laugh.

"What can you tell us about Robert?" Rachel asked.

"I am sad to say he has not made any significant improvement in four months."

"How long do patients stay in a coma? Is there a normal length of time, Lauren?" Mary asked.

"Weeks, months, and sometimes years," Lauren answered honestly.

"Is there a test you can do on Robert to predict when he might come back to us?" Rachel asked.

"We have done an EEG test. And we have completed other tests that can give a doctor a pretty good idea how close a patient is to coming back to us and, to a certain degree, how he will be when he does. The doctor will go over those tests with you. In the meantime, do you want to see Dr. Robert Wilson?"

"Yes. Please," Rachel answered excitedly.

"Please follow me," Lauren said as she started walking into the intensive care unit.

Rachel reached down to hold Mary's hand as they followed Lauren into the room to see Robert. When they walked closer to his bed, they separated and stood on opposite sides of his bed looking down at him. Mary watched Rachel put both of her hands up to her face before she began to slowly shake her head from side to side as tears welled up in her eyes. Rachel reached her right hand down to touch the left side of Robert's stoic face before she leaned down to kiss his forehead, his right cheek, and his lips. She ignored the tears that dropped from her eyes as she stood there, watching him lie motionless, with his eyes closed only inches from her.

Lauren gently touched Rachel's left shoulder as she stood by her left side. "I believe we will see some improvement in him now that you are here, Rachel. Your love for him is deep, and he will respond to it. The more time you spend talking to him and reminding him of the special things you have done together or the things you *both want to do together*, he will come back to you. I also suggest saying a lot of special things privy to only the two of you to strike a special nerve within him, and pray."

"Thank you, Lauren. This is going to be a long process to get him back to the life he once enjoyed, isn't it? Please be honest with me."

Lauren motioned for Rachel and Mary to follow her back out into the hallway. Once they were out in the hallway, Lauren turned to them and said, "Patients who are in a coma can hear what we say, so it is important to only say positive things near them to stimulate and encourage their recovery. Comatose patients have told their nurses and doctors that they either heard positive things that encouraged their recovery or depressing things about their having missing teeth or a heavily scarred face that made them want to avoid coming back to life."

"Good points. Thank you so much for telling us," Rachel said.

"Do you think it would be a good idea to post a sign near his bed to let people know he can hear what they might say and request that they keep their comments positive to aid in his recovery?"

"Yes. We can have that done immediately. Good point, Mary."

"Thank you, Lauren."

"You're welcome. Any more questions before we go back inside?"

"Yes. Please tell me what to expect from him physically when he wakes up?"

"Good question, Rachel. If he woke up today, it will be months before he can be like the person he was before he got hit in the head. We have a medical saying that happens to be true for comatose patients, and that saying is *'use it or lose it.'* People that sit around at home, or lie around without getting up to exercise different parts of their body, will lose the use of those inactive body parts. It doesn't take long to lose muscle mass. Physical movement or physical therapy is necessary to keep our body active."

"Will Bobby need much physical therapy when he wakes up?"

"Yes. And he might need a speech therapist to teach him to talk. He will definitely need a physical therapist to regain the use of his legs and his arms."

"Seriously, Lauren?"

"Yes."

"Please explain this to me in layman terms for me to understand," Rachel asked.

"Let me try. Let us assume there are only thirty days in each month. Some months have thirty-one days, while one month has twenty-eight, and some years twenty-nine. But just for my explanation, we will use thirty days. Okay?"

"Okay."

"If we multiply 30 days times four months, we get 120 days. Right?"

"Right."

"There are 24 hours in each day. If we multiply the 120 days that he has been totally inactive by the number of hours in each day—24—we get 2,880 hours that he has lain there without moving his legs or his arms. That is a very long time for the brain to be in total disconnect from his arms, legs, and his body. The longer he lies here without moving his arms and his legs will add to the hours he will need to spend with a physical therapist. Understand?"

"Yes. Crystal clear. Thank you for explaining this to me in layman terms. Wow."

The three of them went back into the room and stood around Robert's bed and watched him lie there motionless.

Rachel looked down at Robert. "Wake up, Bobby, we have work to do." She looked at Lauren and smiled.

"I need to check on some other patients. You know how to call me if you need me. I will soon make it back around to this room again. Okay?"

"Okay. Thank you so much, Lauren."

"You are very welcome. Bye."

"Bye."

Rachel looked up at Mary. "I am so sorry to drag you up here with that prognosis. I know you must get back to Joe's Crab House. I guess we can—"

"From my conversation with Lisa Phillips, I figured this was going to be a long drawn-out nurturing process, so I called and quit my job before I drove to your home to come up here. Thank you for thinking about me, though."

"What are you going to do for money?"

"I have a piggy bank." Mary laughed at the expression on Rachel's face.

"A piggy bank? Is there more to this story?"

"Not today." Mary looked intently at Rachel.

"I guess this all relates back to your earlier comment when you told me you might be more than a waitress?"

"There she is—the woman with a steel trap for a mind. Nothing gets by you, does it?"

"Not too much. But do not worry, I will not press you on your deep dark secret."

"Careful, you will start to make me believe you are a natural brunette." They both laughed out loud.

"Bobby might wake up faster if he hears us laughing like this," Rachel said while laughing.

"Speaking of us laughing. Do you think it would be a great idea for us to get the nurse to bring in a television set for him to listen to 24-7?"

"Great idea, Mary. I knew there was more than one reason I asked you to come up here with me."

"You mean other than my charm, bubbly personality, and ability to drive a car?" Mary laughed.

"I believe there is a much bigger reason you have not considered."

"What would that reason be, pray tell, Rachel?"

"I will not jinx it. My lips are sealed."

"Now that sounds mysterious or precarious."

"Not really. To me it is hopeful and, with my knowledge of the Holy Spirit, very possible."

"Knowing that you are bringing in the big guns gives me something to look forward to."

"It does not get any bigger or better than the Holy Spirit." Mary nodded in agreement.

*****

Rachel never asked Mary how she was able to afford to buy clothes, cosmetics, food, and stay in her hotel room for the two weeks they have now stayed in Maryland. She was starting to feel a little guilty for being the reason Mary is incurring these expenses but didn't know how to bring up the subject. She thought she would leave it alone until the Holy Spirit led her into that conversation.

Mary and Rachel alternated staying with Robert while the other took a break to walk around the hospital or sit outside to enjoy a cup of hot coffee and welcome the light breeze that blew against their face. This was a great time for Mary to reflect upon her past, present, and future.

Over the last two weeks, when it was her turn to stay with Robert, a nice-looking man would slowly walk by the hospital room doorway and look in at her. On occasion, she looked up toward the doorway to see him standing there watching her. When she looked at him, he would turn around and walk away. He did this a few times every day for two weeks before he finally came into the room and stood on the opposite side of Robert's bed, looking at her. Mary looked at him and raised her eyebrows.

"Hi. Your husband, boyfriend, or just a friend?"

"The fiancé of the girl who is usually in this room with me."

"Is it okay if I just say hello to Robert and say a silent prayer for him?"

"Yes. I am sure he would love for you to pray for him. Do you want me to walk away to give you some privacy with him?"

"No. Please stay." He was temporarily mesmerized by the kind look in her eyes and impressed with her offer to let him spend quiet time with Robert. Even without makeup or lipstick, he couldn't help but realize she was an attractive woman. If she wore lipstick and a little makeup, she would easily be an incredibly beautiful woman who would turn men's heads when she walked by. The way his eyes fixated on her as he studied her face made him suddenly realize he was making her uncomfortable.

"Why do you wish for me to stay?" she asked.

"Your offer to give me alone time with Robert touched me. You have kind eyes. I try to surround myself with kindhearted people." He smiled at her and watched her get ready to say something to him.

"You are an unusual man, sir."

"May I ask why you say this of me?"

"If you really do surround yourself with kindhearted people, you already know the answer."

"You speak from your heart."

"Just like you do." Her eyes smiled at him when their eyes met.

"Do you mind telling me your name?" He figured her to be about 5'5" tall, maybe 150 pounds that was distributed perfectly for his liking. He also liked the hazel color of her eyes and the way she wore and styled her shoulder-length black hair to only cover a small portion of her forehead, instead of styling it to hang down her face to cover a portion of one eye, like a lot of woman do. He liked her.

"Mary Shipley. May I have *your name?*" Judging from the height of her dad, she knew he was 6'0" tall and two hundred pounds, with black hair, hazel eyes, and sparkling white teeth. Her heart told her to find out more about him. She did not come up here looking for a romance, but in five minutes, this man has stirred things inside her heart that she has never felt before today. Feelings of love do reside inside her heart, but feelings of romance never have. She never trusted the truthfulness of a man or his ability to be *loyal to only one woman. Surprisingly* he spoke to her from his heart, which, in her mind, put him in a unique class of 1 percent.

"My name is Stanley Spring."

"May I ask how you know Robert Wilson?"

"We were classmates at Johns Hopkins University School of Medicine."

"I am impressed."

"Impressed from knowledge or just impressed?"

"What does that mean?" Mary laughed.

"Most people do not have a clue about XYZ college from XYZ medical school. The name just sounds like it is—"

"Johns Hopkins University School of Medicine is ranked number 1 in the nation, for your information." She looked at him triumphantly, with her eyes wide open, waiting on his response.

Stanley bowed at his waist toward her and held out his hand apologetically. I owe you a humble apology, Mary Shipley. I am sorry. Please accept my hand and my apology."

Mary reached out and accepted his hand out of courtesy. When her hand joined his hand, she felt a flutter in her heart that convinced her that something was happening between their hearts. Looking into his eyes and feeling her reaction to their hands touching melted her heart. *Could it be that I am meeting the love of my life on this impromptu trip with Rachel?* she wondered.

"Answer me honestly, how did you know Johns Hopkins University School of Medicine is rated number 1?"

"My college classmates were checking out schools to attend."

"What college did you attend?"

"Harvard."

"Whoa. Look who is throwing around impressive words now. Did you graduate from Harvard?"

"Would you ask a man that question?"

"No. Wow. That was a bad choice of words, was it not?

"Yes."

"I cannot believe I asked you that question. I am sorry. I seem to be digging myself a hole. I am not good at this. Tomorrow might be a better day. May I come back tomorrow to see you and try again?"

"I do not control who comes in or out of this room. You are not good at this? What is this?"

"Us."

"I did not know there was an us between us. Please explain this to me."

"I like you, and it has been a long time since I met a woman that made my heart react the way it does with you. I am a little flustered, and I have temporarily lost control of my conscious thoughts, making me say things that make me look and sound a little scatterbrained. Maybe tomorrow will be a better day."

"I love your explanation. Keep speaking from your heart when you talk with me. Okay?"

"Okay. I promise you I will. We are good. I am forgiven?"

"Yes. We are good. I like you too."

"Please tell me if I ever hurt your feelings. No walls will ever be built between us if we discuss any issues that may arise between us when they happen. Deal?"

"Deal. I like this understanding between us, so there is an us between us after all." Mary smiled.

"I love to see you smile. Did you attend a specialty school after Harvard?"

"Yes. I attended and I graduated from Harvard Law School. And before you even ask, which I know you will, I did take and pass the bar exam to become an attorney." They both laughed out loud.

"Do you have a significant other?"

"Before I answer it, I want to ask you a question that you must answer truthfully. Deal?"

"Yes."

"Shake on it as our stamp of approval and our own unique seal." She reached out her hand toward him for him to take it and shake.

"You just want to hold my hand again, don't you?" Stanley laughed out loud.

"Is this your clever way to avoid answering me truthfully?"

"No, ma'am. I will always answer you truthfully. I do love what happens when I hold your hand." He joined his hand with hers and immediately felt the same reaction as before. Their hands felt like a matching pair. From the look in her eyes and the sudden flushed look on her face, he was sure she felt it too. While holding her hand and looking into her eyes, he said, "Ask me your question."

Although she did not want to remove her hand from his hand, she tried but met his resistance. He did not want to turn her hand loose. She wanted to hear his answer to her question, notwithstanding the many butterflies she felt flying around in her stomach, making her behave like she was back in high school.

Her heart told her to go for it, so she asked, "Are you asking me these personal questions because you have a genuine interest in me, or are you just asking out of curiosity?"

"I have a sincere and genuine interest in you."

"Tell me honestly if your answer is not only truthful but comes from your heart?"

"Yes, Mary, my answer is truthful and comes from my heart."

"Please keep what we discussed between us until I tell you it is okay to reveal the things I told you. Okay? I did not come up here looking for a romance."

"I did not come into this room looking for a romance either. I tried to resist coming in here to speak with you because I did not want to risk getting my heart broken but standing this close to you was all it took for my heart to take control over my brain and my body. Take a chance on me, Mary."

Rachel had come back into the room and stopped a few feet inside the doorway when she saw their hands joined together. She quietly stood and listened to their conversation before she walked closer to them.

"Hello." Rachel looked at Mary and then at Stanley. "May I ask you a question?"

Stanley released Mary's hand and turned toward Rachel. But before he could speak, Mary said, "Please let me introduce you to my friend Rachel Rice."

"Hello, Ms. Rice. My name is Stanley Spring. Yes, you may ask me anything."

"Where did you hear and learn that saying, 'Take a chance on me'?"

"From this guy." Stanley pointed to Robert.

"May I ask who Bobby said this to?"

"Who is Bobby?"

"I call him Bobby." Rachel pointed to Robert.

"Okay. You had me going there for a minute. To answer your question, I liked it when he said it. I told him one day I would use his saying if I ever found a woman I cared that much about to ask her to take a chance on me. I used it today when I met Mary. I did ask her to take a chance on me."

"What does that mean?"

"Well, it means—"

"I know what it means, but what I don't know is who did he say it to and why?"

"He told me that he was looking for one very special woman. He had to consider her to be the woman of his dreams, and when he found her, he would make sure he asked her to take a chance on him. I often wondered if he ever found that special someone, and I wonder—" He stopped talking when he saw tears running down Rachel's face. "Did I say something wrong?"

"No. You said everything right," Mary answered.

"I do not understand?"

"Rachel is the fiancé and love of Robert's life. She did take a chance on him when he asked her to."

"Wow. It worked! He asked you to take a chance on him, and you did? Praise the Lord."

"'Take a chance on me' has now worked two out of two times," Mary proclaimed before she leaned across the bed railing to receive and give a brief kiss to the new man of her dreams."

Stanley looked down at Robert and said, "Thank you very much, Bobby."

"What am I missing here? Why do you say it has now worked twice, Mary?"

"Stanley asked me to take a chance on him, and I am going to. That makes two out of two for that saying. I cannot jinx it anymore. It came true. Congratulations, Mary."

"This was it? You had this feeling about this trip for me?"

"Yep. The Holy Spirit knows everything," Rachel answered with a smile.

"Holy Spirit?" Stanley looked at them with a confused look on his face.

"I will tell you later and teach you how to communicate with it."

"Is this voodoo, Mary?" Stanley asked.

Mary and Rachel burst into laughter, looking at Stanley.

"Are you laughing with me or at me?"

"We would never laugh at you, Stanley. Never," Mary told him assuredly.

"You mentioned the word *spirit*. How do you communicate with a spirit?" Stanley asked.

"I see where you are getting the impression of voodoo," Rachel volunteered. "Let me see if I can make this understandable for you. Okay?"

"Okay. Please try."

"Did you ever start to do something, and your brain seemed to be telling you, 'No, do not do it?'"

"Yes. I have experienced this many times. Occasionally I listen, and on other occasions, I do what I want to do anyway. Later, I realized things would have been better for me if I had listened, especially when things turned out so badly in a business deal. Is this what you mean? Is this the Holy Spirit trying to keep me away from a bad deal?"

Rachel reached her hand across the railing to encourage him to do a high five with her. It only took him a couple of seconds for him to catch the meaning of her extended hand when he reached his hand out to complete a high five with a big smile of accomplishment.

"I will be more conscious of the Holy Spirit talking to my thoughts in the future. Thank you for telling me about the Holy Spirit."

"You are very welcome," Rachel answered.

"Did I hear you correctly, Rachel? The Holy Spirit told you Mary would meet me on her trip up here with you to visit Robert?" Stanley asked.

"The only thing I knew for sure was she was going to meet someone who very well could be the love of her life on this trip," Rachel answered.

Mary walked around the bed to stand next to Stanley. "I can honestly say I was not looking for any kind of relationship when Stanley walked into the room and started speaking to me. It was when he shook my hand, and I looked into his eyes that I knew we had a deep connection." She looked up at him and stared into his eyes for a couple of seconds before she continued speaking, "I was sold on him when he said, 'Take a chance on me.'"

Stanley leaned down and gently kissed her lips. He stood up and looked down at Robert. "Wake up, buddy. Time to wake up, *ding, ding, ding.* Come on, Robert, open those peepers. Rachel wants a kiss. She has been here by your side going on three weeks. Time to wake up."

Rachel leaned down to rest the right side of her face on his chest. And while looking up at his face, she cried, "Oh, Bobby. Please wake up and talk to me. I miss you so much. Please wake up, Bobby. Our two-second-kiss rule is hereby waived. You can kiss me as long as you want to. Wake up, Bobby." She raised up her face to kiss his forehead, both of his cheeks, and left her lips pressed against his for a very long time. Just as she was about to remove her lips from his lips, she felt his lips move like he was trying to kiss her back. She kissed him again to be sure, and when his lips responded, she squealed and yelled, "Yes. Oh yes, Bobby. Open your beautiful blue eyes and look at me. Open your eyes, Bobby. I felt you kiss me. Please open your eyes. Look at me, Bobby." She kissed him again and felt his lips trying to kiss her back. "Kiss me, Bobby. Kiss me." She kissed his lips repeatedly, trying to get a bigger response from him. "Get the nurse and doctors in here," she yelled out.

Nurse Lisa Phillips and Nurse Lauren Jaco came running into the room with a puzzled look on their faces, looking at Mary, Rachel, and Stanley "Tell us why you called us to this room?" Lisa asked.

"Bobby kissed me," Rachel said excitedly. "He must be ready to open his eyes and come out of his coma. Please help him."

LOVE WILL FIND YOU

Dr. Mike Leafley, who is forty-seven years of age, stands 6'7" tall, and weighs 233 pounds, with brown sandy color hair, blue eyes, a brown stylish pair of eyeglasses, and white perfectly shaped teeth, walked into the room and stood next to Robert's bed and looked down at him. He did a series of tests, including a reflex test on his legs and on the bottom of his feet that failed to produce a single response.

He looked up at Rachel and shook his head from side to side before he spoke, "Nothing. He does not exhibit any signs of voluntary movements. If you think you felt or saw any kind of movement from him, it was nothing but an involuntary reflex movement. He is not able to give voluntary responses to anything yet. Please let the nurses or me know when he opens his eyes. Okay?"

He turned and spoke to the nurses before he started walking toward the door to leave the room when Rachel leaned down close to Robert and whispered something into his right ear before she pressed her lips firmly against his lips. Immediately she held up her right hand high into the air and started clicking her fingers rapidly with excitement to get the attention of the others in the room.

Mary yelled, "Wait. He is kissing her back. I see it too."

The doctor walked back to the bed with both nurses and stood there, watching Rachel kissing Robert. But the doctor could not see a voluntary response from Robert. He was shaking his head sideways and about to let everyone know the slight feeling Rachel feels on her lips was not a voluntary movement from Robert when Lauren said, "I just saw his big toe move, and in my professional opinion, the movement of his toe movement is voluntary. I believe he is about to finally wake up."

This was all Rachel needed to hear. She leaned down closer to his right ear and whispered something to him that produced movement again in his big toe. She kissed his forehead, she kissed both his left and his right cheek, and kissed his lips one more time. This time, her kiss did not evoke any response. The nurses and the doctor shrugged their shoulders, shook their heads, while they raised their eyebrows and looked at Rachel before they turned and walked out of the room.

Rachel disappointedly laid the right side of her face on his chest and placed her left hand over his right hand and stared up at his motionless face. A tear slipped out the side of her eye and fell onto his chest. "Please don't leave me, Bobby. Please come back to me. Please open your eyes. Please. Please. Please open your eyes."

Bobby was unable to move his hands, arms, or legs, but he did move one finger on his right hand that was underneath Rachel's hand before he opened his eyes and looked at her. Rachel initially thought she was just seeing things before she slowly lifted her face off his chest for a closer look. She stared into his open eyes and whispered, "Welcome back, Bobby. Keep those beautiful blue eyes open." She turned to look at Mary and yelled, "He is awake. Please ask the nurse and doctor to come back to check Bobby."

Rachel now wished she had asked Lisa and Lauren more questions about this miraculous moment when Bobby did open his eyes. She never wanted to believe that he would not be able to wrap his arms around her and hold her when he woke up from his coma. Nor did she allow the nurses' words to sink into her heart and mind to believe he would need speech therapy and physical therapy. Notwithstanding the warning from the nurses, she was not mentally prepared for his inability to speak to her. But she did feel blessed, however, to see his blue eyes one more time. And now she knew he did try to kiss her before he moved his finger to let her know he was about to wake up.

Lisa, Lauren, and the doctor came rushing back into the room and looked down at Robert. The two nurses hugged Rachel in a group hug. "Finally! Now begins Robert's long journey back to an active life. You will enjoy every movement and every step he takes back to you. We are so happy for you, Rachel."

"Thank you for everything you have done, Dr. Leafley, Lisa, and Lauren. My heart is full."

"You are very welcome, Rachel," Lisa answered, while Lauren and Dr. Leafley nodded their head in agreement. "When his kisses get better, you will have one more thing to keep looking forward to," Lisa said. Everyone in the room smiled and nodded their heads in agreement.

Dr. Leafley stepped closer to the bed, and while looking down at Robert, he said, "Welcome back, Dr. Wilson. Do you feel up to answering a few questions?"

Robert tried to speak, but distinguishable words could not be understood coming out of his mouth. His facial expression told Dr. Leafley most of the things he suspected and needed to know. Robert stopped trying to speak. He nodded his head and looked at Dr. Leafley.

"Good. I am going to ask you a series of questions. Blink your eyes one time for yes and two times for no. Okay?"

Robert blinked his eyes one time.

"Good. Ready?"

Robert blinked his eyes once.

"Is your name Robert Wilson?"

Robert blinked his eyes once.

"Do you know where you are right now?"

Robert blinked his eyes two times.

"Perfect. You could not know. You were asleep when you came here as a patient. Do you know how long you have been here as a patient?"

"Robert blinked his eyes two times.

"Do you remember being a medical student at Johns Hopkins University School of Medicine, located in Baltimore, Maryland?"

Robert blinked his eyes once.

"This is great news, Dr. Wilson."

"You are now a patient in Johns Hopkins Hospital." Robert tried to smile.

Dr. Leafley reached his left arm around the back of Rachel to gently pull her closer to him. "Do you know who this woman is?"

Rachel held her breath, waiting for his eyes to blink his response.

Robert's eyes misted up as he tried hard to speak. His face exhibited a lot of frustration before he realized that he had personal emotions that he did not know how to utilize or control. He finally surrendered any additional futile attempts to speak to Rachel. He blinked his eyes one time and shifted his eyes to her.

"Thank you, God," Rachel whispered out loud.

"I am going to stop my questions for today to give your fiancée time to speak with you. Sleep when you feel tired. Do not push yourself. Okay?"

Robert blinked his eyes one time.

"A physical therapist will work with you every day until you are able to ambulate on your legs and use your hands and arms. This is a slow process, so do not get discouraged. Okay?"

Robert blinked his eyes once.

"A speech therapist will work with you every day until you are able to talk fluently. Okay?"

Robert blinked his eyes one time before the doctor turned and left the room with the two nurses.

Rachel placed her left hand on top of Robert's right hand and leaned down to softly kiss his lips. She lifted her head up to look into his eyes before she spoke, "Bobby, please do not try to talk. Just listen to me a few minutes. Okay?"

Robert blinked his eyes one time. He did manage to lift his index finger on his right hand high enough to allow it to fall on top of her left hand, covering his. He could only give her a partial smile, but that was big enough to touch her heart.

"I was so happy and relieved to finally learn you were alive. When you didn't show up to meet me for dinner, and months passed, I thought you had found a good-looking nurse or doctor and dumped me, or you were in an accident and died. I was not able to be a daughter to my dad, not able to be a good teacher to my students, and not able to be a friend to anyone. I was so miserable without you. I resigned my teaching job and was working on my thirty-day notice to the school board when I got the news you were alive." Rachel stopped talking when she saw tears slowly trickling down his face. She lowered the bed railing to allow herself to lean the top part of her body closer to him. She kissed the left side of his neck and laid the left side of her face onto his chest so she could admire his handsome face and watch his eyes close as she and he drifted off to sleep.

CHAPTER 21

Stanley Spring and Mary Shipley

Robert and Rachel had fallen asleep for almost two hours before Robert opened his eyes. He was unable to physically adjust or move his body, but he could move his eyes enough to see Rachel asleep lying on top of him. He closed his eyes and thanked God for his being unable to move his body this one time, because he would never want to stir or move to wake Rachel from a deep sleep she so desperately needed. His heart was full of love for Rachel. He felt blessed to have a woman like Rachel in his life to love. His eyes filled with happy tears just seeing her sleep so soundly on top of him. Her left hand was resting lightly on top of his right shoulder, with the right side of her face lying on his chest. He loved looking at her beautiful face. He knew when she had rested enough and did open her eyes, he would be the first thing she saw looking back at her with love in his eyes.

When he felt her eyelashes tickling his chest, he knew she was about to wake up. Seconds later, she raised her head up and looked into his eyes. "Awe. There he is! There is the blue-eyed love of my life," she said as she crawled, inch by inch, up toward his pillow and kissed him on his lips. "I want a lot more kisses from you, buster." Seeing his face turning beet red and the muscles straining in his neck, she covered his face with both of her hands and said, "Do not try to talk, Bobby. Please save that strength."

He blinked his eyes one time.

*****

Robert worked with his speech therapist over the next two weeks and learned how to talk using a raspy sounding voice just above the sound of a whisper. Not one person ever experienced any difficulty understanding the words he spoke. The doctor and the nursing staff were elated to see the progress he had made in just two short weeks. He was driven by sheer determination to return to his life as a doctor so he could begin living his life with Rachel by his side.

Instead of resting after a strenuous day with his physical therapist, he periodically continued to do the exercises he was learning. He was far ahead of the projected recovery schedule set for him by his doctor and his physical therapist.

Rachel was seen with a smile on her face every day. She was jolly and happy like a kid at Christmastime, now that Robert was awake and had mastered the art of kissing her like he used to. Every time they kissed, she thought about the two-second rule she had imposed, before he was hospitalized, that kept her from allowing his passionate kisses from pushing her emotions too far. Robert did not possess Rachel's ability to limit kissing. He was a typical man ready to experience now what married couples experience instead of waiting for their wedding night. She visualized how hard it must be for her friends who must resist the natural desires of men. The choice was simply to resist until a marriage certificate was in her hands and a wedding ring on her finger, or learn how to live with bittersweet regrets raising a child as a single mom if the man turns his back on her and walked away. The blessing would be a child to love for the rest of her life, but that would also include a lot of sacrifices experienced by single mothers. Robert's kisses did test her ability to resist the temptations of Satan telling her to relax her newly imposed kissing rule and submit to Robert. She prayed for strength from God to enforce her two-second-kiss rule until she was happily married.

Stanley Spring had become a daily visitor who spent quality time with Robert, Rachel, and Mary. Robert and Stanley often laughed about things that happened back in their medical school days. Rachel loved hearing about the good ole days and watching the closeness between Stanley and Robert.

Rachel watched Mary light up when Stanley focused his attention on her. It did not take an Einstein or a rocket scientist to know Mary was smitten, big-time, with Stanley. Mary's heart now belonged to him. Mary started wearing a conservative amount of eye makeup and a light touch of red lipstick that did not go unnoticed. Her face was instantly transformed from a cute face to a beautiful face. Once she looked at her face in the mirror after applying these changes to her face, she realized these minor changes were going to improve the quality of her life. She now had an aura of confidence shown in her eyes and a glow to her face. Something unexplainably good was happening to Mary. Stanley was the reason for this and the extra energetic bounce to her step.

One day, Stanley walked into Robert's hospital room to speak with Mary but did not see her in the room. He did see Rachel, however, standing in front of the window and looking outside, so he walked over to speak with her. "Hi, Rachel. Mary taking a break?"

"Yes. It has been a long tiring day. Gone are the days when we can just sit in the room and watch TV or read a good book. Mary and I are constantly talking with the physical therapist, speech therapist, nurse, doctor, or Robert. She needed a break, so she went down to get a cup of coffee and walk around."

"May I speak with you in private for a few minutes?" Stanley pointed to the hallway.

"Yes." Rachel walked into the hallway and turned around to face him.

"May I ask how you and Mary met?"

"She was a waitress at a restaurant where I went to eat one night."

"A waitress? Do you mind telling me the name of the restaurant?"

"No, I don't mind telling you the name. The restaurant was Joe's Crab House. Why?"

"Did she ever attend Harvard University or Harvard Law School?"

"Not that I know of. Why do you ask these questions?"

"Just curious."

"Why are you curious about Mary?"

"I like her."

"Like her as a friend or hoping for something more than a friendship?"

"First, there has to be an attraction."

"From your questions, I am assuming she already passed your initial eye test."

"You do not waste words, do you? Frank and Earnest. Hello, Frank."

"She is my friend. I don't want to see you hurt her."

"Has she been hurt before?"

"Haven't we all?"

"Good point."

"You never answered my earlier question."

"Which was?"

"Why did you ask about Harvard University and Harvard Law School?"

"Did you ever go to college?"

"Yes. I graduated from MIT."

"Impressive school. I take my hat off to you. Congratulations."

"Thank you very much."

"What was your major?"

"Oh no. You are good at ducking the one question I have asked you. Why?"

"May I ask a special favor from you about that one question?"

"You can ask, but I am not sure I will grant your favor."

"Fair enough, but I need to ask it anyway."

"Okay. Ask me."

"I will never deny asking you about Harvard, but could you do me and possibly Mary a huge favor by blocking out my question from your mind until a much later date?"

"May I ask the reason?"

"I may be talking out of school by revealing the subject matter of Harvard, especially if you do not know anything about it. And if you mention it to her, it may destroy any chance I might have for Mary and me to be more than friends. Okay?"

"Do you have a strong reason to suspect she is a Harvard graduate?"

"Harvard?"

"I get it. Okay. Your secret is safe with me."

"Thank you. I am in uncharted territory when it comes to love. This is my first potential romance after so many years of school. There are a lot of things about her my heart loves."

"How ironic. A heart doctor who has yet to experience a deep true romance where the heart is all in."

"Sounds like you have been talking to Mary about me. Has your heart been broken?"

Rachel pointed inside the room toward Robert, who was lying in his bed trying to take a nap. "My heart is his now. I am all in with Bobby. I have never been in love before. When he went missing from me, it almost killed me. I was useless as a daughter to my dad, useless as a teacher to my students, and useless as a potential friend to anyone. I cried myself to sleep every night for four long months, not knowing if he had found someone else and dumped me, or if he was in an accident and dead."

"You just gave a very graphic definition of being in love with Dr. Robert Wilson—Bobby to you. I could see the pain in your eyes as you told that brief story and the deep love in those same eyes when you looked toward him. Thank you for that."

"Thank you for sharing what you have shared with me today. It means a lot for me to get to know some of Bobby's friends. Thank you for trusting me with how you feel about Mary and about a subject we are not at liberty to discuss until." Rachel smiled at him.

"Robert has great taste in women. I am happy for him."

"I try to show him every time he wakes up. Oh, by the way, I just thought about something of interest to you."

"Mary?"

"Yes. Mary. She made a comment to me before we got ready to drive up here weeks ago."

"About?"

"I forgot how we got on the subject or what led into her comment when she said, 'You may find out I am a lot more than a waitress,' followed by her saying that she might tell me about it one day. So—"

"So this might be about Harvard?"

"Yes."

"I would bet everything I own she never lied to me. Thank you for telling me this."

"Telling you what?"

"Touché." They both did a soft high five and smiled at each other as Mary walked toward the room.

"Leave you two alone for a few minutes, and I come back to see you playing cutesy." Stanley, Mary, and Rachel burst into laughter.

Nurse Jaco and Nurse Phillips walked toward the room just as the laughter started. "Hey, we have rules against this kind of laughter in or near a patient's room, you guys," Lisa said with a straight face. She turned to look at Lauren, who couldn't hold her straight face any longer and burst into laughter.

"If you include us in the laughter, it is okay," Lisa said as she laughed out loud. This made the three of them continue to laugh. They had more reasons to be happy now that Robert was out of his coma and getting stronger every day.

They all walked back into the room and stood a few feet away from Robert's bed to talk.

"Did you hear a voice?" Rachel asked out loud. She turned around and looked down and saw Bobby looking up at her with his blue eyes open with a partial smile. She lowered the bed railing in front of her and leaned down to begin kissing him all over his face until her lips locked onto his lips. She put her hands under each shoulder to pull him closer to her. She heard the gasp from the ladies behind her when they saw Robert reach out his arms to pull her even closer to him.

"The healing power of love," Lisa and Lauren shouted at the same time.

"Oh, Bobby. I love you so much."

"Am I too late for dinner?" Rachel burst into laughter at his comment and that caused everyone in the room to laugh. "I take that as a yes," Robert said jokingly. The laughter in the room got a little louder.

"How are you doing today, Dr. Wilson?"

"Better. My thanks to you, Lauren, and Dr. Leafley."

"You are welcome. I know you know that my name is Nurse Phillips, and this is Nurse Jaco. We need to take your vital signs and record them on your chart before we call your doctor to update him on your progress. Okay?"

"How long was I in a coma?"

"Please hold your questions and relax until we get your vital signs recorded. Okay?"

Robert nodded his head in agreement. Nurse Phillips and Nurse Jaco both took his vital signs and recorded them on his chart.

"I need to call your doctor with your vital signs and get his orders. You need to eat so you can get stronger and gain weight. And you need to continue doing the exercises your physical therapist has shown you how to do. You are making great progress with your speech therapist and progressing nicely with your physical therapy. You will soon regain full use of both your arms and legs. We are really proud of you."

"Careful. My head may not fit through that door the next time you roll me out of here for x-rays. Seriously thank you. I need to hear your motivating comments. I deeply appreciate both of you."

"And we appreciate patients like you who not only appreciate us but tell us. Everyone loves praise and everyone loves to hear their own name spoken about kindly. Thank you, Dr. Wilson."

"You are very welcome."

"To answer your earlier question, you were in a nonresponsive coma about five months. I will give you the exact dates when I get a chance to check your chart at the nurses' station. Okay?"

"Okay. Thank you very much. No hurry or rush. I am not going anywhere."

Stanley walked closer to the side of Robert's bed and looked down at him. "Hello, good buddy. You are looking chipper this morning. How are you doing?"

"Better, thank you. Say, Stanley, how did you find me?"

"I had a choice of television or reading a local newspaper. Your story was on every local television station and printed on the front page of every newspaper within fifty miles of here. You were the talk of the town like you were a celebrity."

"What do you mean like I was?" Robert smiled at Stanley.

"You would think that after several months, you would fade out of the news, but they kept reporting on you like you were their headline news story."

"For real?"

"Yes. For real. Honest."

"Rachel must have found me the same way?"

"Oh no. You haven't heard how they used divine intervention along with their Sherlock Holmes skills to find you?"

"No. Tell me."

"Saved by an angel." Stanley smiled at Robert and then looked toward Mary, who walked into Stanley's arms to receive her first daily kiss. "Mary, please tell Robert how you found him in this hospital?"

"I thought Rachel found me. How did you get involved in searching for me, Mary?"

"Oh, this gets good. You are going to love how the big guy in the sky instantaneously moved people around to form one long chain of people to find you, pal. You have powerful friends in lofty places. I am staying on your good side," Stanley said this with a serious look upon his face without smiling.

"Are you serious?"

"I am as serious as a heart attack, and it does not get any more serious. Tell him, Mary."

Mary cleared her throat and looked down at Robert, who was looking up at her. "Rachel came into the restaurant where I was working as a waitress—"

"Sorry to interrupt you. You worked in a restaurant as a waitress?"

'Yes. It is a long story. I did work in a restaurant as a waitress when I met Rachel. May I tell you about this later?"

"If you want to tell me later," Stanley answered with a doubtful tone to his voice.

"Are you okay with it?"

"Okay with you telling me later or okay with you working in a restaurant as a waitress?"

"Both."

"Why would I not be, Mary?"

"I do not know. You tell me." Mary did not smile as she looked up at him like she was preparing for a fight or vicious argument.

"I do not need to hear your answer to that question, Mary."

"Why?"

"Are you asking me why?"

"Yes. Tell me why?"

"Because there is nothing wrong with working in a restaurant as a waitress. Why would I frown upon this?"

"Because of the things about my life I told you about. You know what I am talking about, Stanley."

"Oh. I get it. Perhaps it was a combination of the tone of my voice or the way I asked you if you really worked in a restaurant as a waitress, like this occupation would be beneath you, or perhaps it was my way of questioning what you told me before? Right?"

"Do you?" She refused to remove her eyes from his eyes until he answered her.

"You would never tell me a lie. I trust you with my life."

Mary gasped at his response as her eyes suddenly became misty, making her look down at the floor.

Stanley put his left arm around her and looked down at the top of her head. Two seconds later, Mary raised her head. She looked into his eyes for only a brief second before she kissed him on his lips. He was momentarily caught by surprise. Just when she tried to pull back from him, he wrapped his arms around her and pulled her close to give her a kiss of his own. Mary had no prior experience to know how to handle the emotions she was now experiencing as her heart seemed to surrender unconditionally to him.

Mary loved the way Stanley rubbed her back as he held her in his arms. It was a man thing. This was her first love, and she was enjoying every minute. Later, she would learn that she was also Stanley's first love. She always wondered, *How does God keep track of us? He sends messages to our thoughts telling us to work a specific job even if it meant moving to a different state or watch a particular movie or eat at a certain restaurant to possibly meet the love of our life or to just meet someone special.* Mary hoped that Stanley would prove to be her someone special.

"Right answer, Stanley," Robert said as he raised his eyebrows and smiled. "They did not teach us that one in medical school." Robert could not laugh out loud yet, but he sure tried, and seeing him try was all Stanley and Mary needed to burst into laughter.

"Now back to my story for me to answer your question, Robert—"

"Before you were rudely interrupted, I must add," Robert said, glancing at Stanley.

"If every interruption ends the same way, Stanley can interrupt me any time he wants to."

"Hmm. You got yourself a keeper, my friend. Congratulations," Robert said without smiling.

"I plan to keep her as long as she will have me. And if she ever decides to leave me, I am going with her," Stanley said, looking down at Mary. "I just stole another line from Robert with that one."

"You just want another kiss," Mary said this just as Stanley pulled her close to him and kissed her. "You keep kissing me like that, and I will never get this story told to Robert." She picked up a pamphlet lying on the bed in front of her and started fanning her flushed face. "Time-out," she said as she giggled out loud.

"Okay. I will stand here like a mannequin and listen," Stanley said with a smile, looking at Robert.

Mary looked at Rachel. "Tell him, Rachel," Mary said, nodding encouragement to Rachel.

"Okay. I was about to leave work to meet you at Cheddar's when a coworker told me to eat at Joe's Crab House that night. She did not demand that I eat there. I still do not know why I suddenly changed our restaurant from Cheddar's Restaurant to Joe's Crab House. I normally do not do those things. You told me to meet you at Cheddar's, and that was what I was going to do until one hour before I got ready to leave to meet you. I kept calling your cell phone to tell you where I was, but my calls were sent to your voice mail. You never answered any of my phone calls all night long. I called all the hospitals and clinics within a fifty-mile radius to see if you were being treated, but I couldn't find you anywhere."

Mary looked at Rachel and pointed to her own front tooth.

"Oh, yes. Thank you, Mary. Now for the amazing power of God."

"Amen to that!" Mary exclaimed.

"I fell coming out of a revolving department store door that led to the sidewalk while I was carrying a couple of packages, and skinned up my hands, my knees, my elbows, and broke my front tooth. A kind woman helped me up and walked me over to her automobile to bandage me up. When she loaned me her mirror for me to see my front tooth, I cried, thinking about teaching my students the next morning and meeting you the next night. I remember making a comment out loud to this woman, saying, 'I wish you were a dentist.' She told me that I should be careful what I wish for as she raised her eyebrows and smiled at me."

"Was she a dentist?" Stanley asked.

"Yep. Dr. Mary Sharp. She agreed to come into her office the very next morning one hour before her office opened to fix my front tooth." Rachel smiled, showing everyone her new front tooth.

"She did a great job. Cannot tell which one was broken. And what an amazing act of kindness."

"Yes. I agree with you, Stanley. I will never forget her kindness and the time she took with me."

"After she fixed your front tooth, you went to Joe's Crab House and met Mary. Right?"

"Yes, Bobby. That was when I met Mary working as a waitress at Joe's Crab House. I noticed that she had a small chip missing on her front tooth. I just came from having my tooth repaired but did not know how to get into a conversation with Mary about her tooth. Well, before the night was over, one of our conversations shifted to a discussion about my white teeth, which opened the door for me to discuss her tooth. I then had the perfect opportunity to refer her to Dr. Sharp. Mary can take over from here and tell you the rest of the story." Rachel nodded and smiled at Mary.

"And as you can see, Dr. Sharp did a great job on my front tooth." Mary excitedly flashed a big smile. "I smile a lot now and do not have to shield my front tooth with my hand. Thank you, Rachel."

"You are very welcome," Rachel responded.

"Mary and Rachel met in some obscure little ole small town called Gallatin, Tennessee. Right?"

"Hey. Watch it, buddy. I love Gallatin, Tennessee," Rachel answered defensively, looking at Stanley.

"Do you know anything about Gallatin, Tennessee?" Stanley quipped.

"Yes. I do. Gallatin is a city named after the US secretary of the Treasury Albert Gallatin. Sumner is the county that comprises all of Gallatin, which has a population of about thirty-eight thousand people."

"That is a nice-size town with thirty-eight thousand people," Stanley said with raised eyebrows, looking at Rachel.

"You will love this little town when you come for a visit," Rachel answered with a smile and satisfying nod of her head. "You will not be disappointed when you visit Gallatin. In addition to the city of Gallatin, there are other surrounding cities for you to visit, such as Nashville, which is the home of country music, located only thirty miles south of Gallatin. Where else can you find famous musicians and singers who are willing to sing some of your favorite songs, pose for a selfie, and give you their autograph?"

"I was too quick to judge Gallatin. I am honestly impressed," Stanley said with a slight bow.

"The General Jackson Showboat, which is a gorgeous-looking boat, is also located in Nashville. You can sit back on comfortable cushioned chairs and enjoy a nice dinner cruise with live entertainment."

"Okay. I am convinced." Stanley waved a white handkerchief in the air to signify his surrender as everyone broke out into laughter. "Gallatin and Nashville are must cities for me to visit and take Mary on a dinner cruise."

"The four of us will have a lot of fun," Mary said as she raised her eyebrows and tilted her head slightly, looking from Robert to Rachel, waiting to hear Robert agree to visit Gallatin and Nashville.

"Come on, pal, please tell me you and Rachel will go with us?" Stanley pleaded.

"Yes. We are in, and we look forward to spending the evening with you," Rachel said, looking at Robert.

"Robert? Does she speak for you? Will you go on this trip with us?" Stanley asked.

"I want to make one thing crystal clear when it comes to my home, my relationships, and people speaking for me. I make the rules for me and my home, so anything Rachel says, we will do."

Rachel put one knee up on the bed. "How do I get on this bed with him after that comment?" Rachel laughed hard and louder than any of the others just as Lisa Phillips and Lauren Jaco came back into the room. Rachel looked up at them, shook her head, and collapsed on top of Robert, saying, "Busted."

The entire wing of the hospital must have heard their roar of laughter that increased in volume every time Rachel tried unsuccessfully to get up off Robert, who had his arm around her pulling her back down. Robert was laughing harder than his capabilities and harder than anyone had seen him laugh before. They each wished they would have thought to record this happy moment on their cell phones so they could watch it on their phones in the future.

"You guys need to sell tickets and take this show on the road," Lisa said, looking at Robert.

"Rachel is assaulting me," Robert said with a smile, looking at Rachel.

"And with your arm wrapped so tightly around her and pulling her down, I can see you are trying your best to help her get off you," Lauren added while laughing hard."

"Busted. Confine him to his bed without dessert," Rachel said while laughing and pointing at him.

"You do not know how happy we are to see you having fun with your fiancée and your friends after you spent so long in a nonresponsive coma. Laughter is not only good for the soul, it is free medicine that doctors cannot prescribe for healing," Lauren said to Robert and the others in the room.

"I agree with that statement, Lauren," Mary said.

"I never saw this side of you. You are a hoot," Robert said, smiling and holding Rachel with one arm.

Rachel slid off him and stood next to his bed. "I am a hoot? You have not seen nothing yet, Dr. Wilson. Now may I finish my part of this story?"

"If I allowed myself to dwell too long on you and what I want to experience with you, my dear, my blood pressure, pulse, and heart readings would wreak havoc on every machine hooked up to me." He looked at her and repeatedly raised and lowered his eyebrows to entice her to get back on the bed.

"Oh no. I am not getting back up on that bed with you." Robert laughed so hard hearing these words from Rachel, he had a coughing fit.

Lisa and Lauren immediately jumped into action, using their nursing skills to stop Robert's cough and calm him down. Initially and surprisingly, they experienced a little difficulty getting Robert to relax and focus his attention on their commands. Once he concentrated on their request to take slow deep breaths, his vital signs started to come under control and show the numbers they were trained to produce. They had never seen him so excited and happy. Robert waved his hand and nodded his head to let the nurses know he had gotten control of his breath and was now okay

He looked up and smiled at Rachel. "Okay, please continue your story," Robert said while Lisa and Lauren stood flanking Mary.

Mary looked down at Robert. "If you could have seen the look of expectation, followed by the look of disappointment, in Rachel's eyes every time the front door of Joe's Crab House opened, you would understand the kind of love she has for you in her heart. It bothered me when I went home that night. You not showing up to meet her did not make any sense to me. The night before I was to see Dr. Sharp about my tooth, I did not sleep very well. I kept thinking about all the hospitals and clinics she called hoping to find you. This stayed on my mind and would not go away."

"Did you figure that part out before you went to see Dr. Sharp?" Robert asked.

"No. A little voice in my head told me to tell everything to Dr. Sharp and ask for her help."

"Did you?"

"Yes. She finished working on my tooth, and I asked her if I could talk to her about Rachel. She never hesitated even for a second to think about it. She asked me to go with her back to her office. I told her my concerns and, after she thought about it for a few seconds, zeroed in on the answer to find you."

"How?"

"Dr. Sharp told me that the love I described between you and Rachel convinced her that you must have been seriously injured to keep you from meeting her for dinner. She said if she was ever seriously injured and was a member of the military, she would want the VA hospital to treat her. That was when she asked which medical school Robert graduated from. I told her you graduated from Johns Hopkins University School of Medicine, located in Baltimore, Maryland. She remembered that they also have a Johns Hopkins Hospital, which is their teaching hospital and biomedical research facility of the Johns Hopkins School of Medicine, and it was also located in Baltimore, Maryland. She also said the hospital has around thirty thousand staff members, making it the largest hospital in the world when you consider staff members. She suggested that I start my search at this hospital to find you. I followed her suggestion and found you."

"Incredible. Rachel, Dr. Mary Sharp, Joe's Crab House, and Mary Shipley were all used in a domino-like chain to find me. If you remove even one person from this chain of people, I stay in a nonresponsive coma for who knows how much longer. Thank you all so much."

"Bobby, I just remembered something. You were already air-lifted to Johns Hopkins Hospital when my coworker told me to eat at Joe's Crab House instead of Cheddar's. God used my coworker to lead me to Mary. God not only loves you, but He also kept a close watch over you, for me."

"You are right. God was counting on you to obey your coworker—and you did—to find me.

"It runs chills up and down my back every time I think about how many people God used to find you after that one spontaneous act of kindness by Dr. Mary Sharp."

"The part that blows me away is how fast God used the Holy Spirit to communicate with your coworker to get you to change from Cheddar's to Joe's Crab House. Think about how close you came to eat at Cheddar's instead of Joe's Crab House, Rachel. You never would have met Mary to find me."

Mary was standing there deep in thought for a few seconds before she spoke, "I would love for the four of us to visit Nashville, Tennessee, for a dinner cruise on the General Jackson Showboat, and more importantly, I would love for the four of us to visit the city of Gallatin and Dr. Mary Sharp to let Robert meet and thank her for her act of kindness and for being the indispensable person in a chain of people God used to find Robert."

Robert looked at Rachel before he spoke. "Is this something you would like for me to do?"

"If I said no, you would not go?"

"That is correct, my dear. You decide. You are my travel agent. This is your call."

"Do you love me that much that you would let me influence or control your life, Bobby?"

"If you were not in my life, I would not have the life I would want to live, so my answer is yes."

"I do not know what it is you see in me, but I pray it never fades from your heart. You make me the happiest woman on the face of this earth. You make me feel loved and important."

"Touché. I have never been loved the way you love me, Rachel. I never want to do anything to ever lose your love. You are my rock and the love of my life. I am the happiest, luckiest, and the most blessed man alive. We are a team that will conquer anything we have to conquer together the rest of our lives."

Rachel had tears running down her face when she said, "Hold me, Bobby. Please hold me." She leaned the top of her body across his chest to rest the left side of her face against the left side of his face. He wrapped both of his arms around her and held her as she asked him to do.

Mary was in deep thought, thinking about what she just heard discussed between Robert and Rachel and wondered if she would ever have that kind of love. She looked up and allowed her eyes to meet Stanley's eyes for several seconds before she kissed his lips.

"Do you want to take a walk together and let these two love-birds spend a little alone time together?"

"Yes. That would be nice, Stanley."

"Okay." Stanley glanced down at Robert. "I will see you when we get back, Robert."

"Okay, Stanley. It looks like Rachel will be leaving shortly to spend the night at her hotel, but I will definitely be here for us to talk when you get back. Bye."

"Bye."

CHAPTER 22

Stanley Needs Alone Time

For the last few months, Robert worked with a speech therapist and a physical therapist daily to help him regain his speech and the use of his arms and legs. He chose a strenuous physical exercise program to accelerate his progress. Neither his personal physician, speech therapist, or physical therapist had any idea he possessed the drive and bulldog tenacity that lived inside him. In just a few short months, they stood speechless with their mouths wide open, shaking their heads in disbelief. His rapid progress defied every known medical study. Perhaps his desire to go home to begin his life with Rachel was the only motivating factor he needed to drive him daily to recover faster than his planned medical schedule.

Instead of allowing himself to drift off to sleep when Rachel left for the evening to return to her hotel room, he chose to exercise in his bed until he fell asleep from sheer exhaustion. Some of his leg and arm strength returned, but because of his extended inactivity, his legs were still a tad wobbly and not quite strong enough for him to walk by himself. He had religiously followed and exceeded a recovery plan outlined by his physical therapist, but he was a tad disappointed with his physical achievements. Although his physical therapist and his doctors were pleased with his progress, he frequently expressed to them his displeasure, even after he heard them say to him today, "You have exceeded the goals we set for you. We are proud of your progress and proud of you. Frankly you are close to being discharged to go home."

Robert smiled to himself after hearing words that he had waited months to hear from them. He promised to start each future day of his life remembering to give thanks to God for a second-chance blessing to live the life he had previously hoped to live with Rachel.

Rachel had a smile on her face as she walked into his room and up to his bed to kiss him on his lips. She eased back from his face and looked into his eyes, saying, "A penny for your thoughts."

"Hello, love. My thoughts are always about you."

"Any particular thought you care enough about to share with me?"

"My promise to God."

"A secret or is it possible to share your promise to God with me?"

"I will never keep any secrets from you."

"Aww. I will never keep any secrets from you either. I would love to hear your promise to God."

"I promised God that I would start each future day of my life thanking Him for the second chance He gave me to live the rest of my life with you."

"Do you want me to remind you of your daily promise to God?"

"Yes. Please remind me, Rachel."

"Okay. And to remind myself to remind you, I will make the same promise too. You are that important to me, Bobby."

"How can we seal this promise so we will always remember it?" Robert raised and lowered his eyebrows rapidly with a big exaggerated smile on his face.

"Men. Is that all you men think about?"

"Is there anything else?" Robert tried to laugh out loud but could not. He started coughing like he did before when Lisa and Lauren had to do something to bring his cough under control and calm him down. He looked at Rachel with a look of concern.

"God is very disappointed in you right now, Bobby. You know better than to even think about that until we get married. Shame on you."

"You are right. I am wrong. I am sorry."

"How about using a pinky promise? We will not break a pinky promise. Will we?" Rachel asked.

"Absolutely not. Great idea. A pinky promise it is." He stuck out his pinky finger, and she wrapped her pinky finger around his with a big smile.

"I love the things we do together, Bobby." She watched him for what appeared to be about two long minutes before he looked at her. A brief second later, he quickly looked away. She saw a look in his eyes that she had never seen before. "Today is the day I get to see that look. Eh, Bobby."

"What look?" he asked without looking at her.

"The look that says I hurt your feelings, and you are going to pout a little about it and not talk to me. That look. Please look at me."

"Is it okay if I take a nap?" he asked without looking at her.

Rachel sat on the bed and scooted closer to him. "Bobby, you are a very smart man. Answer this one question for me honestly. Do you believe it is hard for me to keep the rules we both agreed to until we are married, or do you think it is only hard on you? I live for our wedding night when *our* two-second-kiss rule will be forever waived. The chemistry we have for each other takes my breath away. The rule is hard for me too. So hard I could not restrain myself without *our* rule. It is *our rule.* I gave you a choice that would probably kill me if you elected to take me up on it when I offered to let you find another woman to love, if that is the one thing you really must have to be happy right now. Do you want that in your life instead of me?"

"No. But please promise me one thing."

"I hope it is something I can promise. Please tell me what you want me to promise?"

"When I get out of this hospital, and the doctor tells me I can return to work, please promise me you will marry me immediately. Can you make me that promise?"

"Yes. I want that too. We both agreed not to keep secrets from each other. Can I get a pinky promise on that?'

"Yes. I'm sorry. I wanted my own way. But honestly, I do not want to break our rule before our wedding night. Thank you for being strong. And thank you for talking to me instead of walking away. Do I really take your breath away?"

"Yes, you do. But remember that life is not measured by the number of breaths we take but by the moments that take our breath away. And you take my breath away, Bobby. I love you."

"I love that saying, and I truly love you, Rachel."

"A friend of mine, Vivian Dorman, told me about this saying. I bet the first few months after we get married, I will be late every day to teach my class, and you will be late making hospital rounds."

"A problem most men would die for." They both laughed out loud and glanced toward the sound they heard coming from the vicinity of the doorway to see the smiling face of Stanley.

"Is this a bad time for me to visit? I can come back another time."

"Hi, Stanley." Rachel hoped off the bed with a smile. "It is always a good time for you to visit."

"I have a nagging question on my mind. I would love to talk to you about my concerns."

"Would you like for me to leave and let you and Bobby talk?"

"No. I would like to get feedback from you, too, if that is okay?"

"Okay with me." Rachel glanced toward Robert.

"You know me, buddy. I am always open to talk with you. Shoot. Tell us what is on your mind."

"My heart tells me everything about Mary is right. Yet in the back of my mind, I wonder if this is too quick to be falling in love with her. I came to visit you and met her in what is considered a chance meeting. Is it realistic to fall in love that quickly? I know so many guys who were blessed to meet the right woman, and over a period of a year or two, they gradually fell in love. Mary immediately impacted my heart so fast that my heart fluttered when I first looked into her eyes. Is this infatuation? Is this something that will pass once we spend time away from each other? I could not live with the guilt of breaking her heart if I am heading down *that road* with the hint of uncertainty that lies deep in the back of my mind. Please be frank and honest with me. More importantly, please keep this conversation between the three of us. Am I out of line discussing this with you, Rachel?"

"Why?"

"Mary is your friend."

"Our conversation will stay confidential, and my comments will hopefully serve to keep the two of you together. No harm and no foul. Okay?"

"Okay. Thank you very much. I trust both of you. One of my friends made fun of me for telling him I am falling in love with Mary. He said people don't meet and fall in love that quickly. Please help me to understand my feelings."

"Chance meetings make up a very high percentage of long-term relationships that lead to marriages."

"I hear what you are saying, Rachel. The reason I have these doubts is because I have never met anyone who met someone and instantly fell in love. Have you?"

"Do you trust Bobby's word?"

"Yes."

"Do you trust my word?"

"Yes."

"Stanley, we are all the proof you need. I went into a coffee shop to read a newspaper article about a job and to eat a sandwich. The coffee shop is a very busy fast-paced place, where you are lucky to find a table or booth without a long wait. I saw an empty booth and reached my hand out to set the newspaper article on the empty table when Bobby literally ran into me, trying to claim the same booth. Seconds later, another couple tried to sit down in this same booth before I told them we were about to sit down. Bobby sat on one side of the booth, and I sat on the other side. We were immediately compatible and comfortable with each other. But I was skeptical about meeting him for lunch or dinner when he asked me until I heard him say, 'Take a chance on me, Rachel.' And to this day, I am so glad I did."

"Wow! That is an awesome story, Rachel."

"God brought the two of you together, Stanley. Remember, before we left my home to come up here, my inner voice told me Mary was going to meet someone. God gives each of us free will to accept or reject any gift He sends to us. Mary is your gift."

"Okay. You have removed all my doubts. Thank you very much for sharing your story with me. It means a lot to me. Robert has always been a good guy and a good friend to me. I am not surprised God matched him with you, Rachel. I am blessed to have two very special friends like you."

"Aww. You just want to see me cry happy tears," Rachel responded with a giggle. You are so sweet and very kind, Stanley," Rachel said these comments from her heart.

"Ditto. You are special to us. We love you like a brother. Stay safe and healthy so the four of us can make good memories together and share them with our children. Okay?" Robert said to Stanley.

"Okay. I can finally stop wrestling with that question." Stanley shook his head with a smile.

"Stop wrestling with what question?" Mary asked as she walked up behind Stanley.

Stanley turned around with a smile on his face. "Good morning, Mary. I did not hear you come in."

"Should I wear a bell?" Mary said with a giggle amid the laughs from the others.

Stanley ignored her question as he opened his arms for her to walk closer for a morning kiss. "Aww. That is how I hope to start every morning. You look beautiful, and you seem chipper this morning."

"Flattery always works on me. Thank you. Now out with it. Stop wrestling over what question?"

Robert raised his hand to get her attention. When she turned to focus her attention on him, he said, "When will be a good time for us to make plans to visit Tennessee? Please give that some thought and give us a projected date so the four of us can stop wrestling with that question. Okay?"

"Seriously? You really do want to visit Tennessee?"

"Yes. I want to thank the people who helped you find me. I also want to experience something I have never done before…"

"And what would that be, Bobby?" Rachel asked with a look of curiosity.

"A dinner cruise with live entertainment aboard the General Jackson Showboat."

Stanley, noticing that Mary was deep into a conversation with Rachel, gave him a chance to make eye contact with Robert before he mouthed the words, "Thank you."

Robert raised the thumb of his right hand and nodded his head at Stanley with a big smile on his face. Robert used his index finger to motion Stanley closer to him. "I have an idea to run by you when we get a chance for a few minutes of guy talk."

"You are piquing my interest. You want to leave the subject matter a mystery until we talk?"

Robert glanced over at Rachel and Mary. "What are you two cooking up?" Mary said with a smile.

"Nothing, dear," Stanley replied, looking sheepish.

"Would you two men like some alone time? Rachel and I would welcome an hour of ladies' time to get a cup of coffee and see what kind of trouble we can get into."

"Great idea, Mary. Do you mind giving us a few minutes to talk?" Robert asked.

"No problem. Come on, Rachel. Grab your purse. Let's give the guys some alone time."

Robert raised his hand to get Rachel's attention. When she stopped and turned to face him, he said, "Do you remember our agreement?" Robert raised his eyebrows and waited for her response.

"How could I ever forget that agreement?" Rachel rolled her eyes as she walked closer to his bed, looking back at Mary, saying, "We agreed to never leave each other to run an errand without a kiss in case one of us never made it back to the other. The last thing we want to treasure is the memory of our kiss." Rachel leaned closer to Robert and kissed his lips. "See you when I get back."

Stanley and Mary were looking at each other and appearing to be in a slight trance until Mary spoke. "I want the same agreement between us, Stanley. If you do?"

"Yes. I love that idea. Any reason to kiss you one more time daily will always work for me." Stanley and Mary both walked toward each other to close the distance between them to seal the new agreement with a kiss. "This rule gives new meaning to saying hello and good-bye." He smiled at Mary.

"Yes, it does. I love this agreement, and I love you, Stanley."

"Have fun and be careful," Stanley told her with a smile.

"Bye, guys." Rachel waved over her shoulder and disappeared out the door with Mary.

"I am all ears. Let me hear your genius idea," Stanley said with a smile and raised eyebrows.

"Our visit to Tennessee will make memories for all of us. During our visit, I thought it would be a great idea to meet Dr. Mary Sharp and invite her to our engagement party when we simultaneously get on one knee and propose to the ladies in our lives. What do you think about this idea?"

"I absolutely love it. We need the right forum to pull this off."

"You are right. Let me explore some options with Rachel."

"How in the world are you going to get into that conversation without tipping her off?"

"Not a good idea, is it?"

"Your idea about our dropping to one knee simultaneously and then popping the marriage question is brilliant. Mary would have legitimate mixed feelings of gladness for you and Rachel, along with a little depression and sadness just standing there watching you pop the marriage question and wishing I was also down on one knee popping that same marriage question to her. Simultaneously proposing marriage will make this a historic moment with pure euphoria. I love it."

"Rachel is not going to be easy to fool. We need a reason for her to come to a hotel ballroom." He looked at Stanley and raised his eyes questionably.

"We can give them a hundred reasons for needing a conference room or a ballroom and pull this off. I am getting excited just thinking about it. It will be easy to come up with a reason to attend a ballroom meeting or ballroom cocktail party in Nashville."

Stanley swiped his left thumb and middle finger together to generate a snapping sound before he pointed to Robert, saying, "Our friends will be gathered in a ballroom, talking, laughing, and dancing with each other when the four of us walk into the room. We will talk to a few people in the room, but our close friends will act like they do not know us. Oh, this is genius, even if I say so myself."

A woman came into the room without speaking and stood behind Stanley with her arms folded across her chest appearing to be angry. The conversation between Robert and Stanley abruptly stopped before they turned their attention to her. She drilled holes into Stanley with her eyes for a few seconds, appearing to be pouting like a wounded teenager, before she looked away from Stanley and glanced at Robert. She nodded to him without speaking, then she hung her head and shook it sideways a few times before she glanced up at Stanley with one eye.

"I sat in the restaurant alone for an hour before I walked to the elevator and rode it up to this floor. I then walked the length of two long hallways to find you in here having a great time without thinking about me, sitting downstairs in the restaurant, waiting for you. Are we having lunch today or not?"

"Yes. I am sorry. I lost track of time"

"Let's go." She started walking toward the door, looking back angrily at Stanley.

"I have to go, Robert. I will be back." Stanley turned and disappeared out the door with his angry mysterious visitor.

Rachel and Mary were laughing about something when they stepped out of an elevator on Robert's floor. They walked past a few other elevators on their way to the room when Mary noticed one of the elevators they were about to walk past had its doors still half open and about to close when she caught a glimpse of Stanley standing inside the elevator, with his arm around a woman about her age. The woman with Stanley did not see Mary stop to stare at her. Nor did she observe the shocked look on Mary's face as she stood there with her mouth wide open. Mary grabbed her own stomach and reached out for Rachel's shoulder before she closed her eyes and collapsed into Rachel's arms. Rachel dropped her purse when she reached both of her arms out to catch Mary to prevent her from falling face-first onto the floor. Mary's purse was wedged tightly between their bodies.

Rachel saw a young man walking by them in a hospital gown, and yelled, "Sir. Please help us. She just fainted and needs a chair or a bed to lie on for a few minutes. We are visiting my fiancé, Dr. Robert Wilson, in intensive care."

"Yes, ma'am. I know Dr. Wilson. Please let me carry her to his room and get her the help she needs. Follow me, please, ma'am." The orderly put his left hand around Mary's back and reached his right arm down to lift her legs to carry her in his arms like she was as light as a feather. He gently laid her down onto the spare bed that was added to Dr. Wilson's room for Rachel, and called for a nurse.

Lisa Phillips and Lauren Jaco came hurriedly into the room and saw Rachel pointing toward Mary.

"Please tell us what happened to her?" Lisa asked.

"She fainted into my arms in the hallway."

"Do you know why she fainted?" Lauren asked.

"No. She stopped laughing and grabbed at her stomach and fainted. I am glad I was standing near her, or she would have hit her face on the floor in the hallway."

"That was going to be my first question, if she hit her head. And you answered it, so my next question is—" Lauren stopped talking when she was interrupted by Rachel.

"Please explain fainting to me. Why does it happen?"

Lisa and Lauren alternated naming all the fainting reasons to Rachel, beginning with fear, emotional trauma, severe pain, a sudden drop in blood pressure, low sugar because of diabetes, going too long without eating, hyperventilation—rapid or shallow breathing—dehydration, standing in one position for too long, standing up too quickly, physical exertion in hot temperatures, coughing too hard, straining during a bowel movement, seizures, or consuming drugs or alcohol. Lisa and Lauren did a high five and smiled.

"Thank you. If you were not around to help me, and I was by myself, please tell me what I should do if a friend of mine or a stranger happens to faint in my presence?"

"Great question, Rachel. Play it safe and always call 911. The operator will ask you a series of questions to know how to give you instructions to help a fainting person."

"Oh, that kind of help would be comforting to me. Thank you so much."

"If the fainting person wakes up, be sure to ask them if they have any pain in the area of their jaw or chest region to rule out a heart attack," Lisa said to Rachel

"If so, do I call 911?"

"Yes. Immediately. And if the person is awake, keep them lying on their back and elevate their legs above their heart, loosen their belt, collar, and restrictive clothing. Try to keep them in this position for a few minutes to lessen the chances of them getting up and fainting again. Okay?"

"Okay. Will Mary stay unconscious exceptionally long?"

"Not normally. We took her vital signs and found nothing alarming. If she is not alert in a couple of more minutes, we will start running tests. Okay?"

"Thank you, Lauren. I am glad you two are here to help me."

"Me too," Mary said while trying to roll out of the bed. She was unconscious for about ten minutes.

"Whoa. Take it slow and easy, Mary. No fast movements. Okay?" Lisa said in a comforting voice. "Do you know where you are?"

"Yes. Johns Hopkins Hospital in intensive care, visiting Robert Wilson with Rachel Rice."

"Okay. Slowly, come up to a sitting position and stay in that position for two minutes. Okay?"

"Okay."

"Tell me why you fainted?"

Mary was about to speak when Stanley entered the room and walked up to the bottom of her bed. "Taking an afternoon nap?" Stanley asked with a smile, waiting for her reply. His smile disappeared when he saw an angry look in her eyes, glaring at him. "Are you okay? Can I do anything for you?"

"Yes to your question asking if I am okay. No to your question can you do anything for me. I need to get up and go alone to my hotel room for the afternoon. May I get up, Lisa?"

"Only if I can walk you around the hospital floor one lap to make sure you are okay. Deal?"

"Deal. Please get me out of here."

"Do you want to talk?" Rachel asked.

"Tonight at the hotel. Okay?" Rachel nodded in agreement.

Lisa gently held Mary's arm and started to lead her out the door when Stanley stepped in front of her. "I am sorry for whatever happened to you, Mary."

"I do not need your pity," Mary replied hatefully.

"Hey. Give my buddy some slack, will you?" Robert said in Stanley's defense.

Mary turned around and walked over to Robert and looked down at him with misty eyes. "Honorable men are hard to find. You are an honorable man. I am glad we met. Get better." She abruptly turned and grabbed Lisa's arm and disappeared out the door.

Stanley looked at Rachel. He opened his hands with the palms of both hands facing up before he asked, "What in the world did I do to her? What happened for her to be in bed needing a nurse?"

Lisa walked back into the room with Lauren. "We need to bring Mary's purse to her. Do you know where it might be, Rachel?"

"Yes. It is on the ledge behind the headboard of the bed she was lying on." Rachel walked over to the bed to retrieve the purse and handed it to Lauren while Lisa answered a question from Stanley.

"Why was Mary lying on the bed when I came into the room?" Stanley asked.

"She fainted. The orderly called the nurse's desk for us to help her and we did," Lisa answered.

"Fainted. Do you know why?"

"She was about to tell me when you walked into the room. She suddenly clammed up." Lisa shrugged her shoulders, opened her hands, raised her eyebrows, and shook her head, bewildered.

"Does this make any sense to you, Rachel?"

"Nope." Rachel's was exasperated. "It makes no sense to me. When she saw you today, it was like she was looking at a real Martian from outer space. Never saw that side of her before. Earlier, for some unknown reason, she turned white as a sheet, grabbed her stomach, and fainted into my arms."

"Rachel, before I leave for the day, may I talk to you in the hallway for a couple of minutes while the nurses are talking with Robert?" Stanley asked.

"Sure." Rachel turned and led the way out into the hallway and turned to face him.

"The nurse mentioned an orderly called the nurses' station to come help Mary. Right?"

"Yes."

"Why was the orderly in the room?"

"He carried her into the room."

Stanley blinked his eyes a couple of times as he shook his head rapidly a couple of times from side to side before he gave her a confused look. "I am beginning to understand. Let me see if I have this correct. It must have been when Mary and you left the room to give Robert and me a chance to talk that Mary fainted somewhere, walking with you, which prompted you to call for an orderly to help Mary. Right?"

"Partially correct. We were on our way back to the room when she fainted."

"Do you mind telling me exactly where she fainted?"

"Why do you need to know this?"

"Because I am trying to figure out what made her faint."

"I do not see how that is going to help you, but—"

"Sorry to interrupt you, but this information might prove to be very useful. Trust me and tell me where you were when she fainted?"

"On this floor in front of the elevators. How does that help you?"

"Oh no." Stanley looked up at the hallway ceiling and closed his eyes. "Lord, please fix this for me."

"What is there to fix? Why did you say oh no?" Rachel asked with concern in her voice. "Tell me."

"She must have seen me on the elevator with Penny. Oh boy. The elevator jerked about the time someone bumped into Penny. I put my arm around her shoulder to keep her from falling, and I bet Mary saw me on the elevator with my arm around her."

"Who is Penny? Why would you risk being seen on this floor with another woman? I asked you not to break her heart." Rachel turned and walked angrily back into the room and stood next to Robert, with her arms folded across her chest.

"Hi. Did somebody take your visitor pass away?" Robert asked, looking up at her with a smile.

Rachel looked down at him with a look he had never seen on her face. "No."

"No. Just no?"

"No. I need to leave for a little bit to check on Mary. I will be back." Rachel leaned down and gave him what amounted to a peck on his lips and turned away angrily and walked out the door.

Stanley walked back into the room and stood next to Robert. "Should I be wearing a helmet?"

"You tell me. What in the world got into her?" Robert asked Stanley.

"The same thing that got into Mary."

"Oh! Thanks, buddy. That sure clears this up for me." Stanley blew out a long breath of air and hung his head.

"Oh my. I can get myself into one big mess after another trying to help others. No problems in my life living on my own and minding my own business. I am going to have to learn how to say no."

"Anything you want to talk about?" Robert asked.

"I am so thankful God didn't make me a woman. I would probably be living in a red-light district as a very busy call girl. In that line of work, I would never need to say no."

Robert spontaneously burst into laughter hard enough for him to start a coughing fit he could not handle without the help of his two nurses, Lisa Phillips and Lauren Jaco.

"I can see I am on a roll here today. What else can I do to cheer you up, good buddy?" Stanley made this last comment just as the nurses were almost successful in stabilizing Robert's coughing spree. But after hearing Stanley's last comments, Robert's coughing started up again, which prompted the nurses to chase Stanley out of the room as Robert coughed, choked, and laughed even harder.

Thirty minutes later, Stanley stuck his head in the door to eyeball Robert to see if it was okay to come back into the room. Robert smiled at him and motioned for him to come in. Stanley only had to stand next to Robert's bed and look down at him for Robert to start laughing and coughing once again.

"Easy, pal. You are going to get me banned from your room," Stanley said with a serious tone to his voice. Robert fought to control his emotions by shaking his head and blowing out a long breath of air. "I like you and want to visit you until we can do some things outside of here together."

"Your comments were funny and just caught me off guard and unprepared. Besides, we always need to laugh. And I needed you over the last few years while we were building a great friendship."

"I needed your friendship too. We have been through a lot together. But I hated that my funny comments brought the nurses running into your room. After today, I am not so sure Rachel or Mary will welcome me back into your room. I am sorry about all this, Robert."

"It will blow over and soon be forgotten. Do you know what is going on with Mary or Rachel now?"

"Unfortunately I do. Penny."

"Mike's wife, Penny? Is she the girl who was here earlier?"

"Yes."

"Penny seemed irritated because you were late meeting her for lunch and not too happy knowing your reason for being late was visiting with me. But how does she figure into the sudden change of moods with Mary? And why is Rachel upset over any of this?"

"Mary fainted outside of the elevators located on this floor."

"And?"

"And Penny and I had just gotten onto an elevator, and while we were trying to work our way to the back of the elevator, it jerked or bounced, causing her to lose her balance. I reached out my arm to steady her and to keep her from crashing into other people. I bet Mary saw that part of what happened."

"I am not seeing a problem in what you just told me."

"Mary must have concluded that I had my arm romantically around Penny. She must have concluded that I was doing something I should not have been doing behind her back, and this image in her mind was too much for her to absorb, and she fainted." Stanley looked at Robert and raised his eyebrows, waiting on his reply.

"Mary didn't say anything to you about this."

"No. She must have too much class and pride to confront me. So she chose to run away."

"How does Rachel figure into this?"

"I asked Rachel where Mary was when she fainted. When she told me outside the elevators, I put two and two together and tried to explain, but I only got to tell her a fraction of the story before she got upset and asked me, 'Why would you be seen with your arm around another woman on this floor?' She angrily walked away to come in here to stand next to you. I figured the best thing for me to do was to let them both cool off and explain it later."

"She was upset and a little short-tempered with me," Robert admitted.

"Women! Unpredictable but we can't live without them, can we?" Stanley asked.

"Neither of us want to try. Do we?" Robert asked.

Stanley said, "No. The goal for every man is to always try to make them feel loved and needed, because they are."

"We are both on that same page, Stanley. Men have it easy compared to women. Our job in life is simple. We get a good education to earn a decent wage to support, protect, and love our families. Women are groomed by their mothers to be the mother of their children, wife to their husband, cook, taxicab driver, house cleaner, grocery shopper, tutor, accountant, maid, laundry expert, and disciplinarian."

"Well said, Robert. You might have missed a few jobs and errands women are responsible for doing, but you painted a clear-enough picture for me to know men have it easy compared to women."

"Back to our discussion about Penny. How do we get you and Penny together with Mary to clear up this understandable but very unfortunate misunderstanding so we can continue implementing our plans?"

"I believe that will require Rachel's help."

"Do you have a plan?"

"Rachel could ask Mary to have dinner with her, and while they are eating, I could walk up to their table with Penny. I would sit down next to Mary so she couldn't run away, and Penny could sit down next to Rachel."

"Clever idea, but how do we pull it off? Do you have instant access to Penny?"

"Yes. Penny has no idea what her visit today caused in my life with Mary. Penny would not hesitate to help me save my relationship with Mary."

"Especially since you are doing what you are doing to save her relationship with Mike."

"She doesn't owe me anything. You know how I am."

"I know how you are. You do not do anything expecting or wanting anything in return."

"Yep. I am just not built that way. My rewards are heavenly just like your rewards are, my friend."

Robert nodded his head and held up his thumb with a look of admiration on his face for Stanley.

"Well, we have a game plan minus the key player. We need Rachel."

"You need Rachel to do what?" Rachel asked, now only a few steps behind Stanley.

"Perfect timing. We did not hear you come in. Perhaps you two ladies do need to wear a bell," Robert answered in his raspy voice.

"You will not have to worry about a bell for Mary. She flies home tomorrow morning." Rachel narrowed her eyes into an unfriendly look as she glanced at Stanley.

"Why?" Stanley asked.

"Why? Do you really have to ask why, or do you want to see a copy of the surveillance picture of you in the elevator with your arm around some other babe?"

"Why did she not talk to me instead of assuming something was happening between me and Penny?"

"Could you not detect something was wrong between you and her when she woke up?" Rachel asked.

"No. I assumed she fainted in the room. I did not know an orderly carried her from the elevator to the bed that I saw her lying on. I assumed he was in this room at the time she fainted."

"You know what they say about assuming things?"

"Yes. I heard the definition of assume many times. Please tell it to Mary," Stanley said.

"I see your point, Stanley. Problems cannot be solved when one party to the problem runs away."

"Mary is the first romantic relationship for me. Relationships do not come with instructions. The only way I know how to be in a relationship is to be unconditionally all in. And that means totally committed with both feet on the ground, ready to work out any problems in the relationship. Relationships do not have a chance of working out when one party has one foot in the relationship and the other foot out the door, ready to walk to the nearest airport to fly away at the first sign of trouble."

"All relationships require a little work," Robert stated earnestly.

"Tell that one to Mary. She is the one who is leaving without giving me a chance to explain who the woman in the elevator is and what happened. I believe this is a reasonable request. Isn't it, Robert?"

"Yes. She will be making a terrible mistake if she flies out of here tomorrow."

"I believe Mary really loves you, Stanley. I do not know enough about her history to explain what is prompting her to choose between not talking to you about what she thinks she saw that has apparently broken her heart versus packing a suitcase and running away." Rachel raised her eyebrows and looked at Stanley, waiting for his response.

"I want a mature relationship with a woman who not only loves me but trusts me."

"We all want that, good buddy. And I believe Mary wants that too," Robert said assuredly.

"Ghosting is unforgivable to me, Robert."

"Do you think Mary is going to ghost you?" Rachel asked.

"Ghosting? What is ghosting?" Robert asked.

"Ghosting is the practice of ending a personal relationship with someone suddenly, without any explanation and without future communication. It is a horrible dating habit normally reserved for one-night stands or flings," Rachel answered while looking at Robert before she glanced at Stanley.

"Since you will be here for another two to three months before they discharge you, I am going to use some of that time to get myself mentally back together. I will not disappear too long." Stanley reached his hand down to shake hands with Robert. Glancing up at Rachel, he detected sadness in her eyes.

He watched her tilt her head slightly to one side, as though she was trying a spot a deeper sadness in his eyes. "There is nothing to read in my eyes or my mind, Rachel. I am a total blank screen after what just happened to me in my brief romantic relationship with Mary, and it will be blank for a long time. Take care of yourself and take care of Robert until we meet again. Okay?"

"Okay." Rachel sniffed back tears. "I am sorry, Stanley."

"Me too. Bye."

Before Rachel had time to reply or react to this moment, Stanley disappeared out the door.

"Boy, that all happened too quickly for me to follow. I did not know what to say or do. How do we fix this, Bobby?"

"You are asking me?"

"Yes. Talk to me about this so I can help Mary."

"How can I help you?"

"I do not know. Do you know anything about Penny?"

"Yes. What do you want to know?"

"Everything you know. Who is she? Why was she here today? Why did Stanley have his arm around her on the elevator? Does Stanley have a romantic interest in her? Does she—"

"Whoa. Slow down with the rapid-fire questions. I can only answer one question at a time. Okay?"

"Okay. I'm sorry."

"No problem. Please ask me one question at a time."

"Who is Penny?"

"Stanley and I went to medical school with a guy named Mike Spencer. Penny is his wife."

"Penny came here today for what reason?"

"Stanley was supposed to have lunch with her today but forgot about it. She waited downstairs for over an hour before she came up here looking for him. She was not too happy."

"Does Stanley have a romantic interest in her?"

"No. He agreed to have lunch with her to discuss a problem she needed his help with."

"Problem? Do you know what kind of problem she needed him to solve or help her with?"

"Why?"

"The subject matter could be very important to Mary. It would be to me."

"Seriously?"

"Yes. Why are you hedging about giving me the answer?"

"Because I do not have Stanley's permission to tell you."

"You would keep this from me?"

"May I ask you a question without you getting mad at me?"

"Try me."

"Do you think Mary will be satisfied knowing there is nothing romantic going on between Stanley and Penny."

"Hard to accept just that explanation when she saw him standing only twenty feet away from her with his arm around her."

"Stanley told me before he left that the elevator slightly jerked or jumped, throwing her off balance and into another guy. He reached his arm out to steady her, and it might have looked like he had his arm around her, but it was not like that."

"Okay. Assuming she accepts that explanation, why were they having lunch together?"

"I'm sorry. I cannot tell you without getting permission from Stanley. If you told me something in confidence, you would not want me telling it to others, would you?"

"No. Is it bad?"

"Rachel!"

"Okay. I will leave it alone, but I am not happy about it since Mary is my friend and needs to know."

"We each owe it to our significant other to talk about our concerns. Do we not?"

"You should have been an attorney. I agree. I need to speak with Mary before she boards an airplane on what could turn out to be a one way flight home with no way back into Stanley's heart."

"Love will find you when people are right for each other. Talk to her. Convince her to stay. Stanley is a solid stand-up guy. Once he closes the door on their relationship, I do not see him giving her another chance. If she stays, however, she has a chance to patch this up and live the life of her dreams with Stanley. She is at a crossroad in her love life. Her next decision will change her life."

"How committed are you to stand behind Stanley?"

"I am 1,000 percent behind Stanley. I watched him around women in our medical classes and when we socialized together enough to know he is not the same guy when he is around Mary."

"Please try to explain what you mean a little better. Your words will help me in my conversation with Mary."

"He keeps everyone at arm's length and seems to be an expert at ignoring flirtatious comments from good-looking women. He is the same in class, cafeteria, restaurants, meeting rooms, elevators, and car rides when we allowed women to ride with us to attend social events that included dancing. He rejected all female invitations for a one-night stand. He is always a perfect gentleman. Mary is the only woman he has allowed to get close enough to penetrate his armor to reveal the romantic side of him. She lives inside his heart, and that has made him more comfortable and much more relaxed than I have ever seen him."

"Wow! That is a graphic crystal-clear picture of love. Rachel exhaled a long slow steady breath of air and looked at Robert. "We have to get these two back together, Bobby."

"Do you or does she know how to get in touch with Stanley?" Robert asked her.

"No. Do you know how to call him?"

"No. I never had any reason to."

"I am going to leave you early today to spend the rest of today and tonight with Mary. I will say a prayer asking God to guide my every word to her. Please say a prayer for me." Rachel leaned down and kissed him on his lips. "Sleep well. I will see you in the morning and hopefully have Mary with me." With a heavy sigh, she said, "Bye."

"Bye," Robert replied, just above a whisper, and watched her disappear out the door.

CHAPTER 23

Mary Waits for Stanley

Robert was sitting up watching the news on his television set when Rachel walked in with a triumphant smile on her face. "Hello, early bird. You are up mighty early. Miss me?" she asked.

"Good morning, love. Yes, I missed you. You look beautiful, and contrasted with the mood you were in when you left yesterday, you now seem to be back to your chipper and bubbly self. Is there a special reason, or are you just happy to see me?" Robert spoke these words with an exaggerated smile on his face.

Rachel turned slightly to her right and pointed behind her with both hands. "She is the reason." Both of her hands pointed to Mary.

"Good morning, Robert. Do I have that same effect on you?" Mary said as she raised and lowered her eyebrows rapidly while looking at him with a big smile. "Come on, Robert, admit it."

"Okay. I will admit that it is a good morning—no, a great morning—seeing you standing here in my room. Welcome back, Mary."

"Thank you, Robert. I didn't fly home this morning, but I still have flight plans for tonight."

"I am deeply saddened by that plan. I did not sleep very well last night worrying about you."

"Worrying about me?"

"Yes. Well, Stanley and you, because of the way you looked at me yesterday through misty eyes, and your last words to me sounded like they were farewell comments. I did not want you to fly home today without giving Stanley a chance to speak with you. Your flight home could change the rest of your life."

"Can you tell me where he is?"

"No."

"No, because you do not know where he is, or no, you do not want to tell me?"

"No, I do not know where he is."

"Do you know when you will see him again?" she asked in a stern matter-of-fact voice, as though she was cross-examining him in a court of law.

"You sound just like a lawyer the way you phrased that question."

"Thank you. And your answer to my question is?"

"See. There you go again sounding like an attorney. Are you an attorney?"

"Are you purposely dancing around my question?" Mary asked, sounding exasperated.

"No. I do not know where Stanley is."

"Do you mind telling me the last thing he said to you before he left?"

"He said, 'Since you will be here for another two to three months before they discharge you, I am going to use some of that time to get myself mentally back together. I will not disappear too long.'"

"Did he say or do anything else before he walked out of this room?"

"He shook my hand and said something to Rachel."

Mary glanced back at Rachel. "Do you mind telling me what Stanley said to you?"

"No. I do not mind telling you. I was kind of in shock hearing what he did say to me. I guess I had an intense look on my face, trying to read his mind after he told us he was going away for a while. I might have had misty eyes. I can be a crybaby." Rachel half-giggled out loud, looking at Mary.

Mary did not giggle or laugh. She just cleared her throat and continued to stare at Rachel for a few seconds before she finally spoke. "And he said?" she asked this in a stern impatient-sounding voice.

"Yikes, lighten up. I am getting to it, grouch." Rachel appeared to look a little upset as she diverted her attention away from Mary's piercing eyes to look at Robert as she continued to speak to Mary.

"He said, 'I am a blank screen and will be for a long time, so do not try to read my mind.'"

"What did that mean?" Mary asked in a more demanding tone of voice.

Robert said, "Mary, we want you to be our friend. Is this how you speak to your friends?"

Mary looked at him without emotion or expression, searching her mind for the right words.

"I agree with Robert. Your questions are kind of curt. I would expect this from an attorney inside a courtroom. If you are not an attorney, you sure missed your calling. Are you an attorney, Mary?"

"Yes. It is a long story that I would rather discuss with you another day, if that is okay with the two of you? Please keep this confidential until I tell you otherwise. Okay?"

Robert said, "I cannot wait to hear that story. Your secret is safe with me. Thank you for telling me."

"Yes. Your secret is safe with me too," Rachel confirmed. "Thank you so much for telling us."

"You are welcome. I will write to you and explain everything. Now back to Stanley. Do you know what he meant with his comment to you, Rachel?"

"No. I do not know. I can only guess that he felt empty inside and very upset over losing you."

"Losing me?"

"Yes. I told him you were flying home this morning and that upset him."

"Oh boy." Mary shook her head slowly from side to side and hung her head. "What a mess," she said while looking down at her shoes. She raised her head, and while looking out the window, she took in several long breaths of air and slowly blew out each one as she tried to plot her next move. The look of sorrow unquestionably covered her face.

Robert and Rachel remained silent to give her time to sort through her thoughts. They watched her blow out long breaths of air and felt badly about the sudden unexpected turn of events in her new love life. Her eyes now had the look of hopelessness or sadness.

She blinked her eyes a few times before she turned to face Robert and Rachel. "Did he say anything else that I should know?"

"He said for me to take care of myself and take care of Robert until we meet again."

"And that is it? He then turned and walked out of our lives?" Mary looked from Rachel to Robert.

"Please tell me there is more to this story," she continued to look from Rachel to Robert like she was watching a fast-moving tennis match, hoping something different would happen. Her usual calm-looking face now looked worried. With her elbows by her sides and her arms half bent, she opened her hands with her palms facing up in front of her, looking at Robert and Rachel, asking, "What do I do now?"

"You know everything that we know, Mary," Robert told her as he raised his eyebrows, looking at her.

"Do you know how to get in touch with Stanley?" Mary asked as she looked from Robert to Rachel.

"No," they answered and simultaneously shook their heads.

"Seriously?"

"I never had a reason to call him after medical school. We lost track of each other after we graduated. I was later airlifted by helicopter to this hospital and confined to this bed before he came in to visit me."

Mary looked at Rachel, raised her eyebrows, and shrugged her shoulders, as if to say she did not have any additional information to add about the whereabouts of Stanley.

"The only reason I came here this morning was to ask Stanley one question that only he can answer. And since we do not have a positive iron-clad guarantee when or if he will return, I am in a quandary over what to do."

"How can I help you with your dilemma?"

"I am not sure you can. You do not seem to know him well enough to help me."

"Try me."

"Frankly I do not think you have the answer my heart needs to hear to persuade me to cancel my evening flight back home." She looked apprehensively at Robert and slowly shook her head from side to side, waiting for him to say anything hopeful. She refused to look away until he spoke.

"If you leave without talking to Stanley, I believe you will be saying goodbye without any hope of a relationship with him."

"Well, I hate to leave and go back home without hearing what he has to say. It is a long shot. But I am asking you to speak candidly with me and tell me anything you feel I should know. Will you?"

"I do not believe this is the time to err on the side of caution."

"Okay. Please tell me everything you think I should know about Stanley. Who is Stanley Spring?"

"Stanley Spring loves you. And every day I know about, through today, he has only loved you."

"Wow! I never expected that comment to come from you as an opening comment. I find it hard to believe that I am the only woman Stanley Spring has ever loved?"

"That is hard for a woman to believe when she meets him, but one thing I know for a fact is there never has been nor will there ever be anything romantic between Stanley and the woman you saw him with in the elevator."

"How do you know this for a fact, Robert?" Mary asked with a look of hope in her eyes.

"She is the wife of a classmate of ours. He was supposed to meet her for lunch to help her with a serious problem, but he lost track of the time when we got carried away discussing something we both want to do with you and Rachel."

"He had his arm around her in the elevator."

"You only had a fraction of one second before the elevator doors closed to form your opinion of what you believe you saw. You did not witness them walking into the elevator. The only thing you know for a fact is you saw him with his arm around her. You do not know why. Right?"

"Right. But I *do know* what I saw with my own eyes—he had his arm around her."

"This is a good example of why the experts say eyewitness testimony is sometimes the worst."

"What are you trying to say?"

"You are supplying assumptions to a one-second snapshot picture in a long one-minute story that you did not witness from the beginning to the end. Not quite fair, is it?" Robert asked.

"Maybe not. Do you have more of this story to tell me?"

"Ah, there is the lawyer side of you seeking all the facts. Good for you."

"Convince me that I am jumping to conclusions." Mary almost sounded like she was begging.

"They entered the elevator walking side by side, intending to walk to the back of the elevator when it jumped or jerked. She lost her balance and was about to bump into a much older man when he reached out his arm to steady her balance. If his arm was around her, it was not done in a romantic way."

"How certain are you?"

"I am 1,000 percent certain."

"Why did Stanley feel compelled to talk to you about his arm being around this girl on the elevator?"

"Because Rachel told Stanley that you saw him on the elevator with his arm around another woman, and this caused you to faint." Mary glanced over at Rachel.

"Yep. I did tell Stanley what you told me yesterday about why you fainted," Rachel confirmed. "Stanley felt it was important enough to tell me what really happened."

"Do you believe him?"

"Yes."

"Why?"

"Over the years that Stanley and I were together in medical school, he always kept everyone at arm's length. He was an expert at ignoring flirtatious comments from good-looking women. He was the same in class, cafeteria, restaurants, meeting rooms, elevators, and car rides when we allowed women to ride with us to attend social events that included dancing. He was never romantically involved with any woman in our classes or any woman who attended our school. And he rejected all female invitations for a one-night stand. He was always a perfect gentleman. You are the only woman he has allowed to get close enough to penetrate his armor to reveal there really is a romantic side of him. You now live inside his heart, and that seems to have made him more sociable to others, and now he is comfortable living inside his own skin."

"I do not know what I was expecting to hear, but it was not anything close to the words you just told me. I guess I have been so afraid to open my heart and unconditionally trust men that I almost made a monumental irreversible mistake by letting the most honorable decent man I have ever met get away. I may at times be dumb, but I am never stupid. Thank you, Robert."

"Stanley was afraid you were going to ghost him."

"Ghost him? Why would I ghost Stanley?"

"Please look at this from his point of view, okay?"

"Okay." Mary focused all her attention on Robert's face and prepared to listen to his every word.

"If you flew home today, as Rachel thought you might, that would leave no opportunity for you and Stanley to talk. That opens the door to the classic definition of ghosting. Right?"

"Right. Ghosting is very cruel. Isn't it?"

"Yes. If you are the one getting ghosted."

"I bet he does not have a very high opinion of me right now. Does he?"

"He loves you."

"He might not today."

"Remember, you have two major romantic things going for you."

"I cannot even think of one right now. Please give me a clue to save me from a restless night of sleep."

"You are each the other's first love."

"And the second?"

"You are the only woman he has allowed to get that close to him. You broke through his armor and touched his heart. He kissed your lips and fell deeply in love with you."

"I am the only woman that you know about. Right?"

"He has had plenty of opportunities to tell me if there was another woman in his past."

"Has he ever told you about even one other woman?" Mary asked.

"No. Wait a minute. Yes. He did worship and love one other woman."

"Now the truth comes out. Who?"

"He loved his mother." Mary playfully threw one of the marshmallows she was eating at him and burst into laughter, along with Rachel and Robert. "I love men who love their mothers."

"Well, Stanley is your man. You do not leave anything to chance with your questions. Do you?"

"No. Not wise to leave anything to chance. I try to ask everything I need or want to know."

"I am going to keep my eye on you. I know Rachel told me you were a waitress, and now I learn you are also a lawyer."

"Rachel did not lie to you. I worked in a restaurant as a waitress when I met Rachel."

"I do remember that part. And the part where she referred you to Dr. Mary Sharp to repair your front tooth. It looks like she did a fantastic job. I cannot tell which one was repaired."

"Thank you for that comment, Robert. Rachel found her first. Thank you, Rachel." Mary glanced over at Rachel and smiled.

Rachel nodded her head at Mary and smiled.

Mary laughed out loud at the sequence of events being discussed.

"It is good to see you laugh, Mary," Robert admitted as he nodded his head and smiled at her.

Rachel flashed her front teeth at Mary. I will never forget how badly my tooth was broken off before Dr. Mary Sharp fixed it. You know, every time I look in the mirror, I still expect to see my broken tooth."

Robert shook his head and said, "The shock of seeing your broken front tooth in the mirror with everything you had going on in your life must have felt like you were living your worst nightmare."

"I had to teach a class full of students the next morning and meet you for dinner the next night. Dr. Sharp calmed my anxieties and literally kept me from losing my mind."

"Do you want to share the plans you and Stanley were cooking up that involves Rachel and me?"

"I would have to kill you if I did share that plan," Robert said, smiling at Mary.

"You cannot share *any part of your plan*?" Mary asked.

"Okay, I will share one part of our plan with you."

"Thank you. Knowing part of a plan is better than not knowing any part of it."

"Stanley and I want to visit Dr. Sharp and briefly say hello and thank her for everything she has done for you and Rachel. That is all you are getting from me."

"Thank you for telling me that much of your plan and for talking with me today."

"You're welcome. I am going to take a nap now. Please go cross-examine Rachel." Robert laughed, looking at Rachel.

"Thanks, Bobby. I thought you loved me," Rachel said, laughing and looking at Mary.

"More than life itself, dear." Robert winked at her and closed both of his eyes like he was sleeping.

"Please tell me you are staying and not flying home?" Robert asked Mary.

"I am staying." Robert opened his arms for a hug. Mary leaned down to hug him and whispered into his ear, "Thank you for telling me the things you told me about Stanley. If you talk to him before I do, please tell him I will never doubt him again." Mary held onto his hand while she stood up and looked into his eyes. "You are a good man, Robert."

"Thank you. You are a good woman, Mary. Stanley is a good man who deserves a good woman like you in his life. You two will enjoy a long happy life together."

"May I quote you?"

"Yes."

"From your lips to God's ears. God brought us all together for a reason only He knows right now," Mary said this as she raised her eyebrows and tilted her head slightly with a closed-mouth smile.

"God brought us together to be blessed and be in His master plan," Rachel said, looking at her intently, as though she was soliciting a response from her.

Mary looked at Rachel with a questioning look in her eyes. Rachel could see the wheels turning in Mary's mind. Rachel did not feel like this was an uncomfortable standoff. Conversely she felt Mary was trying to decide what to do with this part of her life, so she felt God would want her to look at Mary with compassion and this understanding look in her eyes. Silently she prayed for God to give her that kind of look. Mary blinked her eyes a couple of times before she took two steps forward into Rachel's open arms. She whispered into Rachel's left ear, "I almost made the mistake of my life, did I not?"

"Almost."

"But good ole common sense encouraged me to stay here."

"Wrong. Common sense had nothing to do with your decision to stay," Rachel replied honestly.

"No? Really?" Mary tilted her head slightly, looking at Rachel, and waited for her additional answer.

"No. The Holy Spirit kept you here. It communicated with the thinking process of your brain to give you the suggestion it wanted you to follow, and you followed it. God the Holy Spirit, who is one third of the Trinity, lives in your heart and in your mind to guide you. You did good. Praise God."

"Remind me to tell you about the day the Holy Spirit talked to me inside of a courtroom. I did follow that message from the Holy Spirit, and it did change my life and the life of another person."

"Awesome. I want to hear that story. Speaking about the Holy Spirit, do you remember when we discussed the Holy Spirit with Stanley?"

"Oh, yes, I remember. Stanley called it voodoo stuff. Right?"

"Right. He called it voodoo because of the word *spirit* used in the name Holy Spirit."

"One day you and Stanley will get on your knees and give thanks to God for the Holy Spirit as it guides everything you do in your life," Rachel spoke with emotion and strong conviction in her voice.

"I did not make fun of the Holy Spirit. Did I? I don't know enough about it to do that. Please correct me if I am wrong." Mary looked away from Rachel to look at Robert before she looked back at Rachel.

"Well." Rachel looked up at the ceiling with a questioning look and back to her with only one eye.

"Come on now." Mary put both of her hands on her hips, tilted her head, and stared at Rachel in shock at what her facial expression was insinuating. Mary then glanced at Robert, who was looking at her with a blank look and a straight face that seemed to imply that he agreed with the message Rachel's face was implying that Mary did make fun of the Holy Spirit. Mary felt her blood pressure rising in anger.

They did not know how badly Mary felt betrayed by Stanley. Nor did they realize how sensitive she was to being teased, to being the brunt of a joke, or being criticized. Mary was wearing her feelings on her sleeve, especially after the incident with Stanley. It would only take one more thing, such as their teasing, for her to give Rachel and Robert a piece of her mind to end their relationship. Her pride would not allow her to ignore negative innuendoes or negative comments. She reasoned to herself that they both had this coming to them as a tsunami begged to be released as she cleared her throat to speak. Rachel lost her poker face and only beat Robert's laughter by a split second. Neither of them knew it was not a split second too soon.

Mary's eyes expanded to the size of a small plate while her mouth dropped open. She shook her head from side to side, glancing back and forth at each of their faces until she finally figured out they were only playing with her. She almost vented a lot of unjustifiable anger at them. *Wow. I better get a grip*, she thought to herself. She promised herself she would never tell them how close she came to unleashing a lot of suppressed angry feelings from the loss of her parents. Feelings even she did not know she had.

"Sorry, Mary. I could not resist. I owed you *that one*."

The three of them laughed, hugged, and exchanged high fives.

"Good one, Rachel. You had me going there for a minute. I thought I was losing what I had left of my mind."

"No. You are not losing your mind, Mary."

"Thank God."

"Yes. Thank God. God is good."

"All the time," Robert added.

"Speaking of God, may I try to explain the Holy Spirit to you?" Rachel asked.

"May I say something before you do?" Mary asked.

"Sure. What is it you want to say?" Rachel asked.

"Well, I am not ready to go into detail yet, but let me say something about what happened in my life recently pertaining to the Holy Spirit. May I?"

"This is what I was supposed to remind you to tell us. Right?"

"Yes."

"I would love to hear it."

"Me too. Count me in," Robert chimed in.

"I had an unexpected communication with the Holy Spirit when I was faced with a major decision to forgive or prosecute a young girl who was charged with two counts of vehicular homicide for causing the death of my parents. I walked over to where she sat, with her face looking down at the table, and asked her to stand up. She asked me if I wanted to hit her. She could not believe I just wanted to hug her. The death of my parents was an accident. No gun or knife involved. Just a car that any of us could have driven and any of us could be sitting where she sat waiting to be sentenced to twenty years in prison. I just wanted to hug her, but when I hugged her, a voice inside my head screamed at me, 'Help her. Do not prosecute her.'"

"I cannot imagine God giving you that option after you just lost both of your parents," Robert said.

"Wow! What in the world did you do?" Rachel asked.

"I hesitated and actually said sarcastically out loud, 'Oh yeah. I am going to ask the court to change their plans to send her to prison for twenty years and instead give her probation. Right. Sure, I will.' The girl I was hugging asked me to tell her what was going on. Before I could answer her, the Holy Spirit seemed to yell, 'Do it! Ask the court to give her probation.' I asked and they did give her probation."

"You did?" Rachel asked with raised eyebrows, looking at Robert.

"Good for you, Mary," Robert said, nodding his head up and down.

"The whole courtroom started buzzing with an unbelievable aura of excitement. That is a moment I will never forget," Mary said as her eyes got a little misty looking at Rachel.

"You are going to make me cry," Rachel said as she opened her arms and stepped closer to Mary.

They both choked back tears as they hugged and rocked back and forth. They both glanced back at Robert to see the tears that had formed in his eyes and started to slide down his face.

"Wow! I wish I could jump up out of here to give you a big hug. Bless you, Mary," Robert said with his eyes filled with happy tears and his heart filled with happy emotions.

"There is a lot more to this story about the girl you saved from prison, is there not, Mary?"

"Yes. May I tell you the whole story over dinner at our hotel?"

"Yes. Whatever you tell me, may I tell it to Bobby?"

"Absolutely. I have no secrets from Robert," Mary said, looking at Robert, then to Rachel.

"You could teach a class on just your personal experience with the Holy Spirit, Mary," Rachel said.

"While I know there is only one God, and I often hear about God being three persons or a Trinity, do you know anything about this to educate me?" Mary asked Rachel.

"I do," Rachel answered.

"Please tell me everything you know about the Trinity," Mary asked and waited with anticipation.

"I learned about God the Father, God the Son and God the Holy Spirit. This is the three persons that form the Trinity. Okay?"

"Okay. But I still do not understand how God can be three people."

"The Bible speaks of God the Father, God the Son, and God the Holy Spirit but emphasizes that God the Father and God the Son live as one true God with a Holy Spirit they can send to live within all who believe in them. Is this where you get confused?" Rachel asked.

"Yes. I have heard this enough to believe it, but I cannot explain it. How can I explain it to someone?" Mary asked.

"The problem is created when you use your human understanding to explain a heavenly being or heavenly spirit that has the ability to be everywhere at the same time. Understanding God the Father and God the son requires the faith of a child. Children accept what we tell them because they trust us not to lie or mislead them. God wants us to have this same kind of understanding about His existence that in the spiritual world is beyond human understanding. God as the Spirit can and is everywhere, which is how He is able to answer every prayer and send heavenly angels to be with us in our time of need. Trust in Him.

"I have heard some complicated definitions explaining the existence of God," Mary replied.

"Oh, you mean the one where God is three coeternal consubstantial persons or hypostases—the Father, the Son Jesus Christ, and the Holy Spirit—one God in three divine persons, right?"

"Yes. I needed someone to paint me a clearer picture of God, and you have. Thank you."

"You are welcome. I am glad I could help. I was afraid I would have to give you a detention or send you to the principal's office," Rachel said and laughed out loud.

Robert spontaneously erupted into laughter so hard at Rachel's comment, he started coughing uncontrollably. His face and neck turned beet red as he gasped for air that did not exist. Out of desperation, he pressed the call button for a nurse. Rachel saw that he was in serious trouble, gasping, heaving, wheezing, and fighting desperately for even a tiny breath of air. The only thing she knew to do was to put a cold washcloth on the back of his neck and on his forehead, but these things did nothing to get control of his coughing. Rachel was so scared she panicked and yelled at the top of her lungs, "NURSE!"

Lauren Jaco and Lisa Phillips came running into the room, well trained to handle any situation. They were assessing Robert as they approached his bedside, and without the need to speak with anyone in the room, they quickly calmed him down and brought his coughing under control.

Lauren and Lisa looked at Rachel. "You did the right thing to press the call button."

"I did not press the nurse's call button." Rachel glanced at Mary. "Did you press it?"

"No. I did not know he needed a nurse."

"I did," Robert whispered. He looked at Lauren and Lisa, then to Rachel. "She is the reason for my attack."

Lauren and Lisa looked away from Robert and focused their attention on Rachel. "Busted. He just threw you under the bus." They all laughed out loud.

"Yeah. I see how it is. Our honeymoon just got cancelled before our wedding."

"I can see now that we need to move our nurse's desk into this room where the entertainment is. You guys need to sell tickets." Lauren and Lisa made everyone laugh.

Lisa and Lauren checked Robert's vital signs before they returned to their nurses' station.

Robert breathed out a long sigh of relief. "I am not as strong as I used to be. Am I?"

"No. That was scary to me. I did not know how to help you. What caused this reaction with you?"

"You."

"Me?"

"Yes. Give Mary detention or send her to the principal's office. I never expected that from you. It cracked me up. I am sorry but it was funny to me. The teacher in you took over, and *bam*, there was the voice of authority. Go see the principal! That was so funny."

"I guess so. It made you almost choke to death." Rachel glanced at Mary. "I guess that *would be funny* to a nonteacher. Would it not?"

"Yes. It cracked me up too. My laughter suddenly stopped when I saw him fighting for air. I sure am glad you are okay, Robert. I was scared watching you gasping for air. Thank God for nurses."

"Amen, Mary. They do not pay nurses enough no matter how much they make. Nurses, firefighters, and police officers should be the highest-paid professional people in the world, the way they put their lives on the line every single day for our safety," Rachel said vehemently.

"Mary looked at Rachel for a few seconds before she spoke. "I can tell that you really believe in the power of the Holy Spirit to guide our lives. You do, do you not?"

"Yes. With all my heart, Mary," Rachel answered with a lot of emotion and feeling in her voice.

"Thank you for spending the time to talk with me about the Holy Spirit. I do believe the Holy Spirit does live inside each of us and does communicate with us to help us make good decisions. I will be more conscious of the Holy Spirit before I hastily make any decisions. We all need divine guidance."

"Good advice for everyone, Mary."

"Will you help me learn how you communicate with the Holy Spirit, Rachel?"

"Did you have something specific in mind?"

"Yes. If I am trying to make a major decision in my life, should I sit down and consider the pros and the cons out loud or silently to myself, or should I write my choices on a sheet of paper?"

"That is a good question, Mary."

"The lawyer in her strikes again," Robert said, raising both of his fists in the air.

"Does not take much to impress you does it, Robert?" Mary teased with a smile.

"I can spot professional excellence. I am keeping my eye on you." Robert smiled, looking at her.

"Hey. No talking when school is in session. You do not want to upset the teacher. Do you?"

"No, ma'am, *Uncle*," Robert said as he laughed, looking at Mary.

"I try to block out all distractions and sit in a quiet place to relax with a sheet of paper. I draw a line down the center of the page and list all the good things on one side and negative things on the other side. The important thing to do next is to embed your list of options deeply in your mind by reading your list over several times, out loud to yourself, without trying to decide what you should do. Say a special prayer asking God to help you decide what to do. Once you give this question to God to handle, do not take it back. Your job is to now focus on your daily life. While you are focused on other things in your life, your subconscious mind and your conscious mind will join together to focus on the Holy Spirit, who will then guide you to make the right decision when you need to make it. One of the options you listed on your sheet of paper will pop into your mind, and that is the one you are supposed to choose."

"For real? This method works for you?"

"It works for me every time. I tell people, 'If you need a decision from me right now, my answer is no. If you will give me some time, I will think about it and get back to you.' I avoid being rushed. I make my list and pray for guidance as I read my list of options out loud several times to embed my list of options into my mind. After I do this, I ask the Holy Spirit to give me the right answer. Once I give this to the Holy Spirit, I do not take it back. I wait for an answer. If an answer does not come to me, I was not supposed to do what I prayed for, so my answer would be no. If I am supposed to do whatever I prayed for, the confirming answer will be crystal clear in my mind. Once this is done, my job is to dismiss this from my mind and go about living my life. Surprisingly after a short period of time, when I am watching a movie or doing something else, *voilà*, the decision I should make pops into my mind to guide me. The choice I should make will be crystal clear, leaving no doubt."

"That's it?"

"That's it. Your life will be forever blessed and guided by the Holy Spirit."

"Thank you, Rachel. Now I want Stanley to walk back into this room and into my life."

"You are welcome. Let us join hands and say a prayer for God to bring the love of your life to you."

"Okay. Even if the love of my life is not Stanley, I welcome and pray for the opportunity to meet the love of my life while I am here without any commitments or schedules. Can I get an amen?"

"Amen," Rachel said, looking at Mary, then toward Robert, who nodded his head in agreement.

"Thank you both for being such special and dear friends to me. It means more than you know."

"You are very welcome, Mary. You are also incredibly special to Rachel and me."

"Do you want to join me for a walk and lunch while Bobby spends time with his therapists?"

"Yes. I would love to join you. Bye, Robert."

"Bye, Mary."

"We will see you in a couple of hours. This kiss will hold you until then," Rachel said, giggling.

"Bye, ladies. Have fun." Robert waved as they disappeared into the hallway.

CHAPTER 24

Robert and Rachel Discuss Ladybug

Robert was sitting up on the side of his bed, with his left arm lying outstretched on his movable tray table and his right hand wrapped around a glass of orange juice, watching television when Rachel walked into his room.

"Good morning, Bobby. I am impressed with the way you are improving with each new day. You must be about ready to get out of here and go home. Are you?" she asked with a big smile. She put her left arm around the back of his neck, hugged him, and gave him a brief kiss on his lips.

"Yes, I am ready to go home. And I am always better when you are here. Will you help me move this food tray out of my way so I can get into that chair?" Robert pointed to the armchair next to his bed.

"Certainly. I will even help ease you down into the chair, even though you do not need my help. I just want to feel your arms around me, even if it is going to be for only a brief minute."

Robert sat upright in his chair, looking into her eyes. "You get more beautiful every day."

"Thank you, Bobby. What a nice thing to say. I needed to hear those words this morning after my restless night's sleep or lack thereof. But I honestly believe you need an eye exam. Better yet, do not get one, or you might take too close of a look at me and run away." Rachel giggled.

"Remember what I told you. If you ever decide to leave me, I am going with you." He reached up and gently pulled her down to sit on his lap. He brushed a few strands of her blond hair back from her face and tucked it behind her ear. He observed the look of love in her eyes looking back at him, and a minisecond later, he was rewarded for his kind words by one of her more passionate kisses that stirred every dormant emotion within his body. "Wow. If we were in a hotel room instead of this hospital room, we would be *on* the bed beside us instead of sitting on this chair after that kiss."

"Notwithstanding how much I truly love you, Bobby, we will never occupy a hotel room before our wedding night. I feel the same things you do. And I want to experience the same romantic things you do. It is not all you. I will never trust myself in a hotel room with you before our wedding night. You make me feel things I have never felt before in my whole life. And I long for the night when I can ignore the natural fears all single women feel in romantic situations like this before their wedding night. I have even envisioned our life together and the beautiful children we will make together. Help me to be strong and resist these temptations. Help me guard and protect this dream that is really *our dream*. Will you help me?"

He fought to control the emotions within him that her words and kisses poked alive. His eyes were now showing the emotion his heart was feeling and that always caused the macho man within him to avoid her gaze. Seeing how her words and kisses impacted him touched her heart. She saw the veins in his neck strain as he sat with his head down, nodding. She now knew he was too proud and too emotional to speak.

"Your heart just spoke for you," she said. "Do not try to say anything. Just sit here and hold me for a few minutes. I love you so much, Bobby. Just hold me. Okay?"

He nodded his head, and using his right hand, he guided her face to rest against the left side of his neck. She folded her right arm against her body and reached her left arm around the right side of his body and closed her eyes to enjoy the comfort of being held in his arms. He leaned the left side of his face against the top of her head and closed his eyes. Robert slept for over an hour. He kissed Rachel's waiting lips and said, "You are my ladybug, Rachel. Do not ever for-get it," he whispered.

"Ah! You remembered the poem about the ladybug? Really? Do you remember it?"

"Yes. The 'Ladybug Poem' and you cross my mind often. How could anyone forget *that* story after hearing it even *once* or reading the words to the poem, Rachel?"

"Do you often think about me? Do you think about the 'Ladybug Poem' more than me?"

"You are my first thought in the morning when I open my eyes. You are my last thought at night, after you leave here to return to your hotel to sleep. You are often in my thoughts, Rachel."

"How sweet. Thank you for saying kind and nice things about me and to me, Bobby."

"Everything I tell you is true and comes from my heart."

"I want to print out the poem of the ladybug, laminate it, and put it on our home refrigerator."

"You will never need my approval to post anything. Please tell me the 'Ladybug Poem' again."

"Okay. The author of the 'Ladybug Poem' is Aileen Fisher."

LADYBUG POEM
How brave a ladybug must be!
Each drop of rain as big as she!
When large drops fall, she never sighs
Or sits and longs for sunny skies!
Can you imagine what you would do
If raindrops fell as large as you?
Could you just smile and calmly do
The work that God has given you?
Author: Aileen Fisher

"I love the words to that poem. Aileen Fisher is gifted. I will research her work to see if she has any other masterpieces we can laminate and post. And you, my dear, also have an amazing gift from God."

"I do? Please enlighten me. What gift?"

"Your plate is never too full to help people. God called you to be a teacher, and you answered His call to help hundreds of children over the years. The love within you attracted you to read the 'Ladybug Poem.'"

"You are very kind and sweet to me, Bobby. Thank you."

"My kindness to you is only a fraction of what you deserve. I could never match the kindness you show to everyone, including me."

"God blessed both of our lives the day we each decided, independently, to eat breakfast in Gallatin, Tennessee. It is a miracle we found each other when we stop to consider how busy they are during their peak hours of breakfast, lunch, and dinner. I am the blessed one to have you in my life."

"We need to make a pact or a promise to each other to always remember how we did meet and never lose sight of the fact that we met as a blessing from God. Okay?" Robert asked her.

Rachel nodded her head and whispered, "Okay."

"What do you hear from your traveling companion, Mary?"

"The other day, she went into the cafeteria downstairs to eat lunch and met a guy."

"Is there more to this story?" Robert's tone sounded like he was interested to know more.

"Yes. But I only have a bare sketchy outline without details. She now lives on a love cloud."

"That happened rather quickly?"

"Not any faster than you and me."

"Good point. Okay, please tell me what you know," Robert asked, looking at her with raised eyebrows.

"Okay. I will tell you what I know, which is not much." Rachel hesitated speaking long enough to look at him for confirmation and to be sure he wanted to hear the few details she knew about Mary.

"I am all ears." Robert winked at her and smiled.

"Mary told me she slid her tray along the railing in front of the food and drink items and stopped at the cash register to pay for her selections. She spotted empty tables to her left, and when she stepped out to walk toward them, she literally collided with this new man in her life. I am going to freeze this story right where it is now just long enough for both of us to realize how God had His hand in their meeting. I will always remember this is a similar way to how we met. I am sure we both remember that wonderful day?"

"Absolutely. God had a plan for them to meet the way they did. Awesome story so far."

"Amen. The way they met gave me goose bumps. God has a unique way of bringing people together. We cannot deny God's involvement when we consider how they met.

"Chills ran up and down my back and actually made me quiver just hearing that part of her story. Every person God creates is important to Him. And knowing He created each of us for His pleasure should make us more determined to be the best we can be to show Him our gratitude for giving us life."

"I agree with you, Rachel."

"God immediately assigns an angel to each person He creates. That one fact alone should tell each of us how much He loves us and how important we are to Him." Rachel's eyes suddenly became misty.

"Do you think our whole life is planned for us when God creates us?" he asked.

"God is love, all knowing, all powerful, and without limitations. I would not doubt that for a minute. I often wonder what prompts people to move from one state to another state. What prompts us to choose one restaurant over another like we did, and Mary did? Why do some people take weeks or months to create a deeper and more meaningful relationship beyond a friendship? Why do we choose one church over another church or one grocery store over another one?" Rachel asked and then added, "I believe the Holy Spirit lives inside each of us, and therein lies your answer as to how or why, Bobby."

"Bingo. Thank you, Rachel. I temporarily forgot about the Holy Spirit and how it governs and guides us every day. We tend to ignore thoughts that we did not consciously think about or put in our own mind. We have not learned that when we are faced with a decision that can alter our daily lives, the Holy Spirit quickly and simultaneously puts a useful thought about it in our mind to help govern and guide us. But because that thought quickly popped up in our mind before we had a chance to consciously think and put that thought in our mind, we ignore it to our own detriment. Sorry to interrupt you, Rachel."

"That is okay, Bobby. It takes time to differentiate between our own thoughts from those thoughts quickly put into our mind by the Holy Spirit. Eventually we will learn."

"Especially when those thoughts seem to be screaming at us to not do certain things. Right?"

"Right. I am glad we both listened when we got the urge to eat at the same time and place, or we never would have met. I am especially glad I listened to what I thought were my own mental instincts when the Holy Spirit urged me to take a chance on you when you asked me to, Bobby."

"The silent voice or silent conscious thought we now know as the Holy Spirit becomes our greatest trusted inner friend when we learn how to listen and follow it," Robert said with a nod, looking at her.

"Do you wonder how involved our guardian angel is when these quick decisions must be made?" Rachel tilted her head slightly, watching him.

"Yes, I have wondered about it ever since you told me about God assigning each of us a guardian angel to watch over us from the minute of our birth. I wondered if they stood in our room watching us during the night when we sleep? Do they ride with us in our car? How active are they in our daily lives?"

"I have wondered the same things you do, Bobby. I remember reading about angels catching people who fell off a ladder or fell out of a second-story home window. I have also read where people were caught in an ocean undertow and about to drown when they felt a hand pulling them to safety."

"Do you think we can become a guardian angel when we die and go to heaven?" he asked her.

"No, Bobby. Humans can never become angels. Nice thought, though, isn't it?" she asked him.

"It is just hard for me to believe anyone like Lucifer or Satan could live in heaven with God and one day become delusional enough to think he was just as good or perhaps more powerful than God."

"Yeah, look how that plan worked. Satan quickly became known to mortal men as the devil."

"How could he ever think he was just as good or perhaps better than God?" Robert asked.

"Delusional. He learned quickly from that error in judgment when God tossed him and a few of his so-called friends out of heaven," Rachel said with a big smile. "God is and always will be in control."

"Lucifer is now retaliating against God. He is said to be on the prowl with a mission to seek and recruit every vulnerable person to his dark side of life. What other tidbits do you know about him, Rachel?"

"I know he is evil and the father of lies. I pray every day for God to keep me focused on Jesus."

"This is interesting, Rachel. I am going to make new rules for everyone who comes into my room."

Nurse Lauren Jaco had been standing in the open doorway, waiting for a chance to speak but did not want to interrupt the conversation about God and the devil. She changed her mind and entered the room when she heard Robert change the topic of conversation to that of making new rules for his room.

"Oh, pray tell, King Robert. Please tell me your new rules. Do these new rules require that I bow to your throne?" Nurse Lauren Jaco asked as she walked into his room.

"Oh, hi. No. You have King Robert privileges and exempt from my new rules. I trust you are doing good."

"I feel honored, King Robert. And to belatedly answer your question, I am doing fine, thank you for asking. May your hardworking servant ask how the king is doing?" She reached for his arm to take his blood pressure and pulse. Lauren glanced over at Rachel and nodded. "Hello, Rachel. How are you doing?"

"I am fine, Lauren. Thank you for asking," Rachel answered, then glanced toward Robert.

"I am fine too. Thank you so much for asking," Robert answered.

"You are both very welcome. What kind of information is Robert wanting to learn from you?"

"He is trying to find out the identity of the new love in Mary's life?"

"Really? I thought she was an item with Stanley. No? Not him anymore?"

"No. They were just in the process of building a friendship. I believe now she feels like she was delusional to think it was more. They knew nothing about each other's likes or dislikes. He never asked about her favorite color, favorite flower, best movie, places she would love to visit, number of children she would love to have, nothing. About four months ago, when she left the hospital without speaking with him, he subsequently left the hospital and never tried to contact her, Robert, or me. After being depressed for four long months, Mary wants God to send a new man into her life.

"Do you have a husband and children?" Rachel asked.

"I have a thirteen-year-old daughter named Taigan, who has dark hair and brown eyes. She must want to be a cheerleader, the way she loves cheering at sporting events. I also have a nine-year-old son, who has blond hair and blue eyes, by the name of Braedon. He is crazy about football and baseball. Braedon's love of sports has fit in great with my boyfriend, named Justin, who loves all sports. We have been together for four years now. He is a caring man who works hard and blends in nicely with our family. When everything is in sync, we all love to travel. It is sometimes hectic finding the available time to take a break away from work to travel around the kids' school hours and their sporting events."

"You must be doing something right if Justin is still hanging in there with you and the kids after four years. Congratulations on finding your Mr. Right."

"Thank you, Rachel. Yes. We are all very happy together. Dating multiple people to find the right one when you have children is not an envious life for a single mom."

"How do you balance everything to ensure cohesiveness and have this happiness you speak about?"

"Great question, Robert. To ensure our cohesiveness and to make our time together memorable and special, we always eat dinner together and do fun things like play a board game, four nights out of each week, around our dining room table. These memories are particularly important to me as a mother. We also love traveling and praying together. Every special moment bonds us as a family. I am finally content and incredibly happy with my personal life."

"People who pray together stay together. Right?" Robert asked as he tilted his head slightly.

"I believe so, Robert. You and Rachel appear to be very close. I pray you both stay that way throughout your careers. Distractions and temptations are always around you. Women will try their best every day to get you to notice them so they can be the one to replace Rachel." Lauren looked away from Robert to look to her right to glance at Rachel.

"I love how you interact with your children and how they include Justin. I will try to emulate some of the things you mentioned into the life Rachel and I will live together. Thank you, Lauren."

"You're welcome," Lauren answered with a nod and a smile as she continued to look at Robert.

Robert smiled at her and asked, "How do we find out the name of the new man in Mary's life?"

"Why?"

"I am curious to see if I know him?" Robert replied.

"If you don't know him, perhaps I do," Lauren said as they both turned to look at Rachel.

"Good morning. Who is about to be thrown under the bus?" Lisa Phillips asked as she walked into the room and stood next to Lauren. "Please tell me what I missed," she asked, looking at Lauren.

"The name of the new love in Mary's life," Lauren answered as she turned to look at Lisa.

"New man? I thought she was involved with Stanley. Something happen I do not know about?"

"Stanley never contacted Robert, Mary, or me when he left over four months ago, so I think she moved on."

"Oh. Holding back on us. Eh, Rachel?" Lisa said with a slight giggle. "Fess up. Who is he?"

Rachel's eyes enlarged from the shock of the question being asked of her. She pressed her lips tightly together and stood there with a slight-red glow to her face, blushing. She looked at the faces of Robert, Lauren, and Lisa with a confused look on her face. "If you expect to find out his name from me, the rest of this story will stay a mystery. I will have to find out tonight from Mary and let you know tomorrow if there is another guy. Okay?"

"No. Call her. We want to know now. Give me her number. I will call and ask her," Robert insisted.

"Let it go. Let me ask her tonight. Please," Rachel pleaded.

"Lauren and I will now take your vital signs and record them before we leave. Okay?" Lisa asked.

Robert answered by saying, "Okay by me. How does my blood pressure, pulse, and temperature look today? When do I go home?"

"Your vital signs are almost textbook normal, Dr. Wilson. You have progressed nicely. Your physical therapist is ready to discharge you. And the way you eat tells me you are close to being discharged from us."

"Thank you, Nurse Lisa. You nurses have taken great care of me. I will miss you when I am gone. But for now, I am going to take a nap. Bye, ladies." Robert smiled as he climbed onto his bed and looked back to watch the nurses walk out the open door.

Rachel quickly walked back to him and gave him a brief kiss on his lips before she turned to join Mary, Lauren, and Lisa, who were waiting for her just outside the open door.

"Bye, Dr. Wilson," Lauren said with a smile.

"Bye, Dr. Wilson," Lisa said with a smile and a wave while she stood just outside the doorway.

"Bye, Ladybug. Bye, Nurse Lisa. Bye, Nurse Lauren." He flashed a big smile and waved to them before he turned to fall face-first onto his pillow.

CHAPTER 25

Stanley Finds Love with Gwen

Stanley Spring was sitting alone in kind of a hideaway corner of the hospital cafeteria sipping on a hot cup of coffee thinking back over the last few weeks of his life, when his mind drifted to Mary Shipley. He met her by chance and violated his self-imposed rules by letting her get close enough to penetrate his vulnerable heart and develop what he felt, at the time, were feelings of love for her. By conscious choice, he never allowed himself to focus his eyes on the eyes of any woman more than a brief couple of seconds, to ensure against the possibility of any romantic feelings igniting in his mind or heart before he met Mary.

Sheer exasperation caused him to blow out a long breath of air and slowly shake his head while he looked through a large floor-to-ceiling window only three feet to his left. How can life change so fast and drastically without being in a car accident or vicious argument, he wondered? *I was happy with Mary one morning, and no longer a couple in the afternoon. She suddenly left me without any conversation, to live the rest of my life with a lot of unanswered questions.* He smiled to himself when a familiar voice within his head reminded him of a message he used to live by, "Keep your distance from women, dummy."

He closed his eyes and whispered low to himself, "God, it is me. I know you have not heard from me since my childhood days, when I asked you for child things. I am learning how to communicate now with part of your Trinity, God the Holy Spirit. Please guide me in my quest to listen and obey the messages you send to me through the

Holy Spirit to mold me to be the person you created me to be. I ask this in the name of your son, Jesus."

Stanley slowly opened his eyes and knew he had miraculously received a miracle that cleared some of the cobwebs from his mind. He saw his brief relationship with Mary and knew now that it lacked one crucial and essential ingredient: friendship. Without a solid friendship where each party knows a lot about the other person, the relationship is usually doomed to fail. *Our relationship could never be classified as each other's first love. We liked each other but never had a prior love experience with anyone. We did not know how it felt to be in love with someone. Our time together was usually spent in a hospital room in front of other people. We never spent any time alone to take a drive, play a game, or watch a movie together. We were a long way from anyone classifying our relationship as each other's first love.*

I hope Mary sees our brief relationship the way I do. Notwithstanding any of these thoughts, she has a big issue to work through if she fainted over my arm being around another woman in a crowded hospital elevator. Jealousy will kill every relationship. Trust must be in the heart of each person for any relationship to coexist, without one person trying to control the other. People who truly love someone will not only trust them, but build them up, make them laugh, and make them feel loved unconditionally.

Sitting here trying to find answers to matters of his heart made him remember when he was a kid and fascinated with just a picture and a model of the human heart. Ironically the passage of time did not dwindle his love and fascination of the human heart. He recalled cutting out pictures depicting different views of the human heart and taping them to the inside of his bathroom and bedroom doors. In strategic places inside his closet and on the walls of his bedroom, he taped colorful pictures of the human heart to view and enjoy daily. The thought that kept him inspired and motivated daily was his visualizing wearing a long beautifully monogrammed white coat that had the name "Dr. Stanley Spring, MD, Cardiologist," in black letters above his heart.

"Compete in sports, and you will compete in life" was a common phrase that he heard almost daily from his dad. While Stanley had zero interest in playing a sport to become a professional athlete, he did play a lot of baseball, basketball, and football when he was a student in high school and in college.

God did gift him with a photographic memory. Words he read were forever etched into his brain and available for him to instantly recall. All he needed to do was close his eyes for just a few seconds to allow his mind to retrieve the words he wanted to recall. His mind would see the page number, and the exact words, like he was holding the book in his hands and reading the words he wanted to recall.

Dr. Gwen Greyson walked into the cafeteria and saw Stanley sitting alone at a table, staring out the window. She walked over to him and said, "Please tell me how to get assigned to your team so I can find time to sit alone and relax like you do during a busy day." She smiled and raised her eyebrows.

Stanley stood and smiled back at her. Perhaps for the first time since knowing Gwen, he looked into her eyes longer than customary for him, before he asked, "How are you doing, Gwen?"

"I am doing okay. Thank you very much for asking me. How are you?"

"Great."

"Great? Just great?" She looked at him suspiciously and narrowed her eyes to look at him more intensely. "We have known each other too long for you to sneak that one by me. Care to talk about it?"

Stanley rolled his eyes and shook his head. "Even you wouldn't believe this one."

"I can rule out women immediately, so let me think about this for—" She stopped wondering when she saw his facial expression. "No way. You! Really! A woman? Please tell me everything." She giggled out loud as she sat down without an invitation and looked at him with her eyes enlarged and her eyebrows raised, waiting to hear all the intimate details about a woman in Stanley's life. "Talk to me. I want all the intimate details. Don't leave anything out, or I will haunt you." Gwen giggled again.

"Why do you want to know about my love life?" Stanley said as he sat down across from her.

"Why?"

"Yes. Why?"

"Because I care," she replied honestly and suddenly wished she had not used those words.

Stanley had always prided himself on his ability to never hold the gaze of a female more than a quick second or two to avoid close intimate relationships, but today, he could not force his eyes to look above, down, or away from the tender look he saw in her beautiful green eyes. *She is beautiful*, he thought to himself. His mouth opened, and spontaneously, out came the word, "Wow!" He had no time to think of a reply that would make sense or seem intelligent to her, so he just said, "Well, in my defense, you have never told me anything about your love life?"

Gwen could not resist. She had to ask, "Why did you just use the word *wow* when looking at me?"

"Is this your clever way to avoid my question?" Stanley asked as he smiled and laughed nervously.

"This is the first time in almost five years I heard you laugh. You should laugh more often."

"I guess that requires reasons to laugh. I normally do not have any reason to laugh."

"Well, we will have to fix that."

"I would welcome any opportunity," Stanley admitted, while his eyes continued to focus on her beautiful green eyes.

"Honestly, Stanley? Would you?"

"Yes. I believe so."

"Whoa. There is a long distance for the mind and heart to travel from believing to knowing. Do you know which one you mean?"

"May I answer your question after you answer my question?"

"I will answer it now. My answer to your question is, you never asked me," Gwen answered honestly, and for the first time in five years of knowing him, his eyes were focused on her eyes without looking away. She remembered he never did look into a woman's eyes longer than a brief second. Not even when she danced with him. Her heart instantly liked Stanley and, over several years, fell hopelessly in love with him. Seeing him look at her without looking away made her heart react like it did when they worked together on class assignments in med school. Her love for him never faded after med school. Her love intensified for him over the last year they worked together as medical doctors. Her heart belonged to Stanley Spring, and she would wait the rest of her life for a chance to be held in his arms and to be the intimate significant other in his personal life. She was all in. She loved him dearly and unconditionally.

Stanley allowed his eyes to slowly look her over from head to toe. Today he saw what his college classmates raved about when they spoke to him about her. She is an extremely beautiful woman, thirty years of age, 5'5" tall, weighs 128 pounds, neatly wrapped inside a well-conditioned athletic killer body. He loved the way she styled her blond hair to accentuate her gorgeous green eyes. She is a well-spoken conservative woman who worked alongside him for four years on medical school projects. They were and are very compatible and familiar with some of each other's likes, quirks, and idiosyncrasies. Neither of them discussed their personal lives with each other or with anyone else through four years of medical school. While they were very friendly, they kept each other at arm's length, except the few times they danced together when their med class got together on short social events. His eyes never saw her the way they see her today, and he wondered how he spent four years in med school interacting and working alongside of her without really seeing her the way he sees her today. *No man in his right mind could ever ignore her the way I did.* Any man in his right mind would consider himself to be the luckiest man alive to have her in his life even as a friend. If she were his wife, he would think he had died and was now living in heaven. *Wow. Where did that thought of wife come from?* he wondered.

"Hello. Earth to Stanley. Where did you go, Stanley?"

"Sorry. I was traveling back down memory lane to our med school days. Sorry. Thank you for your answer to my question. If I had asked, you say you would have told me. For real?"

"In a heartbeat. How about that answer? As we both sit here on a path to become licensed cardiologists in a heartbeat. What a hoot. Eh?"

Ignoring her comment, he asked, "Why would you have told me about your love life?"

"Do you really want me to crawl out on a thin ledge to answer that question?"

"Yes," Stanley answered.

"Why?" Her heart immediately started pounding a little faster, just like it did when she was in med school dancing, sitting, or standing close to him. She nervously ran her tongue over her lips like a woman would do if she was expecting or hoping to be kissed. Today was the first time they ever sat down and talked about anything personal. She wanted to hear his answer before she foolishly said things she might regret.

"You do not really want *me* to crawl out on that same thin ledge with you. Do you?" Stanley asked.

"Yes." Oh, how she wanted to tell him how she had gradually fallen in love with him over the last five years, but she had too much pride to crawl out on that ledge today without knowing if she would be crawling into welcomed territory. Transferring to another hospital would be her only option if she made a fool of herself. "And while you are crawling, please tell me why you said wow to me earlier."

"Because…" Stanley started and quickly stopped talking to carefully choose his next words. He liked how cheerful Gwen was with lay and professional people, and he loved being around her. Today he was surprisingly awestruck sitting here, looking at her. *How did I miss this?* Unconsciously he shook his head from side to side while his eyes traveled up to her blond hair, down to her lips, and back up to her eyes. *Mary opened my eyes and opened my heart to unfamiliar romantic feeling of love before she dumped me and ran away.* After that happened, he promised to leave his mind open and his heart ready to love the next woman God put in his path. Now he wondered if God had answered his prayer by sending him Gwen. *She is perfect in every way. Witty with a charming personality, love and kindness in her heart, beautiful smile, natural beauty, gorgeous green eyes, and a well-conditioned sexy-looking body.* Just as he was ready to answer her question, she got up from the table and started to walk away. "Gwen."

"I am going to get a glass of ice water. Maybe then you will be ready to answer my question?"

Stanley had no chance to respond before she walked away. His eyes quickly scanned up and down her body. Spontaneously he blew

LOVE WILL FIND YOU

out a short breath of air and said, "Wow. She worked by my side for *years*, and I even danced with her a few times over our four years of med school together and never saw her as being a beautiful woman with a body that would turn any man's head. Why didn't she date another medical student? Was she holding out for me? If so, why me, Lord?"

He got up like a gentleman when she returned to the table to sit back down across from him. He sat down when she took her seat. "Thank you, sir." She looked at him and smiled.

"You are very welcome." Stanley smiled back at her while raising his eyes to look at her.

"Miss me?" she asked jokingly as she took a sip of water, followed by a mouthful of ice chips to chew on.

"Wow!" without forethought, again, he impromptu blurted out this same word—*wow*—and felt embarrassed. He was mesmerized by seeing the kindest look he had ever seen looking back at him through female eyes. He knew now that his two-second rule saved him from dating and falling in love before today. He felt his heart beating at an alarming rate. The voice within his head whispered, *Gwen is my gift to you. Protect, cherish, and love her always.*

"Please tell me why you again just said the word *wow* when you looked at me?"

He was now ready to obey the voice within his head and to declare his love for Gwen when he answered her with one word, "*You.*"

"Me? Would I be asking too much for you to be more specific?" Gwen asked.

"That would require me to be blatantly honest with you. Are you sure you want this from me?"

"Yes," she answered honestly, just above the sound of a whisper, looking nervously at him.

"Do you know what you are asking of me?" Stanley asked hesitantly.

"I believe so."

"I could always find out by asking you a direct question." He watched her intently.

"That is one way." She swallowed another mouthful of water and tapped the outside of her glass to allow a few more ice chips to slide down the glass and into her mouth. She looked up, smiling at Stanley.

"Will you be blatantly honest without playing games?"

"I am getting too old to play games. Aren't you?" Gwen answered while chewing on ice chips and watching him fidget in his chair, getting ready to ask her his big question.

During his silence, she tried to guess which question he would ask her. She did not have a clue.

"Do you love me?" Stanley asked.

Gwen spontaneously opened her mouth in total disbelief at his question. She sprayed ice chips across the table, into Stanley's face, and onto his white medical coat. She sat there staring at him with a shocked look on her face. She put her right hand over her heart and grabbed for napkins with her left hand to hand them across the table for Stanley to wipe the water from his face and off his medical coat. "Talk about *Frank* and *Earnest*? Hello, *Frank*." She laughed embarrassingly at her comment and felt totally embarrassed. She watched him wipe the ice and water from his face and off his medical coat. "I'm sorry. I never expected that question from you. You caught me totally off guard. Please forgive me." She sat there with a half-smile and questionable look on her face that revealed to him that she was not sure what she should do next.

"I am the one who should be asking for your forgiveness, Gwen. Please forgive me. I asked you a question normally reserved for a much deeper relationship. I am like a fish out of water when it comes to relationships. I don't know how to be in a relationship. Will you help me?"

"Who do I help you with in your relationship?" Her heart was now beating faster than it ever had before as she waited anxiously for him to answer her question. Stanley was now sitting back in his chair, away from the table. Her arms were outstretched more than halfway across the table toward Stanley, with the palms of her hands facing down on the table. Her face was above her arms, and more than halfway across the table, when Stanley decided to lean forward in his chair. His face was now only about six inches to the right of her face.

"You." He leaned in toward her and lightly kissed her lips. His kiss was not offensive nor an intrusion into her professional or private life. Conversely it was an answer to a daily prayer of hers for five years, and today, finally, God answered her prayers. Without hesitation, she kissed him back. She was stunned, not only by his kiss but by her own impromptu impulse to kiss him back. She coiled back by removing her arms from the table and sat back in her chair. Her face must have looked flushed from the way her heart was now racing. Overthinking what just happened instead of remembering he kissed her first, she allowed herself to feel embarrassed by believing she would now have to tiptoe around him the rest of her career. She looked to her left and behind her to see who witnessed one of the biggest mistakes of her career. She needed time to think. She had to get away from the man she truly loved. *One more minute, and I'm out of here*, she thought to herself as she turned slightly to her left and put her left foot out to make a fast exit before she said some things she would regret that would permanently destroy any hope of a future relationship with him. Just as she was about to get up, he put both of his hands on the top of her right arm that was still resting on the table to prevent her from getting out of her chair.

She shot a stern look at him that sent a message to leave her alone. Her mouth was open without any words coming out. Her eyebrows were still raised when he said, "Please let me speak first. Okay?" He did not know her feelings were hurt. Nor did he know she was about to run away. He looked at her and swallowed hard. Just before he began to speak, he saw her mouth open, so he waited on her to speak.

"Please say whatever you need to say before I go. Just as the song says, 'You have five minutes.'"

"Okay. Hey, I love that song too. Funny you would reference that song now."

"Nothing about this is funny to me right now, Stanley." She glared at him.

"Okay. I'm sorry. I want to answer your earlier question. Today, for the first time in more than five years, I looked at you longer than my two-second rule, and I spontaneously and unintentionally said the word *wow*. The word just popped out of my mouth. Why? Because I saw *you* for the first time. Flashbacks came to me earlier today, during the times you were saying, 'Hello, Stanley. Where did you go?' I remembered the way you graciously spoke with kindness to both students and people of authority. I admire everything about you. I believe you are a beautiful person on the inside and on the outside. I love you, Gwen Greyson."

His words hypnotized and froze her in place. She continued to stare at his mouth, wondering if he had more to say to her. In her wildest dreams, she never envisioned hearing Stanley Spring tell her that he loved her and that he felt she was beautiful. She waited five years for him to show any interest in her.

Stanley took advantage of her silence to continue speaking. "I never allowed myself to notice any females during med school. I refused to do so until I passed my medical boards to become a medical doctor and started to work in my chosen specialized field of cardiology. But today, with my blinders removed, and I saw the real you, I wondered if it was too late for me. I had flashbacks of dancing with you in medical school, and I tried to remember how it felt holding you in my arms. I cannot believe I avoided loving you in medical school and, again, over the last year working with you here at the hospital. I have now crawled out here, on the proverbial limb, without a safety net because I believe you are worth the risk of a heartbreak if you leave me dangling. I will never regret crawling out here. A chance to love you, and hopefully for you to love me, is well worth this risk. It is not like we just met. We have known each other and worked together for five long years. A long solid history of working together and years of having fun together. My heart and I love you unconditionally, Gwen Greyson."

Tears had filled her eyes and started sliding down her face and onto her white medical jacket as she continued to sit there, listening to his words. God chose today to surprise her by answering hundreds of her daily prayers over the last five long years. Noticing that Stanley had stopped talking, and it appeared her romantic life was about to finally change, she swallowed hard and ran her tongue over her dry lips and looked up into his eyes and stared at him through her tear-filled eyes

"Please say something," Stanley asked softly.

"I now know with certainty that God does answer prayers." She paused to sigh and blow out a long breath of air before she wiped happy tears from her eyes. She looked across the table at him. "Okay, I will crawl out on that thin ledge with you. You want honesty? I will give you honesty. I fell in love with you years ago and promised myself that I would wait for you, no matter how long it took for you to notice me. I knew before you held me or kissed me as the woman of your dreams that you would always be my *first love*. I cried myself to sleep many nights, but I will not tonight." She forced a smile to spread across her face. "Thank you for your kind words and the gift of your love for me."

"Thank you and thank God," Stanley said just above a whisper. "I was afraid I had missed my chance to win your love. I know we danced together in med school, which means I held you in my arms while we danced, but I cannot remember how it felt holding you."

"Do you want to find out now?"

Stanley stood up as he opened his arms and stepped toward her. "You will never have to ask me twice to hold you," Stanley said as she walked two steps into his arms.

Gwen feared her heart might come through her chest wall the way it raced with these feelings of love. Never in her wildest dreams did she ever envision today would be the day she would be held and kissed by Stanley Spring. "Thank you, God," she whispered out loud and unintentionally into Stanley's left ear.

"Ditto for me, too, whatever you are giving thanks for." They both laughed as their lips met.

"I will always try to hug you with my face on the left side of your face so our hearts are touching," she said.

Hollywood movie producers would pay a fortune to film this spontaneous romantic love scene where two hearts were drawn together like a magnet in search of love to make their dreams come true.

Stanley was not just any man to Gwen. Stanley, to her, was the crème de la crème of men and the man of her dreams. "Please pinch me so I know this is real and not just a dream," she whispered to Stanley.

"It is *me* who should ask *you* to pinch *me*. *You* are the real prize in our relationship. You are the whole enchilada. You are the real deal. I am a little slow when it comes to love, but eventually, I would have figured it out, and if you were with someone else when I did, the depression would have probably come close to killing me. I almost let you get away," he whispered into her ear.

His words caught her by complete surprise and rendered her speechless as they touched her heart in a big way. She felt overwhelmingly happy and felt like shouting joyfully. She wanted every woman to feel this kind of love.

She impulsively reached up and gently pulled his face down to give him a special kiss that she held in her heart for five long years. She held nothing back in this kiss that spoke volumes about her love for him. When their lips parted, they stood silently exploring in rapid fashion the other's eyes, hair, and mouth before they simultaneously opened their mouth at the same time to utter one word, "*Wow.*"

It only took one quick second for this word to register before they both roared with laughter, as though one of them had just told a funny joke.

"The word *wow* is now going to be our secret word to always make us reminisce and smile."

"I like that idea, Stanley. You do realize it will be hard for us to top that kiss?" Gwen said as she tilted her head slightly, looking at him and waiting for his reply.

"But we will. The love we have for each other will ignite our passionate emotions to top that kiss." Stanley smiled at her and blinked his eyes rapidly. "I have an idea. Why don't we go away for the weekend somewhere?"

"Thanks, but no thanks. Nice try."

"What does that mean?" Stanley asked with a shocked look on his face.

"It means I will never sleep with you without hearing the words *I do* in front of a preacher. Remember, I am getting too old to play the games lovers play."

"Women," Stanley said exasperatedly as he blew out a long breath of air.

"Oh, I get it. Please listen closely to me for just one minute. You have other options, Stanley."

"Options? Oh, you mean options to date another woman without limitations?"

"Ah, I see you are aware of other options. Use those option available to you if you want or expect that in any women you date before marriage. And before you say anything, I do understand. Most men want the whole enchilada because they are more impatient than women. Once a woman says she loves a man, bingo, the magic word has been spoken, and a man expects and wants a complete relationship that includes sleeping with the woman in his life. I get it. I do not go along with it, but—"

"Whoa. Stop. Time-out. I am not most men. I do not want to sleep with you."

"You do not? Oh great! Now you are going to tell me you are gay?"

Stanley laughed out loud while looking at Gwen's disappointed face. "No. I am not gay."

Gwen shook her head from side to side and smiled sheepishly at him. "Well, I did not know."

"No problem. I do want to sleep with you but not before we get married. You are not a sleep-around woman, and I am not looking for an affair. I want to settle down and raise a family with you."

She pushed back slightly from him far enough to look into his eyes. "Who are you? What have you done with Stanley?" She paused to laugh. "Thank you. I can finally relax around a man, and I am glad that man is you."

"Me too. I will be a perfect gentleman. But be warned. I will turn into a tiger on our wedding night."

"Women dream about a special day in their lives when the man of her dreams drops down onto one knee to ask her to marry him. Based on the subject matter of our conversation, is this your clever way of bypassing that romantic question women wait a lifetime to hear a man ask her?" Her heart began to race rapidly as she held her breath, eyeing him and waiting patiently for him to answer.

"I cannot sidestep that question, eh?" She noticed that his eyes seemed to be smiling at her.

"Not something that important, Stanley. Every girl grows up dreaming and hoping one day she will be asked that question. Is this my day?"

"Conditionally."

"Conditionally? What in the world does that mean?" She wrinkled her forehead and looked at him.

Stanley laughed as he gently placed each of his hands on her shoulders. "Conditionally means my heart wants me to ask you to marry me now and not wait until I have an engagement ring in my hands to ask you. I want to get on one knee and ask you to marry me now with the understanding that I, or hopefully we, can shop for your engagement ring tonight. That is why I said conditionally."

"You can wait until you have the ring you want me to wear if you prefer. I have waited five long years to hear you ask me. We can wait, unless you really want to ask me today. Do you?"

"Yes. I do. May I?"

Suddenly her heart was racing excitedly like a kid gets at Christmastime. "Yes," she blurted out.

"I have not asked you yet." They both burst into laughter after she yelled the word *yes*. He got down on one knee and reached out his hand to take her left hand into his two hands and looked up into her eyes. "Gwen Greyson, will you complete my life and make me one of the happiest men on earth by agreeing to be my wife? Will you marry me?"

"Yes! Yes! Yes! I will marry you." She cringed and looked around her to see who she disturbed with her outburst. She waved to a few tables across the room. "Sorry."

Stanley stood up and looked into her eyes for only a brief second before their lips met.

Word had quickly spread earlier like wildfire about Gwen and Stanley sitting closely together in the cafeteria. A small group of doctors and nurses who heard about their meeting rushed to claim their viewing position from the upper wing of the cafeteria. They stood quietly for the last twenty minutes, watching the two people they loved and respected the most find love. Over the last five years, Gwen tried hopelessly to hide her love for Stanley from her medical school classmates and her medical team at the hospital, but she was not able to hide this kind of love that seemed to radiate from her heart and shone brightly in her eyes. Her eyes gave away a secret she mistakenly thought was her closely guarded secret.

She did not have a clue her coworkers were talking and saying loving things behind her back, such as, "She has been in love with Stanley for almost five years now. How can we help these two find each other?" Today they were watching Gwen and Stanley not only find each other but find a special kind of love only God gives to deserving people.

"You two get a room," someone yelled from the overhead balcony group. The laughter and cheers that followed the words *get a room* sounded like a large stadium crowd cheering for their favorite team.

Stanley and Gwen were frozen in place, locked into each other's arms, watching this small body of people clap, cheer, and yell things that touched their hearts and moved them emotionally. They held each other close and continued to look up at the people who viewed them as two deer caught staring into bright headlights of an automobile, as they laughed hard and pointed at them playfully.

"No use fighting it or trying to hide our love for each other now," Gwen whispered into his ear. I am not ashamed to love you." She watched his face and waited anxiously for the longest ten seconds of her life, wondering if he would be ashamed to love her publicly.

Stanley did not make her wait much longer for his answer when he immediately waved to the group and put his left thumb in the air as a sign of victory or triumph to show that he had won her love. He then shocked the entire group when he leaned down and kissed her lips. He drew back from her far enough to look into her eyes before he said, "I will never be ashamed to show my love for you, Gwen."

Seeing his public expression of love for her made the same lips he just kissed quiver. Instantaneously she pressed her lips tightly together and nervously sucked in a big breath of air as her defense mechanism to help her hold off the biggest tsunami of happy tears these people would ever see. She has never felt this happy, and without any prior experience to know how to react to this kind of attention in public, she felt like she was in a raft floating in deep water without an oar. Frantically she searched her mind for a prior happy experience to emulate that feeling and experience to keep her from making a fool of herself but quickly realized her past was void of prior happy public experiences. "Please help me, Lord."

Stanley looked down when he heard her speak these words and saw that her eyes had filled with tears, and one tear had just started to slide down her face. Fortunately she was not facing the upstairs group. He cupped her face in his hands and whispered, "I am going to hold you in my arms until that group goes away. Okay?" She blinked away more happy tears as she shook her head in agreement.

He leaned down and lightly kissed her forehead before he wrapped his arms around her and held her close. He glanced upstairs at the smiling group of supporters and simultaneously lifted his right thumb into the air and waved goodbye to the group. They waved back to him and blew kisses as they turned to exit the cafeteria. They were witnesses to how love found Stanley and Gwen.

"Coast is clear, my dear. Our admirers have vacated the premises. You are now all mine." He smiled.

"Thank you. I have waited five years to hear you tell me that I was all yours. And for your act of kindness in helping me with our admirers, I owe you one."

"I will never keep score. You will never owe me for doing anything for you."

"Me neither," she answered honestly. "I waited a long time to hear words of love from you."

"Which words?"

"I am all yours. I confirm to you I am truly all yours."

"Really?" He rapidly raised and lowered his eyebrows with a mischievous look in his eyes.

"Down, tiger. Besides, did you hear it? No. Neither did I."

"Hear what?"

"I now pronounce you man and wife. Did you hear it?" She giggled as she dried her eyes and smiled.

He stared at her for several seconds before he opened his mouth to speak, "Old Mister Webster could never define what's being said between your heart and mine."

"Oh! I love that song by Keith Whitley. I love all the words. Do you know the words?"

"I have heard them. And I love the song. I bet you know all the words. Do you?" Stanley asked.

"Yes. I do. The name of the song is 'When You Say Nothing at All.' It is a beautiful song."

"Your audition time is now, my dear. The stage is yours. Sing a verse," Stanley urged.

"The smile on your face lets me know that you need me. There's a truth in your eyes saying you'll never leave me. A touch of your hand says you'll catch me if ever I fall. Now you say it best when you say nothing at all. How is that?" Gwen asked with a big smile on her face.

"I love the song, and I especially love listening to you sing it. The sound of your lovely voice is mesmerizing. You are multitalented, my dear. Among other things, you do sing beautifully."

"Thank you, Stanley. Do you think I am just being silly by wanting to make this song our song?"

"No. Our hearts will always react favorably to this song, and to me, that is both precious and sweet."

"Thank you, Stanley.

"You are welcome."

"Do you mind if we sit for a few minutes and talk before we head back to our labs?"

"No. Good idea." They both sat down on the same side of the table.

"I am going up to the counter and get a glass of ice water. May I bring you anything?"

"No. I am good. Take your time."

"Did you miss me?" She giggled as she watched Stanley respectfully stand until she sat down.

"Yes. I like it when you are with me or near me. Do you drink a lot of water every day?"

"I drink eight glasses daily Your prior comment was a sweet thing to say. Thank you."

"You are welcome. You are going to be a good influence on me."

"I hope to be," Gwen answered honestly.

"I believe you will be, Gwen."

"Me too. Stanley, I am curious, what made you realize you loved me today?" she asked.

"I tried hard to resist loving you or anyone by not looking at you longer than a couple of seconds."

"We all talked about you a lot in med school. Girls were so frustrated with you for not noticing them. They literally threw themselves at you. I watched them do it repeatedly. So why me? Why today?"

Stanley now knew that he will one day tell her all about Mary and how she opened his eyes and touched his heart before she suddenly dumped him and ran away without giving him a chance to experience the feeling of being in love. Mary was a friendship that fell apart before there was any real chance for love. Lovers talk about having that wow feeling *when they meet the love of their life. Women talk about feeling butterflies in their stomach that made them feel giddy. He felt nothing with Mary. Today unmistakenly he felt love in his heart every time he looked at Gwen.*

"Sorry. Another trip down memory lane that I will tell you about one day. To answer your question, I get these thoughts from time to time within my head that I believe are thoughts of divine intervention that come directly from God. One day, I will explain this in more detail."

"Okay. I would love to hear about it, especially if these thoughts come to you from God."

"May I explain this to you tonight over dinner?"

"Absolutely. But could you possibly answer the one question I just asked you, now?"

"Yes. I am sorry. Today when you sat down in front of me, the voice within my head told me, 'The woman sitting across from you right now is my gift to you.' I looked into your beautiful green eyes longer than my typical two seconds and impulsively blurted out the word *wow*."

"Today?"

"Yes. But it is much deeper. Let me briefly explain a little more to you now. It's important. Okay?"

"Okay. I would love to hear more."

"When I looked at your beautiful green eyes today, my heart took me on a trip down memory lane, reliving all the times we spent together in med school. I was on this mental trip down memory lane when I got distracted from our previous conversation, which caused you to say, *'Hello, earth to Stanley.'* I was trying to remember how it felt with your face against mine and how it felt holding you in my arms when we danced. I remember wishing those nights would never end."

"I wish you would have told me how you felt. I would have slept better and lived my life without some of my anxieties. I always worried about someone else loving you instead of me."

She never dreamed this would happen again when she picked up her glass of water and swallowed a big mouthful and began chewing on ice chips, listening to him say, "If you had found someone else and were not available to be in my life after I opened my heart and poured out my love for you, I would have purchased a mule."

"Why would you purchase a mule?"

"I would bend over once every morning and once every evening to allow it to kick my butt for allowing you to slip away."

It only took a fraction of a second for his comment to register in her mind. Her burst of laughter could be heard throughout the cafeteria while she, once again, sprayed ice chips all over him. Stanley laughed so hard at the cute expression on her face, he was immediately paralyzed and unable to move out of the way or lift his hands to deflect the barrage of ice chips being sprayed against his face. When they finally stopped laughing, they shook their heads, marveling over how God had brought them together in med school and kept them together into their careers to enjoy moments like this, until love found them.

"Ice chips are now your secret weapon." And with Stanley's comment, they both burst into laughter. Stanley was feeling the happiest he has felt in a long time. Gwen's earlier comment about giving him something to laugh about just registered on his mind to make him realize she has given him many reasons to laugh. Unlike his brief relationship with Mary, he had slowly built a solid friendship over several years with Gwen before he ever realized he was in love with her.

Gwen helped him remove a few ice chips, and giggled like a schoolgirl. She put the chips into a cup and gave Stanley a big smile. "I will keep a full cup close by just for you." She loved how her eyes were getting accustomed to romancing with his eyes.

"You have made this day memorable and one of the best days of my life, Gwen. This day jumps ahead of Santa Claus and the Easter Bunny. It may also match my graduation from medical school and passing my medical boards. I will always have your back and try to show you how much I love you."

"You have taken some of the same words right out of my mouth." She saw Stanley smile like he had just thought about something funny. "Go ahead. Say it." She smiled at him and waited.

"Surprised there was any room in your mouth with all those ice chips." He laughed hard out loud.

"Cute." Gwen removed a handful of ice chips from her glass and playfully threw them at him.

Stanley laughed. "What did I ever do that made you want to wait five years to be in my life?"

Gwen pointed to her chest. "My heart jumped out of my chest five years ago to be with your heart. I was waiting for it to return with your heart to live in me forever."

His facial expression and his sudden quiet demeanor told her that the words she just chose to say to him impacted his heart, leaving him speechless. He would later say that her words were the sweetest words ever spoken to him by a female. Her words would live in his heart forever. With love in his eyes, he looked at her and said, "Old Mister Webster could never define what's being said between your heart and mine."

"Our song does say it all, doesn't it?"

"Yes. Thank you for choosing our perfect song."

"You're welcome. I never dreamed, when I woke up this morning unattached, that I would return to my home in a relationship with you. Our romantic relationship is solidly built on a five-year friendship. I feel like I have known you forever. We are both so blessed."

"May I buy you a nice dinner at a place of your choosing, tonight?" Stanley asked with his head slightly tilted to one side, with one eyebrow slightly raised, waiting for her to answer him.

"Yes. May I have a hug before we go back to work the rest of this day?"

"Absolutely." Her heart started to race with the mere thought of being held in his arms again. She envisioned the day when she would no longer need to hold her emotions back when they kissed. She smiled to herself when she visualized the passion she would put into their wedding-night kiss that would even make her own knees buckle and him needing oxygen.

"What were you just smiling about?"

"I promise to tell you one day, but not today. It is a woman thing." She smiled.

"May I have the subject matter so I will remember how to ask you later?"

"A wedding-night kiss." He started to speak when she held up her hand. "No questions."

"Tonight is a big night in both of our lives. Once you select the engagement ring you would like to own, I want to ask you again to marry me so I can simultaneously slip the ring onto your finger and stare at it, and you, all night.

"Your term *all night*, and every future night, will never include a sleepover until our marriage."

"I would not have it any other way, my dear."

"Just checking. I am overwhelmed with the privilege to pick out my own engagement ring. This is a genuinely nice touch, and I do thank you, but I will not be awestruck over a ring to relax my principles."

"Just for the record. I will never expect or want you to relax your principles. I want our wedding night to be special, so I will never ask you to break that rule."

"Okay again, who are you? What did you do with Stanley?" She laughed out loud, looking at him.

Stanley folded his arms across his chest before he looked defiantly at her. "You will have to beg me to stay overnight at your house before we get married."

Gwen's eyes smiled at him. "Are you trying to use reverse psychology on me?"

"You are too smart for that one, eh?"

"I will give in and beg you to stay with me all night long on our wedding night. Deal?"

"Deal."

"May I walk you back to your lab and wait for you to come get me when you are ready to leave?"

"Yes. I would like that. Plus it will give everyone something to talk about." They both laughed.

Stanley turned slightly toward the exit before he reached his left hand down to hold her right hand with their fingers intertwined. Their hands fit together perfectly. Stanley now believed God had created Gwen for him to love and for him to protect her the rest of his life.

Gwen closed the door to her office and sat on a cushioned chair behind her desk. She placed her elbows on her desk, interlocked her fingers, closed her eyes, and rested her forehead against the tips of her fingers as a tsunami of happy streamed down her beautiful face. She took in a big breath of air and slowly blew it out as she continued to shake her head in total disbelief of what has now proven to be the most wonderful day of her life. "Thank you, God."

CHAPTER 26

Mary Steps into Love

Mary Shipley walked into Robert's hospital room and smiled at Rachel before she glanced toward Robert and asked, "Good morning. Any word from Stanley?"

"I am sorry, kiddo." Robert's smile was forced.

"You would think after four long months of not hearing from him, I would give up and go home, but I hate to close that door to the unknown. Do you have any thoughts, suggestions, ideas, or hopeful words?" She looked away sadly from Robert to focus her attention on Rachel.

Rachel saw the sad expression on her face and heard the pain in her voice. "I hate seeing you look so sad, sweetie. I feel responsible. After all, it was me who asked you to come up here with me. I felt it was appropriate for you to meet Robert since you were the one who found him. Kind of bittersweet, isn't it? My comments enticed you to come, and for that, I am humbly sorry."

"Did your comments come from God? Did you make up the things you told me?"

"No. The voice within my head, although silently received through my thoughts, told me clearly that you would meet a man on this trip up here with me. The message to me was so strong I assumed it meant you would meet the man of your dreams."

"Well, my trip and my visit up here are not over yet. There are other men up here besides Stanley."

"May I give you my thoughts?" Rachel tilted her head slightly. "Do you want to hear it?"

"Sure, why not? Especially since it appears you are going to tell me anyway." Mary giggled out loud.

Mary put her sunglasses on her face and then, with a heavy sigh, pushed them up to rest on top of her head before she refocused her attention back on Rachel.

"Stanley has surprised me with his long absence and, more importantly, his insensitivity to at least call the nurses' station to let Bobby or me know he is okay and when he *might* come visit us again. We are all in limbo. His silence makes me wonder if he is nursing a broken heart to the extent his daily life as a cardiologist might be temporarily derailed over losing you. I then wonder if he even possesses that degree of sensitivity? If not, he must have moved on with his life. He has no reason to contact Bobby or me if he has moved on. You might want to consider doing the same thing and return to your home and your former life. We will miss you, but—"

"This morning—sorry to interrupt you. But let me interject something at this point because it fits. Okay?"

"Sure, please go ahead and say what you feel is important at this point." Rachel looked over at Robert.

"I agree. You are not an interrupting-type person, so this must be important. Please tell us."

"I am amazed at how sweet the two of you are to me. Thank you."

"You are very welcome," they both answered at the same time.

"This morning, I got on my knees and prayed to God about my life. I literally had tears running down my face. I literally begged God to take the reins of my life out of my hands and tell me what to do. 'Let me feel your presence in my life as you guide my life. You told Rachel that I would meet a man on my trip up here. Is that man Stanley? Do I move on from Stanley? Will I meet someone else? I am so confused right now, you are going to have to make this next introduction—if there is a next introduction—more dramatic than my initial meeting with Stanley. Did Rachel get your message, meant for me, wrong? Should I pack my clothes and go home? I am slightly depressed, but I do feel an inner peace and comfort being on my knees and turning my problem over to you to handle. This problem

LOVE WILL FIND YOU

is now in your hands. I will not take it back into my hands for me to mess things up. Please tell me clearly, without any room for doubt in my mind, what I am to do. Please help me?'"

"You said all of that to God this morning?"

"Yep. I sure did."

"You have come a long way. I am so proud of you."

"I will bite. You have raised my curiosity. Why do you say that?" Mary asked.

"Why? You have taken matters into your own hands. You are now on a one-on-one with God. You verbally reached out to God, and He will answer you. Spend a few more days up here with us before you make any life-changing decisions. Okay?"

"Okay. I am going downstairs for a cup of coffee and some meditation with God." Mary turned and started walking to the door. Looking back with a big smile, she said, "I will be back."

Mary stepped into the elevator and pressed the button for the lobby as she decided to not only have a cup of coffee but to eat lunch in the hospital cafeteria. Once the elevator doors closed, she stood there, watching the floor numbers go down, and thought about the day Stanley stood in this same elevator a few months ago with his arm around a woman. *Seeing this made my heart race until I fainted. Jealousy? Me? Am I a jealous person? I was that day. How deep does jealousy run through my body?* she wondered. *Did my jealousy permanently chase Stanley away from me? I will never blame him if he decides to never come back to me. My jealousy was inappropriate and probably set off alarm bells in his mind. I then compounded this huge concern in his mind about my jealousy by refusing to even discuss my feelings with him. He must be thinking that I packed my clothes and flew back home to resume my previous life without him in it. His silence does speak volumes. I believe he has closed the door to us. After four long months, which is one fourth of a year, perhaps it is time I close my heart to him.*

Doctors cannot afford to have jealous wives sitting at home wondering which day a female nurse or female doctor will catch their husband's eye and destroy their marriage. I blew up that ship with our relationship in it before it had a chance to sail. Looking on a brighter side, now I wear lipstick, a little mascara, and light facial makeup that has changed

my face from a plain Jane to a pretty face. It is time for me to say next.
She smiled.

Trust issues with men, along with my newly discovered jealousy issues, are major insecurities in a healthy relationship. These two issues must be disclosed and addressed immediately in any new relationship for me, or it is doomed from the beginning. I do not believe any man can be trusted. And until I get a grip on that insecurity, I am not ready to unconditionally trust men. If any man wants a relationship with me, I need to immediately let him know about my men insecurities and my jealousy to see if he wants to work through these issues with me.

She reached her right hand out to hold onto a small gold horizontal bar attached to the right side of the elevator, about waist-high, and closed her eyes. Mary opened her eyes, and while ignoring the half dozen people who were staring at her, she stepped out of the elevator onto the main floor and walked into the cafeteria. She selected a tray and took her place at the rear of a long line of people who were sliding their trays across the top of three round gold horizontal bars mounted in front of each food item that led all the way to the cash register. She selected her drink and the items she wanted to eat for lunch and stopped at the register to pay the cashier. After putting the change she received from the cashier into her purse, she picked up her tray and searched for empty tables to her left. She took one step toward some empty tables and collided with a young man who was about to walk past her. This man was coming from the restroom, heading back to his table without a tray in his hands. Quickly he placed his hands over the top of her hands to steady her tray and keep her from falling.

"I am sorry. I didn't know you were going to step out when you did. Please let me carry your tray to a table for you and get you a fresh cup of coffee since I spilled your coffee all over your tray." He expected to see anger in her eyes, but instead, he saw the look of innocence and friendliness in a beautiful pair of hazel-colored eyes looking back at him. He is an expert when it comes to eye colors. Hazel eyes combine the two colors of brown and green, which is the perfect combination of elegance and sensuality. People with hazel-color eyes are in touch with their inner emotions and tend to be more introverted. Once you get past their tough introverted exterior, they are funny, spontaneous, and witty. People who have hazel eye color have a need to compliment people, almost overly so. If they are going to be a part of your life, they have an inner need to match you emotionally, physically, and spiritually. They must be in sync with the people they spend a lot of time with. If they are part of a family, active in a friendship, or active in a group, it is important that they feel they are a significant part for them to feel comfortable enough to stay connected to the family, the friendship, the group, or you.

"Please forgive me for stepping out into you. I should carry and use a side mirror before I make such sudden moves." Mary realized his hands were still covering her hands.

"I can manage." She tried to turn to walk away with her tray but met resistance. Suddenly because of her independence, slight irritation with this stranger started to rise within her. She was ready to give him a piece of her mind and tell him to get lost when she saw something in his eyes she had never seen in any man's eyes. Before she spoke, a voice within her head said, *Be still and trust this man.*

She could not shift her eyes from his eyes. She unexplainably abandoned any desire to walk away with her tray. She found herself reluctantly complying with his request for her to let go of her tray and follow him to a nearby table. He set her tray down on a table next to what appeared to be an abandoned tray full of food and a drink. He arranged her food items next to that abandoned tray. He picked up her tray with the puddle of coffee and took two napkins from the abandoned tray full of food and wiped up her spilled coffee.

"Ta-dah! Partial mission accomplished." He looked down at her and smiled. "Please do not go anywhere. I will be right back with a fresh cup of coffee for you. Okay?"

"Who does this tray belong to?" She pointed to the tray he took the napkins from and waited for him to answer her.

"A very special friend that you will like instantly. Trust me."

"I do not trust any man, so please do not ask me to trust them or you. Besides, I do not know you."

"Fair enough. I will get you a fresh cup of coffee, along with a clean tray, and come back to properly introduce myself. You can then let your heart decide if you want to be one of my trusted friends. I hope you do."

"Why?"

"Look in the mirror."

"Oh please. Men say kind things to women until they trade us in for a younger model when we get a few wrinkles, add a few pounds, or get older, while they ignore their own wrinkles and beer bellies."

"I am not just speaking about your pretty face. I am speaking about the look within your eyes that tells me you have a kind heart. I believe even you know this to be true." She started to speak when he put up his hand to stop her in midsentence. "Hold that thought until I return with your coffee. Okay?"

"Okay. Thank you." She smiled at him as he started to turn to get her a fresh cup of coffee.

"There it is. Your first of many smiles in our new beautiful relationship. Nope. Do not say it. Hold that thought until I return."

"We do not have a relationship. We—" She stopped talking and just watched him walk away. She whispered to herself, "Lord, is he the new love of my life? I am only doubting why you would offer a blessing so quickly for me. I am so unworthy. I have not thanked you for helping me through the death of my parents or for keeping me mentally focused to pass the bar exam. You made me an attorney against all odds, and I will always be eternally grateful. My heart is full. And thank you for helping me save the young female driver who drove the car that ended the life of my parents on earth. I know they are with you in heaven. The young girl deserved the big break you gave to her through me. You made me look good, when all the glory belonged to you. I promise to stay in closer communication with you and pray to you every day. Please guide what I do and what I say to this new man in my life. Thank you, God."

"Thank you for not running away," he said before he set the clean tray down on the table in front of her food. "I also have a fresh cup of coffee and two napkins." He set those down in front of her right hand. He stood up and looked at her until she looked up at him. Once he had her attention, he bowed slightly at his waist, with his left arm folded across his stomach, like a butler would do, and extended his right hand toward her with his fingers in the air like he was hoping to do a high five. She literally shocked him when she quickly raised her left hand to meet his right hand in the air to complete a high five with him. "Wow! I never saw that one coming. Score one for the pretty lady with a quick mind. Thank you. Twice."

"You're welcome. Why twice?" she said questionably, with a smile in her eyes looking up at him.

"Once for not running away while I was gone to fetch your coffee. Twice for being so quick-minded to complete a high five that I did just to be funny. You surprised me in a good way. I have a good feeling about you. We have the potential to be great lifetime friends." Mary listened to him and leaned forward to take a sip of her coffee when he asked, "Do you love me yet?" She practically choked on the mouthful of coffee. A little ran down her chin. She reached for a napkin to wipe her chin and protect her blouse.

"Love you? I do not even know you. Who are you?" She felt embarrassed. "Thank goodness for the napkins." He sat down next to her in front of the tray full of food that she thought somebody had just got up and left on the table. She looked sheepishly over at him and forced a smile.

"I might as well eat this food somebody left here. Right? Cannot let it go to waste. Can we?"

"Please tell me this is your tray and food, or I am out of here."

"Oh no! Here comes trouble. Remember, you made me sit down here and eat this food." He laughed.

"No. I will not be—" She got interrupted when he put his left hand over her left hand resting on the table next to her tray and put his right arm around her shoulder and gently pulled her closer to him.

"Hey, buddy, what are you doing sitting here eating *that food* with your girlfriend?" A large man was now standing in front of their table, looking angry and speaking in a loud, stern, angry voice.

"I am sorry, pal. I just took one look at her pretty face and sat down here when she told me to. Do you blame me?"

Mary started to say something in protest when he pulled her even closer to him, laughing. Mary turned and glared at him. She was embarrassed and stunned. With a shocked look on her face, she frantically searched her mind for the right words to use to end this charade. She continued to stare at him while she tried to get her mind working to choose the right words to give him a piece of her mind. She was more than a little angry and wanted to say something legal and so cutting and curt that he would never forget her words. *Be still*, the voice in her head told her. It was then that she noticed his eyes looked unusually friendly and seemed to be smiling. It was during this brief hesitation when she got a longer and better look at his handsome face. *Why does my brain suddenly go AWOL?* she wondered. *I am a lawyer, and lawyers are known to be a client's mouthpiece. Why now? Why fail me now? I need to speak up and let this stranger standing in front of my table know I do not know this guy sitting next to me, and I never asked him to sit down next to me to eat another person's food.* She was about to finally speak her mind when a voice in her head again whispered, *Be still.* She now understood why Felix chose that moment to climb into her mouth and bite her tongue. *God is involved in this charade.* She just closed her mouth and continued to stare at the handsome face of an exceedingly kind man sitting next to her.

"Ma'am. You need to find *me tomorrow.* I will sit anywhere you want me to." The big man smiled at her.

"Please forgive us, ma'am. I have known Ed an exceptionally long time before we hooked up again at this hospital. We played these kinds of jokes on each other in college and in med school. I could not resist this opportunity when I saw him sitting here with you. I never saw him chummy up to even one of the hundreds of available females who frequent this hospital. He has always been a loner. And I have never seen you with a man until Ed. Tell me the secret. How did you hook up with each other?"

"I am not following your comment about me not being with a man before today."

"My apology to you again, ma'am. I did not make myself very clear. I did not realize who you were until I got a closer look at your face."

"Have we met before today? If so, I am sorry. I do not remember you."

"No, ma'am. I have watched you come into this cafeteria alone or with the same woman with blond-color hair every day over the last few months and wondered why any man would ever let you two eat alone. So when I saw you with Ed today, I had to come ask if you are available to date. Please tell me he is your brother, and he is trying to play a trick on me sitting here with his arm around you."

"I am sorry. I cannot tell you a lie. He's not my brother."

Mary's heart melted along with her embarrassment and anger after hearing the things he just revealed to her about the history he and Ed enjoyed together. Surprisingly she was not uncomfortable with this man's arm still around her shoulder. Turning her face toward him, she whispered, "Do you want your arm back?"

"No. You keep it."

"How long?" She studied every square inch of his face before looking into his eyes. She did not feel nervous or uncomfortable. She wondered what this mystery man was going to do or say next. His boldness intrigued her. *What did he see in me so quickly?* she wondered.

"It does not matter. You can afford to pay my price for having my arm around you."

"You have definitely raised my curiosity. I must ask you to tell me your price?"

"No money or expectations."

"No expectations? Never thought I would ever hear those words ever come out of a man's mouth. Ah. I get it. You're gay."

"Nope."

"Okay. Let me try asking my question this way. Will I be offended in any way by your price?"

"May I show you what I would love to receive from you?"

"Before you do, you know about my mistrust of men. Right?"

"Yes, I do."

"And knowing this, you still want to show me rather than tell me. Right?

"Right."

"You are hereby forewarned that your demonstration better not offend me in any way." Mary folded her arms across her chest to guard against anything he might insinuate to be an open invitation to invade her privacy.

"I will now collect your first payment." He leaned his face closer to her and lightly kissed her lips. Boy, was she shocked, especially when she heard applause and cheers break out all around her from nearby tables and from the big guy who was still standing in front of her table.

Looking up at the stranger standing in front of her table, she asked, "Are you still here?"

"I was not about to leave a front-row seat to what will be one of the greatest future love stories ever told. I am happy for both of you. The medical world will never believe it about him."

"Should your story about him embarrass me or make me happy?"

"Deliriously happy. You do not know who he is, do you?"

"No. Please tell me first who you are and then tell me who he is."

"My name is Jim Ott. You are sitting next to none other than the famous Ed Cox."

She turned to face Ed. "You have some explaining to do, but for now, no more unauthorized payments from me to you. If you do not agree or understand, I am walking away from you now."

"Yes, ma'am. I do understand and will always obey your wishes or instructions. I apologize to you."

"Accepted. Thank you. You are forgiven."

"Please tell me you are not involved in a relationship or going through a nasty divorce to unleash an angry boyfriend or husband on me." He glanced his eyes up at Jim, then back to her and waited anxiously for her response.

"No. I am not married nor am I going through a nasty divorce. I met a man here at the hospital a few months ago and began a short-term friendship that abruptly ended. So I am not involved with anyone."

"That is great news to me. You just made my day. Thank you." He smiled at her.

"Why?" Mary asked.

"Because—"

"Sorry to interrupt you. First, please answer those same questions you asked me and then tell me why."

"I have never been married or engaged, and I am not in a relationship. I do not know the acceptable thing to say or do to begin a relationship that would evolve into a romance or marriage. God knows everything about all of us. I joke with Him about arranging a possible relationship for me. I tell Him that just crossing my path with the potential love of my life will not work—she must fall onto my lap. But colliding with you worked for me."

"Honestly? You said these things to God?"

"May God strike me dead in this spot if I am not telling you the truth." He made an *x* across his heart and raised his right hand up toward the sky.

"Wow. You have clout with the Almighty for Him to work that fast. You and your story impress me."

"Mission partially accomplished. I aim to impress you." Ed changed his facial expression to show a look of deep concern. "Do you honestly believe God answers prayers?"

Mary avoided answering his question by asking, "Do you believe God answered your prayer today?" Mary tilted her head toward the table and raised her left eye to look closely at him and waited for his response.

"I cannot draw landscapes, buildings, people, or animals, so I did not have the capability of drawing a picture of you. But I do know we met the only way possible for me. I am really a shy person. Once you stepped into me, God took over, and God does not make mistakes. You make me feel unusually comfortable. I cannot believe I am sitting here with my arm around you. I love God's choice in women for me. Are you as new to romance and love as me?" he asked her.

"Yes," she whispered. "I have a personal concern that I must tell you about. Is now a good time to tell you?"

"Any time is a perfect time for you to tell me something you want me to know. I will always listen to you."

"I rode up here with a friend of mine to visit her fiancé, who is a patient in this hospital. One day a man walked into the room to visit this same patient. He introduced himself to me, and we talked that day and many future days to begin building a decent friendship that included a few kisses."

"That is one way for a friendship and romance to begin. The way we met is a better way. Do you agree?"

"Yes. I do agree. Well, one day I went down here to eat lunch with the fiancé of the man we were visiting, and on our way back to the room, we stepped out of our elevator, and as we walked past the bank of elevators to our left, I happened to glance into the open doors of one of these elevators and saw this new man in my life standing inside the elevator, with his arm around a woman. Seeing this caught me by complete surprise, and I fainted. I later refused to even talk to him about it. I chose to end the brief friendship that we were building without giving him a chance to explain. I might have been wrong to just walk away. No man wants a woman in his life if she has issues of jealousy. Do you think I do?"

"I am not a possessive or jealous man, but honestly, it would bother me if I saw you standing in an elevator with another man's arm around you. If that is jealousy, I am a jealous man."

"Are you saying this to make me feel better, or do those words come from your heart? Please be honest."

"I will always speak from my heart," Ed answered her just above a whisper as he looked into her eyes.

"I promise the same thing to you. Can we make a pinky promise on it?" she asked.

"Absolutely. I love it. I have never done a pinky promise. This will serve as a binding contract. You probably don't know a lot about binding contracts?"

She ignored his comment by saying, "Communication is the name of the game. It saves relationships, especially between married couples. Please do not ever clam up on me. If I do anything that irritates you or rubs you the wrong way, please tell me immediately, or at least before that day ends, to avoid the slimmest chance of us building a wall between us. Okay?"

"Oh, I love that idea. Not just the big things but little things, too, right?" Ed asked.

"Yes. Little things start to grow and fester into bigger things. And before we realize it, we have stopped talking intimately with each other and drift apart. Eventually an insurmountable wall is built between us, and I do not want that to happen in any relationship I am in. Do you?" Mary asked.

"No. Is that what happened in your last relationship?" Ed asked.

"Kind of, yes. The failure of that brief relationship was my fault, but—"

"I do not agree. He knew where to find you. Sorry to interrupt you."

"Well, in one way, I can see where you are right because he could have reached out to me over the last few months if he had deep feelings for me and wanted to save our brief relationship."

"Do you miss him?"

"Not really. At least not from a romantic point of view. Friendship maybe, but nothing romantic. We never spent any time alone to build even a strong friendship. We never sat down close to each other to talk like you and I are doing today. We never shared any of the things you and I are discussing today. We never had a reason to do a pinky promise. So hey, no pinky promise, no possible romance. Right?" She laughed.

"Right," he said as he, too, laughed out loud.

"Thank you for telling me about hazel-colored eyes. Do you mind telling me something about people who have green-colored eyes?"

"No. I don't mind telling you. Thank you for your interest in eye colors."

"You're welcome. I have always been fascinated with the different eye colors and how these different eye color people behave emotionally. Please educate me."

"God blessed us with a very quick, compatible, and highly unusually close relationship." Ed smiled at her.

"And although quick, I believe in our case, it has been a good thing. Right?" she asked.

"Yes. I love you and what we are building. Whoops. I said it, didn't I? I'm sorry." He bowed his head.

"Do not be sorry unless you are sorry. Are you?" she asked, sounding concerned. "I feel the same way."

"You do? Honestly? Do you feel the same way about me?" He sounded surprised.

"Yes. I do," she admitted.

"Wow. Admittedly this *has* been fast for me. And for what you have told me, I believe it has also been fast for you. In my daily prayers to God is a standing daily request for Him to not only allow me to meet the woman of my dreams, but when I do meet her, please make our paths collide into each other so I am certain she is sent to me from Him. I am such an introvert. This is the only way I could ever meet the woman of my dreams."

"Do you consider me to be the woman of your dreams?" she asked.

"I do. Everything with us feels right. You have made me believe in something I felt was a myth. I now do believe in love at first sight. Whoops, I said it again. Did I not?" He bowed his head again and peeked at her.

"Thank you for not keeping these kinds of feelings from me. If you feel something this intimate, and you believe it to be honest, please tell me. Okay?"

"Okay. I promise. I have always been shy and extremely intro-verted around women, especially good-looking women with real class, like you. The real me would never have the courage to do the things I did to meet and kiss you. My guess is God did not want me to let you get away. I will blame my temporary change in personality and aggressive actions on Him." He bowed his head to look down at the table after saying these very private and intimate things to her. He was now reluctant to turn his head to even look into her eyes.

Mary reached over to gently put the palm of her right hand under his chin. She turned his face toward her as she kissed him lightly on his lips. "You are a very kind and sweet man."

"Thank you for saying such a nice thing to me, Mary."

"You are welcome. Is this a good time to set some ground rules on kissing?"

"Yes. Any time is good for me. Please tell me the rules you would love for me to follow?" Ed asked.

"Well." She stopped talking to study the look in his eyes.

"Go ahead. I am a big boy. But what?" He watched her showing a cautious half smile.

"We have never been in love before. If you agree, this might be a good time for us to take things slow and learn not only *how to be in love but how to be in a loving relationship with each other*?"

"I agree. This borders on being brilliant. I like what I am hearing, Mary."

"I want to learn *how* to be in a relationship with you and *slowly* learn how to love you the way God intended for us to love each other. May I ask you to help me?"

"You just made my heart jump when you said you wanted to learn how to love me in a relationship that God intended for us to live together. I will always respect you and go slow with you. Does this sound good to you?"

"Oh, yes. Thank you, Ed."

"You are welcome."

"Is it true that you can look into my eyes and read the feelings I have in my heart? Can you do this, Ed?"

"No. I wish that were true. I read the typical things most people do. I have never been in love, so this is my first chance to experience that feeling. I believe we will both discover that being in love with someone while we are in an active relationship with that person is the best relationship to be in."

"Aww. You are such a sweet man."

"I want you to keep noticing that in me. Thank you." They both smiled, hugged, and briefly kissed.

"What color eyes are the most beautiful?" Mary asked.

"The most beautiful color of eyes is those that see the beauty in others. And experts say our eyes are windows into our soul," Ed said.

"I like that saying," Mary answered. "What does it say about green eyes?"

"Obsessed with green eyes, eh?" Ed teased.

"No. I just think green is a very beautiful color." Mary smiled and stared at him. "What?"

"You're a mess."

"Good or bad?" she teasingly asked. "Careful how you answer that question." She giggled softly.

"Always good. Never bad. Could not be bad with you." He smiled and pulled her closer to him.

"I am impressed with how you are always spontaneously very kind and sweet to me, Ed."

"For me to just say you are welcome does not explain how and why I interact the way I do with you. You seem to wear your heart on your sleeve and guard it. There is nothing pretentious about you. You speak from your heart and seem to relax your guard around those people who do the same when speaking with you. 'What you see is what you get' seems to be your philosophy that guides the way you live your life. You make loving you and being your friend easy. I love my new relationship with you."

Mary did not try to stop the happy tears that were forming in her eyes as she sat there mesmerized by the love she saw in his eyes and mesmerized listening to the complimentary words coming from his lips. Only her parents have said the wonderful things she was now hearing Ed say to her. Only her parents have been so kind to her. She dried her eyes and looked at Ed. "God has blessed both of our lives by bringing us together to do His will."

"May I impose upon you to tell me more? I like it when you speak about God."

"Okay. Life has a way of blocking out important memories. We were given a gift of each other, and it is important to always remember this gift from God when we are living our busy lives. It is our job to never allow this gift to fade into oblivion. I do not want to lose the way I feel today. Do you think I am being silly?"

"No. I want the same things you do. And I believe it is our job to remember God's gift to us and protect and cherish this relationship, or we might lose it." He stopped talking and looked into her eyes as she opened her mouth to speak.

"We must always remember our love began as a special gift given to us by God." She stared at him as he started to smile like he had remembered something. "Are you thinking what I am thinking?" she asked.

His eyes lit up as his smile broadened, looking at her questionably. "Pinky promise?" he asked.

"Yes." A smile spread across her face as she held up a pinky finger that he quickly encircled with his own pinky finger. "Our pinky promise will serve as our own unique reminder to keep the love we feel for each other alive. This is especially important to me, Ed," she said as her voice cracked with emotion.

Whatever is important to you will always be important to me. Okay?" he answered and asked honestly.

"Okay. Thank you, Ed. I believe you were about to talk about green eyes. Shall we?" she asked.

"Yes. I almost forgot. I was engrossed in making another pinky promise with you. I love talking with you."

"Thank you for being such a breath of fresh air into my life. Just for the record, I love talking with you too."

"Do you have any legal training?" he asked.

"Why do you ask?" she answered with a concerned tone to her voice.

"'Just for the record' is a legal term lawyers use in a courtroom. Hearing you say it made me wonder."

"Hearing you ask me this question makes me wonder how you know this term is used in a courtroom?" she asked him.

"Clever. Asking a question with a question to avoid the question. What are you hiding?" he teased.

"Back at you. What are you hiding, Mr. Cox, or is it Dr. Cox?" she asked.

"You win. You started the first question, and now you get the last question to get them all answered. You are good. You belong in a courtroom," he answered with a smile and a light laugh. "It is Dr. Cox. And I have no experience inside a courtroom. I believe it is now your turn to fess up."

"You sure know how to quickly put a girl on the hot seat." She smiled at him and blew out a big breath of air.

"I want to answer every question you have about me. Okay?"

"Okay. I detect a but coming about now. Right?"

"Look who is clever now." She smiled and remained silent for a few seconds to study his facial expression before she continued speaking. "I am a Harvard Law School graduate with a law degree, and I did pass the bar exam to practice law. I have not decided if I want to work for a law firm or open my own law office to practice law. This is a perfect spot for me to temporarily freeze our conversation about me professionally for another day, if this is okay with you?"

"Yes. Thank you for sharing this much of your life with me. I look forward to hearing the rest of your story."

"Thank you, Ed. Now for a distraction." She giggled. "Green-eyed people." She smiled, watching him.

"Okay. Nice distraction. Green is the color of nature. People with green-color eyes have the perfect blend of civilized nurturing qualities mixed with raw, unbridled, fantastic instincts. They have mastered the battle between calm and passion to be experts in the art of unconditional love. Their partner must not just show his love but prove it. Experts say a green-eyed person's partner must be a saint on the street and a devil in the sheets. Green-eyed people are not only compassionate but very loyal."

"Wow! Do they sell green contact lenses?" Mary giggled slightly at her own comment and quickly turned her giggle into a belly laugh when she witnessed Ed howl with laughter at her comment.

"It wasn't that funny. Was it?" Mary asked teasingly.

"Your expression, along with your quick wit, made it very funny to me."

"Well, I am glad I could entertain you."

"Me too. And you did. Awesome for you to be that quick-witted to think about a green contact lens and put those thoughts into words with the facial expression you just used. Very funny. Thank you."

"Unintentional on my part." She smiled. "But you are welcome. Speaking about colored contact lens, do you know anything about people with blue-color eyes?"

"Yes. Do you want to learn about people who have blue color eyes for any particular reason?"

"No. I love the color of blue. I am simply curious to learn something about people with blue eyes."

"All right then, but before I continue, I must use a little legal jargon on you by saying I need to make the record again. Since you know what that means? Right?"

"Yes. You are advising the court of something you feel is important for the judge to know. Right?"

"Correct. To make the record, and surprisingly to me, I loved how your kiss ignited something inside me. I am new to intimate relationships and to kissing. I am overwhelmed at how well I am getting along with you so easily. I cannot believe I actually put my arm around you, even as a joke, and it is still around you."

"So this explains why Jim Ott told me the medical field would have a hard time believing you were in a romantic relationship. Right?

"Yes."

"Cool. I must confess that I am more than a little shocked that I held my tongue during everything that happened between us today. The voice within my head kept saying, 'Be still. Trust this man.' I am glad I did."

"Me too. But I must ask if you are serious about hearing voices inside your head?"

"Yes, but not a verbal voice. More like a strong thought that I know I did not consciously create myself. Haven't you started to do something when your instincts told you not to do it?"

"Yes. Is this what you mean by voices within your head?" he asked her.

"Yes. I have learned that this silent strong voice or thought is the Holy Spirit or God trying to get me to listen to His guidance. There are a lot of us who believe in the Holy Spirit. Do you understand?"

"I do understand what you are saying to me. And I understand about your strong belief in God."

"God is a Spirit capable of being everywhere at the same time. God is part of a Trinity consisting of God the Father, God the Son, and God the Holy Spirit. God the Son is Jesus, who came down from heaven to live as a man for thirty-three years to die on a cross for our sins. Three days later, He rose to ascend back to heaven."

"This is the first time anyone ever told me that story so concisely. Please tell me more about this Holy Spirit and how it works? Do you mind?"

"Please make a mental note about my last comment to realize that Jesus defeated death. The grave could not hold Him. He rose from the grave and remained on earth for forty days to prove to His disciples and to the world that He is the Son of God and that He will one day come back to take all His believers with Him to heaven."

"You must believe what I told you about Jesus and believe that He is your Lord and Savior."

"You are speaking about me having faith. Right?" he asked her.

"Yes. I like to think of it as having the faith of a child. Children believe the things parents tell them because they believe their parents will tell them the truth."

"Faith?"

"Yes. Faith of a child is crucial and vital in our personal relationships and in our relationship with God. We cannot see the air that we breathe, but we know it exists, right? Could I convince you that air does not exist?"

"No," he replied.

"Keep that same faith in God until you can positively show me that I am wrong about the air and God."

"I can see I am going to learn a lot from you, Mary."

"I believe I will learn a lot from you, too, Ed. Please tell me more about people with blue-color eyes."

"People with blue color eyes are said to be intriguing, striking, and passionate people with a diversified broad-range personality. Their partner needs to be sometimes rough, and sometimes sensitive, and occasionally they must be simultaneously loving, strong, and warm."

"I did not think the eyes told us that much about someone, but they obviously do?"

"Yes. This is extremely useful information when it comes to choosing our companions and life partners."

"This is fascinating information to me. What is the most common human eye color?"

"Brown."

"Brown? Seriously? I never would have guessed the color would be brown. Why?"

"There are so many shades of brown, and surprisingly every brown eye is different. No two brown-eyed people have identical eye colors."

Mary leaned back from him to look up into his eyes before speaking. "No way! For real?"

"Yes, ma'am. You will not find two brown-color eyes the same. If you find this preposterous, do you believe that God made every snowflake that falls during the winter months different?"

"Yes. I believe it because God said it. No two flakes are identical."

"I bet you will not believe my next statement to be true."

"Try me. I have no idea where you are going with this, but please tell me," Mary asked.

"There are billions of stars in the sky, and God gave each one a different name. True or false?"

Mary just looked at him and smiled. "My answer is written in my eyes and my smile. Can you read both correctly to pass this part of my quiz?"

"Both your eyes and smile are beautiful. Yes. I can easily read each one to know the answer to your question is true." He laughed. "If a person didn't know anything else about God, knowing the answers to these two questions would make it hard for anyone not to believe in the power and glory of your heavenly God."

"Our God. Not just my God. Right?" Mary slapped him lightly with her right hand on his chest.

"Right. I do believe in my God, your God, our God. The one true living God in heaven. How am I doing?"

"Better." Her eyes smiled at him, showing genuine expressions of love.

"I am not the outspoken believer you are today, but after being around you a little more, I might purchase a pulpit and start preaching the Word of God."

"I noticed you did not laugh when you said this." Mary looked at him and studied his expression.

"No. I am so impressed with the belief you have in your heart for God, I want to possess that belief."

"Boy, does that give me something else to look forward to with you. You are now making God proud."

"My first goal is to make *you* proud of me."

"You had me an hour ago." Mary paused to look at him. "Your first goal is to always put God first."

"Do I have you?" Ed asked.

"Yes. But if you ever want all of me, you must marry me and put God first in your life because He is first in mine. Deal?"

"God brought you into my life just the way I asked Him to. I will commit to do my part to invite God to live in my heart like He now lives in your heart. I will research everything I can to learn more about the Holy Spirit to hopefully acquire the love you have in your heart for God. Deal?"

"Deal." She sat still for a long minute, staring into his eyes without speaking. Her heart did flips inside her chest while she sat quietly looking into his eyes. Simultaneously his heart fluttered as he studied her face. Their mutual romantic feelings for each other slowly escalated as they continued to look into each other's eyes.

"I love—" Ed suddenly stopped speaking.

Mary wondered what he was about to say after he said the word *love*. She ignored this thought to shift the conversation away from love or romance. She did not want their initial conversation, after they just met, to evolve so quickly into expressing romantic feelings. She wanted romantic conversations to evolve naturally over time.

"You were finishing your comments about brown eyes before I interrupted you. I am sorry."

"You have my permission to interrupt me any time. People with brown eyes tend to be optimistic and highly creative souls who are known for their ability to be committed to whatever they chose to do in life. Their partner needs to be just as committed to them. They believe that you expect their loyalty, and you also expect their total acceptance of you, because they believe you are offering them the same things. This relationship needs to be on equal footing. When it comes to intimacy, pleasure must be a two-way street."

"Now that will make me look at brown-eyed people differently. Any other eye colors left to discuss?"

"Yes. Gray."

"Gray or grey?" Mary asked.

"Great question, Mary. Grey is the British spelling of the word. Gray is the accepted spelling in the USA. They are both accepted, however. It is a neutral tone between black and white," Ed said

"How do you make the color gray?" Mary asked.

"Another great question. Combine equal amounts of black and white together to get a neutral gray. If you want a darker or lighter shade of gray, vary the amounts you combine of white and black. Have you ever heard of primary gray?" Ed asked her.

"No. How do you make that color?"

"Blend equal parts of red, blue, and yellow to get this color," Ed replied to her with a smile.

"Is gray considered a depressing color?" Mary asked.

"Yes. Too much of a gray color creates sadness, depression, loneliness, and isolation."

"You just chased me away from gray walls in our home." Mary laughed out loud with Ed. "I have never seen a gray eye in a human being. It must be very rare. Is it?"

"Yes. Gray-colored eyes are so rare that it comes as no surprise to me that people with this eye color play their cards close to their chest. It takes a lot for people with this eye color to open their lives to scrutiny. But once they let you in and show you their world, you will see that the world they have created for themselves is usually a wonder to behold. Their partner, therefore, needs to be highly creative by nature. Gray-eyed people see both sides of the same coin and seem to know when someone is trying to con them. They are creative and very expressive with an incredibly unique personality."

"Wow. Thank you for sharing this information with me. We have probably accomplished more today than we could have over several months of dating. Do you want to exchange telephone numbers and set up a day soon to meet again?" Mary asked. She looked in her purse and removed a piece of notebook paper and looked at him with a smile, saying, "Let me give you my cell phone number and the number to the hotel room where I am staying. I am glad I took the time days ago to write these numbers into my pocket notebook. Meant to be. Eh?"

"Yes. Everything about us is meant to be. Do you mind walking me back to my office so I can give you my numbers? Then you will know how to find me."

"Man cave," she teased.

"My home is my man cave. I cannot wait to show it to you. My office, however, is just a standard office."

While standing behind her chair, he gently slid her chair back from the table to allow her to stand. She looked back at him just as the light within the room captured a gentle look of love in her eyes. The meeting of their eyes froze him in place until he heard her say, "Thank you. You keep impressing me, Dr. Cox."

"I will strive to impress you daily," he answered while thinking about the gentle look of love in her eyes.

"What?" She gave him a curious friendly look.

"Nothing. But I will never apologize for being fascinated by the gentle look of love I see in your eyes."

"Nobody has ever said this to me. Thank you. Ed."

"Perhaps they have never seen you in love before."

"Before you, your statement is true. But I think you are only saying these nice things to get this." She took one step closer to him and placed a hand on each side of his face and pressed her lips against his. "That is your reward for being the sweet man you are and for saying such nice things to me. I will get on my knees tonight to thank God for sending you into my life. I never want to lose this feeling. Thank you, Ed."

"I need to get on my knees in prayer and give thanks too. We have both been blessed," he said slightly above a whisper while holding her close to him.

"I can see I need to carry a notebook and a calculator to keep a record of the kisses I owe you for the kindness you show to me. Right now, we need to get out of this cafeteria," she said, laughing.

He immediately reached out his hand to accept her hand into his. The feeling of their hands together felt good enough to make Ed give a fleeting thought of confirmation that they truly were meant to be together.

Jim Ott was standing in the hallway, talking with a small group of people, about thirty yards away from the exit door of the cafeteria when he spotted Mary and Ed leaving the cafeteria. Instinctively he smiled and waved to them. Mary and Ed smiled, used their free hand to wave to him as they smiled, and continued to walk toward the elevators.

"This feels so natural to me," Ed said to her.

"Which part?" she asked.

"Holding your hand and walking with you in this hospital. I love having you with me."

"I need to be more like you," she confessed, looking up into his eyes.

"Please tell me what I did to make you want to be like me?" he asked.

"I need to be more spontaneous to verbalize the feelings within my heart that I feel for you and about you, like you just did, telling me you loved having me with you. I am sure you would love hearing spontaneous things from me. Right?"

"Everyone loves words of praise and kindness. But honestly, I will always be content just knowing you love me." Mary was not prepared for any man to ever say these words to her, especially not a sweet kind man like Ed. She was immediately stunned and choked up by his words to the point she felt her emotions stirring wildly out of control as her lips began to quiver. She pursed her lips tightly together to quell the trembling. All she could do was stand there and stare at Ed, like she was a deer caught in the headlights, as she tried to fight back a tsunami of deliriously happy tears. Out of embarrassment, she closed her eyes and shook her head sideways, trying to figure out the next thing she should do or say, until she felt Ed's arms wrap around her. She did not resist him gently rocking or swaying with her.

"We have never been in love before. You could very easily be saving me emotionally instead of me saving you, if that is what I am doing for you?" he whispered into her ear.

"You saved me," she whispered. "I need to go before I flood this place with happy tears assured to embarrass both of us. I have never been this happy. Thank you for loving me and for giving me this feeling."

"These emotional tender moments serve to prove me, right? Embrace every heartfelt moment and give God thanks for each one." He tightened his arms around her and pulled her closer to him. "Are you okay?"

She nodded her head without speaking. "Thank you for holding me." She blew out a long slow breath of air, then looked up at him. "I need to go back to my hotel room and give thanks to God for your love and my new life with you in it," she spoke with a shaky voice."

"We both have a reason to be on our knees tonight, thanking God for bringing us together."

"I will blame my emotions on my hazel eye color," she whispered.

"People with hazel-color eyes usually never miss an opportunity to compliment friends, family, and even strangers. Have you ever helped someone through a difficult time in their life when they had nobody else to turn to for help?" He watched her eyes light up. "You have, haven't you?"

"Yes. I helped a girl named Amy, who drove her vehicle into the path of my parents' car and killed them instantly. Amy was a college graduate and just accepted into Yale Law School the day of the accident. Amy was charged with two counts of vehicular homicide and minutes away from being sentenced to serve twenty years in prison before God used me to save her."

He pulled her gently into a nearby doctors' lounge and closed the door. "Please do not leave me hanging without telling me more of *this* story."

"Okay. The voice inside my head, which is the Holy Spirit I was telling you about, screamed, 'Help her. Do not let her go to prison.'"

"Wow. You felt this or heard this?"

"Yes. A clear thought in my head. A thought I knew I did not think up myself. It was so convincing I could not ignore it."

"So what did you do?"

"I convinced the judge to reverse her intention to sentence Amy to twenty years in prison to give her three years of probation. I drove Amy to Yale for her to claim her Yale scholarship that paid for her law school. I bought her a car to travel to her classes during her years at Yale Law School. The car will be a gift from me if she does everything expected of her."

"How does she pay for the other things she will need?"

"Good question. I opened and funded a checking account for her to buy food and have money to live. She will work with me and pay me back when she graduates from law school and passes the bar exam."

"From the way your eyes lit up discussing this subject, I did not want to wait to hear this story."

"You solved a little mystery for me."

"How?"

"I wondered later, after I helped her, why I did so much for a total stranger?"

"God motivated you to keep her out of prison. Right?"

"Yes. No question about that part of this story."

"Please tell me the troubling part."

"I know the Holy Spirit told me to hug her."

"Seriously?"

"Yes. She even asked me if I wanted to hit her or really hug her."

"I can see why she asked that question."

"The second I hugged her, the Holy Spirit told me to question the percentage of alcohol in her system at the time of the accident and ask for probation."

"The Holy Spirit told you all of this while you were hugging her?"

"Yes. I would not have asked her otherwise."

"Interesting. How did that turn out?"

"She had less alcohol in her system required by the law to be charged with driving under the influence. This opened the door for the judge to consider giving her probation, especially since I was the only living relative of my parents. My belief now is my hazel eye color might have played a big part of the compassion I showed toward Amy. Is there a correlation between compliments and compassion?"

"You did not compliment her, but you certainly used compassion. So possibly?" Ed answered honestly.

"I believe that I did show her compassion. Thank you for listening, Ed."

"You are very welcome. I like your logic. Everything you said makes sense to me."

"Thank you for telling me that what I just told you makes sense to you. Your question serves as a reminder to me that I need to physically visit Amy again. She is a sweetheart who has kept in touch with me and has gone the extra mile to do more than I ever expected of her. She will be the sister I never had."

"In that case, this must have been a touching moment for you and her. I am glad she is working out for you," he answered with a nod of his head and a smile.

"It was indeed a touching moment for both of us," she responded to Ed, followed by a big sigh.

They continued to walk. He gently squeezed her hand and led her toward the closed door of an office. "This is my office." He opened the door wide enough for her to enter ahead of him. She entered so quickly, she failed to notice the name on his office door. The first thing she noticed were the expensive-looking framed pictures professionally placed on his office walls. Two expensive high-backed cushioned chairs in blue-and-green color tones were positioned in front of his desk with a brown-colored expensive-looking table between them. A beautiful blue-and-green sofa that matched the office chairs was positioned against the far wall to the right of the door. End tables with lamps flanked the couch. These tables matched the color and style of the table between the two office chairs. The green carpet color accentuated the beautiful furniture and picture frames.

"Did you choose the beautiful furniture, pictures, carpet, and accessories in your office?"

"No. A woman takes care of everything. Most, or perhaps all, the doctor's offices look the same." Ed reached for one of his business cards and wrote his home and cell phone numbers on the back and handed it to her. "Call me any time of day or night. I will answer when I can or immediately call you back. Okay?"

Mary immediately put his card into her purse without looking at it. She looked up at him. "I am suddenly speechless. Perhaps over-whelmed. Meeting you has suddenly, without warning, impacted my life in the best way possible. I will also give my thanks to God. Thank you for a wonderful day. Please call me when you have time to talk or spend with me. Okay?"

"You are not leaving my sight today or any future day without a tentative plan for me to see you again."

"I love the sound of that plan. All family members and peo-ple with significant others should adopt your plan because we never know when there is no tomorrow or next time for us."

"May I call you tonight to chat a few minutes and hopefully make dinner plans?" he asked.

"Yes. And before I forget, I want to thank you for making one of my dreams come true."

"Just one?" Ed said with a chuckle.

"Yes. But it is a big one that I wondered what it would feel like, and now I know."

"I do not understand?"

"I will explain this in more detail at a later time, but for now let me just say, I wanted to feel the same kind of love in my heart Rachel felt in her heart for Dr. Robert Wilson the night she waited hours for him inside the restaurant where I worked as a waitress. She con-firmed to me that men like Robert Wilson are out there in the world, hopefully looking for me. You are that man for me, Ed. I thank God and thank you," she said cheerfully.

"You just described a one-in-a-million kind of love, Mary. Thank you for picturing me in that kind of love."

"You are welcome," she replied with a loving look in her eyes.

"I will call you tonight." She stepped into his open arms to receive a hug and kiss. "Good night, Mary.

"Good night, Ed." She turned and floated on a cloud out of his office.

CHAPTER 27

Mary Shipley and Ed Cox

Rachel and Robert were sitting on the side of his bed, watching television and talking, when Mary walked into the room. "Hi, guys. Hold it right there just a minute." Mary raised her cellphone and snapped a picture of them. "I may frame this one." Mary giggled out loud.

"You look good and sound chipper this morning," Rachel said while smiling.

"Thank you, Rachel. What are you two discussing? Or is this your private powwow time?"

"If we tell you, we would have to kill you," Robert said with a big exaggerated closed-mouth smile.

"Pass. I choose to live." Mary smiled back at him, using her own closed exaggerated smile.

"Anything new with you?" Rachel asked looking at her with a questioning look and raised eyebrows.

"Yes. I met a man. Well, to be more accurate, I ran into a man in the cafeteria, and he might turn out to be my significant other. Not declaring it yet, but after our initial meeting and several follow-up phone calls with him, I am almost convinced that he is the one for me. And just think, Robert, it all happened for me when I went looking for you. Is that not a hoot? I might have found the man of my dreams in a bizarre twist while doing a kindness for Rachel looking for you. This could be a Hallmark movie moment for all of us."

"Tell me everything. Leave nothing out. Especially the kissing and hugging parts," Rachel pleaded.

"You expect to hear about a kiss or a hug so quickly from me? What kind of woman do you think I am?" Mary pretended to be upset over the mere suggestion.

"A woman looking for love. Start with telling us his name, then tell us about the kissing," Robert barked.

Nurse Lisa Phillips walked into the room to take Robert's vital signs. "Good morning, Dr. Wilson, Rachel, and Mary. How are y'all doing this morning?" Lisa asked.

"We are doing good," Rachel answered.

"But we will be doing a lot better when Mary comes clean and tells us the name of her new mystery man, who might just turn out to be the man of her dreams. She met him in the hospital cafeteria, which means we probably know this man." Robert turned his attention away from Lisa and focused his gaze back on Mary. "Tell us his name, Mary."

"Why?"

Robert opened both hands with palms up and fingers pointing toward her. "I want to know if I know him?"

"If you do not know him, Robert, perhaps I do. May I ask his name?" Lisa asked.

"Good morning. Who is about to be thrown under the bus?" Lauren Jaco asked as she continued to walk into the room to stand next to Lisa. "Please tell me what I missed," she asked, looking at Lisa.

"The name of the new love in Mary's life," Lisa answered, looking from Lauren to Mary.

"Oh. Holding back on us. Eh, Mary?" Lauren said with a slight giggle. "Fess up. Who is he?"

Mary's eyes narrowed as she pressed her lips tightly together as she grew angry. She raised her eyebrows and stood there with a slight red glow on her face, blushing. She studied the look on the faces of Robert, Lisa, Lauren, and Rachel before she turned to face Lauren. She was searching her mind for the right words. "You do not know him. Please leave it alone and a mystery for now. Okay?" she answered almost embarrassingly.

"No. Sorry. It does not work that way, Mary. You are among trusted friends. Fess up. Name please."

"Come on, Robert. Please leave it alone for now. Please."

"No problem. Your reluctance to tell us his name speaks volumes. Face it, you are not impressed with this new love of your life. He must be quite an embarrassment to you, which makes me wonder why you even want him in your life?"

"Bobby!" Rachel yelled.

"What? What else am I to think?"

Robert's comments made Mary seething mad. She wanted to say something hateful back at him to hurt his feelings like he just hurt her feelings. Her first thought was to slap his face and walk out of his life. With this thought on her mind, she started walking closer to him. Robert could tell his comment really upset her. Her eyes possessed the angriest look he had ever seen in her eyes before now. Understandably he grew more apprehensive as he watched her continue to walk toward him. When she was only three feet from him, she stopped and stood silently for the longest minute, staring holes though his eyes. She angrily opened her mouth to speak words that would certainly end their friendship when the voice within her head whispered, *Stop. Do not say it. He is your friend. Tell him the name he wants to know.* Suddenly she changed her mind and closed her mouth. Robert, Lauren, Lisa, and Rachel were mentally blown away, seeing this sudden change in her demeanor and had to see this sudden softer look in her eyes to believe what they just witnessed. Mary noticed the bewildered look on Robert's face and noticed his mouth hanging open, looking at her without speaking.

"Do not ask. You would not believe me if I told you." Mary smiled, and that smile totally blew his mind.

Robert continued to sit on his bed next to Rachel, shaking his head. "What did I just witness? Wow! That was some transition to watch. Maybe one day you might explain this to me?"

"Maybe." Mary smiled at his reactions to her demeanor change and waited for him to look back up at her before she spoke. "But if I tell you, I will have to kill you."

Mary started the laugh that made everyone roar with laughter. Robert had gotten better at controlling his spontaneous burst of

LOVE WILL FIND YOU

laughter, but Mary's comment caught him totally off guard as his face and neck turned beet red as he fought hard to get a fresh breath of air.

Fortunately Lisa and Lauren were standing next to his bed instead of down at the nurses' station. They were trained to know exactly what to do, and in seconds, a smile spread across Robert's handsome face. "Your lung capacity is much better than the last time you coughed like that. You could have recovered from this one on your own, but I am glad Lauren and I were here. "Do you feel okay, Dr. Wilson?"

"Yes. Thanks to you two nurses, I am. Thank you very much. You two are the best of the best."

"Why, thank you, "Lauren and Lisa responded at the same time.

Robert looked over at Mary, smiled, and raised his eyebrows without speaking.

"Okay. I will tell you without killing you. You almost did that yourself." Mary laughed out loud, and that started everyone inside the room to start laughing again.

Rachel turned and smothered Robert with her body as she yelled, "Not you, Bobby."

Robert was so stunned by her attack he did not have a chance to laugh.

"Now we know how to control his fits of laughter," Lauren said as she laughed, looking at Lisa before they happily completed a high five.

Robert had regrouped and regained his composure, thanks to Rachel. Looking at Mary, he bowed his head toward her and politely asked, "May I have his name now, Mary?"

"You may. I must admit you definitely earned the right to know his name. Ed Cox is the name of the man who replaced Stanley in my life. Do you know him?"

Lauren and Lisa yelled at the same time, "Yes."

"Is that a good yes?" Mary asked excitedly, not intending to use that high of a tone in her voice.

"You must not have a clue who Ed Cox is if you have to ask that question. Do you?" Robert asked her.

"I know a lot about him. But maybe not the things you feel I should know. Do you care to fill me in?"

"I apologize, Mary. You have met and talked to this man whom I have never met. Doctors do talk to other doctors. My information about him comes from several other doctors who have had dealings with him."

"Please tell me if their dealings with him were pleasant or not so pleasant?" Mary asked.

"Not one doctor has ever said one negative thing about him. They say he is all business and a nice guy."

"I would describe him as a very nice man. Nothing business with me." Mary suddenly blushed at her comment. "You know what I mean."

"No. I do not know what you mean, Mary. Fill me in on the other things he does with you."

"Men. Always got your minds in a gutter."

The room erupted with laughter. "You better quit while you are behind, Mary," Rachel said teasingly.

Mary picked up a white towel lying on a chair, waved it back and forth a couple of times, before she playfully threw it at Robert, saying, "You win. I surrender. Men just do not play fair."

"Okay. I apologize. I will be nice. You can keep all your secrets, and I will still tell you everything I know about Ed Cox through the hospital grapevine. Not from my firsthand or direct knowledge. Deal?"

"There is not a story for the tabloids in my brief relationship with Ed. Just a few kisses, so I agree. Deal."

"Whoa. Even one kiss from Ed Cox might be a story for the tabloids. I will wait to hear your story."

"Do I have to prepare a nondisclosure form for you to sign to ensure that whatever I say remains very confidential and between us?"

"No. I will agree to keep what you say about Ed Cox confidential. You have my word. Okay?"

"Yes. I trust your word. Thank you. Okay, please tell me what you know about Ed Cox."

"In his defense, the things I am going to tell you are things he would never tell you about himself. He earned his position at the hospital by working long hours. He is very well-liked by everyone. By reputation he is friendly but a little standoffish. He is known as a person who likes to keep to himself."

"And knowing all this about him, I am shocked you were able to introduce yourself to him, and he took that impromptu moment to begin a conversation with you," Lauren said.

"I am both double and triple shocked to find out this chance meeting then took off and blossomed into *any* kind of a relationship," Lisa added.

"He is known to be a nice man but also known to have a huge self-imposed wall he mentally erected around his private life," Lauren said as she raised her eyebrows.

"People who know a lot more about him than I do will tell you he is number 1 on every woman's list of available single men, and very standoffish when it comes to initiating a relationship with any woman."

"If this is all true, what in the world did he ever see in me so quickly, Robert? Do you know anything about previous women who might have penetrated this wall he has around him? In other words, has any woman ever been a part of his life?" Mary asked.

"All I know are rumors," Robert answered.

"If you are not betraying a trust, can you tell me these rumors?"

"Yes. Rumor has it he met and married the love of his life."

"I knew it. Married. Boy, I can pick 'em, can't I?"

"Hold on. I need to tell you the whole rumor before you run downstairs to scratch his eyes out."

"Sorry. Your use of the word *married* instantly sent a dagger through my heart. Please continue. I will try not to interrupt you," Mary said.

"No apology needed, Mary. I understand."

"Thank you, Robert."

"You are welcome. To be honest with you, I do not know for a fact if he ever married her. The rumor says he met a girl, and after he met her, he was always seen with a big smile on his face and a positive word for everyone. His friends said this woman made him deliriously happy. Her sudden death almost destroyed him. It broke his heart and killed every instinct he had to even smile. It zapped every positive emotion from his body. He was a dead man walking. He vowed to keep women at an arm's length to avoid the pain he endured when the love of his life died. I am not sure about the married part of the story. I am sorry. I did not mean to upset you or to make you cry."

"I did not know I had that instant tear button inside of me." Mary continued to stare at him as she slowly blew out a long breath of air and shook her head sideways. "Wow. Ed never told me that he had lived through that kind of pain and heartbreak." Mary blew out another long breath of air, trying to compose herself. She glanced over at Rachel and saw a tear sliding down her face too. Next she glanced over at Lisa and Lauren and saw that they too were struggling to control their own emotions over this tragic news of Ed Cox, who they loved and admired.

"From the reactions in this room, it is a given that Ed Cox is well-liked and respected. Do you know him to be an honest man?" Mary asked as she looked at Robert, then to Lisa and Lauren, who were nodding their heads up and down. Mary took this time to eat a few bites of popcorn from the bag she held in her hand.

"People often joke about him being Honest Abe," Lisa offered during the brief silence.

Mary stepped closer to Robert and gave him a big hug. "Thank you, Robert. You just made my day, week, month, and year. Thank you."

"Please tell me how I managed to do all this for you?"

"You told me that Ed is known as Honest Abe, which is the same as saying he is an honest man. Ed told me that he has never been married, and I believed him then, and I believe him now. Hearing you say you were not positive about his being married made my heart flutter with overwhelming feelings of joy. Thank you for that. I want a love I can trust and believe in. I do believe in Jesus, who lives inside my heart. Jesus led me to Ed, who saw something instantly in me to make him want to begin a conversation with me that ultimately led to his trusting me with personal information about his life, and that appears to be a huge leap for him."

"Wow. Thank you for sharing all this with us, Mary," Robert said with sincere emotion.

"Being in love is making me sentimental. I honestly love the new way I now view life and people."

"You have definitely piqued my interest about your new love, Ed Cox. And I love how you are now praying to ask God to guide you. Rachel has always been led by the Holy Spirit. I am touched by the way you feel that same love and guidance of Jesus. Thank you for telling me, Mary."

"You are welcome. Thank you for not making fun of my emotions."

"I do not believe anyone would make fun of what you just shared with us," Rachel said before she looked at the face of each person, watching them nod their head in agreement with her statement.

"Thank you, Rachel. You and everyone in this room make me feel like I am one of you, and I belong here."

"You definitely belong, and you are one of us, Mary." Robert watched her emotional reaction to his words.

Mary looked at each face smiling back at her before she said, "You are my new family, forever."

Rachel slid off the side of Robert's bed to say, "I am first. Give me a family hug." Rachel laughed.

"Second," Lisa called out.

Lauren stepped closer to Mary, saying, "Yep, you saved the best for last." Lauren laughed along with the others, who loved how she phrased her last comment to Mary.

"Thank you very much." Mary turned to face Robert before she asked, "Do you know how Ed's girlfriend died?"

"A tractor and trailer ran a red light, traveling at a high rate of speed and T-boned her car as she entered the intersection. The tractor ran into the driver's door, killing her instantly. Ed reportedly went into a deep state of depression that seemed to turn off every emotion within his body, until God brought you into his life. You obviously made a life-changing first impression for him to let you inside the fortress he erected around his heart."

"Why me? I am nothing special. Why me, Robert? After hearing what you just told me, what in the world did Ed ever see so quickly in me?"

"Let me see if I can answer that question for you since you are putting me in the hot seat and definitely on the spot."

"Sorry. You are right. This is not fair of me. I withdraw the question."

"Too late. I already processed it in my mind, and I want to answer it if you will allow me to. Will you?"

"I will do better than that. I will also allow you to lie about me." Mary laughed out loud, making the others laugh.

"Let me first deal with the obvious thing. Ed quickly observed your appearance."

"Oh, brother. Do you have to start there? I admit that I do have about ten more pounds I need to lose."

"Good men don't care about ten extra pounds. More to love is their motto. Ed is a good man, so you are safe. Besides, I am looking at you now, and I do not see where you need to lose ten pounds. You are simply not hard to look at. Which tells me he was immediately attracted to you physically."

"You are very kind."

"He is very honest."

"Thank you, Rachel. You are also exceedingly kind."

"Continuing my critique of you, once he looked into your eyes, he saw the softness in your heart that we see, and knew right away that you were a good person."

"And you think he could tell this by looking into my eyes?" Mary asked.

"Absolutely. You may not know that one of his areas of expertise is as an ophthalmologist. He knows everything he needs to know about the human eye, including eye colors. He has performed hundreds of eye surgeries. Did you know any of this about Ed?"

"Being confined to this room, how do you know any of these things about Ed?"

"Now the lawyer side of you comes out. Good for you, Mary."

"Are you trying to duck my question?" Mary asked teasingly with a smile.

"I am a licensed medical doctor with my specialty listed as cardiologist. I do have hospital status. Doctors do come in here to speak with me about my injuries and the progress of my recovery. We discuss many things about this hospital, including Ed Cox, who runs this hospital.

"Ed runs this hospital?"

"Yes, ma'am. Ed wears many hats to go with his many different medical degrees. He is a smart man."

"We did discuss eye colors, which was fascinating to me, but he never told me his specialty. I walked with him to his office to get his business card and the private phone number he wanted me to use to call him. I never looked at his business card or looked for his name on his office door when we walked into his office."

"These things were not on your mind at the time. You walked with him to get his business card with his private number, and he gave it to you. No alarm bells or reason to question anything," Robert reasoned to her.

"I stood in his office while he wrote his private phone number on the back of his business card, and I never took the time to read his office plaques hanging on his office wall. I was too preoccupied looking at him. I guess that shows you the level of trust and respect I had for him."

"Yes. It does. He is an impressive guy. But you would not have learned about his medical specialty from his business card."

"No?"

"No. He is the chief honcho of the hospital. He keeps it all running smoothly wearing many hats and being the genius he truly is."

"I am glad you think of him favorably like I do, Robert."

"Absolutely. I really do. And if he talked to you for any length of time, which he obviously did, he also concluded you two had a lot in common. You are a smart woman with a decent head on your shoulders, and exceptionally good-looking."

"Wow! Now you are going off script. I never paid you to say all that."

"I want to make sure I earn every penny you paid me." They both laughed out loud.

"I never dreamed those words would ever come out of your mouth about me. Oh, wait. I get it. I am not blond but, in your eyes, slow." Mary laughed, looking at him, then glanced at Rachel. "He really thinks I am as dumb as a blonde." The whole room burst into laughter.

"Watch it if you still want a ride back home in my car." Rachel smiled and then burst into a belly laugh.

Mary could not resist laughing as she raised her right hand to complete a high five with Rachel. She looked at Robert. "This is the part where you confess that you just lied to me. Right?" Mary laughed, looking at Robert.

"Busted." Robert laughed.

"See. I knew it." Mary rolled her eyes.

"Wait. It pains me, but as bad as I want to, I cannot lie to you. I spoke the truth about you."

"I wish I had recorded your words to play back for me to listen to every morning and every night. Darn."

"Close your eyes every morning and every night to allow your brain to recall my words that are etched into your heart. Those words are my opinion, and they are worth exactly what you just paid me for them." Robert smiled at her before he glanced toward Rachel and then to Lisa and Lauren. "How did I do?" he asked.

"Do you really see me the way you just described me?" Mary asked hesitantly.

"I bet everyone in this room sees you the way I just described you, Mary." Robert glanced at the others for confirmation and watched them nod their heads in agreement.

"I always had the feeling that you thought of me as a bimbo."

"Why?"

"The way I treated Stanley."

"The way you treated Stanley is the reason I could never think of you as a bimbo."

"Really? Please explain that to me."

"You had reasons to be incredibly angry and justified to vent your angry feelings on Stanley. I was surprised when you held your tongue. I was also surprised when you came over to me and said such nice things to me before you turned to walk out of this room. Only a mature responsible person who had complete control over her emotions could do such a thing. You impressed me. Bimbo? Not you, my dear. You are a catch."

Robert's comments hit a nerve strong enough to stun her emotionally. To avoid tears flowing down her face, she looked down at the floor to quickly recapture her composure. She did not want to appear to be a baby. She closed her eyes and just listened to additional comments made about her.

"I agree with everything Bobby just said to you, Mary," Rachel said her comments with emotion.

"I also agree," Lauren said.

"Me too," Lisa added as she looked at Mary and raised her eyebrows before she looked at Robert.

"I am both lucky and blessed to have you guys for friends. Thank you for being my friend." Mary felt the emotion rising within her and had to bow her head once again to get control of her emotions.

"You're very welcome. May I ask how you met him? I know before you tell me, this meeting had to be both memorable and unexpected from his point of view."

"And from mine as well. Neither of us will ever forget our memorable and very unexpected meeting."

"If he shook your hand and was gracious to you, that would probably be very memorable to him. You have us in suspense. Please tell us how you got Ed Cox into a conversation with you?" Lisa asked.

"Yes. Forgetting, just for a moment, anything romantic. Just knowing him, I, too, would love to know how you got him into a conversation with you that consisted of more than a few words. Boy, times like this, I wish I could record what you are going to say," Lauren said while shaking her head, feeling a little bewildered.

"To be honest, he did everything to make our relationship possible."

"Ed Cox?" Lisa and Lauren both yelled out at the same time. "No way," Lisa said.

"Yep," Mary said honestly.

"I want to hear this story," Robert admitted. "The floor is yours, my dear."

"Thank you. To tell you the truth, initially I was a little angry with him and close to giving him a piece of my mind. And then again, on two different occasions, when a voice within my head told me to *be still*. That is my only part in making this relationship a possibility. I managed to keep my big mouth shut."

"I bet that part was monumental for you," Rachel said teasingly and laughed out loud.

"Watch it, blondie." Mary's eyes smiled at Rachel's eyes. These eyes were destined to be close friends.

"This is sounding like the start of a great movie," Rachel said, smiling at her.

Mary smiled back at Rachel, cleared her throat, and blew out a long breath of air. She then looked at the face of each person waiting for her to begin telling her story. "Okay. This is what happened. I slid my tray holding my food and coffee to the register and paid the lady. I saw empty tables to my left, at eight o'clock on a watch, so I picked up my tray and took one step toward the empty tables and literally walked right into him. I had one leg stretched out toward the empty tables and the other leg trying to balance me and the tray holding my food and coffee, when he put his hands over my hands to steady the tray and keep me from falling onto the floor. He had been to the restroom and intended to walk past me to return to his table when I stepped into his path. Once I got control of myself, I tried to walk away from him to the empty tables, but he wouldn't remove his hands from mine. I started to give him a piece of my mind when I got the first message from the voice within my head that said, 'Be still and trust this man.'"

"Wow! Déjà vu all over again for Rachel and me," Robert said to her as he glanced at Rachel.

"Yes. I was thinking the same thing. God chose that way for Robert and me to meet," Rachel said to Mary.

"He did, didn't he, Rachel? I immediately thought about you and Robert when I met Ed Cox this way."

"God does not make mistakes. I love our chances to have a successful marriage, don't you?" Rachel asked.

"Yes. We both met in remarkably similar ways. God must bring introverted people together this way."

"I love the beginning of this story. Do not leave any of the romantic details out," Lauren said, looking at Mary. "Now is the time I wish I did have a recorder. I am happy for you, Mary."

"Thank you, Lauren."

"You took the words right out of my mouth, Lauren. I am happy for you, too, Mary," Lisa said.

"Thank you, Lisa. I was initially upset with myself for not taking my tray and walking away. I just stood there, looking into his eyes. In fact, I have never seen in any man's eyes what I saw in his eyes. I had a hard time shifting my eyes away. And against my nature, I found myself letting go of my tray and following him to a different table about two o'clock on a watch. He set my tray down on a table next to what appeared to be an abandoned tray full of food and a drink. He arranged my food items next to that abandoned tray someone left on the table. He then picked up my tray that had a small puddle of coffee that had spilled from my coffee cup, onto my tray, and took two napkins from the abandoned tray full of food and wiped up my spilled coffee.

"I then unconsciously sat down on the empty chair at the table where he was arranging my food. He looked down at me, smiled, and said, 'Please do not go anywhere. I will be right back with a fresh cup of coffee for you. Okay?'

"I remember asking him, 'Who does this tray next to me belonged to?' 'A very special friend that you will like, instantly. Trust me.'

"I bet he wished he had set my tray down and ran out of the cafeteria before he heard me say, 'I do not trust any man, so please do not ask me to trust them or you. I do not know you.'

"'Fair enough,' he said. 'I will get you a fresh cup of coffee, along with a clean tray, and come back to properly introduce myself.

Let your heart decide if you want to be one of my trusted friends. I hope you do.'

"I asked him why?

"'Look in the mirror,' he said to me.

"'Oh please. Men say kind things to women up until we get a few wrinkles, add a few pounds, or get older, while they ignore their own wrinkles and beer bellies. That is when they trade *us* in for a younger model.'

"Several ladies in the cafeteria clapped, laughed, cheered, and even whistled hearing these comments from me."

Lisa and Lauren did a high five while laughing and shaking their heads. Rachel burst into laughter and grabbed her stomach before she walked over to also complete a high five with Mary.

"Good one, Mary," Rachel confessed.

"What did he say to you after those absurd comments from you?" Robert asked.

"Absurd? That is exactly how men are to all women," Mary answered vehemently.

"That gets *no admission* from me." Robert winked at her and smiled. "Continue with this *fairy tale*."

"This is a *true story*." Mary emphasized her last words and paused to let those words sink into Robert's brain as she looked defiantly into his eyes. "May I continue, *my lordship*?"

"Please do." Robert bowed sarcastically from his waist. He pressed his lips tightly together and smiled his biggest smile yet at her. "You don't even have to say master or, Mother, may I?" He winked at her.

Mary looked at Rachel. "You have work to do to make him more women friendly."

"Yep. He is a challenge, but nothing a good woman like me cannot handle." Rachel leaned toward Robert and gave him a kiss. "Be nice to her, Bobby."

"Nice? I am being nice. I am always extra nice to her. After all, she is the one who found me. Thank you, Mary. Please continue with your *true story*." Robert fake coughed and rolled his eyes.

Mary shook her head and, while blowing out a disgusting breath of air, glanced at Rachel and said, "I swear if I had it to do over again, I would have disregarded my phone call to this hospital and let him be unfindable." Glancing at Robert, she shook her head from side to side. "Lord, what in the world was I thinking?"

The room erupted in laughter as Mary kept shaking her head in playful disgust, looking at Rachel. "I will pray extra hard for you, Rachel." Everyone in the room laughed just a little harder.

"You love me, Mary," Robert said to her while raising only one eyebrow, looking hopefully at her.

"Love you, or do you really mean what would I love to do with you right now?" Mary walked over to the window and looked down at the street and looked back at him. "Hmm. I will fight the temptations to roll your bed over to this window and—" Her additional words were lost in the roar of laughter.

"Cute. Real cute, Mary. Truce. I will be kind and quiet while you tell the rest of your story."

Mary looked at him questionably, cleared her throat one more time, before she continued, "Ed said, 'I see you have a fan club. Congratulations.' Ed then bowed his head.

"'Thank you, Ed.' Other women love it when one of us tells it like it really is to a man."

"'You are welcome, I think? The look you have within your eyes tells me you have a kind heart. I believe even you know this to be true.'

"Before I could speak, he put up his hand and said, 'Hold that thought until I return with your coffee. Okay?'

"I said okay. He came back with a fresh cup of coffee, napkins, and a clean tray.

"He then said, 'You surprised me in a good way. I have a good feeling about you. We have the potential to be great lifetime friends.' While listening to him, I leaned forward to take a sip of the hot coffee he brought to me when he asked, 'Do you love me, yet?' I practically choked on the mouthful of coffee I had in my mouth as a little ran down my chin. I grabbed one of the clean napkins he just brought to the table and wiped my chin to protect my blouse. Then I just sat there and stared at him in total disbelief."

"What in the world did you say to him?" Lauren asked as she glanced over at Lisa.

"I said, 'Love you? I do not even know you. Who are you?' I felt embarrassed. Thank goodness for the clean napkins. He then came around the table and sat down next to me, in front of the tray full of food that I thought somebody else had left on the table. Neither of us spoke a single word. I forced myself to look at him. I was feeling angrier at him than I have ever felt in a long time. I decided to simply stare at him until he looked me in the eyes. I wanted him to see my anger, and I wanted him to hear the shortest and cruelest tongue-lashing he has ever heard or received. He turned slowly toward me until his eyes were looking into my eyes. Never in my life have I ever seen a friendlier pair of eyes looking back at me. My anger melted, and I literally forced myself to smile at him. I was frozen in place, watching him open his mouth to speak to me.

"'I might as well eat this food somebody left here. Right? Cannot let it go to waste. Can we?'

"'Please tell me this is your food, or I am out of here. I mean it. I am getting up and leaving now.'"

"Oh, Mary. I do not blame you one bit," Lisa said to her while showing a little anger of her own at the attitude of Ed Cox. "I would have given him a piece of my mind and walked out. Did you?"

"No."

"No? Why?" Lisa asked.

"Because even you will not believe the next thing he says to me."

"I give up. I cannot even guess. Tell me," Lisa asked.

"He said, 'Oh no! Here comes trouble. Remember, you made me sit down here to eat this food.'

"I had enough of this guy at this point, so I said, 'No, I will not be—' He interrupted me by putting his left hand over my left hand that was resting on the table next to my tray, and he put his right arm around my shoulder and gently pulled me closer to him."

"You got to be kidding me. He does not sound anything like the Ed Cox I know. You must be with an impostor," Lauren said.

"I agree with you. This does not sound like the Ed Cox that I know either," Lisa confirmed.

"This big guy walked up and said, 'Hey, buddy, what are you doing sitting here, eating that food with your girlfriend?' This guy spoke in a loud, stern, angry voice.

"I was a little frightened and ready to run. Ed Cox must have sensed it the way he pulled me even closer to him and started talking to this big guy."

"What did he say to him?" Robert asked.

"'I am sorry, pal. I just took one look at her pretty face and sat down here when she told me to. Do you blame me?' I again started to say something in protest when Ed pulled me even closer and started laughing. I remember I turned toward him and glared at him. I was embarrassed and stunned. I continued to stare at him, trying to get my mind to work."

"I bet you were hot as a firecracker at him," Rachel said.

"Yep. I was more than a little angry and wanted to say something legal, curt, and hurtful so he would never forget my words. Finally my mind worked. I was ready to lay into him when that same inner voice seemed to yell at me, 'Be still.' It was then that I noticed Ed Cox's eyes looked unusually friendly. Not scared. Not concerned about this big guy about to pounce on both of us. He was cool, calm, collected, and smiling. *Bam.* It hit me. I got a longer and better look at his handsome face and realized why my brain suddenly went AWOL. It baffled me for the longest time. Here I am, a lawyer, and lawyers are known to be a mouthpiece for someone, so why now? Why fail me now? It was not like me not to speak up and let this stranger standing in front of me know that I do not know this guy sitting next to me, and I never asked him to sit down next to me to eat another person's food. I was finally ready to speak my mind. Suddenly the mystery became crystal clear to me. I now understood why Felix chose that moment to climb into my mouth to bite my tongue. God was involved in this charade. I just closed my mouth and continued to stare at the handsome face of Ed Cox, just wondering what he was going to do next."

307

"Wow. This is sounding like a script for a movie," Robert said with his eyes opened wide.

"The big guy standing in front of me said to me, 'Ma'am, you need to find me tomorrow. *I* will sit anywhere you want me to.' He then burst into laughter along with Ed Cox. He confessed to me that he has known Ed Cox for an exceptionally long time when they played these kinds of jokes on each other in college and in med school. Ed always chose to be a loner. They lost contact with each other for a few years. Recently they hooked up again at this hospital. He could not resist the opportunity to come tease Ed when he saw him sitting here in this cafeteria next to me, especially when he remembered that Ed used to be a loner. He had to come closer to see what Ed saw in me."

"Did he ever say why he was a loner?" Rachel asked.

"No. But he did tell me that he noticed me come into the cafeteria over the last few months and never saw me with a man before today."

"Wow. Sounds like you have two eligible men after you. Do you?" Lisa asked. "Please do not leave us dangling here. What happened next?"

"He then said he came over to ask me if I was available to date since Ed was known to be a loner. He asked me if Ed was my brother and just sitting here with his arm around me for show?"

"Oh, that is a hoot. What did you say?" Robert asked.

"I said, 'No. I am sorry. I cannot tell you a lie. He is not my brother.' My heart melted along with my embarrassment and anger after hearing the things the big guy just revealed to me about his enjoyable history with Ed."

"Did Ed Cox have his arm around you this whole time?" Rachel asked.

"Surprisingly yes. And his arm was not uncomfortable. I remember whispering to him, 'Do you want your arm back?'

"He looked at me and said, 'No. You keep it.'

"'How long?' I remember studying every square inch of his face before I finally looked into his eyes. Surprisingly I never felt nervous or uncomfortable looking into his eyes while sitting so close to him.

I wondered what this mystery man was going to do or say next. His boldness intrigued me."

"Totally out of character for him. I am shocked. He is always so standoffish," Lauren said.

"What did he see in me so quickly?" Mary asked Lauren.

"That is now a two-way street. You allowed him to sit very close to you for a long time, with his arm round you. Perhaps he saw in you what you were seeing in him, love," Lisa answered her with raised eyebrows and a big smile. I cannot wait to hear what happened next.

"Next he told me he knew I could afford to pay his price for having his arm around me."

"What! He plans on charging *you* for putting *his arm around you?* The nerve," Rachel said.

"I know. I said, 'Your price?' That comment has now raised my curiosity way too high for me not to ask. 'Please tell me your price?'"

"Can you believe this guy?" Rachel said disgustingly. "What did he say?"

"No money or other expectations?"

"I never thought I would ever hear those words ever come out of a man's mouth." Mary looked at Rachel.

"You got that right," Rachel said as she slowly tilted her head to steal a look at Robert with one eye.

You will never hear even a part of that sentence come out of my mouth."

"You are partially trained. There is hope for you, Robert," Mary answered with a smile.

"Hey. I thought we had a truce?" Robert teased.

"My bad. You are right. My apology. Back to my *true* story. I was stunned by Ed's reply, so I said,

'I get it. You are gay.' I sat there and stared at him, waiting for his response. Everyone in the room erupted with laughter at Mary's comment.

"He calmly said, 'No. I am not gay.'

"I said, 'Let me try asking my question this way. Will I be offended in any way by your price?' He laughed and told me that he would like to show me what he wanted to receive from me.

"My guard was nine miles in the air at this point, so rather than say or do anything to run him off hastily, I asked, 'You do remember about my mistrust of men. Right?'

"'Yes, I do.'

"'And knowing this, you still want to show me rather than tell me. Right?'

"'Right.'

"'You are hereby forewarned that your demonstration better not offend me in any way.' I folded my arms across my chest to guard against anything he might insinuate to be an open invitation to invade my privacy and said, 'Show me.'"

"Good for you," Lisa said as she glanced at the faces of the other ladies, who were nodding their heads.

"He said, 'This is my first payment, and it is due now.' He leaned his face closer to my face and lightly kissed my lips. I bet he was shocked when he felt me impulsively kiss him back."

"You did not!" Lisa and Lauren both yelled at the same time as everyone in the room clapped and laughed.

"I did and immediately heard applause and cheers from people sitting around us at nearby tables and from the big guy who was still standing in front of us.

"When our lips parted, I remember smiling and saying, 'Paid in full.' I looked up at the big guy and asked, 'Are you still here?'

"He said, 'I was not about to leave a front-row seat to what will be one of the greatest future hospital love stories ever told. The medical world will never believe this story. Not about him.' He pointed to Ed Cox.

"'Should the untold things you know about Ed Cox embarrass me or make me happy?' I asked him.

"'Deliriously happy. Especially with your life hooked to his. You do not know who he is, do you?'

"'No. Please tell me.'

"Ed said, 'Before you tell her anything, I must get her to answer one question for me. Okay?' Ed looked at me. 'Please tell me you are not involved in a relationship or going through a nasty divorce to unleash an angry boyfriend or husband on me.'"

"Ed Cox asked you that question?" Lauren asked.

"Yep. He sure did."

"He must have been smitten with you immediately. Was he?" Lisa asked questionably.

"I cannot believe we are talking about the same Ed Cox," Lauren said, looking bewildered.

"I cannot either. This is unbelievable from everything I have heard about him," Robert said.

"I answered his question by telling him that I was not married, and I was not going through a nasty divorce. And I did tell him that I met a man here at the hospital a few months ago and began a short-term friendship that abruptly ended with nothing more than a few kisses. So I am not involved with anyone."

"What did he say to your comments?" Robert asked.

"He told me I just made his day."

"This is a story for Hallmark movies," Robert said, shaking his head slowly. "I am impressed and happy for you, Mary."

"I have never met a man like him before," Mary revealed while gazing past Robert out the window.

"Anything specific?" Robert asked as he watched her stare out the window.

"After we sat down next to each other, I instantly felt amazingly comfortable being with him. I have never sat that close to any man before in my life. I did not want to leave his side. I kept wishing he would think of another reason to kiss me. Is that not crazy? How does anyone fall in love so fast? There it is! I said it. I met, kissed, and fell in love with Ed Cox within a few hours of meeting him for the first time in my life. Do I need a shrink?"

"If you do, you better schedule that first appointment for one more person. I suspect he is now telling his close friends a similar story of how he met and fell in love with you," Robert answered honestly. "Is there more to this story?" Robert asked.

"Yes. We sat there for more than an hour talking about eye colors," Mary admitted.

"I expected him to know a lot about eye colors. I mentioned to you that he did hold several degrees. He enrolled into several post-graduate courses, one after the other, and aced them all. I suspect that he loved talking with you about eye colors. The man is a walking genius with a photographic memory."

"Awesome. He knows everything about every different shade of eye color. Before he would answer my question about each eye color, he first wanted to charge me a kiss," Mary confessed and immediately blushed. "Honestly I was shocked that any man, especially Ed, would agree to *my terms* on kissing."

"I would love to hear these terms." Robert laughed out loud and seemed to enjoy it when others in the room laughed too.

"Well, I did not want to sit in a cafeteria and continue kissing a man I just met, every time he told me about a different eye color. Kissing should be spontaneous and special, so I told him how I felt."

"Good for you, Mary," Lisa said vehemently.

"Did he agree with you?" Robert asked.

"He said, 'I agree to no more kissing at this table today.'"

"Just like that? End of kissing story?" Robert asked.

"Not quite."

"I thought so. Way to go, Ed," Robert said triumphantly.

"Not so fast, Robert. He wanted to add an addendum to our verbal agreement."

"Which is what?"

"He asked, 'Is it okay if we exchange a kiss when we part from each other later today?'"

"And you said?"

"I said, 'Yes. A brief kiss on the lips when we meet or part would always be welcomed by me.'

"He added, 'Plus a kiss to commemorate a happy circumstance during any day for either of us?' He looked at me with a hopeful expression.

"I immediately agreed to his additional terms. I would agree to any legitimate reason for him to kiss me again." Mary looked suspiciously at Robert, then glanced at Rachel, Lisa, and Lauren. "Go ahead, say it." Mary shook her head and abruptly walked over to look out the window.

"You have rewritten the dating handbook, Mary. No need for you to feel guilty or shameful in anything you have done so far in this relationship with Ed. God is moving in Ed's life and in your life. It is your turn to be blessed, and speaking for myself, I am glad I am privileged to be a witness to the spontaneous things God is doing in your life. You are a testimony for every single person who is looking for love to hear or read about your experiences. Once your relationship with Ed is consummated in marriage, tell your story to the world."

"I have got to hug you for those comments, Robert. May I?"

"Yes. I welcome a hug from you anytime, Mary." When their bodies parted, Robert said, "I will keep my ears open and let you know the feedback from the gossip mill circulating this hospital. Believe me, it will circulate quickly and predictably make the tabloids," Robert said with sincerity, a nod, and a big smile.

"Thank you for talking with me, Robert. Your friendship means a lot to me," Mary confessed.

"You are very welcome. I hope everything works out for you."

"Thanks. Me too. I do not like being in the dating world. Did you like being in it?"

"Not really. I am glad *that* part of my life is shored up. I was blessed beyond what I truly deserved when God sent Rachel into my life."

"I myself am cautiously optimistic as I begin to tiptoe into a new relationship with Ed. Everything feels good right now. Naturally I am skeptical and waiting for the other shoe to drop. I keep waiting for bad news to rain on my rose-colored visions of life with Ed. I live with this bad feeling that something or someone will destroy the love I feel in my heart. I will pray every day that I am wrong."

"I am not privy to your past, so I cannot see the hills, valleys, dips, curves, or potholes you zigged, and you zagged around to get where you are today. I do not know where your pessimistic feelings come from. I am getting the impression that your past life has not been smooth or without its share of bumps and bad breaks, so all I can tell you is to focus on the positive things and try to block out the negatives. That might be too big of a task. I do not have all the answers, but I do know you have quality friends in this room who have your back no matter what you may face in your future. Okay?" Robert answered her with a look of concern on his face.

"Okay." Mary was caught totally off guard by his comments. Emotionally she has been through the wringer and did not expect any kindness or support from Robert. His kindness was so over-whelming she teared up and looked away from him to grab a tissue.

"Too much in one day for you?" Robert asked her hesitantly.

"No. Not really. I feel the need to tell you something about my past that might explain some of my unusual emotions. I had two supportive and very loving parents. They were each very successful in their careers and very active role-model parents and supportive of me. They encouraged me to achieve everything I was able to achieve in my life. Shortly after spending a wonderful weekend with them, I remember feeling so comfortable about my life, my achievements, and where my life was heading, when I received an unexpected phone call from a police officer informing me that both of my parents were just killed in a head-on car accident. I dropped the phone and collapsed into a minicoma. I have never been able to adequately describe the gut-wrenching pain that raced through my body as I dropped the phone and drifted into la-la land. I needed boatloads of counseling and a lot of alone time to mentally find a reason to get out of bed. I never realized that kind of emptiness and loneliness existed. I kept thinking about all the special occasions in my life that my parents will not be a part of. I never dreamed they would not be at my wedding, never hold their grandchildren, or celebrate their birthdays or graduations. The day I landed face-first on my kitchen floor, I broke my nose and my front tooth."

Mary was oblivious to anyone being in the room while she told her story to them and oblivious to the tsunami of tears freely flowing down her face. She held a handkerchief she used to dry her eyes and glanced up, for the first time, to witness every person in the room allowing tears to freely run down their faces.

Rachel was wiping tears from her eyes as she successfully man-aged to walk closer to Mary and stood by her side. Mary uninten-tionally looked up to allow Rachel to see the sadness and pain in her eyes. Rachel also grew up like Mary, without siblings. They each represented the sister that the other never had, until now. They hugged each other like sisters would, and that proved to be exactly what any doctor would have prescribed for the emptiness and pain they each felt in their own ways.

"Thank you, Rachel," Mary whispered into Rachel's ear.

"Please try to always remember that we are sisters in life with Jesus Christ in our hearts. Okay?"

"Thank you, Rachel." Mary finished wiping tears from her eyes. "Today has been overwhelming."

"Do you want to talk about anything?" Rachel asked.

"I never told you until recently about my becoming an attorney. May I tell you now?"

"Yes. I would love to hear that story and anything else you want to tell me," Rachel said with a smile.

"You are so kind and sweet to me, blondie." They both burst out laughing at the word *blondie.*

"I did attend and graduate from Harvard Law School. Ironically the same month I passed the bar exam and was sworn in to become an attorney, my parents were simultaneously killed in that car accident. I handled their estate and some of the legal matters associated with the young girl who drove the car that sent my parents to heaven. Normally when I do not know exactly what to do with important matters, I learned to back away from everything and do nothing. This is why I accepted a job as a waitress to figure out what to do with the rest of my life when you came into my life."

"Wow. God's perfect timing to bring you into my life just when I was about to lose contact with Robert. I did not know when we met that I was about to become a depressed person for several months. I often think about a two-letter word—*if*—that is so small but means so much."

"You got that right. *If* for this or *if* for that," Mary said.

"Exactly. Dr. Sharp fortunately fixed my broken front tooth that same morning we met. I immediately saw your broken front tooth and wondered how to get you into a conversation with me so I could refer you to her."

"God took care of that dilemma," Mary said. "God led *me* to comment about your beautiful front teeth, and that opened up a discussion with you that led you to refer me to her." Rachel nodded in agreement. "If we did not have a need to discuss your teeth or mine, we would not have been two of the people to find Robert when we did. He might still be in a coma." Mary looked toward Robert. "He is so lucky to have us in his life."

"Okay, ladies. Yes. I am lucky and blessed to have both of you in my life." Robert smiled.

"How did God know so far in advance who to move where and precisely when? We all know now you were ultimately chosen by God to find Robert." Rachel paused to look at Robert. "Be nice to her, Bobby."

Rachel looked at Mary with a confused look on her face. "I never really thought about the sequence and the precise movements everyone had to make on cue to find you. This plan had failure written all over it if one person did not do her part. The people involved acted out this Broadway play without a script, and it worked only by the grace of God." Rachel started shaking her head. "You are a very lucky man, Dr. Bobby Wilson."

"I am lucky to have you in my life. But before I agree to your Academy Award performances and buy bouquets of flowers or rose petals to lay at everyone's feet, may I hear the sequence of events acted out to find me in this Broadway play, Rachel? I have never heard the sequential story."

"Yes, you may. Mary was self-conscious about her broken front tooth. When she saw my new front teeth and made her appreciative comments, I referred her to Dr. Sharp." Rachel nodded toward Mary.

"Yes, you did. And if Dr. Sharp had not taken the time to speak with me, I never would have found you, Robert." Mary looked from Robert to Rachel.

"Oh, okay. I see now where you are going with this. God brought your lives together for a purpose you never saw at that time. God knew years ago, before you settled the estate of your parents and put your legal career on hold, that you would work as a waitress to meet Rachel. Now that part is almost mind-blowing if you pause long enough to think about it. I see now why you want to see God's day planner. Wow. That is planning pretty far in advance." Robert raised his eyebrows and shook his head, glancing from Rachel, Lisa, Lauren, and to Mary. "This is nothing short of a Hollywood movie revealing how God uses several people to change lives."

"I can add a bonus to this script," Mary pledged.

"How?" Robert asked.

"God simultaneously added a bonus just for me by orchestrating a crash meeting between me and Ed. God told Rachel I would meet what has turned out to be the love of my life on my trip up here to meet you, Robert. I call that a win-win." Mary put her lips together and smiled broadly from ear to ear without showing her teeth. "Now let me finish this amazing story of how we found you, Robert."

"I am all ears. Please continue." Robert smiled and bowed his head toward her.

"Rachel referred me to Dr. Sharp. I told her I needed ideas to help me find you. She could have ended our search for you by saying she did not have any ideas. She stopped what she was doing and took me back to her office and asked me the right questions to point me in the right direction of Johns Hopkins Hospital to find you. Do you see how easily this plan could have fallen apart by one person in this chain not doing her part?"

"Wow! God *does* move in mysterious ways." Robert shook his head and looked down at his folded hands before he looked back up and added, "I agree with everyone that everything had to happen in that precise order to find me. I am impressed, amazed, and very grateful," Robert admitted.

"Lauren and I have never heard the sequence of events to find you until today," Lisa admitted.

"Please keep us updated on how things progress with Ed Cox, and I will let you know anything I hear through the hospital rumor mill. Deal?" Robert asked.

"Deal. I am going to say good night and go back to my hotel. Thank you for speaking with me. I want to thank all of you for being my friends. I will see everyone tomorrow. Bye."

"Bye, Mary," Robert, Rachel, Lisa, and Lauren said as Mary waved and disappeared out the door.

CHAPTER 28

Dr. Robert Wilson Goes Home

═══════════════════════════════════════

Robert and Rachel were sitting on his bed talking when, during the conversation, Rachel asked, "Are you ready to get back to your life as a doctor, and us?" She carefully studied his face to detect any negative facial reaction or perhaps a look of indifference when she mentioned the word *us* to him. She was understandably concerned about their future together after what she had endured only a short few months ago when she wrongly concluded he had dumped her for another woman and moved on with his life. She braced herself and held her breath, praying to God to not allow his answer to break her heart. When he looked at her, and his lips started to move, she tensed up and dug her fingernails into her legs and waited to hear his words.

"Yes. I am ready to resume my life as a cardiologist and begin my life as a husband to you."

It had been what seemed like a lifetime since a happy feeling was a part of her life. Hearing the word *husband* coming out of his mouth, unexpectedly and voluntarily, simultaneously grew her eyes to the size of plates. She briefly looked away from him to allow his words to register in her mind and heart. Once she was sure she heard him correctly, she almost gave herself a whiplash turning her neck so quickly back to look into his eyes. Her mouth unconsciously opened without any words being spoken as her lips started to quiver because of the happy emotions now racing through her. Being unable to speak, she could only stare through her happy tears into his eyes, knowing she just heard words spoken to her that were every woman's dream to hear, and those words just rendered her speechless. She felt like screaming joyfully.

"Are you happy?" he asked.

"Deliriously happy, Bobby. I am floating on a love cloud."

"When you are happy, I will always be happy."

"What can we do to always feel this close to each other, Bobby? Is it even possible for us to design a plan where we have close daily communication to a point we never allow distance or anything to set in between us? How do we make this work for us to have a uniquely close bond? How, Bobby?"

"I want what you want, Rachel. I do not want to lose this either. A pinky promise, perhaps, with a vow to always spend a few minutes each night talking about our day with each other?"

"If this becomes hit and miss, we must agree to immediately plan a getaway trip for a weekend to keep that spark of love for each other alive, with hugs and kisses without a two-second rule."

They both laughed at the mention of a two-second rule as they completed a high five and laughed out loud.

"Are we good?" he asked.

"We are good. I love you so much, Bobby."

"I love you more."

"If you do, then we are really good." She giggled, then laughed out loud looking at him. "And to fully answer your question asking if we are good makes me confess that my hearing you say the word *husband* on your own, without any prompting from me, made my heart full. Your words choked me up, knowing you *do* want me by your side as your wife to build our lives together. Thank you for saying what you said to me, Bobby." Without another word being spoken, she opened her arms and impulsively wrapped them around him as her lips found his lips to suppress any additional words he might try to say to her.

Unable to speak with her lips pressed against his lips, he did not need any coaching to respond instinctively and aggressively to the second-best kiss of his life. He felt his emotions rise to a level forbidden by Rachel, but he could not resist trying to lower her down onto the bed.

When she felt him pulling her down toward the bed, she pushed back from him to look into his beautiful blue eyes. Once she had his full attention, she asked, "Why do you want to push me down onto the bed when you know we cannot do the things it will lead to, Bobby?"

"Guilty without an explanation, Rachel. I will never apologize for wanting to hold you in my arms. Never." He leaned closer to her and gave her a kiss he had stored up just for her.

When she tried to stand up and felt the weakness in her knees, she realized she could not stop Robert from pulling her back onto the bed and rolling her over onto her back. Rachel consciously surrendered to her own two-second-kiss rule, especially after hearing him say the word *husband,* as she focused on how deliriously happy she felt over now being kissed by the man of her dreams. She knew now how some of her close friends felt when they related stories to her about losing control of their emotions just before they completely surrendered to romance, the guidelines that they vowed to keep. They were both breathing hard and kissing each other so passionately they were oblivious to the presence of Nurses Lisa Phillips and Lauren Jaco, who had verbally announced their visit when they each entered the room, carrying several inflated colorful balloons.

Lisa and Lauren stood flanking Robert's bed for only a few seconds before they both started making exaggerated noises people make when they clear their throats.

Rachel and Robert turned their faces sideways, with their mouths opened wide toward the noises, but no words were spoken. Their guilty facial expressions told it all.

In unison, they both yelled, "Get a room, but not this room." Then their laughter was all that was needed for Rachel and Robert to burst into laughter.

"Busted," Rachel yelled out.

"Yep. Busted on my last day in this hospital. What is my punishment?" Robert asked.

"Well, for you, Robert, we are kicking you out of this hospital and ordering you to continue being a very successful cardiologist and verbally telling Rachel you love her every day for the rest of your life."

Lisa and Lauren turned toward each other and did a high five with big smiles spread across their beautiful faces.

"I accept your punishment for my sins, and I will comply," Robert said, smiling.

Mary Shipley walked into the room and stopped in her tracks with a peculiar look on her face, wondering what she had just missed. "Should I go get Ed and come back?"

"Cute," Rachel replied to Mary's comment. "How much notice do you need to say your goodbyes and pack up before we drive back home?"

"Honey, I am ready when you are. Knowing today was Robert's release date, I packed up last night."

"May I ask how you are leaving things with Ed?" Robert asked.

"Ed wants me to move up here and open a law office near him."

"Have you consulted with your protégé, Amy?" Rachel asked.

"Who is Amy?" Robert asked?

"Her future employee when she graduates law school and passes the bar," Rachel answered.

"You are talking about many years into the future. Aren't you, Mary?" Robert asked.

"No. On her law school breaks, she will be an asset to any law firm. I chose her for mine."

"Cool. Something tells me this is a mutually good deal for both of you. Right?"

"Right, Robert. She will work wherever I need her to work with me."

"I love how you answered that, Mary. Work with you and not for you. Good for you."

"Coming from a man who will show this same consideration to those who work with him. Touché. And I know you will also show your employees other valuable considerations they each deserve. Right? I like your style, Robert."

"Thank you, Mary. I like your style too.

"May I ask you a question about Stanley Spring?"

"Yes. Ask me anything you want about Stanley."

"Have you heard from him?"

"Yes. I have heard from Stanley."

"You have?" Lisa and Lauren asked at the same time. "When? Fess up."

"Stanley has hospital privileges regardless of the hour, and late one night, recently he came in to see me."

"Oh no you don't. You know the definition of fess up. All of it, Dr. Wilson," Mary said.

"I do not want to say anything that might hurt your feelings, Mary."

"You cannot hurt my feelings, Robert. I am in love with Ed Cox. Remember?"

"Okay. Stanley finally fell in love with a doctor who has been in love with him since their medical school days." Robert looked at her and raised his eyebrows, as if to say, *That is all.*

"I will hurt you, Robert. Details! What does this babe look like? How strong is their relationship? Hold nothing back from me, Robert."

"Geez. What a grouch. You missed your calling. You would have been a perfect fit as a general back in the Hitler days."

"Robert." Everyone in the room burst into laughter, hearing the tone used by Mary.

"Okay. She is a doctor who also specializes in cardiology. She is madly in love with him and has been for going on five or six years now. She is a blonde, with a beautiful face and athletic figure."

"So this relationship has been going on for many years. Right?"

"No. He had no idea he loved this woman until they recently sat in the cafeteria talking. It was during their conversation that two things happened that changed both of their lives."

"Which was? Please tell it all," Mary pleaded.

Robert nodded his head and held up his right hand, as if to tell her more was coming.

"Sorry." Mary smiled and bowed her head without comment.

"No problem. To continue with my comments, let me add that Stanley also mentioned that on one occasion, Stanley said something Gwen thought was funny enough for her to spit ice chips she had been sucking on onto his face and all over his medical coat, and they had fun laughing and cleaning up the ice chips. Stanley then declared to her that ice chips was her secret weapon."

"Cute. I love that story. She sounds like a hoot," Mary exclaimed, laughing.

"The other thing he mentioned was he remembered dancing with her in med school and working with her on medical projects. When he mentioned to her that he recalled dancing with her at med school dances but could not remember how it felt to hold her in his arms, she said, 'Do you want to find out now?' She got up and took one step into his arms and then told him she had been in love with him as far back as their med school days.

"Stanley fell head over heels in love with her on the spot, especially considering all their personal history together. Stanley hesitated to tell me the last part of his meeting with Gwen until I pried it out of him."

"Oh, boy. Now we get to the intimate details. The floor is yours, sir," Mary said excitedly.

"The entire cardiology department wanted to see these two find the love they all knew they had for each other. Gwen and Stanley really believed the love they felt for each other was being hidden from everyone. But neither of them had a clue that everyone who worked in cardiology knew about the love interest they had for each other. A nurse went down to the cafeteria to bring back her lunch when she happened to see Gwen and Stanley sitting at a table in the cafeteria, talking. Quickly and quietly, a small group of nurses and doctors rushed down to the cafeteria and spied on them from the overhead section of the cafeteria, directly above their table downstairs. For the longest time, they watched them talk, and then hug intimately, before their lips met for their first very passionate romantic kiss. The nurses in the above group were holding one another's hand as they excitedly jumped up and down, laughing and giggling like high school kids. This small group of doctors and nurses, who had gathered in an overhead section of the cafeteria, started clapping and cheering. This group started yelling cute sayings like 'Get a room,' as the group hugged one another and laughed excitedly seeing these two doctors find love. That day was an especially happy day for Gwen, Stanley, and everyone in the cardiology department who watched these two doctors experience how love brought their hearts together and how love found them.

"Before the overhead group dispersed to head back to their cardiology department, they could not resist yelling out, 'We love you.' Stanley looked at the faces of each person as he raised his eyebrows and his thumb high into the air as sign of his victory of finding the love of his life."

"Do you know how Stanley and Gwen reacted to the overhead group?" Mary asked.

"Yes. Stanley mentioned that they were both speechless They waved to the group. Stanley took Gwen into his arms to shield her and made a few friendly gestures to the group and held her until the group went away. That is all I know. End of intimate romantic story. Sorry." Robert laughed.

Mary glanced at Robert, then to Rachel. "Thank you, Robert. I am happy for Stanley."

"I am too. It appears everything is working out for you too, Mary."

"Yes. I am also happy. Thank you, Robert."

"You are welcome."

Lisa and Lauren stepped closer to Robert. "Time for us to make our hospital rounds and say goodbye. We both hate to see good patients like you go home. We feel like we have made a new friend in you, Robert. Thank you for being so kind to us. We will honestly miss you," Lisa said half of these parting words, and Lauren finished.

"I never had a joint message before, and I think that is so sweet, and it touches my heart. You two ladies are the best of the best in the nursing field. I was blessed to have you two assigned to me. May I get a goodbye hug?" Robert asked.

"Absolutely," Lisa said as she stepped into Robert's open embrace. "You take care of Rachel and tell her you love her every day. Goodbye, Robert."

"Goodbye, Nurse Lisa."

Robert turned slightly to his right to give Lauren a hug.

"Goodbye, Robert." While he was holding Lauren, she said, "It was my pleasure to meet you. Good luck with your new practice. Take good care of Rachel. Goodbye, Robert."

"Thank you for always being there for my every need. You two have saved me on more than one occasion, and I really appreciate both of you. Goodbye, Nurse Lauren."

Lisa and Lauren hugged Mary and Rachel and said their good-byes before they walked out of the hospital room door to make their hospital rounds.

Mary glanced over at Rachel. "Your prophecy has come true for me, Rachel. I met and fell in love with Ed Cox on this trip up here to find Robert. Stanley fell in love with Gwen Greyson. And you rekindled your made-in-heaven relationship with Robert." Mary nodded and smiled. "Do you ever wonder how God does what He does so far in advance? How does He know? How does He move people from one place to another so far in advance to make it all work out perfectly for love to find each of us? How?" Mary asked.

"God is all-knowing. To me it means the day we are created, God can see our whole life up until the day of our death, and *that date* is immediately entered into our book of life as the day our life on earth is over and the day we will leave this world. Only God can extend that day," Rachel answered with conviction in her voice.

"Do you really believe this to be true, Rachel?" Robert asked

"Yes, Bobby, I do."

"Interestingly we are all born with freedom to choose our own path in life, but God does give each of us His choice for every decision we are about to make." Rachel added.

"How do we get these choices from God?" Mary asked.

"Good question," Rachel answered with a smile on her face and love in her eyes.

"Do you have an answer to my *good question*?" Mary asked while smiling back at her.

"Yes. Do you remember when you told me that you got on your knees and prayed for God to take the reins of your life and guide your decisions?" Rachel asked.

"Yes." Mary had a confused look on her face when she looked back at Rachel. "Meaning?"

"Did you feel God was talking to you convincingly in your mind that day? So convincingly you felt He answered you and gave you a direction with so much clarity you knew what to do with your life? Right?" Rachel asked

"Wow. Right. Yes. It happened just like you said. So it is that mental thing you mentioned, the Holy Spirit that lives inside each of us to guide our lives, if we learn how to listen to it? Right?" Mary slowly shook her head as her eyes enlarged, and her mouth dropped open before Rachel answered her. Her face lit up with a glow to signify she had figured out what happened.

"Bingo. Talk to God the way you did that day, and ask for guidance each and every time you want His help reaching decisions on trivial or important matters." Rachel raised her eyebrows and smiled. "You figured this out for yourself. Right?" Rachel asked.

"Yes. I have my own genie who lives inside me instead of in a bottle." Mary laughed. "Does every person on earth have their own genie? I do not mean to make fun of this or make light of the Holy Spirit helping *me* and a lot of lives in this room. I am asking this as a serious question. Please forgive my laughter for which I humbly apologize." Mary's eyes became misty.

"I believe we all know your heart, Mary, but thank you for saying what you just said. And to answer your question, every person who believes Jesus Christ is the Son of God, who died on a cross for our sins and three days later rose from a grave to spend forty days on earth with His apostles, before He ascended up into heaven to sit at the right hand of God to judge the living and the dead *and* who asked Jesus to be their Lord and Savior, is actually inviting the Holy Spirit to descend upon them from God to live inside them."

"Wow. That is a mouthful. How do you know all of this, Rachel?" Mary asked.

"I am simply giving you my opinion based on my reading of the Bible."

"I would have a hard time cross-examining your opinion since I have to admit that I have also heard what you just said to be true, and

I heard that God does give each of us free will to accept or reject His choices for our lives. Hearing you tell me how and where we receive these choices God gives to us is comforting." Mary had her hand on her heart. "Thank you, Rachel."

"You are welcome," Rachel responded as she nodded her head in agreement.

"Not many of us pause or even think about the possibility of another route to achieve the new thought we just created in our mind. God, however, simultaneously, just as quickly as we think about doing something, prompts the Holy Spirit to give us options for doing or not doing the thing we just decided to do. This is where the *choice* comes in for us to choose the idea of the Holy Spirit idea, which is God's choice, or ignore the Holy Spirit to do it our own way. We have these options on every thought we create in our mind," Rachel answered.

"You are saying, in lightning speed, God gives us the choice He hopes we will make on any idea we are thinking about doing. The Holy Spirit *always* provides options in our subconscious mind for us to consider. Is this right, Rachel?"

"Exactly. But unfortunately, most of us react impulsively to the new thought we just created in our mind. We do not stop even for a few seconds to consider any additional thought or options on the subject before we impulsively react," Rachel answered. "And right now, I am so proud of you, Mary. You have grown in your faith on this trip, and God has blessed you with Ed Cox."

"Thank you for saying this to me, Rachel."

"You are welcome. It would please me very much if we could stay in touch with each other after we return to our homes. I would love to have you as a close friend of mine."

"My promise to you is to stay in touch with you so we can become closer and better friends. Besides, I have never met anyone like you before. I like you, blondie."

On hearing the word *blondie*, they burst into laughter.

"Cute. I am going to wear earmuffs on our drive back home," Rachel teased, making them laugh harder.

"There is nothing wrong with telling a person who is pushing you for an answer that your immediate off-the-cuff answer is no, but if they give you time to think about their request, your answer could be yes," Robert volunteered.

"I like that answer, Robert. Doctors are so smart," Mary answered.

"Thank you, Mary."

"You never stop impressing me, Bobby. I am so proud of you," Rachel said.

"You inspire and impress me, Rachel."

"Aww, that comment is so sweet of you, Bobby. Is there a particular reason, other than I love you with my whole heart?"

"Yes. Other than the many ways we love each other, foreseeing the kind of spiritual life we will live and share together, Rachel."

"Thank you, Bobby. Let us get you checked out of this hospital and find my car so we can get on the road to start living that life."

Rachel and Robert held hands as they walked out of his hospital room, with Mary following closely behind them.

ABOUT THE AUTHOR

William McNulty served in the United States Marine Corps for eight years. After his honorable discharge, he met and married Cathy Carter, who subsequently gave birth to two daughters and one son.

Working as an insurance adjuster during the day afforded him an opportunity to attend and graduate from a night college and law school, all while raising three children. Bill practiced law for twenty years before he retired to pursue other endeavors and become a writer. His first published book is titled *The Holy Spirit Conquers Vengeance*. His second book is titled *Dreams Come True*.

His fourth book will be titled *Finding Love Again*.